Children of Vampires

Little Reason

By Darren DiGiovanni

Fractured and broken, even my brain remembers all the battles of life. Never surrender to the struggle.

Chapter One

The Visitor

February 1989
126 Rooting Hills Road, Summerville USA

"Why are you going out this late?" Her tone carried annoyance. Standing inside the entry to the house she was pissed. Her left hand on the backside of the front door, she wouldn't allow him to leave. Trish's demeanor was selfish even at the late hour.

She didn't include the expanding lack of concern he harbored toward her. He had the nerve to think tonight was his. She'd been fed up with all his failures for years now. Presently, she had come to the regrettable and sobering realization that there was no better place for her to go. He was a miserable provider, but she would make him pay for that.

Shaking his head, Brian was resolute in his mission to escape for the night. There was nothing she could say that would stop him. Brian had suffered her abuse for days. The nagging never changed, and tonight–no matter her reasoning—he would not be swayed to stay in the house. If luck was on his side tonight, by the time he returned, Trish would be three sheets to the wind. Though she tended to be a violent drunk, she always seemed more manageable if he was drunk as well.

Shedding an annoyed breath, he stopped in front of her blockade of his exodus. "I'm just gonna get some drinks with Jimmy."

"I hate that fucking idiot." She moved under Brian's chin. Easily seven inches shorter than this pathetic man she called her husband.

He was carrying his good leather jacket, and she knew what that meant. It suggested more than 'just drinks.' She'd met him the first time at nineteen, when he was in that jacket. That had been fifteen years ago now.

She knew he thought the stupid thing was his lucky charm. A curl of her lip, she thought on that heated drunk night. A million nights since then and she was still stuck with this loser.

"You don't even remember this morning, and what you said?" Trish huffs out an indignant breath. "Said you'd take me to my mom's house, then to work in the morning." Her finger poked him sharply in his throat.

"Just like every promise. Just another lie, one after the next. You make em, you brake em." Trish bullied the five-foot-ten man, as if he stood a foot shorter than her. He wasn't leaving her again alone in this pitiful shed they'd called home for eleven years now. A two-story house, living room and kitchen to the right on the first floor. Upstairs there were two small bedrooms and a bath. All this clutter as if lived in for over forty years. None of its neglected spaces had aged well since the twice mortgaged house was theirs. The so-called neighborhood, even further removed from the modern world. Their house sat like an island in some forgotten and unmanaged woods. Run down and poor, the only other house barely visible, was on the far side of those thicket-filled woods.

Trish hated being left here. No car, no friends, and not a drink to be found. She knew there wasn't any more liquor, having finished the last of it just the night before. Many of them were tossed in the overgrown yard or dotted in the trash piles, spread about the overgrown property.

Behind Brian was the staircase leading upstairs to her cold bedroom. "You're not going to take me to work in the morning?" She knew that no matter how this conversation went she would face his retribution.

"Well, I changed my mind. Isn't that what you always bitch to me about!?" Aiming his derision, he meant to draw some reaction before he left. He never got the last word, and he really didn't expect it now. Pushing the finger from his soft pecs, he glared back at the abrasive snarl she was giving him.

"Just shut up. I told you already, and that's just that." Brian's eyes avoided hers as they narrowed and burned up through his skull. Fighting to get around her, he pushed his arm through the leather jacket's worn and heavily faded sleeve.

Her shorter body was half his weight, but still he had to muster some effort simply to move her from in front of the door. Trading places at the door. Taking hold of the door handle, he forced it open. With her barely out of the way, he slammed the already damaged door against the wall between the stairs and his portal out.

Harsh and biting cold, the night's icy touch flooded into the widened space. Their interiors, only lukewarm to begin with, now found all the more wanting. Brian, realizing the temperature, closed the other flap to his jacket before attempting to zip it over his larger belly.

The silence behind him was telling. She hadn't mocked his failing attempt to close the clearly lacking fit of the youthful garment. Before he moved out the door, he frantically patted every pocket. A heavy blink and turned lip said it all, as he found only a half-empty pack of cigarettes but no lighter .

"Looking for 'these,' asshole?" Trish's self-righteous lip curled at his loss. Holding the only keys they had up in the air, she stepped back to the staircase behind her. Between two fingers, she waved them as Brian turned back to her. A growing snarl of an expression peeling across her cheeks.

"You're not going anywhere, you fuck!" She was prepared to start this battle, even if no one won.

"Just give me the fucking keys, Trish." His jaw and teeth tightened. Wanting to take a swing at her, Brian worked an audible breath before he grabbed at her hand, and the keys.

Having learned through numerous unfortunate bouts with Trish, striking her was folly. Mouth narrowing and dry, he was already parched from the night's endeavors. Thinking his speed was better than hers, he swung out to snatch the prize. Brian instantly seethed with his first miss, and she jabbed with her empty hand into his beer gut. Though diminutive to his overweight belly, she'd always been able to inflict greater than she received.

Given the forced delay, Brian straightened his shoulders. While remaining a foot inside the doorway, he tried to relax and calm the anger boiling up. Though it was harder, it was his best bet to simply stand there. He assured himself she would eventually tire of the argument.

What had been proven out in her history would surely happen again. She would either throw the keys at him or attempt to hurl them into the dirt and tall weeds outside. Her best throw had led to a two-day search in the woods around their house. It was an unpleasant reminder, yet it had ended that fight.

Holding out a flat up turned palm, his tone was just short of fortified.

Conveying a rigid conviction, "Give me the damn keys, Trish." It was as good as she was going to get.

Getting off on her control, Trish waved the rundown-truck keys in the air. A small pattering of her feet, she excelled at pushing his buttons. A step closer before dancing away, she continued to shake them like Christmas bells for him to grab at.

The passive-aggressive tease caused his head to lower halfway. She relished the effect she could draw out of him as he passed that oh-to-familiar boiling point.

It was at that very moment a slighted pang of delight mingled with her anger. Some small pinch in her brain had found vindication in the entire episode.

His feet still hadn't stepped out the door behind him. His strained gaze at the top of his lowered head and palm still hung there. She had control right now, and the flavor was grand.

"You're not going out and wasting all my money." She had proven it repeatedly, to great effect. An old argument as she made more money than he did, and it ate him up.

"You're not wasting it on fucking beer and dope and 'fucking' around on me." Trish's aim tapered in. The bullying hand and key lowered. Her lips tightened as she stopped. Positioned forward in that same hand was the point of the key. She used the truck key as a weapon and jabbed at him.

"Yeah." She glared at him. "Don't think I didn't know. You mama's-boy piece of shit." She added. It was an insult she loved to bring out in arguments. The childish insult never failed to strike a nerve in Brian's defenses.

"Told you a hundred times–I'm not cheating on you." His clean-shaved face revealed more than it was meant to. Now under her accusing stare, every flinch of his disguise was laid out for any to see. She was testing him, yet he was still unsure of just what she knew.

Her fury was genuine. He didn't want to look away, but had to. Drifting slightly, his gaze was still wide when a fleeting distraction arrived at the outer corner of his right eye. Somehow, lurking in his peripheral, was someone sneaking in the kitchen.

Off to his right and a step down, sat their long living room. Angled toward the stairs was the back of the couch, centered in the large room.

Facing them on the opposite wall were some cabinets and a tv. Its static filled picture was the sole light flickering in the room. Yet, with that poor illumination, a portion of that light reached into that dim section, entering the kitchen.

Distracted in that instant, Brian abandoned Trish's bitterness as his head turned fully. His focused attention turned completely. Late to any of the details, he swore he'd seen someone moving in the kitchen. A small breakfast island in the kitchen was its central feature as there were just a few useful cabinets. Icebox, filthy stove, and a small window over the sink. Their kitchen had found little use over the last few years. Somewhere, unseen against the left corner of the back wall, was a door leading into the backyard.

Though he couldn't confirm nor see the door, Brian thought it ludicrous. If he entered there, the very idea that someone was in their house ignited a fire. Amending the disbelief, he'd been positive of the fact he'd seen a tall silhouette moving.

The back door out into that untidy and overgrown yard was almost always left unlocked, but the shape he saw had gone to some darker corner right of the island.

Putting in suspension their entire argument, he leaned past his wife's determined and weaponized key.

"What the fuck was that?" His demeanor had flipped. No longer hesitant, Brian pushed from her and stepped off the singular landing. After stepping down, he moved to the closet under the stairs and snatched up an old, dented aluminum bat. All within his first breath, Brian hadn't lost a step as he continued across the remains of the living room.

Like a dog on the scent, he aimed for the darker kitchen. The intruder, whomever it was, could now expect to find pain for the mistake.

"What are you talking about?" Trish's voice gained an exasperated tone yet remained at the entrance. Whatever Brian's newest ploy was to end the conversation, wasn't working on her. Glowering at him, she watched as he marched through the living room straight for the kitchen. Once upon a time there'd been two swinging doors separating the rooms. As if from some remote audience chair in a horror flick that she'd watched too late at night, Trish was hit with an uneasy chill. Odd as it was, it crept along the hairs on her arm. Like so many spiders, the feeling wouldn't leave after reaching her neck then back.

Under her over processed blond tips, her brain acknowledged the sensation was more relevant. Cursing the dim light of this house, she was faced with an answer to a question that hadn't been asked. As Brian centered his attention within the kitchen, a feeling of other specters visited her ears. Unconnected to his search, Trish heard several creaking boards.

Standing with her back to the open door, the bottom of the staircase loomed large. She hated to admit where the location of the noise had come from. Reluctant and fearful, the sound she'd heard came from up in the depths of the second floor. Pushed through a drawn breath, she turned her head up in that direction.

At first, the only avoided location was up there as all lights upstairs were off. Then, one molecule at a time, she detected something new and unwelcome. There was a clattering whisper, which lived in the darkened framework above the top step. In those surrounding shadows up there, Trish pointed her gaze.

A thickening shape, possibly an outline, was somewhere beyond the top step. Though having no hard edges, it was more than a feeling. Even without a direct view, she was sure of some change far above.

Having lived in this house countless years after they were married, Trish continued dreading the childish dark specters that haunted some of the corners. Whether meaningless, or the residue of some former trauma, she had never been prepared to identify it.

She was unable to free herself of her vulnerable self. A frailty that'd always lived deep, refusing to speak of, surfaced as she watched. Tightened in, and around her throat, the emotion was growing to be a physical thing. Its power able to pull the air from her lungs, Trish struggled to speak. Even though the battle was hers, and she had the means to Brian's escape in her hand, she now fought contrary to her hatred of Brian's actions.

"Brian…" Her voice never rose loud enough. Trish's eyes wanted to reject the shadows that so effortlessly swallowed her attention. She knew to look away.

"Brian please?" Her feet locked to the ground; her arms moved into her center. Protection of her vital core was unconscious.

A step back, Trish found the swinging door headed to close. Before she could acknowledge it, the movement of her body absently drove it shut faster.

The latching, though loud, was lost to other concerns. Remaining in her head and at the stairs apex, she wanted to look away, yet a fear of the results of doing so loomed.

What was heard in her doubt was the screams and pleads within her bones, but there needed to be proof. Drifting back into a cavernous corner of some childhood dream, she'd never willingly gaze at it till now.

Fingers pulling at the corner of her collar, she added a level of urgency to her calls. "Brian, I think someone's upstairs."

Not hearing any of her words, Brian was growing frustrated by his own imagination. Circling the kitchen island, he'd found nothing more than a back door slightly open. The gloom was the only occupant and a chilled winter's air moving a lonely curtain over the sink.

The threat for Brian was easily brushed off, the solution nothing more than slamming the back door closed. Retreating through the kitchen, he came into the living room once more. Bat, still in hand, his boots stomped his return. The idea of beating some prowler to death was as easily erased when thoughts of a growing night's endeavors arrived back on his mind.

Jerking his younger-sized jacket closer to his larger waist, he absently headed back for the front door. The six-inch step up to the entry level was still occupied. A quiet Trish was here. She had a lost expression, puzzled and distant. The statement on her face was no longer one of conflict. This was a troublesome idea for Brian. Though she didn't look at him, he was forced to pull the exit back open with her in the way. The goal in Brian's head was leaving the house before any more obstacles arose.

Turning the knob, the door only traveled a few inches. A new barrier at its base caused his breath to slip. The back of Trish's bare heel had landed squarely in the door's path. He was about to unleash a world of hurt, but immediately discovered she wasn't even looking at him. Trish's gaze and her full attention was aimed elsewhere. Like some cornered or caged wild animal, her considerations were far from centered on him getting out behind her. Either unwilling or deceitfully quiet, she was locked somewhere twenty odd feet up the staircase. To Brian, it was uncharacteristic of a sober Trish. There had never been a ploy such as this one she'd tried to trick him with. As he watched her, she gave little concern to his questioning gaze.

Her eyes never fluttered as he stood around to her side now.

On the second floor of their run-down house, Trish did her best to resolve the impression of an intruder. Powerless to get a word out, she needed Brian to look. Her arm finally rose to point the location out. A narrowing finger, still with the truck keys, pulled his judgment in the same direction.

Surfacing once more, Brian covered his restlessness with an irritated sigh. Offering her concerns nothing more than a fleeting glance, he was aware of the bullshit she was capable of.

In the last feet before his gaze reached the top of the steps, he at least wanted her game to be false. Having found no intruder in the kitchen, he finally arrived in the area. As before, an uneventful space of nothingness. Still, he knew she was immovable on something she'd decided on.

"WHAT? WHAT? What in the hell are you pointing at, you psycho?" His increased language was a lot, but the frustration had already been mounting. He was fed up with all this drama, whatever it was.

Brian lashed out again. "What? The bulbs are out. I'm NOT changing it tonight." His tone was harsh but his eyes now looked at his watch, then her hand. She still had the keys. There was a small hope inside him she would lay into him. An inkling of that hot-headed fury she owned so well was sometimes useful. It would give him the chance to storm out, but still, he needed those keys.

"Do you hear me?" Returning to her gaze, Brian was unsure of the strings to her confusion. Seeing no fitting reaction to her mindset, he gave the first flinch. She was being overtly strange, and he was a bit off balanced by her intensity.

Strangely, Trish was unwilling to fight him, as he'd pulled on the door. Brian stood beside her a moment longer as she even refused to find anger in anything he said. She hadn't yet ventured from the distant spot filled with a colorless gloom.

Fights between them were more than common. Alas, he knew the more convoluted ones had nothing to do with nights out or the amount of money either of them wasted. There was a profound difference in the center of her gaze. To get a better look he came around her. There he still refused to react to his call.

"This is stupid," Brian's cynical streak cut the mystery. He'd already looked at her paranoid dilutions in the distance and hadn't seen anything or anyone.

A blotchy and flushed expression tightened over Trish's face and neck. Her throat even felt too small, as she swallowed. Why could he not see the truth? She knew there was movement in that remote void upstairs.

"Hello nut job, this is earth calling you." His hand shifted, preparing to block if she telegraphed a swing. "Can you move your damn foot?" His tone lowered slightly to see if she played with him.

There was nothing, not a shred of disdain, not a curled lip to give her sharp retort. There were just those cheeks, burning red as she seemed lost to some unknown trip.

Had he not promised his 'friend' a visit, Brian might have stayed to investigate this new plot of hers.

"I won't be long, just a couple of shots with Lance." He tapered in on her glassy eyes. Trish was working this game for everything; however, Brian shrugged it off. "I'll be straight home after we hang for a bit. I promise. Okay?" His timbre changed yet again as he stepped away from her.

Trish said nothing. Even though she knew he'd more than screwed up. The idiot had made an error telling her the wrong name from earlier. At this moment, it all meant nothing to her.

If she might simply make a shape out of that darkness, her brain could stop fixating on those unlit corners. Alas, the shadows said nothing, patience, or even an ounce of longing. There were no facts she could translate to him, even if her lips would move.

Grabbing Trish's pointed hand, Brian pried the key free as well placing the bat in the now opened palm. He was no longer interested in joining her new delusional game.

"Go nuts with the bat, okay." The sting of his forced sarcasm hadn't hit home like he would have thought. Added to the peculiarity, her arm dropped as if no longer powered, nor was it heard as he pushed her body and foot from in front of the door.

Trish wanted to storm up the stairs. She could do as she'd done a million times before, especially when left alone in this godforsaken house. She could turn every one of the house's lights on. Then she might discover this sensation was merely a crumb of nothingness.

Possibly a window somewhere was left open. The reason for any shift in the darkness was simply the jostling of an unseen object upstairs. 'No,' she knew it wasn't this. A physical chill was calling; it was sustained through the fear in her lungs and spine. Even now as she fought to clarify her imagination, the shadow seemed to expand down a step. She wanted the cause of her anxiety to be nothing more than the side effect of a pill taken earlier, sadly every nerve in her body said different. The vital air she needed appeared hesitant to come, as it too vanished. Left standing there in its place, a pained, sickening sense of a prowler.

The trance broken, "PLEASE! Will you just listen to me?" Her paralyzed voice cleared. Lost in Trish's volume was a remnant of the previous irritations with Brian. She was already cleansed of that earlier pettiness and needed help.

Her mind late to her foot or the surroundings was no longer blocked by Brian, nor a closed door. Turning 180 from the stairs, she searched for the empty spot where Brian had been. A lingering blink and Trish brought her hand up to find an old bat in hand. The memory for its use or reason was found to be empty.

Outside was night, with a soft mist of rain falling. The living room remained flooded with the only light found there, the face of a silently flickering tv. A tremor and a touch of nausea filled inside her. Trish's stomach shifted as the prickles of fear commanded that she should run. However, the irrational wasn't yet understood. One idea at a time, she needed to find Brian. Trish dropped the bat uselessly to the floor before continuing.

Brian was taking the only vehicle they possessed. Her car, still not running, had weeds growing higher around its abandoned spot in the yard.

Trish knew the nearest person was buffered by a stretch of convoluted woods. A narrow tree-lined dirt driveway was the only exit, and she wouldn't dare traverse it at night.

She made the quarter-mile walk every day to get to their mailbox, but not tonight. It was out by the main road, but that was always under the shine of daylight. This avalanche of fear was spiraling out of control in her mind, and she wasn't having it. With a hand on the door frame, she saw the porch outside, wet and empty.

Pathetic and angled against the dirty siding, the light only forecast the hope of getting to Brian before he left her. Resolute, Trish wasn't deterred as she moved quickly out the front door. Almost in tears, she needed a warm body to stay home with her. Realized too late, the soul of that person could even be a cheating idiot.

She'd have to make a plea for him to stay. Out the door, Trish slipped on the icy wood outside their doorway. Corrected, her bare feet ignored the chill.

The porch, an aged planking in need of a well-deserved layer of paint. Though a bit off level, the ten by ten was the home of two forsaken barbecue pits, a questionable picnic table and scattered debris. Dotted about everywhere were countless ashtrays.

Its perimeter, at a foot high, lined an ocean of feral weeds covering most of the yard.

At its drop-off, two steps down, Trish halted. Her panic tormented her, it told her that she would only find taillights down the driveway. Shocked, there was no truck rumbling up the night's dirt road. It wouldn't be disappearing as it exited away from this secluded home. Instead, just a few yards from the porch, was the stationary miracle. He hadn't left her yet, still lingering just behind his truck, was her target. Discovered to her astonishment, Brian hadn't as of yet gotten into his truck. He hadn't left her, thankfully.

A wave of joy bubbled up, as Trish's shock was considerable. Sliding her hand on the wobbly railing at the deck's edge, she cocked her chin. An airy but constant drizzle was falling. The chill, holding the night, quickly found bone on anyone not wearing layers. For miles around, there were no other light sources to be found. A haze rested low in the rain and felt to thin it even further.

Trish felt herself holding there on the porch. Under the view atop the steps, she found a puzzling sight. To her confusion, Brian was kneeling on the wet, cold ground of the driveway. One foot back, he supported on the other, bent in front of him.

His location was oddly stopped short of his truck. Not on its driver's side nor the passenger-side, but a few feet directly behind it. At that faint distance in the night's cloak, his details were beyond the clarity of the porch light. He was only a blurred man, unmoved and tight.

Though deliberate, Trish stepped down the first of the two steps tense. Head remaining at pause, she wanted a reason for his delay. He sought a reason why he hadn't left her here yet. Her own arms were tight against the cold. Crossed over her chest, she looked for further clues and the degree of the misfit.

His head was straight, his back stiff, but for some unsettling reason, both his arms hung at his sides. The meaning and purpose, anything but clear to what ailed him.

He was in his favorite jacket, and it was continuing to get soaked. This alone caused Trish's curiosity to bend. One of their stupidest fights had been over that dumb leather jacket of his. He'd always overly protected it from any damage. It was a known quark of this man, even one she'd once claimed to love about him.

Dangling from his right hand were the keys to the truck. A harder squint of her eyes, Trish watched his motionless fingers. Surprised and unsure of her next words, she came down to the last step before the dirt.

Undecided, she reached her arm out, still three yards from his bearings. She wanted to call him, but another step found a layer of mud under her bare toes. Immediately looking down at the freezing ooze of filth, she grimaced. Repulsively, it pushed through her unpainted toenails, but she said nothing. Gritting, she continued her approach. Nervous steps crossed the expanse, and she came close to feet now. Two feet from his still unmoved position.

A step more and she could reach out to his shoulder. Behind Brian, her numbing feet came together. Landing quiet in the uncaring rain, Trish watched, distressed about the reasons for his incongruent actions, .

Eyes locked and mouth parted, Trish tensed when he finally moved.

Brian's body remained. His head, plus less of his shoulders, pivoted around. Eyes and face angled; they moved up onto her unsure gaze. Pupils and facial musculature pressed they were drawn in an afflicted expression, yet still numb.

The leering spheres were ones that had little match for Trish. To know where they originated could help. Perplexed, she leaned into the space left over. Traded were her fears of the dark, for a level of distress she was ill-equipped for. Her brain had no care of the bite of winter on her frame, only the concerns before her.

What was playing out before her? He was saying nothing, yet, screaming a pain she didn't understand. It had to be added to the blurred colors of a disturbing night she wanted over. A hand already out to him, she began its withdrawal.

The words would fix it, only if she knew how to frame the question.

Brian's body static, Trish forced one more step closer. The porch light did little to clarify or even lighten the tension of this new situation. Her questions were building up, but it ebbed away to just his name.

"Brian?" Delicately her tilting face looked deeper into the obscurity of this idiot she thought she knew everything about.

The numbness surrounded her and tightened in her throat. Pounding rivers of blood coursing through her veins as they screamed for answers. She didn't understand why Brian was acting this way. He'd been in a rush to leave seconds before, and now this.

Her chilled toe arrived at a small touch to Brian's up-turned boot heel. Her attitude moved further into the black, as the porch light was useless and angled squarely behind her.

"You're scaring me, you asshole." The collection of words seemed to have no meaning to his expression. "What's going on Brian?" She allowed a tremor of emotion into her plea.

Pressed deeper into the mud behind him, Trish was met with a pungent and wildly unfamiliar odor. Habit or alarm, her right hand came to cover her mouth before giving a disapproving shake of the head. A transitory scan of the area found no source or location for the smell. Too dark to even see the front of the truck her efforts were returned onto Brian.

However quick she'd been, before coming back to him, his head had turned round and away. Short brown hair, his head was wet and dripping. Rebellious, her hand rose once more. She could take a pause on his head; it had been cherished in their youth but now, she just needed contact. She could land on his shoulders, but the decision was halted inches from any contact.

She wanted to plead with him. To ask him to stop whatever nonsense he was doing. Her fall-back to anything he did was curses and accusations of things in the past. Yet in this moment, there was fear. A plea to stay home was next, but there was something much more here that was taking place.

Fingers offering a tremor, her right hand finally came to rest on his shoulder. There, Trish let her nails turn in on him. He hated more than anything being pinched. Trish, aware, expected nothing more than a harsh swing or the equivalent in profanity.

She'd been on the receiving end, as well as the cause of wild swings. Theirs was a battle of equals, and on many a night, a reason to get a point across. This was far and away a deviation she didn't like.

Harder, she was sure she drew blood. Her nails, able to find space between jacket and neck, she pinched deeper. There was no reaction even as time piled up her work. Surrendering the attack, Trish took a single step around his right arm.

Off the side of his back, she discovered someone missed until now. There was a minor form here. Its shape, oddly standing inches in front of Brian's lost attention. Rigid and stark, under the tower of Brian's bent shape, was the smallest token of a girl. Even in the stolen light that reached out from the porch, her shape was withered. Her hopeless-looking face was hushed and turned down toward the ground. No older than seven or eight her sunken eyes subtly shifted up ahead of Brian. Slow and powerless the emotionless orbs rose higher without help from her head.

The vacant stare traveled in eternity as those eyes offered their pain to Trish's arrival. Her pitch-colored hair was wet and weighed down over the tiny, framed shoulders. Its thin strands spaced out and ended uneven around what torso could be seen.

Drained by it all, Trish plunged round her husband to draw up the lost creature. What fears and trepidation that had been preying on her every nerve and fiber, since this day had begun, instantly melted away.

Clear in Trish's scan, this thing was a wisp of a child. Face marred and covered with a film of dark smudges; the refined details remained clouded at these lower light levels. Though a ghostly figure of a girl, she stood squarely in front of Brian's limp arms and his carelessly staring eyes.

Dropping to her own knee, Trish twisted the meager girl's frame toward her. Its lifeless and defenseless muscles unable to object in the effort. Caring hands on both sides of her frozen skin, Trish feared there was more to her pain. All these concerns were beset by the sad state the girl must have been living.

In that flash, she scrutinized her every inch she could see. Only after, was Trish at least thankful to see no blood or apparent wounds to be outwardly found. From her downcast face, she saw the girl's arms remained limp as if cumbersome weights locked them in place. Eyes, deep set in a malnourished face, the fact she stared motionless outward was proof of some dire abuse.

Head nodding back and forth, Trish couldn't understand the tattered clothes hanging from the sum of a girl. Soaked and covered in misuse, the resilient scraps softly flapped in the dreadful chill. There was no getting past the neglect standing before her and it was disheartening.

Every strand of cloth barely held to each other. What concealment the rags offered the child held none of the elements at bay. Most notable to Trish was the lack of color in her pale flesh. It was obviously distressing, even in the dim light.

Closer to the girl, she felt the torment and loss deep within its wild eyes. She wanted a word, a living noise to come from her lips, but all that was left in its space was a want. Focusing on her faintly blue lips, Trish looked for help about the abuse.

A moan of agony would help, but nothing was said. This child stood a statue of abandoned grief and she had to intervene immediately.

Wasting no more time in the chilled wet air, Trish came over the lost spirit. Hands positioned under the arms she firmly drew her into her heart. Pulled into both arms and bosom she gave what warmth could be immediately offered.

Tied to her and turning toward the house, Trish further examined the tattered and worn clothes. Not simply overused, a fact obvious to her gaze. The clothes were clearly meant for a smaller frame, even for an infant. Worse, several slashes ran the length of the garments as if she had been in them her entire life.

The clothes took a back burner for Trish. Better light, told of bones easily pressing against her pale skin. She was surely emaciated to the point beyond any criminal level, and Trish couldn't believe anyone capable of this.

"Oh my God Brian." Though she hadn't looked back at him, she was baffled by his unbroken silence.

"Where did she even come from?" Trish was afraid to hold her too tight. Frightened if she did, she would break the frail creature. "Shit, you feel like you're frozen solid, child." The struggling emotions to understand the limits any human could go to, burned in Trish's face.

Heading back for the open front door, Trish cautiously felt the girl's forehead. Moving on to her cheeks and round her neck, she verified the worst.

"Damit, I think you're probably hypothermic." Before the first step onto the porch, Trish glared back to Brian for help. "Help me get her inside already!" She wanted to smack the idiot in the head and call him entirely new levels of harsh names. However, that could wait until she did something about the girl's low temp.

Before crossing the slick decking, Trish returned her efforts back to the stray orphan. Reaching the limit, between warmth and the dry security of the house, she entered. "Sweetie, I'll get you some warm blankets and something to eat."

Chapter Two

The Unwanted

Carrying the weightless flesh-and-bones into the living room, Trish immediately noted that Brian still hadn't followed. He'd been an asshole over several things, but at this moment, she would be hard-pressed to list them.

Still, she thought 'why continue?' The growing irritation thickened on her already stressed mind. What if he had gotten back in his truck after finding this girl? Trish's jaw tightened even more with the consideration. She would murder him in his sleep.

Again, she needed to put the revenge on the back-burner. Her first priority was the wet body in her arms. With no kids of their own, and not by choice but because of biology, this moment felt oddly welcoming.

Headed for the couch, Trish left the door standing open. Her full attention was down on the staring eyes of the innocent. Her own gaze was lost in those pearls of peculiar black. Their shape was unnatural. Trish's intent was to nurse the soul back from the edge.

Immediately, she came around the side of the couch to its front. Placed in the center of the fifteen-by-twenty-foot room, this was the oldest piece of furniture they possessed. Older than even their dresser upstairs. The couch was a faded aqua and had more cigarette burns than she wanted to admit to.

Nonetheless, it had piles of blankets all over it. Trish, pained to admit the reason for so many, because it wasn't for warmth. Not even because Brian slept there most nights, but to cover up the fact, she'd set fire to the entire face of the cushions.

Before sitting in the sofa's clutter, Trish's gaze sprung up. Alarmed by the awful sound of creaking floorboards inside of the front door, she glared. The door had been left open; the outside porch light sliced a brighter wash on its side of the threshold. Meanwhile, the dim television's glow was weak, parting it's half of the scene. At first, Trish saw only a silhouetted man looming in the entry, as her fury and fear mixed, she saw it was simply Brian standing there. He stood blankly. A foot inside the opening he waited. Lumbering inside, Brian gave all the appearance of an accident victim.

His facial declaration was continuing to be one of bafflement and loss. Watching his eyes, in the glimmer of the tv behind her, they said less. A trauma seemed to live in that space between logic and understanding, but she troubled to know why. What awareness there might've been was elsewhere. Trish looked at him, and the information given said there was no one in control.

Her own state of confusion swelled as she thought about going to inspect him. His pants soaked; his jacket dripped with the winter's heavy flavor, yet no reaction. Continuing to dangle, from a purposeless grip, were the unused truck keys. No more a thought to him than his blank face.

Besides these things, his mouth said nothing as it lay slightly open. His clean shaved chin, as well all his face, appeared vacant of the warm blood needed to move.

She'd been with him all day. Confident in her knowledge that he hadn't had one drink today, she worked her thoughts. Eyes adjusting to the lower light levels inside, she stared longer at his numb face. Brian's eyes looked bloodshot. What was more, they laid as fixed saucers, seeing nothing. His gaze straight forward, they lingered on the staircase, venturing nowhere, and offering her little clue to his logic.

"Brian, are you feeling, ok? Do you even hear me, you idiot?" She wanted some reaction but received no explanation. Forced to wait for a waiver in his eyes, she was again led to think of him as a lost cause.

Before she asked him for more, a shift in her rescue pulled her attention back down into her cradling arms. Though perplexed, her thoughts returned to the girl she held. A better use of the moment could be spent on the needy child waiting.

Trish's own eyes, wider than any other time, drew in everything around them. Nerves and anxiety heightened; she noted a shift in the shadows to her right. Only aware of a vague movement from the corner of her eye, her head snapped quickly toward that half of the room. Reignited were the fears of that sensed visitor atop the staircase.

It was within the kitchen now. A fleeting unnatural collection of shadows was moving. Stealthy as before, it had instantly vanished before she could center on anything of its type. Electrified and invisible fingers felt to wander across her every inch of open skin. A twitch in her neck started off the tremors that traveled unstopped. The phantom in her visions had returned her to the paranoia living within these walls. The needling wave of charged shivers found a home. Flooding into her nervous system, it ramped up her heart rate to a painful level.

Brian erupted in a coughing spasm as the muscles encircling his lungs fought back. The experience was no different from the traumatic seconds after being forced unexpectedly underwater. Sharp and violent, they continued where he stood at the entrance of the house.

What trance he'd been in was ultimately terminated. He was again aware, but unsettling aches continued to inundate his body's every fiber. Free of those hefty depths, Brian fought to regain control over the weakness. The moment forced him to bend forward as his skipping heart rate found rhythm once more. 'Was it possibly all a delusion, a flash of some drug taken months or years ago?'

Brian was not weak, and he was no child afraid of the shadows. His brain screamed at him to stop the foolishness; to 'man up' as his father had pounded a thousand times into that boy he once was. Shaking the covering of dust, he could see clearly once more.

He was in control of his actions, though at a loss to explain the recent unfolding of events. Not even sure of his location, he took a quick inventory of the whole. A counterclockwise twist of his head and neck, Brian used his palm to help produce a pop in his vertebrae. Following the adjustment, an uncontrolled need to shake his arms out. The action allowed the truck keys freedom from a ringed finger, falling unnoticed to the floor.

Arriving in his own skin, Brian looked about. He was back in the house. An open door behind, and the stairs dark as before were ahead of him. To his right, the tv still glowed. He found Trish. Though she was in front of the couch, she was not seated. Her leg stood but she was arched over something. A figure unseen by him, blocked by the height of the sofa.

A gesture in his movement, he spoke but fell immediately silenced.

As the tv's staticky picture flashed brilliantly, a figure moved from some corner. Faster than his full attention, it moved from the living room to disappear into the kitchen. A blur of a shape, it was now and forever a fact to Brian. Proof of what he'd thought before was not a lie.

Enraged, the figure had escaped his earlier search; this time he knew it wouldn't end the same. The revelation crystallized; it hadn't been his imagination. Condoling himself on that pyrrhic victory, there was truly an intruder nearby that he would now have to deal with.

This was his house, he wanted to take this new opportunity and give it an ending his father would have been proud of. Fists balled, he just needed his feet to obey commands and lurch forward.

"Give me the fucking bat, Trish! It's gone far enough, and I swear if this is some cheating ass boyfriend of yours, I'll…" The irony was not lost on him, though ignored. Before leaving his chilled space by the door, he found the bat resting just under the rung of the first step leading upstairs.

Dipping, he grabbed the slugger and entered the living room. Trish had obviously dropped the bat earlier. This was fortuitous for him now as he passed behind the couch headed for the kitchen. Swiftly he crossed the length of the room, avoiding other piles of work shoes and piled clothes.

He'd been sleeping down here so many nights that it was just easier to pile his stuff along the wall. Blind to his mess, all attention was placed on the whooping he was about to bestow on some unsuspecting halfwit.

Twisting the warmer metal shaft in his still damp and chilled hands, he tightened his grip. Fingertips tingle as he choked down harder on the weapon. "You came to the wrong house, asshole. We're not taking visitors till tomorrow. You know, when your funeral procession passes by." The banter was something he'd heard weeks ago, outside his favorite bar. Still, he thought it was cool to repeat.

"Hide and seek, mother fucker." Brian's tone leveled out the statement as he could see nothing, when the tv's glow dimmed dramatically.

Marching up to the living room's divide and the kitchen entrance, Brian considered anything moving. Met at that transition was a motionless darkness, as well a bleak taste in the air. Only wanting to give a slight pause, he subconsciously sensed the area was anything but empty. The fugitive notion couldn't be worked out in his brain. Distinctly, Brian knew the impression was nothing more than paranoia he should ignore.

Matching the sensation as best as he could, Brian took a half step over the two rooms' divide. If it the same, it was a feeling he knew well when out deer hunting. A nervous rhythm he could use, one that told him that there was something, just something his eyes couldn't see yet. Though he might be blind to its approach, he'd get the first attack in.

The longer he waited, just one foot in, the thunder in his chest kept information from his brain. The room, though unmoved, was anything but tranquil to his confused sight. Fortifying his spine, his left boot finally joined him in the kitchen. He would start his hunt. Closed lips, he concealed a troubled swallow.

Stepping closer to the inside edge of the breakfast island, he could barely make out the window over the sink. Each step leading him to the right, and around the nuisance of an island. It only collected dirty dishes and bags of nothingness that were best tossed, anyway. Brian had threatened a multitude of times to rip the eyesore out of the kitchen.

Automatically, his feet continued over the darkened floor without thought or measure. The weak light from the living room couldn't reach through the double opening any better than the house's space-heater could heat it.

Cautiously he needed to go round the counter to see in-between the island and the sink counter. Switching the base-hold of the bat to his offhand, Brian felt sure he was pursuing the ever-moving shadow. Yet, there was a distinct difference with each step. The space he conquered never seemed to be any clearer.

Any hope of being under the influence of large sums of alcohol tonight, over. He'd hope to even find some weed in that distant daydream he'd planned out.

'This was not the plan for tonight,' Brian's alter ego sadly verified. His 'friend,' would surely start to wonder by now, if he would show up at all.

Brian could just walk away like before; the idea of turning and leaving was available. He could go back to his truck and speed up that dirt road, hit the main road and do eighty all the way. It was a fertile consideration, but now he was curious to know who Trish was cheating on him with.

Tendons and muscles flexed; the call for physical violence was stronger than he understood, and the pounding in his blood vessels was slightly intoxicating. The rage, currently swelling inside, needed to be satisfied. Soon he'd have some gratification knowing the answer to previous question.

Taking precedence, was this new necessity of his, to situate the old bat squarely across the face of some idiot who might be fucking his wife.

The island, almost completely circumnavigated, Brian scrutinized one of the last options. In a deeper shadow, behind a missing section of their counter, was the last hiding place available to an intruder.

In his mind, it was the sole remaining area. The concealed corner in the kitchen was small, but a person could hold up in it. Corrected in the imagination, at least a thinner man might.

"Come on, come on out." Muttering over his breath, he cursed whoever built the stupid house. The moron had placed the only light switch for the kitchen, on the far side next to the rear door. Luckily it was just in front of him as he stood between the sink and island.

That last spot and it would be all over. The mystery man would be unveiled, and he could lord it over Trish's head forever. However, first he needed to find the man's eyes. He wanted to witness them as he beat him to death. Reaching his hand out for the switch, he hesitated an inch over its location. At the back door, he was positive he'd closed it when he searched the first time.

It was open just a sliver. A missed fact, that is till now, Brian's face burned red with fury. The trespasser had some nerve, even if he was stupid enough to leave evidence of his entry. The scenario said nothing of this man's fortitude. What was it to venture this far into strange woods, just to get into Trish's bed?

It was easily a half-mile from the main road. Brian, oddly, hoped he was smart enough to hide whatever car he'd traveled in. Parking somewhere off the paved street was the best hope of not being found out.

Through all this, he couldn't help pondering the very idea of someone so brazen. Someone clueless enough to enter even knowing Brian had guns in the house. At that second, Brian's lip gave a curious grin. The bat in hand was a toy. Why didn't he have his gun? It was the tool needed for the job. 'How stupid are you?' His father's voice echoed up from memory.

Jarring, the more prudent notion arrived, 'what if this is a criminal, and he had a gun?' That meant he was wielding a knife in a gunfight, not a winning premise. A downward turn of his grin, he chastised himself.

Focusing around, he looked to at the very least remove one obstacle. No longer would the night's hold have a domain in the kitchen.

Hand crossing the messy area on the counter, his nearest fingers searched where the habit said the light switch was.

Brian heard a disquieting snap, but not the elusive light switch. Its location was in that very corner, he'd assumed. The bat in his non-dominant hand felt more than off balance. Resting tight in his left hand, it would not give the best offensive chance. Nor would it protect him, if he needed a defensive swing, from a lunging man.

Displayed, the heavily dented shaft loomed outward. Now it floated only as an obstacle for someone else to push aside. A frustrated squint, he never turned his gaze away; his every faculty narrowed on that inky but motionless void.

He hadn't yet hit the light switch. A further sign of worry, a nervous bead of sweat found some exit off the edge of his hairline. In need of glasses ages ago, Brian's pupils couldn't penetrate that loathsome gloom with their nonexistent help.

Brave as he preached to be, his step backward told of his shrinking nerves. His will bending, and an inner acknowledgment of fear, Brian hesitated in his hotheaded tempo.

"Is someone there?" The opening was delayed.

Brian wasn't truly prepared for an answer. He found peace in an idea that the man had already sped out the back door before his arrival. Unsure of just what he expected, Brian restored his wandering hand back onto the bat. Joined there with his weaker arm, the two tightened down on the stock.

Unlike all else that had occurred tonight, Brian found an answer offered in the damp kitchen. It simply wasn't what he wanted. Unsure of his ears, he felt a meek and muffled response reach out to him. It was an answer to his open query.

Utter shock and dismay, its origins hadn't come from the corner as Brian had expected. Remote from that specific corner, this utterance surrounded and even floated above him. Even far worse than the moaned words, an icy breath touched his skin. Its caress covered his ears and back of the neck.

"What in the FUCKING HELL!?" More than just the bat, Brian's arms and shoulders joined in the crazed swings. Positive he might have hit something, he only made contact with the counter and all that had collected atop it.

Ending the attack of his bat, his shoulder tightened against his ear for safety. Frantic he worked to rid the sensation as his head shook to escape further contact.

The image of webs and malformed fingers placed over his skin made his skin crawl. The glancing ambush felt as if it now increased to cover the back of his head and neck. Chills and needles spread inward of his flesh, but no amount of rubbing could remove the sensation.

Searching with a stray hand, there was no substance to these irritations. Brian continued scratching at the side of his face to remove the effect. With no physical object to hit, madness caused him to make a new volley of swings with the bat.

Turning round several times, he staggered back blind in the environment. Retreating another step, he found the back door behind him. Now with his dominant hand around the bat, his left grabbed for the kitchen's light switch.

Missing on the initial strike, Brian slapped with his open palm. Without better sight, he needed focus to make his fingers crawl over that section of the wall. Finally, finding the edge of its dirty wall plate, he greedily stabbed at the light's toggle.

Chapter Three

Not Now

The yellowing tinted glow of the fluorescent bulbs flickered and hissed to life. Brian took the seconds needed to look up to the three-foot long tube on the kitchen ceiling. Off-center and missing its cover, the gasses inside of its slender tube struggled to burn.

A smile welcomed the radiance to come. Brian would use the bulbs light to gut the man hiding somewhere in his kitchen.

Popping and sparking, the fluorescent tube heated as always, before it could fully spring to life. It was the lone fixture to the kitchen and the living room. The other room had a lamp, and Brian used it every night. That was until last week. Trish had pulled it out of the wall in some tit-for-tat fight they were having. It now sat bent and smashed in one of the corner piles.

As if counting the ticks of some clock, his anticipated light failed to reach its climax. Its attempt to ignite into a glowing force crashed to nothingness as it dimmed completely. For all that he could see into the living room, he noticed the glow vanished there as well. The constantly running tv picture that usually lit the room faded to black. Worrisome, every point of life was drawn down to nothing. Brian's desires personally felt deflated. This turn of events could only mean trouble.

His anticipated elation crumbled as the last ticks of electricity faded from the tube above him. Numerous times he punched at the light switch, hoping for a different outcome. On the sixth time, a puff of energy shot through the full length of the bulb. The reward for Brian was a brilliant dying flash. The tube gave its last as a fleeting blue spark echoed in the fixture. All hope for some illumination in the house quickly dwindled with that last beacon.

The ink in this blackness was far more pronounced. His eyes blinked deliberately, and his skin was still wet. It took him a moment to orient himself as his eyes adjusted to the darkness. Even though he knew his eyes were open, it was hard to trust his senses in the depriving dark. He wanted that violence he promised his core. He needed it to warm the hate he was feeling at the moment.

The steps needed to rectify the loss of power were anything but new to him, or Trish. The house was notorious for the breaker-box tripping with any added load, the main cause had always been the space heaters. The largest was in the living room but there was also one in Trish's room. Plus, there had been one added in the bathroom upstairs.

A purge of the lump growing in his throat, Brian kept the back door behind him. He took hold of the bat with both hands. Up and ready, no one was getting behind him again.

The breaker was outside in the house's front. Just another stupid decision someone had made when constructing this house.

Choking down on the weapon, Brian leaned away from the door. Prior to a footstep away from it, a sickening shriek passed throughout the length of the house.

The entire structure subsequently fell inert to any movement or voice. While outside, an unwieldy winter gust now increased. Its own looming voice was heard rifling over any loose shutters. The frame of the building held fast, even as an increasing chatter tapped wider over the house's exterior.

Any untrue boards, clad over the surface of its roof or the house's frame, protested. A natural force with its single chorus, drove the weather louder. All the while, other mundane creaks and willful noises added atop the dull.

What had been a lite rain, was extended, and now was becoming more of a threatening storm. Its voice outside grew louder by the second. Its roar heard, the storm felt to be holding the house and forest around them, as hostage.

This was all more than Brian wanted, as a bottomless tug opened in his troubled stomach. It was an unwelcome warning. Tormenting him as it grew, and he was a fool, standing motionless in it.

Thirty-nine years of existence, and he wanted clarity tonight, at least a framework to proceed by. He was beset in some nightmarish play. An actor on a stage where he knew none of the lines, and his brain was begging that it might shake off this fearful emotion.

Somehow, he might purge the ache, only because he knew that it was fear building up. A string had been pulled inside of him as he corrected his nerves. He felt the strain on his logic. Wanted, there was reason to swing desperately. Possibly he might hit something nearby. No longer cold, but his breath and skin spoke of other terms he hadn't control over.

His lungs tapered in rhythm, as he pushed his breath through clenched teeth. His temple throbbed as his warming hands stung from some abuses already forgotten. Though his eyes were wide and continued to search for anything to grasp upon, the surrounding landscape disappointingly lay dark and still.

He wanted to be fierce, even chilling, his weapon swaying in hand. He had nothing inside. No plans to follow or fight to win. All the hard work and curses fell away. He stood solitary in the dank night, his panic gaining control now. It crawled wide over his skin. Multiplying, it had given birth to new alarms as his focus failed too, drowning in the inky abyss.

Absent to him, as he no longer felt the door frame behind, was true clarity of purpose. He was cognizant of a few things, a counter and sink somewhere near to his left side as well an island. To his right, lay a cluttered wall, on it an incomplete pantry cabinet, left by him unfinished almost a year ago. He was a better car mechanic than anything to do with carpentry.

The living room, somewhere ahead of him. It easily might have fallen to some sinkhole without proof or sight.

The noise outside, however strong, was actually just an envelope of static. One which faded into white noise the longer the storm poured. Its separated droning intensified the lack of sound inside the wood- paneled walls around him.

No nagging voice to aim on, nor tv to guide a dizzy footstep. Brian waited. Absent for now was his opponent's whispered challenge. Though its bite had been fearsome, at least with that cruelty, he had violence to hold him up. Anger fed his engine and stopped his thoughts from taking over.

His hands were numb as they continued to strangle the stock of the bat. Upright and ready with both, he felt another significant bead of sweat roll from his brow. A foot reluctant to go, it eventually tapped forward into the blanket of darkness. Soon after, his right followed, but only as far as needed to rest beside the first.

As if moving ahead of his slow approach, a low dragging shuffle moved with him. Its duration was painful even with his troubled march. Stopping, Brian listened.

There was a presence in the foreground, a tease to the sightless. Brian felt quickly thrown off-balance. His head swiveled when unknown murmurs came again. This time from behind him. Its path carried no logic, as it moved in all directions. Its meaningless words passed untethered by any physical laws.

Separate, yet just as foreboding, a drone of hate visited from the other room. Numbers far greater than one, these entities soon built atop the first. None of them was louder than the rhythm pounding outside, however, far more disturbing. The echoing chants one after the next fell away, utterly vanishing in the beat of his speeding heart.

A deviation in Brian's voice, he earnestly appealed for his wife's help. "Trish!?" The bat stopped moving, his feet together he called through to the other larger room. "Trish, gosh dammit, are you there?"

Perished in that space left for her answer, Brian took a normal step but was not even past the island. The unmeasured interval passed, only abandoned for a newer query.

"Trish, will you fucking answer me? Are you okay?" Unconsciously, he leaned forward as if the shorter distance to his ears mattered.

His aggravation only worn skin deep, "Come on, Trish? I know you can hear me; you were right there." The level of his defenses dropped considerably.

"The breakers tripped again; we need to flip it back on." He ratcheted up each word as he stood waiting for her voice. His volume hit a nervous level. "It's in the box outside. Come on, answer me!" He was sure she couldn't deny she'd heard, even if she'd moved upstairs.

His brain wrestled to fill the bottomless chasm under his feet. The shapeless landscape that rolled out before him, hadn't the faintest glimmer of light. He plied his dry mouth with the last of his saliva. Standing there, he wished for any escape to be offered from this phobia.

An idea, stupid as it was, he turned round to find any of the cabinets and drawers. A hand on the island's edge guided him back to the counter. Fumbling around, he immediately pulled at a nearby kitchen drawers.

Opening the stubborn bins, his fingers searched within.

Each drawer was the same, stuffed full of meaningless crap. Old rags, wires, condiment packages, and an endless parade of minutiae he'd never used. What was disappointing was he hadn't found a lighter, matches, or the most elusive of them all, a flashlight.

Quickly moving from one to the next in line, his hand plowed through most of it. Carelessly allowing most of the debris to fall over to the unkempt floors. Then his memory offered other possibilities.

Out of habit, Trish had always thrown all the old lighters into an older cookie jar. It was a leftover from his own mother's kitchen up state. Fondly, it was in the shape of a honey pot with a missing lid. He knew it was tucked into the back of the counter near the right of the sink.

Scattering stacks of whatever lay on the counter, Brian made short work of finding its location. With no lid, his thick fingers instantly dove into the bountiful load of lighters. Though unseen, he knew them all to be different colors, but their brand was all the same. Trish always bought the cheapest Bic lighters, from that gas station several miles up the main road.

Pulling a hand full out, he fumbled with the first group. Dropping all but two to the floor, he laid the bat on the counter to correct his nerves. Amending the missing weapon, he took it back up, and for a moment slung the end under his left armpit.

His right hand never veered from the task. Fighting him he repositioned one of the lighters. The first of them was planted correctly in his palm and under his thumb, but gave little hope. Tossing it into the unseen sink beside him, he positioned the next.

The second lighter was no better. Able to use his free hand, he quickly collected more from the jar. Pulling at the flint strikes best he could, the igniter only gave brilliant showers of sparks. One after the next the lighters disappointed before falling away. Each of their gas reservoirs, proving just as Trish had known, was empty.

"Damn it bitch, why couldn't you have left at least one working?" Brian cursed her stupid habit, only for the fact that all the lighters were dead. Hope remaining, there were easily forty or fifty filling the depths of the jar.

Regardless of spilling ten or so, to the floor, his sixth lighter found hope rekindled. A misfit in a bowl of duds, he'd discovered the one that might offer animation. Regardless of its poor flame, his expectations were bolstered with the mere hiss of the lighter.

Turning away from the sink and the mess he'd left there, Brian focused on what was important.

In the direction of the living room, he came back around the untidy island. Working by the lighters' weakened flame, Brian fumbled forward.

Speed reduced; his efforts bowed to the decaying flame. Justifying his caution, its fluttered life vanished as his fist fought to return it. An anguishing thumb pulled at the wheel.

This was a new problem created as the lingering flash-spots were being burned into his vision.

They were repeated and harsh, but with every ignition of explosive sparks, the darkness seemed to crowd in on him faster. The thick silence was waiting after each flash. The inferior lighter was far from what he had envisioned as helpful. After a fit of effort, it burned once more. Thankfully, this time, it grew into a healthier yellow and white flame.

"Trish! Answer me if you're here, will you?" Even now, her whereabouts were no more important than his need for her to be there. Just a fractured or irritated answer would suffice. "Please, Trish, will you just answer me?" His feet found the conclusion of the kitchen floor. A small strip of metal separated the flooring of the living room from the kitchen.

Their kitchen had a layer of linoleum that gave way here. Stained and overly worn, a dingy orange shag led out into his makeshift bedroom on the couch. Covering most of the living room, the carpet had been shortened. Some time ago, it was after a small fire had spread from the couch.

Glaring blind spots in his vision, he continued. Each time Brian fought to bring back-to-life the lighter, it amassed new holes. His finger had little time to recover fully, before another shudder of the flame called on his anger.

A slightly more confident foot, now pressed atop the turned-up edge of the carpet. He'd tripped over that half-taped-down edge a hundred times and this would not be another statistic added to it. Heedful of any new sounds in the living room, he wanted to see Trish. He wanted to see her spark up a lighter of her own. Searching, the pitiful flame stayed close to his bat and the right hand holding it.

He heard almost nothing. Blocked out in his consideration was the one exception. A stronger downpour was drumming onto the grill outside. The softened drone was a clue in the ink around him. The front door was closed, but Brian couldn't be sure Trish hadn't left that way when he was in the kitchen.

At the closest edge to the couch, he loitered. A slow deliberate turn with the flame, he saw and heard no wife in front of him. The proof was unclear, as his reach was limited. Restricted by both the strength of the puny flame and his continued blinding, anything was feasible.

Another drum beat as thunder in the room. It was the rushing pound of blood in his eardrums. After a deeper examination of the area, Brian discovered an abnormal scent. Not so much stronger than the existing smells left by two unkempt adults, but one distinct enough that it curled his nose and lips.

It was around him, drifting in a stale but strangely unfriendly air. An anchored heaviness was felt to be closing about him.

Returned was the sensation of a nearby breath. Panting anxiously as if it were a creature looming only in shadow. Its impact reaching out, waiting, hungry for his light to die.

Hunting since he was old enough for his late father to push a rifle in his hand, Brian thought he knew most smells of creatures, dead or rotting. This foreign invasion wasn't on his list. However, had he been forced to name it, it was decay.

Harsher than this understanding, Brian drew back a step as the scent intensified, ultimately extending even to his taste.

Swallowing, against the unpalatable rot, he wasn't prepared for the wrenching pulse it caused. A troubling tremor, its extent traveling out over every connected bone and under his soaked jacket.

Reluctantly mixing his hand back to the bat, the lighter shifted uncomfortably. The attempt was folly as his thumb slipped off the fuel lever. A puff and the flame vanished.

Over and over, the sparks flew into the air as he struggled to return life to the dark.

Frantic, Brian's crazed thumb repeatedly jerked against the studded roller of the lighter. Zealously, the pain was ignored, even as a blister matured under its attack.

"Fucking piece of shit!" With a furious shake of the tool, he had to let go of the bat with his right hand. The weapon, ignored in his left hand, lowered to no longer defend him.

"Come on. Come on, I know you have it in you." He could feel the last bit of butane liquid still inside the lighter. Anxiously he growled, his skin was raw from the comparatively small roller. Neither force nor speed returned the flame to the worthless plastic.

"Shit…" His teeth rested atop his lower lip. Brian wanted to curse more, but the fact was he hadn't brought more of the dead soldiers with him from the cookie jar. With a second's rest, he told himself he wasn't returning to the stupid kitchen.

Stubbornness a defining trait, he would continue the blinding shower till it returned. Switching to his weaker left hand, he snarled and huffed.

Beneath the ripped skin on his thumb, it was no longer easy to ignore the raw slicing pain. He continued to force the lighter, hoping every second it would give him some satisfaction. His miserable efforts were finally rewarded. Regained, was a tenuous blaze compared to the void. With the tiniest of flames cresting the rim, Brian nourished it with nothing more than pure force of will.

Its strength dimmed, reducing even as he watched. A slight blue feverish spot was all the plastic tube wanted to deal with him. He arched the sole beacon to the remaining spot he lived in. Its authority could not stretch farther than the end of his bat.

Kindred to a howl of suffering pain, a desperate scream echoed from within the walls of the living room. A sharp blade started and ended like the voice of lightning. It was gone before Brian could focus on the direction of the terror.

While its true location remained a mystery, he thought. The quivered childlike tone was a returned memory for Brian's addled mind. Where his pain emanated from was immediately less important. There was a clearing fog in his thoughts and something new played out. A forgotten fact was once more returned for his consideration.

There was a very real possibility that he'd seen a child tonight. A young, devolved girl, but he hadn't pictures in his head of what the feeling was matched to. No direct memory came forward, none of them ever helping anyone. Nor had he welcomed some stranger's child into his home. He detested his brain's contest; this chilling fear wasn't anything he could swing at. Brian had seen Trish moments ago in this befouled room. Although, with far less light than the equivalent of a spark, evidence was lacking.

The flame fluttered. Then once more it gained a hue of yellow, before widening its reach. As Brian gazed toward the railing and steps, he could see the closet door under those stairs.

Had the noise before been Trish's howl, or was it a child's cry? He wanted to bury the fearful memory of it. There was simply no way the scream came from his wife. Whether reassurance or damnation, Brian knew its call carried more than pain. Yet even the thought of it made him want to cover his ears before it could be repeated.

Fearful, he sensed a growing cowardice inside that was pleading with him to find the front door. He had the keys still; he could simply get in the truck and go. Hands full, he couldn't check his pockets for the truck keys he'd had outside.

A scan down to his wet coat found no clue to the location of those keys.

The stairwell and the back of the couch, Brian stared at it. Coursing quickly beneath him, a foot away, came the withered blur of a child. Seeming to pass by him, with no legs, its form echoed suddenly back into darkness.

A jackhammer under Brian's ribs tightened his organs and crushed his lungs. His brain awash with the purge, his gaze blurred slightly as balance narrowed. Feet attempting to secure a better hold, his idle flame hadn't matched the arc of the ragged figure. Best he could, he tried again to wet his arid mouth. Brian saw nothing more than a fleeting whisper, and in it was the impression of that forgotten child.

Vanishing as fast as it came, his cerebral gray matter hadn't the time to imprint the phantom.

Swallowed by the impenetrable layers of the room, Brian staggered back further. Blind and panicking, he now shuffled backwards toward the tv. His fear of a little girl was ridiculous.

Panting vibrations under his tongue, "Little girl, are you there?"

He needed to adjust her game. The flooding in of trepidation would be better served if it had been filtered through anger or fury. Yet without light, it all melted to an aching discomfort. A confusing game in the dark, and worse, it was with someone else's petulant child.

"Are you there?" He determined a demanding voice was his greatest cover.

Venturing into buried images, a revolting sense of desiccated and pale shapes visited his inner eyes. After he'd stepped off the damp porch, he remembered closing in on someone. He recalled standing over a figure confused and sad.

He knew help was needed. No matter how he tried, the thought went no further. There was an absence of more information, a hole carved out of his mind. Perplexed by his faulty memories, had he seen her enter the house or was it all somehow just lies? He could summon no face, no detail in his thoughts. Standing in the blocks of his memory was just an outlining silhouette of a form. A hungry but ghostly deposit, somehow searing his mind.

"Wake up, Brian." His own voice echoed in an endless room, now inhabited by an invisible creature. His hands and arms washed in needles, plucking the blood through thorns unseen. The swirl of red then white light was painful to his eyes and confused his vision.

He braced against the delusion. It had to be all some drug or alcohol-induced hallucination. There was no other way for this to be reality. Jarred from his thoughts, Brian was pushed out to the thriving darkness again. Unseen, a hardened and shapeless torso grazed him from behind his legs.

Spinning round, the lighter gave a fraught spasm. Too late to swing his bat, Brian petitioned against it. "STOP! What do you want?" He was afraid of the dark, fearful that what tested him was anything but a girl. The feeling was sharp and had a weight that drained his muscles as fast as the last of the lighter's fuel.

Once more the flame hadn't abandoned him as he returned the glow.

Grasping further into his reluctant memory, Brian wanted an account of a kind girl.

Again, a fleeting blur erupted out of the dark. Hitting him from screened-off corners, this attack wasn't understood in his mind.

Spinning round, the shape wasn't set or motionless. Without seeing it clearly, its path was quickly erased from his view.

Whether imagination filled the void instead of fact, death and terror had taken hold behind his eyes. A nightmare of a face that was not living, teased from the darkness. It refused him any rest as every shadow cast by him or the flame was filled.

Brian was cursed in his thoughts as he tried to follow. Left spinning further, he pleaded his own mind to forget all he'd seen. The shape remaining was a stain on the closed windows of his pupils, and it was no impish little child.

Chapter Four

A Child

He'd been standing at the door, wet and in a fog of something he didn't understand. His last thought had been walking to his truck and then. There was a spot on his brain that was lacking. A blank warped hole of information.

Brian thought he'd either passed out or worse. He remembered being soaked, chilled by a temperature that should have never reached bone, but he was cold. A sensation of wandering, as if he'd been on some type of hallucinogen with none of the benefits.

Focusing on that recollection, there had been Trish. He stood at the bottom of the stairs, and she was in the living room. She was standing there alone. No. Brian saw it, though she was by the couch, she wasn't standing straight there. She'd been leaning over. Not for the couch but to someone in front of her.

She was covering something, someone, a child he hadn't seen. Brian couldn't separate facts from the twisted images his hazy brain wanted to give him. What had been at his wife's side?

There were more concrete facts; he was presently surrounded by an oppressive ink and the shadows were malevolent toward him alone. Hesitant to move from in front of the couch, his flame found no location safe. His strongest fist wrapped tight on the base of the bat.

For now, he had light, a weapon and now a fresh purpose.

First, he would go to the breaker box, just off the front porch of the house.

Second, he would find his keys and get to his truck. There, he was certain he had a flashlight that worked.

Looking at his lonely flame, Brian noted the efforts of a strange breeze. Whatever the source, it hadn't come from any doorway or window. Its origins remained veiled beyond his fire, a cruel puff of some foul air.

On the tail of that rotted breeze, Brian heard a faint shuffling. Whatever the form, it was waiting, watching, willing this game, to play out. A child, it was not, yet the breath came inches from his secluded ember. A healthy flame was needed; he pulled it to his chest to be fiercely protected.

"Trish, this is not FUNNY anymore! Where the FUCK ARE YOU!?" The scream wasn't enough anger to give warmth to what had been stolen. Brian's last friend here was only the dying flame.

Waving the aluminum shaft menacingly, he moved forward a step. The advance caused a shift in the darkness. However, what Brian noted above all was the magnitude of what the thing was. This was horrifying and caused Brian's entire body to lurch back. A step too far and he found the end table they used to hold the tv against this wall. The bumped retreat upset his thumb's hold of the fuel button. The result, the same as all the times before, a faltering blue flame returned.

Unsophisticated, he knew anger was his answer. No matter what the outcome, he had to push forward. The threat had pulled away the first time. The shape of the noise always remained a step out of reach; he simply needed to get to the door.

A shield of rage could allow him room. Pounding veins in his head were at capacity in the pitch, he had to go now before either flame left him. The decision was clear, but feet and legs hadn't yet signed on to this suicide mission.

Child or no, whomever played such a vindictive game would rue the day. Getting the response needed, he started his journey, heading for the left side of the couch. Nearing that front wall of the house was the space heater in the corner. Its unpowered shape sitting beside an idle desk Trish had brought home from work.

This time, his move hadn't caused the darkness to shy away in fear as before. Witnessing along with his second hesitant foot was a faint but new distressing moan. Brian waited, his bat ready, while he took in the noise. Unsure at first, his focus attempted to clear his nerves but only gave cause for shivers.

This aching cry he heard was beyond purpose. Wanting to reason this out, he found it impossible, as it was becoming all too much. Growing louder than the hum outside the walls, its pitiless undertone reverberated. Seeming to bounce off the dark-wood-paneling, the groans crawled from under every corner.

Absent were any words, at least ones he might recognize as familiar. Strung out whispers could linger as if waves of thick liquid evil emerged. They splashed over him, and his flame retreated even under his protection.

A transformation followed. Entwined within their overlapping hues was a child's aching but soft laughter. Near the kitchen, its location felt like it never found a place of rest. Going behind the couch, she was low and circling back to him. Its slanted input of laughter neared him, only to ebb away.

"You little fucking brat, are you serious?" Brian wished the lights to miraculously come back on.

Disobediently, his skin crawled from the girl's creepy giggling.

Opened in its closest approach, he responded with a swing of the tip of the bat. Not so hard as to kill a three- and half-foot tall child, but permanently maim? He wouldn't object to silencing the taunts. Enough to teach a well-deserved lesson, one that would not soon be forgotten.

He listened, while the bat remained between them, the sound floating round the living room. Turning toward the kitchen's half of the house, he watched what his light might offer. There was clearly a child playing here. Still, Brian wouldn't stop wondering about her friends.

A drifting boot took another few inches away from him and the front door. Spaced within his next steps, he continued his narrowing swings. Each of them reaching out into the bleak.

"Why are you doing this? Little girl, what do you want?" It was a ploy wherein he could offer her a reason to stop.

"I have food, and we can get you home, I promise. Where's your mother or father?" None of the questions landed, nor did his bat. Other than a skip off of the corner of some cushion, he was coming up empty, with each joust in the shadows.

This was all beyond any child but focusing on details was absurd anyway. He knew it, still; he wished to stop or curb the slight of a girl from her sinister harassment. Denied in his negotiation, he pushed away any further attempts to talk her down.

The left edge of his boot hit the single rise of the entrance, and Brian flinched. A bit shocked he froze there thinking it was another attack.

Flashing into his thoughts. He recalled the location of a working flashlight within the house.

He'd brought one home some months ago. Along with a few tools, he needed to work on his truck's slipping transmission. All of it had been thrown haphazardly into the closet. The very closet, a few feet away now. The coat closet, unseen by the shrinking blue puff, lay under the staircase. This was motivation and a quick ending to the intruder's advantage. He was already facing the correct direction and all he needed to do was find its handle.

The laughter shrank, as did any other sounds. Its power, for once, drowned in the pounding of rain outside. Brian stood there as the courage required, accumulated in his muscles. There continued to live in his bones a chilled vibration that spoke badly of the true state of his nerves.

The door handle was on the far side of an outwardly opening door. Its surface was further into the tormenting darkness of the living room. In-between him and that knob was a typhoon of pitch black. Thick and pulsing, the veins of those shadows were opaque to him, as any distorted beast in his mind could be.

The shake in his hand increased. Holding the lighter and his wrist tight against the wet leather, he hoped to slow the vibration. The curling of his back drew him lower, a creature now himself, he lurked forward. In his hunched shape, he would have to shorten the distance to the closet.

His aim was determined; he looked to the light one last time. Its reservoir unseen but its burn held even against his tremors. Glaring up and reducing the coverage of his view, to advance, was the purpose of his every cell now.

He could see the post at the end of the stairs leading up, and the wall under it as it angled up to the ceiling. The floor ahead of him was empty. Between the back of the couch and the closet, there was no orange shag. The floor planks here were old wood. Smooth and worn, they seemed to creak the least of anywhere.

Brian simply needed to cross, twelve feet, to the closet's smaller door. The living room was long and dark, and the distance might as well have been a hundred feet.

The air was washed as a crack of thunder outside its walls shook the house. The change forced his decision. His looming journey was presented with an abrupt termination of torment. All taunts ceased against his ears and nervous system. All the noises halted; no laughter, no words, no movement, or shuffling shape escaped out of the bleak. Even the rain outside now slowed its endless pound.

An answer found in this; Brian paused his legs. Conscious of every grain of dirt and sand under the souls of his boots, he moved forward. Clinging to his skin was the familiar damp and joining it were the needles of warranted caution. Averse to slowing, he pushed his knees to bend faster. Screaming at his muscles was trepidation. Their voices called for him to lean forward, to draw him across that space quicker.

The foul palate that stayed round him hadn't left but its fever felt less. Though the noise weakened, the rot still seemed to push down on him, over his arched shoulders, holding tighter to his nostrils. The sensation had become overwhelming, physically and in his thoughts. Like a foreign limb, it was over his mouth. Brian felt as if the oxygen in the very air was being sucked from his lungs the further he moved.

Rocking his head against the sensation, his mouth and jaw snapped shut. The preoccupation with the wretched air gave Brian an unwanted hesitation to any swing of the bat. In that pause, and rushing at him was the small, deviant girl. Her dash was aimed straight at him. Fast as she approached, she then disappeared behind him over the path he'd already made. A ghoulish rat of a creature and its glancing rush gave Brian a spasm as he pulled back against the wall. Almost swallowing his tongue, he inattentively swung away at the fright.

"You better not do that again, you little shit. I…" The shudder was broadcasting a newer stage of his rising anxiety. It was a river of fear stinging the folds of his brain.

"I'm not afraid to hit you!" The shout was feeble. Added under his breath, "you little bitch." His lips spat now as they secured his open mouth. Hitting such a 'defenseless' child had become more of a foregone conclusion. One that he wouldn't have liked to admit to anyone else.

In the next step, his waning flame finally came upon the sought-out door casing. It was shut tight, but there was hope inside.

Shifting the two objects in his hands, tragedy struck, but not from the dark room around him. Loss from under his ripped thumb, the gas lever closed from the burn. The already pitiful flame simply vanished without the eke of food.

A worried hunt for the lighter switch began under a flurry of jabs. The super-heated metal of the lighter's roller burned the already tender skin. That raw attack on the plastic sent repeated but briefer showers of sparks.

Blood and broken blisters made him jerk, causing a straightening twitch. His cramped hand then let loose in a throw of the fingers. The resulting action caused the entire lighter to slip any hold he'd had. All grip of the sweat-covered plastic was let loose.

Frantic and voiceless, Brian bent a knee to save the dying hero of the night. As fast as he might be, he was late to slash out and grab it. Astray in the pitch, the lighter spun randomly in the air when the side of his palm nicked the edge. Absent luck, his attempt to catch it sightless merely sent it flying erratically toward the kitchen.

The sound of it striking some unknown surface was followed by it landing on the linoleum floors of the kitchen. The lighter was gone, and Brian now shrunk inside his panic. Wicked and hungry, the darkness engulfed the last holdout in the room. It'd been playing with the taste of fear for long enough. No longer waiting, an undefinable weight lumbered closer to the withering man. An opportunity available, it reached out.

Savage and sharp, a probing jab struck at the center of Brian's lower back.

Reeling from the strike, he swung back wild in desperation. The leverage used against him was far more than the angle of attack could explain. His mind was crazed, but the child's viciousness, if not her devious use of the dark, was without equal.

His bat returned from the swing, having only hit the back of the couch. Lost for which direction to protect, he was left with no good options. Pointing the weapon toward where the front door was only made his back vulnerable. Soon, an attack would come at him from the kitchen's direction.

Hoping to ward off any further assaults, he put his back to the closet and randomly switched back and forth between the two. The surface was rough enough through his jacket. However, the foundation was welcomed as protection.

Leaned against it, his back flattened to take more advantage. The passing blur of consciousness filtered away. Soured thumb and fingers, his left hand fumbled for the doorknob. A transient twist, Brian stepped out as he pulled, then swung the smaller door all the way open.

Protective of further jabs, and already in hysterics, he instantly spun round to position the opening at his back. Both hands around the shaft once more, the closet was behind him. In it lay the last expectations for lighting the room back up quickly.

The bat struck the door jam and slipped from one of his hands. In that lone weaker hand, he continued its angle and an outward jab of his own. Situating its point downward, he was hopeful in stopping another menacing attack.

Stepping into that ominous hole, he felt the touch of the hanging coats first. Brian wasn't turning around, nor was he able to see. A decision was needed here, but what? He could give up his defense.

Crouching with only his knees, he regained control of the bat with his slipped hand. Under the packed collection of coats, he bent inward, his back leading the way the entire time.

He reached his left arm downward to find the distance under him. A twist in his core, he needed to reach anything on the floor. Feet were the first to find a cluttered floor being pushed behind him. Unable to reach far enough, he lowered further. Above the ground, he could bend no more before sitting on the piles under him.

The packed landscape within the closet was going to take a greater effort on his part to find anything, especially the flashlight. No longer benefiting him, he plopped down off his sore feet. His search within the abandoned rejects of this hole could now advance.

In his doubtful mind, without eyes to find the flashlight, he'd have to turn with his back to the opening. He'd have to lower the bat completely as well. The shape was specific if he came across it, but which area? Deeper his search went, yet the only discovery, more forsaken bits of their bruised life.

His sanity at a breaking point, the tip of one of his fingers located what he'd been looking for. Vindication had arrived; but its shape was buried, and he would have to rise off the layers under him. Multiple layers of piled clothes, bags, oddities, and unknown objects held the flashlight captive.

The action of lifting his overweight bulk loosened the tentative grip of the bat. Try as he might, the shaft of the stubborn flashlight remained stuck under some other obstruction.

Forced to pivot away from the exit, Brian let rest the bat with the slightest hold atop its end. Grappling with the tangle of oddities lining the floor was a greater threat than he could have thought.

Endless were the seconds, until finally his throbbing fingers plucked the girth of the flashlight free. His breath and weight crumbled back down atop the debris' surface.

Those actions lightened his hold further on the bat. His grip slid now to the last inches as Brian focused on the new hope. He'd never used the borrowed flashlight before. Its shape, a foot long cylinder with the only difference being on the torch's end. The button to operate it was almost flush against its midsection. Under a blistered thumb, he fought to correct its vital direction away from him. His loosened hand, still resting on the bat's grip, felt a change. Slight in his inattentive thoughts, and from outside the closet's edges, the bat's distant tip rose. Violently, the dented weapon was ripped from his clammy hold, disappearing into the ether beyond.

The assault was unsettling, Brian's mind numbed as his hand sat empty now. Wielded in his other hand, now a flashlight was his only defense. Even now, its use was unpowered. Flooded with anxiety, Brian pushed back deeper into the recesses of the closet. A beacon of stress, his face became engorged, blood blushed and discolored. Instead of words a spattered drool of sounds erupted out of his mouth.

Crushing harder against that filthy, cobweb covered back wall was Brian. Panic and fear pushing him, he continued to hold the un-ignited flashlight pointed outward. All the while, he nursed the stinging right palm and its abused blisters.

Swirling in dread, what more inhabited his house? More than evident to him was that no tiny girl possessed that strength. Correcting his hold, he put both hands tight around the sleeping torch.

A hesitation lingered, but it wasn't a concern if the batteries still worked in the older flashlight. No. The real reason he'd not turned the beacon on was that he was unsure. He wanted a clue to what truly was out there but was the outcome worth the reality. His spine compressed harder against the unpainted sheet rock back here. Desperate, this hole was his last safety, even in complete and utter darkness.

As if an explosion, a crashing racket filled the living room. An eruption outside the doorway took all the darkness to heights of destruction. Then silence fell back to earth.

To his secluded tomb inside the closet, whatever the demolition was, it was unknown to his overreacting brain. Although what followed seemed worse. It was a roaring quiet. One that left an impression of hurt on his eardrums as it peeled his empty eyeballs wider.

Already at the limited recesses of the closet, Brian moved to the corner. Pushing his weight into it, he felt no safer than any of the minutes before. The flashlight's butt pushed harder into his chest. All the while, his eyes closed tight, any expectations unknown or welcomed.

In his retreated corner he felt the bottom line of coats hanging over him. Their lengths mostly even, as each just dangled at his forehead and closed eyes. Motionless, they deceptively existed only to protect him from above.

Distant and away from the opening, a soft, whispered voice of that girl reached through the abandoned space.

'Hide and seek.'

Chapter Five

The Whisper of Now

The odors here were far more hospitable than what he imagined was creating the rot just feet away.

A blistered thumb held tight over the button on the flashlight. Tense, the bones in his finger shook atop the 'on' switch. Waiting for his brain's command to engage, it had no more sensation.

Ultimately, the word was given. Though the proper muscles still worked, he knew the hesitation came from his heart.

Leaver pushed; the tool still had a well-supplied storage of battery power. Even after sitting for so long at the bottom of the closet, its light was instant.

The end of the torch rested firmly in Brian's chest as the other side sent a magnificent beam outward. Aimed straight and pure, the beacon exploded out from the depths. Its force unchecked it reached out beyond the curtain of coats.

Flaring to life, the view from behind the beam was fractured by the clothes waving above him. Pitifully, Brian's wide-eyes and brows dipped to see from under the obstruction. His head lowering, a cautious pain caused his lids to narrow. Bonded, his hands sat firm on the slightly rusted metal, he needed to allow his eyes correction. The journey from that farthest point back in the closet was limiting his sight. Just under the jackets he eked his focus.

The beacon's path was anything but steady in his hands. Over a shifting palm and hanging belly, he searched only the closet feet in front of him.

Brian's thoughts all shattered, he would see the person or persons meant to do him harm and humiliation. His gaze passing the edge of the curtain, he froze for a moment. He wanted to look fully about the area, but his eyes squinted cautiously. His left hand down, the other turned the light to see the hinge of the door.

There was a scene outside the door. One he hadn't known or expected.

His brain aching to work properly, noted the couch was gone. It was no longer resting in the center of the living room. Though his scans had failed to find his attackers, they were still there. They were likely somewhere to the sides of the door frame, waiting as they had when the lighter's flame led him.

The flashlight had power, but it was a diffused and yellowish one. The stream of energy leaving the closet quickly discovered floating through the air fine particles of dust. Their tiny specks drifting in a path aided by unseen breath.

Though there was no longer movement, he watched. No creature or bloody monster staring back at him. Yet Brian was far from convinced of any safety outside the hole he was surviving in. He knew whatever was beyond here, merely mocked him as he tried to stay safe.

The burn of the light set feet out the door, its purpose not yet further than the floor. Sending his light of truth farther, Brian was heedful to missing anything. Without the obstruction of the couch, the newly coveted source reached entirely across the room. His spine was heavy with the hanging weight of his flesh. Brian dragged his legs into action. Arching his head, it came up into the view and level with the floor. A companion to the light, his eyes walked with its journey.

Tapering the farther it traveled, the glow of the flashlight crossed the room. Striking the far wall of the living room, it awaited his scrutiny. Its power was just off to the right side of the tv, the flashlight's illumination arrived unchecked on the paneling.

Nothing but a motionless space echoed back to meet Brian's gaze.

Dropping his raised waist to the ground, Brian watched as the shaking of his hand translated through the beam. He still hadn't heard anything more. As those tiny atoms floated past, they gave him the false sense of peace. Their playful shapes, swirling in an abandoned dance.

Unsure just how long he should sit there, Brian held back every instinct to call out. The back of his head and dark hair, mixed in the reach of jackets from above. He knew not to trust the tricks of the mind, but where was he to move now? The consideration to stand up was next.

Constant, the path of the flashlight remained straight to that distant wall. A tilt of the head, Brian found a need to clarify an oddity found there. As he stared, he allowed lenses within each pupil to narrow. The view, spanning those fifteen feet, rested on the dingy white paint. His interest wasn't the painted paneling, but what was on that section of the wall.

It had been a detail he'd thought missed. Studying it harder, his focus couldn't deny what information returned from its surface. He was unsure, but the proof might have been on that wall earlier today. Although unfamiliar, there were dark lines stretching upward. Framed by the touch of the circular light, it was a prelude to something much more.

Heartbeat continuing its rumbling race, he let the flashlight tilt upward. His shoulders leaning farther out, they passed the arms of the coats. Hand wrapped around the light; the beam moved up over the edge of the tv.

Pupils smashed at the top of their orbit; Brian's already tired gaze was treated to a gruesome sight.

The unbelievable location was also daunting to his mind. The living room had a ceiling equal to the height of the two stories. What he'd discovered oozed and ran down as a stream, its gore increasing covering every inch of its climb.

Brian was looking up at the remains of some horrid act. Displayed there for him to see as the carnage spilled out. It was from that source. The river of vileness dripped down the length of the wall. Neither black nor confused in the yellowed light, it was the aftermath, a red leaching canal coming down.

A troubling dark crimson that turned his stomach. Near vomiting, Brian's mouth gaped open. Gasping, he couldn't fight the need to wretch. Sucked from his lungs, little oxygen returned as the struggle intensified. Draining above all, was some masticated animal carcass. Somehow its shape was skewed now to the ceiling. Unclear of the creature's original form, he fought to slow the bile forming within his throat.

Having gone hunting thousands of times since youth, he'd thought himself immune to guts and gore. Many a time, he alone was left to gut any number of God's creatures. However, sitting here, he found those earned nerves were now absent.

What could have left this profanity? His thoughts and mind thrashed violently against this aberrant evil. There was no way a man could commit such an act of utter horror.

The strength that he might have had returned was now shattered. Subtle in his mind before this moment, his every system now demanded him run, to move. He needed to leave the boundaries of this closet and the house. 'Escape' the animal instinct within him shrieked a call that was hard to disobey.

His spent arm flinched and dropped with the light's power. The usefulness of his flashlight fell back to the space just in front of his isolation. Outside his camp, still no shapes awaited his rabid vision.

The room lay disquiet as it had most other nights. Those nights were largely innocent and free of dangers to him. This night was far and away different. It carried a lingering change, a flavor that said the calm was a lie. It was an unnatural lie with no trust. He knew what waited for him, whatever its shape, a child, Trish's lover or a twisted creature, there was a fight waiting for him.

It would be a battle for his very life. A mistake to draw away from the threat, he would have to face it and kill what looked to kill him first. The question he needed answered was just where this hunter was waiting for him.

Shifting his weight, he pulled one leg up off its knee and tight against his belly. Although an uncontrolled breath betrayed, he placed a hand and the flashlight atop it for support. He was now ready to exit.

Pushing straight away to gain his balance, Brian was still too far inside the confines of the space. As his other hand lifted off the floor, his stability slipped from his supporting knee. The force already warped, it sent him off course and sideways.

Uncoordinated and leaning too far to the side, he fell forward onto all fours. Breath continuing to struggle, Brian's face was near the threshold of the closet. Ears turned, he was immediately aware of the sound of movement somewhere in the living room.

Dragging his legs back forward of him, he came back down on his ass. Settled in for a mere moment, shapes were seen off-center and in the direction of the kitchen. The soft shuffling noise had no outlines to define it, but it had returned to taunt him. It seemed to dance and beckon him to move, to run from it. To attempt escape, that it might take chase.

Without the bat, Brian could only gather up the metal flashlight tighter to his core for protection. Jerking the light back level with the room, he pointed it toward the kitchen.

As before with the lighter, he found no shapes, no creatures. What he found was a shattered couch, piled against the wall in the corner. Yet the threat was all around him, heavy and panting for a taste.

He could make a rush for the truck. He might get cut or stabbed, but with his weight, he could push through it. If able to exit the house, he could just run for the driveway and muddy road out.

His heels dug in, moving in the layers beside him, as his empty hand corrected his seat. He was a fraction from exiting the closet and now lost in the floor's mess.

Piercing the measured edge of the darkness, the faintest of a whisper hissed at him. Its foul shape came over him, caressing his hair and ears as if it a tongue of some fetid breeze. A harbinger of some worshiped and encroaching death, it had found him wanting.

While there seemed to be words, their transient form only visited inside Brian's head. His flashlight moved quickly, twisting one way, then the other. Sadly, the light's search could no sooner locate its source than swat the breath away.

Mingling deeper in his skull, the childish taunt beckoned in a distorted chorus. Calling to him, longing for a violence that lived in him, a violence that it seemed to want set free.

"What do you want!?" The scream tightened his view to slits. "Please–please." It was a descending whimper that he'd meant to set as a howl.

Brian's focus torn; a brutal scourge visited from the muddied shadow around him. Landing against Brian's body, its purpose was pain.

Backed into the cluttered area behind him, his flashlight's passing look was ineffective against the blurred attacker. Single-minded, the foe had proven the safety of the closet was fleeting and worthless. His exit pushed back; it had narrowed Brian's movement.

He'd seen that same small, morphed figure as it flew past. Anchored there, Brian watched the darkness. His view, in the ink of a living room, was rewarded with a girl's figure passing by. The sum of its diminutive stature, hateful, as it disappeared faster than the beam of light could find more detail.

Up on elbows, "FUCK YOU!" Brian's terrified yell sent chills over his own skin. "FUCK YOU!" Shuffling backward to that singular corner in the back of the closet. His meaningless protection, the light, angled and prepared for another attack.

Looking down, he felt warmth. Clothes desperately soaked from the rain outside, he noted a growing spread of heat under the cover of his shirt and jacket. A moment, he allowed the light to make a pass over the area. His leather was sliced, a sizable rip cut to the flesh. Spilling from it was his own life. His blood was so red under his berserk sight.

The pain wasn't there yet. Intellect evaporating, his entire hulking weight plowed upward. Pushing to stand-up onto shaky legs, he made his own path through the hanging coats. His frantic concerns were all primitive now.

Panic-stricken, he started to swing both arms and the flashlight. The efforts only pulled the rod from its mount. Subsequently, all the hanging clothes came fast onto him. A maddened attempt to free his head, the tangle of clothes seemed to cling tighter. Revisiting in horror, the maze of coats drowned his vision in disarray that he couldn't get free of.

An ever-worsening predicament, all vision and light plummeted into the abyss as the flashlight jetted from his hand. The slipped cylinder and its light fell under him and instantly got buried.

Finally, the wooden rod was hurled out of the closet.

Tumbling to the floor, on his knees, Brian frantically searched for his only hope. Through intertwined coats and mixing artifacts, he was left in this dangerous hole alone again. The light under him only failing to show as it was further buried.

"No, no," the fight was real, even as his breath refused him peace. His hand pulled everything he could grip and flung them wild.

The particles of light flashed here and again but continued to evade his panic. Moments of hope teased, as it would show partly from beneath. His fight or flight instincts now trampled his brainwaves, causing stray electrical storms to fire. Every subsequent inhalation grew more and more problematic toward any success.

His vision was spinning. He was no longer sure if he faced in or out of the tightening closet walls. Hands never surrendering, they ripped and tore away sections of the mess. His head pounding, Brian had reached a point where he was extremely light-headed. Yanking up the last coat, the glowing light, and the only weapon he was left with. It was the last means of escape in this fight, the flashlight was his again though.

His position was bent on both knees. Facing outward, from the back of the insignificant space, he had only the light. Its influence on the world around him was a dizzying spin. Atop the confusion, his blood was roaring through his skull unchecked. Unable to budge, its effects were like a hammer on his vision.

Brian felt paralyzed from the neck down. The light pointed to just outside the threshold, as it had when first found. Following the beam, his eyes fought to take control of the light leaving him. Focusing slowly onto the dirty floor, his focus needed effort to clear. There at its shrinking termination, Brian's worry found the circle of light on the ground, and it was not alone.

With no other muscles moving, his reddened orbs focused.

The beam's path carried him just beyond the frame of his confinement. Its power to uncover even the darkest shadows now caressed the bare feet of that murky figure. At its ending, a square foot of occupied wood flooring. It was the gently swaying shape of that small girl, now awaiting his attention.

The flashlight motionless in his limp arm, never had its heavy powers raised higher. The glowing circle, for once, rested unmoved on the floor. Its work intensifying the contours of what now stood looming, hungry, directly over it. Bare, pale-fleshed, and dirty, her feet remained fixed. Her head, moved slowly and with a tick to one side then straight again.

Furthest from his light was the girl's bony flesh and face. Its eyes and scrutiny aimed down at Brian. Her towering shape watched as his eyes raised to meet hers. Hollow caves that were her eyes, made death real. Their purpose and temperature appeared to consume his infinite panic.

Matted and still wet, her hair draped about her shoulders and part of her face, as another twitch came. The sinister summit of her threat was the grin from one side of her thinning lips. As a slithered hate matured in her face, so did both hunger and a lustful need creep into her grin. She'd found food across the threshold of the closet. His wounded chest bled as she glared down on him.

"We can play hide and seek." She said.

Eyes like saucers, Brian could only witness the facts of this guest in his house. The anomalous gore of blood clearly on her face was disturbing. Her jaw, as well as the rags draped over her frail figure were speckled and stained dark. The liquid, more than apparent, was a match for the gore on the far wall.

His will was broken; Brian lay unable to object. He was now the fly in some dreadful spider's web. His remaining means of defense, was reduced to the worst, watching in a numbed terror. He would see everything and regret it all.

Around from behind the unmoved girl, something poured out the nearby gloom. Their shapes were different from hers, and their forms were poisonous to Brian's soul. Shifting outlines, they materialized from around her smiling silence. Crowding over to the small child, they were neither walking nor supported as a man should.

Approaching the closets threshold, and the prey they'd sought out, each brought with it unseen cackles of hunger and anguish. A gaping face, Brian's quivering lips and eyes surrendered hope. No noise escaped from his useless mouth as the repulsion of an undeniable beast came round. Able to observe the sunken wells that carried their gaze back on him, he found just emptiness returned.

Cascading around the child, the creature's mouths opened foul with teeth. All the while, Brian remained aware of the intended abuses he was to die by. In some late protest, his arms came up to stop the feeding. A fruitless attempt to defend, Brian was treated to the girl's laughter. Its echo and his life extinguished before the night finished its close.

Chapter Six

The Dark Step

February 2006

126 Rooting Hills Road, Summerville USA

Clutching Scuff, a stuffed toy dog, under her arm, Simone glared back with a scowl. A level of disgust and hatred rare for someone only seven-and-half years old, she stood there at the edge before the woods. Three-foot six, her hips were even with the winter's surviving weeds.

In front of her, a dirt and gravel driveway. Her dark sienna eyes watched past this and were locked on to the house. Thick lashes moved slowly as she continued her wait. Simone wasn't afraid of night, but standing there she felt unescorted.

Numerous tears rolled down her bruising red cheek, but they weren't forgotten. Around the sides of her jaw, they were just worn trails, meant to be ignored by everyone else. Alas, these tears were unlike any other.

Born of anger more than any other emotions, she let them fall without wiping them away.

She studied that cluttered porch, looking for movement. On it, beside the closed door was a porch light, its yellow glow just to the right. Through a window beside it, all the other lights were off, except that single muted one outside.

It was a lonely source in a strangling wood around her, yet she scrutinized it as if it might dim further. Its power was not dissimilar from what lived within. Only a low-wattage bulb, behind it and inside those walls of her home, was a heartless living room.

An eked-out existence beside the front door, the light hid what couldn't be seen through the small window. That man she hated was sitting in there. Probably slouched over the cushions of the couch, staring at the same program Simone had heard before leaving.

"I hate your face. I hate your stupid face." Simone uttered cold and despondent to any ghost hovering nearby. Over and over the sentiment shaped the snarled twitch on her stiffening nose and lips.

She was wearing a thin jacket and leggings, nowhere near warm enough for the temperature. Simone was watching the door she'd slammed shut minutes ago.

The hateful words held little more meaning than the anger she associated with them. She'd heard them repeatedly by her mommy and Jude, her stepfather, time and again. They'd saturated each other with far worse flippant wishes her entire life, but these were Simone's limits.

Tonight was the first time she'd ever said some of them, and straight at that man's face.

Jude was her stepfather, but would never be her dad. Never would she say those words that her mother had asked. She would never call him daddy. Yet beyond these thoughts, he was alone inside the warm house.

Behind her curled lip, Simone let go of the most important wish she believed in. "I hope you die." She had a history with this one.

A glance skyward she meant it as a wish that she'd trade anything to see it come true.

He had never even moved from the couch, when she screamed and stormed out. Simone had made it more than clear to him, she was running away. Even at the late hour, he hadn't given her more than an unsympathetic huff.

Though she wasn't sure of the reaction she needed, Simone hadn't expected his harsh indifference. Looking at the pinpoint of light, she didn't care now. She hated him and so did Scuff. Her sole friend, Scuff, was a worn but well-loved stuffed animal. Tan fur covered most of his body, all except for a happy black spot over half the left side of his head.

A passing glance down into his hazy, scratched eye, Simone found him gazing back up.

With a sigh, she looked back to the distant door. There, forty feet away, a new flame burned in her fury. Soured further, the damage was placed as part of her view. The porch light that had blazed in the freezing night air turned off.

His last words, when she'd walked out the front door, returned to her ears. Running away from home forever had only merited sarcasm from Jude. "Don't let the door hit you in the ass, but make sure it shuts." These heartless quips were always flavored with a chuckle that he would add to any remark. She hated that evil laugh he used, even against her mommy.

The weight of that light disappearing said it all to her. She hadn't believed he could reach her out here and make her anger worse, but he had. The forty feet between her and the silhouette of her home was the last page written.

Turning away, Simone's face recognized its significance. A trembling chin, she swore, with all that she knew and understood in this cruel world– this was it. This would be the last time she would see that cursed house. She could fare much better than just surviving each night. Hiding most of the day, till her mommy came home, was no life. Long nights, she worked most days, till late morning.

Before letting her sight rise off the overgrown weeds at the woods' edge, Simone focused under the stars. A plastic garbage bag slung over her left shoulder let her feel the weight of the decision she was making. The lumpy shape was stuffed with every meager stitch of clothing she owned. Few other things were valuable enough to mix in the trash bag, but the choices were few to begin with.

Its ticket was shifting on thin muscles and nearby bone. It held the remains of a young life and let her know the load would grow heavier with each step. The plastic had no warmth as a soft breeze reached out to the woods in front of her.

Both hands on the burden, she made sure Scuff was tight under her arm. Forced to pull harder on the line, she positioned the weight closer to her neck. Set on a destination, Simone's diminutive frame leaned forward. She took her first steps into the depths of this new life.

The open sky above her was dotted with small puffs of gray. It was the remains of the past day's clouds, but most had moved on long ago. Somewhere out of her sight and above the horizon, a moon sat hidden. Without it, she still entered the woods.

Even in the crowded shadows of night, Simone felt a sliver of peace. It would be found the deeper she traveled into the small trees nearer the driveway. She'd spent more than a day or two in the dark embrace of this forest. Now that would be tested, as it would soon become her permanent home.

These woods were hers alone, and theirs was the only definition of tranquility Simone knew. That feeling would grow as she moved on trails; she'd laid out over the past weeks and months. This line was only one of many rabbit-sized paths she'd made leading away from the house.

No matter the direction or path she chose, none of the trails refused her a needed calm. The towering trees that lived here had no monsters living under them. Their leaves and branches hadn't a violent intent in the darkness holding them. The wafer-thin souls of her shoes pressed down on a discarded branch and heard the snap. The disgust she'd started with in her expression softened with the sound. Simone knew the voices here were welcoming ones, and all of them she could except. There was no one near that screamed at her for things others had done.

Out here, Simone had only found escape, time after time. The curtain it allowed always welcomed her small hands, and embraced her with no harsh memories.

Correcting the plastic as it slipped, Simone let her eyes drift a few feet ahead of the path she walked. There was no longer a need to be worried about hidden threats. She'd encountered no sinister shadows; never had they walked up to her and struck her square across the jaw.

Any and every scary sound she'd ever heard, were perpetrated by the very ones that claimed to protect her. The man behind her, drinking his loathsome depression from sour smelling bottles, was the worst of any.

A shiver spoke under her jacket as the moon made its first appearance. Low in the distance, she could see its full circle hovering for her to witness. Not offering it a smile, Simone returned her gaze downward.

Her jaw ached as she wanted all her thoughts to leave her. Though her eyes led her forward, her mind remained back there. The woods had their infinite depths, and she knew in this place he could not reach her. Yet each step was slow to make the distance effective.

She still had wanted to think of him as a father. To think he might, in the smallest pieces of his heart, reach out for her with a kind hand. In that same cob-webbed corner of her consciousness, she waited for a shout through the woods building behind her. Every step was a chance to hear a plead.

That he might be able to beckon her back from the front porch was an illusion. Simone hated herself for wanting this. She always wished it to end; she just wanted to hear a pleading voice, the smallest of apologies.

Even against his heavy hand, she needed to be loved. Not to be alone.

A softened gasp broke her sob. Simone wanted to hear him apologize. For nothing else than to say sorry for striking her so hard earlier today.

Letting go of the bag with her right hand, she cupped the side of her bruised chin. Already aware of the injury, she discovered a growing welt and a fury of sharp pain. It wasn't her first. Sadly, the other times had drifted away, both in location and their soreness.

Simone had never wanted them to be real, so she would just ignore them till finally they faded. Though she knew they certainly hadn't vanished. Her reality was anything but a kind one.

She'd been taught over, and over, and over months, then years. This would never change. Jude's abuses were the norm for her now, and he was nothing, if not consistent.

Oh too many times, Simone's feet hesitated. Her own will separated from her heart. She gave the world yet another opening. Another opportunity to prove the discomfort wrong. Her hand returned to the bag, but she refused to turn around.

That disconnect came and went, its dispassionate shape the same as any before it. That stubborn half of her mind reporting an extended heartbreak in the house's silence. A cocked head over the right shoulder. There was no porch light leaking through the growing woods behind her. Simone thought, 'could this be the way it was for all kids?' How was it possible that she alone had it worse from the hundreds, if not thousands of kids that covered the world? 'It just can't be,' the naïve section of her brain was still trying to protect her.

The only audience for her queries were the winter insects. Though few and spaced around her woodland escape, their meaningless answers spoke only of their own woes. Their arrangement, to her, seemed a clamoring but spaced-out blanket that stretched equally over the forest.

Simone had made songs of their wavering melodies before, yet tonight, all their rhythmic performances fell on deaf ears. This hazy, star-filled night, the fire under her ribcage blazed only with hatred.

Returning to her sparse course, she sent the next foot forward.

She wiped the last unwelcome tear away before it could roll down the entirety of her cheek. "Okay fine then, Scuff and I will be just fine without any of you." Tight under her struggling arm, her solitary friend's furry face pointed forward.

The matted and weary head of her stuffed animal never broke character. Its gaze eternally locked open. With a dog's smile, the hard plastic eyes continued undeterred by any of the obstacles the little girl faced. Scuff was forever a partner to her escape, as well as all her pains.

Shifted under her armpit, the black spot and gaze of the dog seemed to look up into her red puffy eyes. Simone's attention dropped down to him. For the time-being, she couldn't share his happy grin.

"We can do better. I don't care when mommy comes home. We'll never go back there again; I promise this time." She narrowed her emotions, even if the affections for Scuff found no objections to her plans.

Its dull scratched-up gaze glared back without a real spoken word. Still, Simone could hear its amiable voice. It was like the one her mother used to imitate forever ago.

Scuff's tone was never angry or forceful as it migrated from her heart up her spine. It would only be heard whispered inside her ears. The happy tones never hurt her feelings, even if it couldn't protect her flesh, it held together her innocence.

"Tomorrow will be different, better for both of us." The words came as a childish bark, but they were never real enough for Simone. Tonight, they seemed to help, even if only a little. An escaped tremor in Simone's lip, she watched his sewn-on grin. His words, like its mouth, were fixed and never changing.

A rip on its back had lost most of the pets stuffing long ago. However, Simone had replaced it with crumpled paper. This had two benefits; it helped to keep his shape more animal-like, but the largest gain was sound. Any movement of the toy offered a shuffling ache of false life.

"We can drink water from the streams and if we need food…" The conversation broke down here.

Simone heeded the lack of food in her bag. It was already heavy, but she hadn't remembered to take anything to eat when she'd stormed out.

The wheels turned in her head, yet her feet continued on the one-way trail in the woods. "We can always wait till he passes out." Though her words were meant for a friend's floppy ears to hear, she was alone with the consideration. Her memories painfully crystal-clear, she knew Jude was a functioning drunk. Yet he was like clockwork when it came to his weekly habits.

If he stayed home on a Friday, which was today, she had a fair chance. After he'd come home this afternoon, he had his normal case of beer. Simone was confident he'd drink every one of those cans until he couldn't stand any longer.

That calculation was also an avenue to her worst memories. She played the history in flashes as her feet sped up the pace. 'When he didn't go out and was home all weekend…' the thought gave a shiver.

Accompanying that picture in her head, came a wave of nausea. "Never. No, it will not be like that anymore. I don't care if I starve, we won't go back. You hear me Scuff?"

The conviction burned in behind the sore eyes. Simone meandered at a slower pace after her trail crossed over the dirt road leading out away from her house. She could take the dirt driveway all the way to the main road, but she'd never been brave enough to go that far.

Her feet were chilled through the fabric of her shoes and short socks underneath. Back into the woods on the right side of the road, she headed for her woodland base.

The woods on this side of the land were much thicker. It led all along the road and even stretched far out around the back of their house. Simone disliked this for one reason–it separated their house from the only other neighbor, closer to the main road.

Slowing her tempo, the space between tree trunks had narrowed. This is where the woods grew in their density. Her trail as it continued was nothing more than a wild animal's impression.

Simone needed to keep an eye out for an approaching fork in the trail. Her sight was well attuned to the low light offered; she gave a passing look as the elusive moon found an opening above her.

Through the trees all seemed to greet her, they beckon only for her company and not her story. This was understood by Simone as she again focused on the path she'd taken over countless expeditions. Tonight was just another, but for one fact, she would refuse to return home.

Absent from her emotions, a faint smile found Simone, even as pain remained under it. Another correcting tug at the plastic bag as it was slipping on her shoulder. Finally found, she stopped at the split in the trail.

One path to the left deviated and headed parallel with their driveway and the road. The other, to the left, was much more friendly to Simone. It was the only one she'd widened from use.

A hop over a fallen limb, she turned to the left, and a narrow tamped down aisle was gladly accepted by Simone. Beyond it was a darker wood's invitation.

Chapter Seven

A Bruised Jaw

Movement forward slowed as her soreness returned, equal to the pain spreading over her neck. Simone hardly progressed as her frustration mingled with a pang of hunger.

"I don't care." There was little food in the kitchen anyway.

She sanded her teeth as Scuff stared at her. Giving a defiant look to her playmate, she knew any harsh words were not helpful. His ears flopped back and forth as she slowed even further.

Simone knew he listened intently to her every declaration. Also, her love for him was the very nutrients that kept him in this world.

The heat on her jaw and neck forced her feet to move again. The first few paces after, led her out of the reach of the moon. Simone felt to be under the protection of the woods, yet it was never enough. The temperature that had been closing tighter around her, was now leaching off what little warmth the jacket could offer.

She wouldn't go back even if it took every ounce of strength in her frail body. Her resolve was acknowledged, yet she knew cracks grew there. Holes in her plan needed mending if she was to survive.

Determined, she weaved in-between more of the hefty trees. This was Simone's own private world. Even had the monster left his lair, this place was hers. Had its fists and hateful eyes wanted to trail after her, it was impossible. Chasing her here, into the strength of the tree's green arms, Simone knew only the fleet-footed deer had a chance. When it came to the forest all around her keeping ground against her escape was unheard of in her mind.

Her thoughts separate from the physical. She ignored the ground below her. It was hard and unforgiving in the cold, dry air. Nonetheless, as she bobbed in her memories, the furry companion was all too happy to rest on her side. Its gleeful expression let her guide them both forward.

Simone's reflection now was being pulled back to the blackened bruise from Jude's steely fist. Its efforts screamed louder even as the chill in the air touched its heated surface. Any mending was beyond her abilities. She knew nothing short of time would relieve the pain. Playing the entire episode behind her eyes, she continued to push between faceless trees. The scene started as a flashing nightmare. She'd only just come out of her room upstairs in the house.

Having come downstairs, she simply headed for the kitchen. It was then that Simone had been caught off guard. Hidden in the living room, just outside the kitchen entrance. That's when everything changed in a blinding flash. Stupidly, Simone hadn't been cautious of the battleground she was descending into. Off the last step and turning round the banister everything shifted violently. Stepping from some unseen corner in the room, the monster was already angered.

Jude grabbed the back of her hair before she knew to run. Stopped cold in her daydreaming the two-hundred-and-fifty-pound man plucked her up like a disobedient pet. His slurring mouth already mid-sentence in some speech he was mumbling about someone else. He was clearly enraged about something, either from his work or her mother. He ramped up in tone and volume. His yellowed teeth chomped as the foul, rude venom dripped out. Holding her in the air he argued, however its aim was not simply from her appearance or deeds.

"Why are you here?" Finally, his addled mind, a split combination of intoxication and twisted regrets found the shape in his hand. The words surely had another meaning, swinging his newly opened beer outward in the air.

The color in his blue eyes already corrupted , he locked onto the broken child. "You fucking shit." A spilling pass of the can's edge came at her head. Simone was only able to grip his hand, holding her hair. She struggled to lighten the pain, as he held her by her long raven hair. The attempt was only to lessen the painful strain. Whining as she'd reached up, the man had little concern for her protests.

"I can't believe I wasted sooooo much time…" The train of thought was all over the place and defective. Jude's grip snagged in her thick hair as he yanked harshly. Her feet landed only for a second as he lifted Simone off her feet again.

Without her mom home, Simone could do little for her safety. Only with her left hand found his wrist. She could do no more than flail helplessly in his shifting gestures. A fight on her behalf would do nothing more than invite a strike.

Timing was no friend to Simone, his first blow made contact. Wild from his significant limb, she hadn't the time to cower against it. Though it wasn't controlled or balled up, his hand had inflicted damage all the same against her thin skin. His grip eventually escaped the knots in her hair. Jude let fall the forty-two-pound child, but not before ripping out some hair on his watch. As she slid from his fist, he no sooner dropped the can from his other hand. Its contents immediately hitting the wall then floor and spraying its full worth over him and Simone.

"What the hell! You think you can just say that to me, then walk away, you fucking bitch?" The goggles in his brain were still fixated on a clearly absent opponent. While his mind floated, his flat palm turned to a clenched fist as he grabbed again for the replacement punching bag.

The hook-shot, low and forced, took its property on Simone's jaw. Jude all the while felt nothing. His rant transformed little as his other freed hand caught hold of her shirt. Pulling it toward his frame, he tilted an angry lip and stone eyes on the blur. He was about to open up on the woman his mind saw, in some past argument still. To his confusion, he again found the small rag of a child under it.

A fleeting second screamed by, as Simone's agonizing howls stopped his follow-up punch. The failures of his own life grew as disgust, lived inside. However, with a hindered intention he hesitated as the ear-piercing cries of suffering washed over him. Curling his head away, he threw her backwards to the floor. "Stop it!"

Her stepfather had sent her to the ground with such force, that Simone flipped completely over. His back to the kitchen, a pissed glance came down to the emptying beer on the floor. Jude merely stood over the beer; a disap-pointed snarl his answer as he leaned against the nearest wall.

His billowing breath was paced out in sickening gasps. His blue eyes drifted behind slow blinks. Jude thoughts were hard to collect as the swirled air around him waited. A glance over to Simone's crumpled state on the floor.

Her whimpering moans, an annoyance.

"You need to watch where you're walking, dumbass." Jude's words were nothing more than a spit of regret. Its shape, a recording he had saved from some familiar existence.

A space between Simone's pain, saw the man's fumbling gaze. She wanted to escape, but he glared at her like he always had. He had the ability to look through her, as if she was a pane of glass as easily broken.

Simone was abandoned there on the ground as he wandered back to the couch. His mumbling had replaced any fuming thoughts he had, and he hadn't looked back at her as she cried. She'd never known a time before him. She would never know another after.

Simone knew little of her real father. It was nothing but random stories doled out carelessly by mommy. When Simone had caught her in times of reflection, it was always brief. To actually reminisce on him, she knew it seemed to be only on those nights her mommy lived in that heaviest sadness.

The story of that person would be forever, a man she gave no name to. A shape from her past, she would never answer questions about.

Compared to her reality, that figure lay as a character in a fairy tale. Whatever his shape, she would think him an impossible person to believe to be real. Still, she loved those stories even if it had been forever since her mommy told her one.

Chapter Eight

The Broken

Swollen and deeply bruised, Simone rubbed the worst of her unwanted trophies. It gave her little to no comfort, but the act of attention was enough for her. Where she found a level of aid was the frigid air she walked in. This section of the woods was slightly more familiar to Simone. Yet that comfort was only good for the trail itself. The shadows further out were covered in tangled walls of thorns, and where they sat empty, other obstacles lay hidden.

A stream farther up the path cut the full length of the forest between properties. On the other side, were less used sections of the forest she had avoided.

Finding a limit to the chilled air's ability to soothe, Simone pulled her jacket open nearer her neck. The mere touch of the rougher fabric was adding to the irritation on her skin. Examining how sensitive her neck felt, a twitch traveled out under the touch. Even when mommy came home, she would do little more than cuss at Jude for new bruises. Simone had even stopped telling her when he'd hurt her.

Some of their fights caused by her were because of this. They'd afterward sink into their own demons. Either way the argument headed she'd end up hiding. Running from his torment and new punishments the second she left.

Simone tapped at the perimeters of the spot on her jaw. Of course, even when mommy hadn't defended the sight of her wounds, she did little to change the dynamic between the two. Instead of even listening to her, her mother would immediately take Jude's side. When it came to her mommy, her stepfather could make her believe she'd done it to herself. It was explained away as Simone seeking attention.

Passing a narrow section on the trail, she was forced to let the bag drop off her shoulder. Stepping out of the tightened collection of trees, the stars opened once more to her. The moon found her as she continued to reminisce about her stresses.

Unfortunately, Simone knew all these lies of theirs, wasn't even Jude at his worst. Those days were reserved for the apex of every other weekend–pay-day. His limits for drink and violence were beyond any reason for Simone to even leave her room.

She'd long ago made a mental list. Things that were best to avoid. The 'when's' and 'where's' of greatest need for caution and what warranted fear made the listing. Although payday was at the top of it, others easily could take its spot on her list.

The second one was both hers and her mother's dread. It was the unplanned visits from Jude's older brother, Steve Shears. Even her mommy avoided coming home if she knew he was over at their house. If he brought his dog Salty, mother would go as far to take Simone to their so-called 'aunt's' house, and hour away.

Another one on Simone's list was if she ever got sick. Defeating as it were, Simone had learned this fact in the hardest of ways. When she got sick, Jude always made things worse.

The trees had become slightly unfamiliar as she stayed in those depressing things. A hesitant foot halted as a cluster of evergreens blocked her path. She hated this section of the woods.

Though most of the forest welcomed her walks, this section was a curving turn that led her further from home. Halfway between the main street and her house it was nearer the stranger's house. The one she'd never seen close-up, as it sat on the other side of the world and her woods.

At this doubtful turn, that circled around the hedge of pines, Simone stopped for a second. Looking straight up into the blanket of stars, she sighed. Letting the stiff chill in the air caress her face, she watched her breath escape far above her lips.

Behind her, all that was left was the occasional small footprint. She never made much noise in the dark, but as she lingered there, she heard the crunch of frosty leaves under her own feet. Her concerns wandering in the surrounding air, and she noticed an unusual smell this night.

Paying little mind to the addition, her gaze returned to the choice. Left or right around the group of tightly packed trees. Tonight, she would choose left around the obstacle. It brought her further away from home, but it would still bring her to where she was headed. The trail she'd been following didn't exist on this section. The bag slung back on her left shoulder, felt heavier than when she left the house. As her feet worked over branches and small saplings, she kept the dark grouping of taller trees to her right.

Repeated in her head, she'd be clear of this murky spot soon enough. She need only walk faster.

There was always some interesting aroma lingering in these woods. Tonight, it had a new flavor, though Simone had to admit it was not a favorable one this time.

A loud snap echoed under foot. Eyes down on the ground, she recalled a not-too-distant occasion, where she'd found a stench. Although it had been during the daytime, she tracked down the smell only to find a huge deer. When she came upon it, Simone was sure it would bolt. They were skittish creatures, and on most occasions they ran. Never closer than a fleeting glance out the corner of her eyes. Yet, that day she was graced by a much braver beast.

Laying completely on its side, the animal never moved a muscle. Walking no different than any other day, she simply came directly up to it. Its head, though cocked to one side, let the massive antlers rest on the ground. Its mouth slightly open, Simone came next to it.

A foot from its still ribcage, she expected it to jump up. Her hand raised up and over its shoulder, she sent her fingers into the fur. The sensation was wonderful, if not an experience she would forever remember.

Coming around to see its considerable eyes, she knew the beast was in deep thought. Those black eyes, unmoving and almost sad, she crouched down beside it.

Simone liked that memory, as she remembered the animal's fur. Under its chin, she had again pet happily over the course hair. Studying its unblinking eye, she hummed a soft tune. She hadn't been sure if the deer was merely resting from some long run or had been waiting for her. It hadn't mattered. The gift was hers and she'd spent an hour talking with the silently listening creature.

That smell from then was not totally unfamiliar to this one tonight. She hadn't an objection to it than either. As long as the deer remained, she ignored the harsh touch to her nose. Simone reminisced on the best part. The antlers had been a welcomed surprise against the touch of her flesh. She'd always thought them to be rough and hard, but they were actually soft. They were the most satisfying sensation she'd ever known.

One direction on their surface, they were as slippery as water, yet the other, gave tingles all over her body. She regretted not staying longer with the creature. When Simone returned the next day, the deer was gone. However, the smell lingered nearby for a week.

Another regret was not following that smell back to her newfound friend. Still, she smiled at the memory as her attention returned to the journey ahead of her.

The sting in her jaw throbbed as she looked again at the vast reach of that void to her right. She hoped to be around it by now, but it continued out into the reaches of the forest. Her thumb pushed at the side of her mouth before Simone opened the tide of self-blame. 'If only I had stayed in my room, none of this would have happened.' She'd been skillfully ignoring the thoughts for most of the walk, but its efforts now had control inside her brain. Beyond the agony and bruises, her feet never slowed. Their angle around the pine grove carried her deeper into the center of the forest.

Eventually, the weight of the bag on her frame was too much. Sliding off her arm, she brought it low beside her. Heavier than before, Simone allowed it the space it needed to drag behind. A sign ahead, there was a possible ending to the cluster of trees. Ducking under the dead carcass of one of the numerous surrounding trees, Simone searched out a path.

A branch of some nearby thorny plant made contact. Its twisted fibers and spiked hunger, anchored into the underbelly of Simone's dragged bag. Unkind, more of the long fingers grabbed hold. Even as their summer roots were ripped out of the ground, its thorns sunk deeper. At first Simone only felt the weight of the bag grow. Pulling against a concealed enemy that was slow to follow, she tugged harder. Taxed, her left arm jerked against the hesitation.

The plastic bag, full of clothes and every worldly possession Simone had, snagged harder. Ruinous, this additional stress pulled back. The plant's main body, feet away and strengthened by a tangle of other trees, refused to let go. A lonely greenery along a forgotten area of the woods, the stretch of vine cruelly bit down. The thorn's grip had found a weakness to exploit. Thin needles and a twisted reach, its extended leash allowed her two more feet before no more was offered.

Simone had found her path once more, only feet away. She need only force her heavy bag to follow through the last of the brush. A step over a half-buried and decaying trunk, her bag fought against her pleads. Allowing her the thought of being free, the bag twisted in her lone hand. Obviously stuck on the log, Simone stiffened her posture back toward the bag. Grabbing it with both hands, she leaned her weight away. Full strength, she jerked against the struggle, hoping to pull the plastic garbage bag to her.

A wellspring of distress was leaching into her muscles, the harder she needed to pull. Her grip choked around the mouth of the plastic bag. More power was needed, and she could feel buried anger coming to the surface. It was an untapped source she'd been fighting for hours. Its strings were linked to emotions that she'd been feverishly suppressing. In her gut, an angry beast screamed to be set free. The weight of the bag was simply another thing hindering her escape. Legs angled away from the bag, she pulled violently to pass the log. Everything within her just wanted to go.

An undeniable equation had been reached between the two forces. Simone's face red, and her teeth finding new pain in her jaw, she felt her efforts begin to pay off. Unable to hold off the human efforts on the flip side of the garbage bag, the vine released. In retribution, the snapped thorn sent a fatal rip up the full breath of the plastic.

Recoiling, all of Simone's energy and anger were focused on the bag in both her hands. The built-up strain now surrendered, sending Simone, her anger, and the shattered remains of the bag flying backwards. Simultaneously, on her flight back, all her clothes were sent sprawling across the bitter February landscape. Laying defeated on the frozen leaves that covered the ground, Simone looked at her hands. Ragged and meaningless, she still held pieces of the plastic. Its usefulness was gone.

All that she held in her hands now was trash. A fitting picture of her existence, if there ever had been. This was a cut too much, too deep into her brain. An inevitable trigger, it had been set in motion earlier and now a perfect storm staged against her. Already shivering and weak, her frame surrendered its last. A final shutter signified she'd abandoned the escape; she was lost and without direction.

Crumbling forward into the thick layer of dirt and debris, Simone broke down. Dropping sideways, her desires refused to support any of her muscles. The bag wasn't the straw to break her back–it was simply the weakest point. Already weary, there was no stopping a replenish torrent of warm tears. Their source, deep in her heart, the flow wouldn't be stopped by closed eyes.

Wilting, she was no different than the Fall's leaves. Without connection to the trees any longer, they lay discarded on the ground. Though they cushioned below her body, they too were dead and forgotten.

Simone's head cradled in her empty hands felt the river begin. Folding her legs into her chest, she lay on her side, balled up in the gloom of her forest.

This time was far harder than any of the times before. The world was so large, and everything in it was set against her slight frame. Simone welcomed the cold, its temperature falling on her in the winter's night. It could freeze her here and at least she might have an ending that was fitting to this night.

She could imagine no other fate to befall her, other than if one of the surrounding trees laid atop her. Darkness behind her sightless eyes, was it possible the earth below her might open and swallow her entirely?

She had nothing other than tears, no other voice than crying. Her moans, a floating breath that carried across the deceased leaves. This was her safe place but none of the trees lent their ears to her pain, nor could they soften the wounds she was living with.

Towering over the scene the bark-covered sentinels all loomed. Their heavy limbs stretched over her, but none of them embraced her huddled surrender. Though she lay deep in the foliage and her sobs echoed, the night's air never changed. All the animals and insects continued unaffected by her presence. Their own voices, untouched by her chain of woe.

Almost directly over the shattered battlefield, a blood moon pressed down. Its unnatural tones tinting even the darkest of shadows. Floating in a cloudless night, the sphere seemed to pause over-head. Its face rendered no empathy for the creatures it touched. The child calling below its breath, still was left abandoned to an eternal drift.

Time lost all meaning as Simone steadily wept there. Head resting on the ground, she witnessed nothing of nature's winter pace. The first change under the moon's sinister weight was the direr colors of the woods. The unbroken whispers of her forest began to leave.

As if one by one their voices grew quiet. A blanket of misshapen silence was filtering into her lonely section of the woods. Tightening under some enduring shadow, the night's chorus drifted further away from her sobs. Taking its place was a thickened and colder air.

The hush entered, it quickly suffocated the last chirps and clicks. The skewed tranquility was anything but a lack of sound. It had shape, weight, and it came close to the broken child. The space between each shadow in the forest grew inward. Its attention now found Simone's small patch and came closer.

No owl, cricket, or animal shape moved along the forest walls or floors. Just the presence of darkness came to her calls. Even the very wind stopped against a wall of unnatural obscurity.

Nothing could be heard except the discourse of a girl's hurt. The only movement was the shaking flesh of a balled-up child. Her last friendly audience, the uncaring trees.

Distant and under duress, the winter's gusts still pushed at the outer perimeter. Its howls silenced as it plucked at leafless branches far above it all. Its freezing tongue, curving and prodding to gain entrance to the dense shadows below.

Above the sorrowful figure, the moon marched further. Its gray light, bouncing off whatever hunted alone in the silence, inching closer to the fallen prey. The spreading ink crawled beside Simone, unwilling to give nature any more room. The call of weakened blood, too strong to be denied tonight.

Simone's attention was centered solely on her own release. Her ears and eyes closed; she couldn't have seen what crawled into her shadows. Oblivious, she wasn't aware of the hunger, now watching her soul exposed. An open wound, she seemed to draw-in evil as it searched to find bare flesh.

A mountain-range of pain drained through her small eyes. Against the harsh chill covering her, she simply allowed the shivering to echo her whimpers.

Something foreign to mankind, unfriendly to the troubles of a child, grew over her. Patient to strike, the fibers of the pitch oozed from other corners. Seeking their own audience at the food, they waited behind the colorless tree trunks.

Finally, a crack on some desiccated limb, spoke first. Then, in sequence, all the other crowded fields stopped their approach. Birthed from the nearest blind void, a soft tone divided the sinking darkness. A shaky tone, it was worthy of its ill history. Rising, it reached out to touch the balled-up child. A hand, unlike man, hovered over the sobbing wreck. While its contact stopped short, its corrupted breath drew in her flavor, only inches away.

The hesitation fixed, the sinister hand retreated back into the shadows. Still, lost on the ground, the warm body hadn't yet seen the threat looming so close.

"Why do you cry?" The voice was from an escaped dream. A lowered cadence that mimicked innocence. The words out of the darkness were covered by her moans. Paused in her pain, Simone wondered if a voice had come from Scuff.

Chapter Nine

The Answer

Her shaky breath as Simone let her eyes crack open. The idea of Scuff talking had been a dream she'd never thought to have come true. The inert animal still laid just under an arm. Released from her trembling sorrow, she allowed for a temporary intermission to her weeping.

"What did you say?" Her brow furrowed as her continuous sniffling sounded in the calm. She took him in hand and looked closely into the floppy-eared gaze. The two half-spherical orbs were equally scratched up. Though hazy and worn, the dog's love was clear as they stared back into her wanting eyes.

A tilt of the pup's head, Simone adjusted her own head to see him better. Every time she would look at him, it was always upon his left eye. The reason was unbeknownst to her. It was just something she had decided on long ago. Her wish for Scuff to speak was persistent since far beyond her memories. A childish one she knew, because toys didn't talk. This wish had died ages ago, yet here it was, when she needed it more than ever.

Unable to simply shut down the tears, the corner of her eye continued its slow drain. With little control over the pain, Simone offered her imagination a moment's break, before returning. Met with no answer from his stitched smile, she again lowered her friend. This time, he was placed center to her balled-up body. Cruelty was her mind, toying with her emotions but tight on the ground she gave it no more thought.

Although tonight, this interaction was unlike any of her dreams and wishes before. This tender voice repeated, but she was sure it hadn't come from Scuff. The spoken touch came from outside her bubble. Possibly from further up the path that she'd wanted to return to before her bag burst.

The voice was too soft to be her mommy's. Simone searched out into the heavier shadows where her head lay. Then with an upward turn along the ground, she narrowed her scan. She was looking for any feet, standing nearby.

"Why do you cry?" The voice quizzed the girl once more. Whatever lips moved, were held back in a faint whisper. Its location anchored closer to the girl's feet as she lay there. Yet the voice was not alone as other larger shapes within the surroundings.

As for the forest the silence was unnatural and fought against the quiet. These words slow and direct had no competition. There was no equal from either unvoiced forest or the cold inaudible shadows. The sound had been no mistake. Simone turned sharply, wanting only to uncover her visitor. Yet the darkness had speed and was helped by her tear-filled gaze. Pushing up to sit straight, Simone brought Scuff just under her chin.

Her curiosity was there, but something inside her said she needed caution. Working to stand on wobbly legs, Simone noted whoever this person might be wasn't close. She thought its shape should have been arm's length away, yet a body for the voice was absent.

Echoed in Simone's head, the question must surely belong to a child. Possibly like her, the soft tone was more likely from another girl, maybe lost here in her woods. Standing straight, she wiped some of the tears from her cheek and chin. A modification to her stuffed-friend's location, Simone's feet shuffled. Their path, a turning circle in the leaves as she spun fully around. Her eyes were already used to the lower light levels. Simone struggled to understand where this girl might be. The call had been nothing of a yell or loud echo. It had been quite the opposite, she thought. A body to fit the voice continued to avoid her pursuit. Where was this friendly voice?

The consideration lingered, as did the premise that another runaway girl could be hiding in these woods alongside her. Her thoughts washed away a thin layer of her gloom. Its interdiction, into the events spread all about the forest floor, was a welcomed one. Even now, the sparks of the gleeful idea matured. Her mind and thoughts sent racing as her search did the same in this impossible idea.

From her own house, and on the deepest nights, she'd made out a transitory light there. It was a star in the abyss, when she did find it, it was merely a flicker in a winter stripped forest. Though fleeting as it might be, it was at the very least proof of life. A sign for a small girl, that outside her little world, was surprisingly other families.

Peering out her mommy's bedroom window on the second floor was the only way to discover that dim light. Sitting for hours, she would endlessly dream of the fantasy beyond. That upstairs window afforded her a bird's eye view through the encroaching forest. Only night afforded her this power though. As for the day, thick woodlands choked off any of the surrounding world and what might be.

She loved that window seat in her mother's room. Simone had certainly spent much of her life daydreaming about the places she might go. With little reference to the true shape of the world, Simone's dreams lay more in the fantastical. She would pretend that the distant house was filled with great teachers and visited by the most colorful travelers. She'd imagined interacting and playing with kids her age and older. Although it was shaped by four panes of dirty glass, the surface kept her body there. Nonetheless, behind them, she was portaled to those worlds in her mind. When she was alone in the house, it was there that she'd escape to places never seen.

Left there other nights, Simone would hear her mommy and that 'man' screaming and yelling downstairs. Time and again, she would vanish through its smudged surface. Out there she would become anything her mind could conceive. To avoid getting hit, in some of their fighting, she'd sneak up the stairs to that room. Perched there, she stared out its powerful edges. That delicate light in the strange house would be her answer.

She couldn't remember actually seeing the house up close. Somehow, it was there just for her though. Her mommy had described it a time or two, alas, Simone never pictured it in the same way each time. Its true shape was meaningless to Simone.

The structure in her mind had no need of a kitchen or bedrooms to her. That light and its beacon was more important. Its flame, otherwise murky and tormented, was a sphere of life. It had let her know that theirs was not the only family in this world. After all was said and done, it may as well have been on a different planet. With her mind trailing, Simone's foot took a step. It had been over three months now. One hundred and twenty-two days, since that 'light' had dimmed, every night after, it was never relit.

Miserably, Simone had never given up, returning one night after the next. She hunted its previous spot, outside those four panes of glass every opportunity she was given. Refused each time, hours wouldn't help to find its burning glow returned. She waited on that windowsill, hoping to be told once more, to dream. Yet, like always and with all things, she was simply ignored. Visiting the window too often, she wondered if it was her fault. She'd called on it too much, too often, looking for it to save her.

Whatever the truth was, she had neglected the real reason she stopped. Having gotten caught one time too many, she stopped visiting that window. That man, the one her mommy had asked Simone to call 'daddy,' he had caught her sitting there. That memory had its own bruises, even if they had healed already.

Her mind slipped back into her freezing body, she was here in 'her' forest. Simone pushed all those thoughts aside. Tonight, there was a possibility of finally meeting a friend. Somehow, that house was paramount to any chance.

She carried a faint smile but it grew as she ventured closer to that gleaming light than she'd ever believed. There was a likelihood that there was now a family living nearby.

Somewhere ahead of her, the darkness gave a moan. There was a meaning behind it. Simone didn't hear a threat that anyone else would have feared. All the chemicals flooding her young brain, centered only on one fact. A girl from that illusion was a few hazy steps away. She was praying on it.

"Come here. Please don't go." Simone's tempered voice reached out where her eyes could not find shape. The moon, larger than the sky, offered little more than shades of black for her to know.

Returning from the darker ink under shifting trees and tormented angles, a voice reached for her "Come here." The caricature was innocent to Simone's ears. Its true shape, seeking her trust, all the while hiding behind a muted despair.

Pulling sore muscles forward, Simone was starting to feel hopeful. There would be a young face smiling back at her. Another step and their meeting would be assured. Her vision was no longer aware of the direction or the familiar shape that guided any other time.

"Where are you? What's your name? I'm Simone." All of it whispers from Simone's lips. She might lose her if there was silence. Only a soft disappointment washed over her, as there was no answer to her wandering eyes.

She took a few more steps. She found tangled branches and unacquainted ground. Her trail wasn't the same anymore, but she wanted to see this girl. Frustration was short-lived, when once again Simone heard the comforting yet drifting hiss.

"Come here." Barely audible, a concealed hunger was there.

Having no face or body to connect with, Simone now gave a hesitation. Stopped, she leaned forward, nearer the darkness calling her. Though she wanted to pursue, she required more. "What's your name?" Her voice was influenced by the chilled air leaching through her thin layers.

Uneasily, she turned her head. Simone was no longer sure of the direction she needed to look. Finding movement in the thickest of shadows, her frustrated gaze tried to penetrate deeper. With a crooked head she tapered her eyelids. Loosened became her smile, Simone was feeling an abundance of confusion with her emotions.

Where her heart lived under her ribs, Simone simply asked it to slow. Its speed was uncomfortable, yet matched to a joy, if she'd been standing at the edge of a beautiful sandbox.

"Do you live in the house by the street?" She twinkled at the idea of having a friend to visit, even if it was that far away.

Without more input, Simone was beginning to worry. Had she imagined the girl's voice? Questioning her mind, she heard a thousand times anything but doubt. Shaking off her reservations, she peered down through her numb shoes. Forcing her toes to wiggle, she was sure she could continue.

She was 'not' mistaken. She wanted to say those words out loud, to just hear them. Regrettably, if the wish was heard, her caller might leave. A nervous grin placed on her face; Simone took another step. What confidence there had been was now a decision she was making.

Simone had to force her legs past a thicker section of brush. Beyond the taller mass of shrubbery, Simone immediately recognized the touch of thorns. A field of them, she could no more turn away from them than escape their hunger.

Unseen barbs, wild and in every direction, they plucked at her clothes first. Scraping against thin fabric, many of the hooks found skin beneath her protection. Undeterred, Simone progressed through them. A goal, larger than their pricks was ahead of her, if she only pushed onward.

Wanting to break through and be surprised, an empty vacuum greeted her. She couldn't lose this friend. It was similar to the deer, and that wasn't going to happen tonight.

Pulling free of numerous snags, she felt warmth rolling from the minor scratches. Some on her legs, while others could be felt through the arms of her jacket. She focused on the distance ahead of her and closed it as quickly as she could.

'Had the words come from Scuff?' The voice in her head was now speaking louder. No sooner did she push it back, than a snarling ache in her stomach growled to be heard. Parsing her attention gradually, the stinging cuts of the thorns made their appearance. Her body's chorus of growing pains had their own voices.

"No," Simone stomped. Jostling them all back, she needed to take back what control she had. Random openings in the canopy found her at the edge of the field of thorns. Finally past the taller trees, streams of glowing rays had begun to reappear. Their touch, now reaching the forest floor, erased many of the harder shadows.

While sufficient swaths of Simone's arena shimmered in the moonlight. During the summer months, storms had ripped through the woods. All around Simone was the result of that powerful anger. Overturned and rooted trees dotted the space in these woods. Broken trunks and indiscriminately tossed branches spread wide around her. With no guide in this section of lost forest, Simone remained persistent. She focused on the unnatural silence. Insistent, a brash wind far above her, fought to be heard. Its power, though, carried little volume over the unseen opponent. Rustling atop the nearby trees, was all swallowed in the noiseless hush.

The only abeyance in the calm was her tender crunch of footsteps. Right then her left, Simone wandered in the frozen time and noise. Her eyes drifted around her, clueless to what followed.

Turns in her slender path changed nothing. Looming over her journey, the unseen and formless was close. A stagnant air that walked with the blinded girl appeared to wait to measure its prey. A thicker canopy quickly reformed ranks as Simone's trail wandered. Its foreign shapes, no longer 'her' forest. Cut from her view, the face of the moon had drifted into a blind spot.

Neither knowing nor being accosted, Simone had traversed more of the forest than she'd ever imagined. Absent of the thought, she traveled completely oblivious of the heaviness holding tight about her.

Chapter Ten

The Darkness Within

Under a massive oak, Simone took a misstep. Landing on her palm in one hand and Scuff in the other, she came back to her sense of reality. She'd been following a suggestion, a phantom. A delusion that would have given anyone else no hope.

Her open hand felt the frost covering the forest floor. The sensation was not as real as the offer of another had promised. This cold texture wasn't a normal feeling, and it was connected to her sadness. There on the ground, she noticed the lack of noise. A hushed burden that was keeping anything from finding her.

Her eyes moved faster than her turning head, she searched both directions ahead of her. Sitting in the soundlessness, her attention moved to her feet and legs. Her mind fighting to exit the fog in her brain, she was given no explanation. Her whereabouts were the next thought. She'd always been so careful to stay on her trail, but this was not one of them.

Following the search of this peculiar world, Scuff's loving-eyes gazed around with hers. His position cradled in her right arm was safe of the ground, but he had gotten dirty in the fall. A drawn breath had given Simone recess from the hard walk. Sitting there, unfortunately, also allowed the chilled ground to seep up into her bones. The minutes were adding up and she was sensing the loss far deeper than the initial collapse. With her other hand cleaned off on her jacket, she drew-up Scuff's attention.

"What do I do, Scuff?" Her heart was alone again. If the dog could talk, it was now that she needed it most. The darkness was different here, even difficult. Her first fearful glance moved outward.

Creeping voids lived here, shapes that didn't belong in her forest. This was a stranger land than she'd wanted to escape to. The tears of earlier were forming once more on the floodgates. The furry friend, she could trust, came back into the core of her rest as she tightened on the ground. Knees and arms retracted; her eyes continued their search. Her breath, floating up, now thickened as it spun round in some silent breeze. Unwilling to turn her head from her formed security, just her pupils made the effort. Halved over the tops of her knees they could go no wider.

While the moon continued its travel, she stayed put. A lost child anchored in the nothingness; she would linger here, unbalanced. Waiting to hear the normal sounds of insects, Simone was suddenly startled.

Out of the murky oblivion, a blurred form moved directly into her view. A tall figure, slender and manly, its details equal to shadows. Unsure if it was a threat, Simone ducked her head below the raised stuff dog.

The discovery of a visitor was joined by tender foliage on the ground aching under its feet. Step by step the body was approaching her. A flash in her subconscious, Simone imagined an adult threatening her. Pushing her own body lower into the leaves, she wanted to be buried. Shaking her head, this was not what she searched for. 'No' to the menace, she continued to rock her head back and forth.

The colorless thing in her mind was not here to help or guide her home.

Buried under folded arms and painful legs, she dreaded emerging into what the night was offering. A second more and she heard the pressure of Autumn's death crunching under strange feet. The body was standing now beside her. Any moment now, she knew a hand would take her, hurt her, even strike her.

Defensively, her left arm rose above her tucked head, to protect. To take the damage of what stood over her. However, as she waited, there was nothing.

After she could wait no more, Simone cautiously cracked her eyes open. Pointed down, they needed to rise above her protection. There was no noise, no voice to begin with–she would have to use her eyes and discover her predicament.

At first, she thought she might find her stepfather. Yet as her vision expanded over Scuff's fur, a surprise was exposed. What she'd known was wrong, everything before now had been a misunderstanding. Possibly a trick to the night's shadows, that was at the very least now apparent to Simone. The figure looming before her was another kid. There hadn't been a towering figure. A fool to some bent moonlight, it had made her think it was an adult. The trees around her must have confused her tired brain.

A rush of glee powered every muscle now. Her legs and arm wanted freedom from the cold ground. The belief that it had been anything other than a girl was washed away instantly. Even as Simone came up, this girl before her looked to be a little older. Perhaps eight or nine years old, yet oddly enough, she looked smaller to her.

Stammering with a nervous but happy tone, "Hi! Hi, I'm sorry, I didn't know it was you." Simone's words of delight spilled out a river.

Seeing another soul to share with was tremendous, even overwhelming for her. "My name's Simone, but mommy calls me 'Simmy.'" It all came out as a chattering purge that had been bottled up forever. "But that doesn't matter. You can still call me Simone–or Simmy." Rambling with no filter, Simone's uncensored grin crossed her face. It pulled painfully at her bruised skin.

Continuing her greeting, up on her feet, she leaned in with both hands. Out in front of her, she reached for the girl, ready to pet her as if she were a newfound pup. "What's your name?" She asked, nearing this stranger.

Simone moved, Her friend drifted backward as easily as a whiff of smoke. Undeterred, she found it only slightly odd there was still a strain to define her companion. The fellow creature stayed in some valley of murkiness. Obscurity that gave nothing more, no matter the calculated efforts Simone made. The girl seemed to be both still, yet perpetually one more step away.

Scuff's ears in hand flopped in the air. Another step and Simone needed a glance downward. Clearing the top of a fallen log, she returned up only to gasp.

"No, please. Wait, don't go!" Panic gripped her. "Hello, please don't go. I don't know who you are."

Another arbitrary turn to see if she'd missed her somehow. The plea cracked in her throat, as desperation returned. Her pitch was higher than before, she pushed it through the void as she begged. "Don't leave me. Please tell me you're still there." Her eyes let loose one larger tear, having only recently cleaned the majority away. Around the edges, more were filling to take its place.

"Why do you cry?" The purr of the child's voice was unexpected, but it came from behind Simone this time.

Slipping as she spun about, Simone thought the girl's playfulness was merely a curious thing. A game of hide and seek, she wouldn't lose her again. Simone wanted dearly to see her face. Awkwardly placed in the night's shapes, the girl was facing away from her. Trying to shorten the seasons between them, Simone called faster. A sore ache in her right foot slowed, but she'd made a promise to herself not to lose her.

"What is your name? Can you tell me that?" The innocence of the question wasn't answered. What Simone could make of the visitor was that she had dark long hair. She also had less clothes on than Simone did. She wore a light-colored dress. It was short-sleeved and its length only above her knees. What might be worse, she didn't seem to have shoes on.

"Don't leave, okay?" Again, Simone crossed back over the same log in the woods. Yet, the stranger was ceaselessly afforded a distance that her feet just could not match. Her clothes, her feet, even her hair, it all had no clarity. No details for Simone to glean information on. The figure survived only a grayed shading of a silhouette.

"Why do you cry?" Again, her voice whispered. A veiled accent snuck into its query. All this and its core hadn't turned round to Simone's longing.

Simone had been trained out of answering that question. The trauma of unmet needs, and the beatings that stemmed from giving her mommy 'reasons' made the answer stick in her throat. Simone peered down at the ground and Scuff. Her bent mind convinced a small lie was probably best here.

"I…" Her hesitation was difficult as she decided. "I fell in the kitchen."

The retreating figure stopped abruptly. Simone's reply seemed to lock it in place. Purposely, the shape came round with a lowered tilt of its head. Round its small shoulder, the sliver of a child gave a glance back to Simone. The air around them both, thinned as a breeze, was allowed to shake each of their hair. From near black shadows, the hungry shape approached the tearful child. Its shuffle in the leaves unheard as the shadowed legs shortened the distance between them. "Can we be friends?"

Simone hadn't yet looked up fully. The request was unseen from the girl's lips. However, the gentle toneless bid was extended to Simone. Its parameters were nothing more than a collection of sounds. Absent, was the logical happy peaks in a child's voice. Missing was the suggestion of a lost neighbor.

Something more sinister lurked beneath, but as Simone's eyes rose, a willing face was found.

A simple expression, thin cheeks, and damp hair framed a set of blue unblinking eyes. Her skin, even in the darkness, pale and wanting. Through all this, as the girl neared Simone, a singular laugh grew from under parted lips.

Skipping a beat, Simone's entire spirit soared. Like a storm that had covered a cold morning, it now cleared away to bring a bright, warm sun. Her gaze far clearer the closer she came, Simone gawked at her beautiful features. The edges of her shadows dropped away. Her height and age almost seem to tease that of hers. Simone couldn't help but focus on some of the facts. Whatever kind of mommy she had; a concern arose about her thin dressing. Her face, at first distinct, was only slender again and much more like Simone's.

Unaware of her own satisfying grin, it was worn larger than that of any birthday she'd ever had. "Are you cold?" A dipping motion of her head tried to pull her in closer. "I know where mommy has a jacket she doesn't wear anymore." Every word from Simone emoted her feelings and desperation. "You can have it, the jacket. She won't know, and you can keep it, if you need." Simone glowed; a final present was accepted by her as the girl stepped closer.

"You …?" The aching voice was long and empty of peace. What might have been a question was contorted under a missing smile on the frail child. It was a misshapen question but easily found home in Simone's ears.

Whatever the true examination was, it was missed; Simone heard what she wanted to. Her answer was something she loved to talk about. "I'm going to be eight in July. July 21st." Simone's volume dropped to only slightly sad, only because that date felt so far away.

A painful five feet still stood between them. Simone moved delicately, so as not to scare her off like some stray rabbit in the woods. Reaching out with an upturned palm, she studied her. This time, the figure didn't disappear or run from her.

"Mommy said I can have a cake too. I know it's months away, but…" A word new to her lips, Simone knew it would feel great to say 'it' for once. "I'm sure she would let me have a friend over."

It was as grand a feeling as Simone could have ever imagined. Beaming, her smile ran like fire on her cheeks. Unfortunately, a flitch from her jaw and neck spoke up. Having buried most of the pain still, needles radiated throughout them. Disregarding most of the payment, she kept smiling. It was well worth the cost, and she had a friend now.

The nameless figure was slow to move, but as the ice broke her hand moved for Simones. The effort seemed herculean, but closed the distance.

Eyelids spreading, Simone watched as their hands had started at feet apart. Then in those wonderful seconds, it was only inches. Finally, contact. To Simone it was a prize she had long dreamt of.

Though colder than her dirt covered palm, the hand was firm and rapped quickly around hers. It felt larger than she'd thought. Before she could examine it, the girl seemed to lead her in a pivoted turn.

"Are you hungry?" Simone's words seemed absent of physical grounding.

The link, now holding the two bodies to the ground, shifted in a single heartbeat. The stranger was leading Simone. Asking in a gentle tug, but clearly, she was guiding them somewhere. While the path felt to be a new-laid route for Simone, she felt confident in her friend's purpose. A sense of direction, far older than years. The stranger was relentless, no matter the tangles she pushed through.

Simone had spent untold hours in these woods . Yet this girl, ushering her forward, used none of this. As if following some bright and unseen beacon, their path was straight.

In a moment of hesitation, she wanted to protest. Simone even considered releasing the hand that pulled her along.

What warning there might have been was extinguished at the sight nearing them. Through the unseen end in the forest, a familiar porch light had appeared.

Despite this being her woods, she marveled at the discovery breaking before them. It was her own house. The very one she'd been running away from. The stranger had led them directly, if not fortuitously, back to its shabby and run-down shape.

Simone had left this hellhole, swearing never to return, and here they were. Turning around to Simone, her friend's eyes narrowed upon her. A foreboding gaze, the purpose spoke volumes.

Surfacing was Simone's hatred for the man that had turned the light back on. She was ready to leave, to walk away once more. Yet when looking back into the masked face standing before her, she found a change.

The smile on the stranger's lips grew as she watched. Just like that, Simone's troubles seemed too far to hurt her. At first reluctant, nonetheless a troubled grin was paid back.

Chapter Eleven

The Darkness that is Home

"We need to go around back." The idea drained Simone of any enthusiasm. Her new friend wouldn't understand the reasons and she wasn't about to explain a life of caution. Still, she needed some excuse to offer the staring eyes.

"My stepfather is…" Any definitions to follow weren't truthful, and she knew it. Shifting between her legs she couldn't work out an easy path through the next few lies. Other than just omitting the entire discussion. The thought wasn't altogether without its merits.

Simone recognized her friend had led her there without explanation. She could do the same for the last hundred feet. A concealed frown on her forehead, she led them to the edge of the trees.

What was great about her trailing friend was that she listened. Her face was not angry or wore a scowl to interrupt her. Simone liked to talk a lot, but it came at a price. Moreover, she knew the figure behind her was nice. She'd said very few things, and she listened to her.

The journey around the left side of the house was quick. Simone only hoped the girl wouldn't think less of her for her house's rundown look. This side of the house was where the driveway led up to an unused and collapsing carport. Past the carport the back yard came into view.

Her back porch was only a small platform a fraction the size of the front one. A five-by-five construction Jude and his brother had thrown together. Covering a sigh, Simone braced herself as she neared the darkened entrance to the kitchen. "Just come on. You'll be ok." The lead up felt covert, but she had little choice. If her friend asked too many questions the entire effort might fail.

"We'll go to my room. There's not a lot to do but we can get out of the cold and play there." The idea of having a neighbor over was a glorious world of potential.

Though there was no light here in the backyard she could find a glimmer of life. The window, over the kitchen sink, allowed the fleeting glow from the tv all the way from the living room. The blue and white light was a suggestion that 'he' might still be awake.

With no sense of just how long she'd been gone, Simone had to consider the light. The glow of a tv didn't mean what it meant for most. The numerous outcomes to this sign were troubled but she would take the chance. He would most likely be passed out. However, with everything that had happened today she wasn't sure. Wavering in her intentions, she led her friend atop the five-by-five landing.

The door into the back of the kitchen was never locked. The reason, she clearly remembered. A few months ago Jude had returned home with his brother Steve, both far more drunk than most weekends. Mackenzie, Simone's mom, had locked both doors before they got home. Jude and Steve busted through the kitchen door. The door had been missing for a week. When he finally took the time to replace it, it never worked right again. The added benefit for Simone tonight was it couldn't be locked properly.

A chilled hand on the doorknob, Simone lingered. She dreaded one fact over any other. They would have to pass through the living room. She hoped there would be no explanation needed. To traverse that most dangerous of arenas, she required a calming breath before she turned that knob. Her entire focus would be to reach the staircase with her friend in tow.

Constructing a forced smile, she gazed back to that quiet mouth. "I need you to wait here." Her head looked down at the rickety boards. A sad collection of mismatched lumber Jude and Steve had used to make the landing.

Her suggested eyes came back to the brilliant blue ones watching her. They were calm windows. An ocean that had lines of black streaks. Had Simone had time to ask she would have babbled on how she loved the color.

Waiting for her reply, Simone found no understanding nor even the simplest of nods. Her request hadn't changed the solemn gaze. "Okay." The promise was a loose one, but it was good enough for her to continue. The blank expression she wore had changed between grins. Simone blindly took it for a good sign. Turning back to her hand hanging on the filthy knob, she counted to five before turning it.

Wetting her parched lips Simone still felt the stress . Possibly the girl standing, a foot behind her, would think this all too much. All she wanted was encouragement, even a word or signal of understanding. The moment passed Simone placed pressure on the steel, but wouldn't push the point with the girl behind her.

Opening it, she stepped aside to allow the door's reach to pass her by. Panic hit immediately; Simone found her friend attempting to walk in before her.

"No. No, you wait here, it's just for a minute. I mean just till I check." The correction was as soft as she could make it and still be heard.

A true misunderstanding was taking place. Simone then had to discourage the girl as she now motioned her head. The implication was clear that she wanted in. A thought passed; it was likely the cold was getting to her. Still, she had to wait.

"No, I said to wait here." A finger pointed to her feet. It was then that she identified the bare filthy feet of the poor girl. Simone knew they were poor, by all measures of what she saw on tv, but this girl seemed worse off.

"I'll come right back and get you. I promise." A second attempt to hear her voice again. Nothing. "Okay? " About to surrender the struggle, Simone made her last attempt. A palm facing her, she placed a smile behind it. Whether the girl understood or not, Simone again pulled at the door. However, this time to shut it behind her. Disappearing within, she made sure to close the door only to the point before clicking.

Inside of the quiet kitchen Simone stood on toes in her thin shoes. The first few steps narrowed both her attention and anxious concerns. Though the interior was quieter in comparison to what she expected, Simone waited a moment more. The house possessed a stillness that was far more menacing. It looked no different than how the night had begun with her attack.

Her acclimated pupils scanned the kitchen's corners first. No looming figure that might jump on her. Next would be the other side of the island. The archway, entering the beast's den, was far less convincing to proceed safely. Though the lights were out in the kitchen, she needed a better understanding. Any knowledge of what she might need to avoid ahead of her. The point at which she could peer into his living room was mere feet away.

From her shadowy branch near the back of the kitchen, Simone gauged the risks. Measuring any noise, she hadn't yet welcomed the warmer temperature. Though much more agreeable than the freezing air outside, she wasn't ready to accept the heat as comfort.

Sliding her shoes, over the distance in three-inch increments, she was now there. The exposed opening at the kitchen's edge Simone glared down. The divide into the living room was similar to that of the stairs. It was an ending to relative safety. The room beyond appeared the same. The only added light source sometimes used here was a heavily stained lamp. To the left of the front door, it was only ever turned on by her mommy. That was when she came home from work early.

Tonight, it was off.

To the left of the border where she stood was two kerosene heaters. One broken, the other was red, and hissing in the corner. Its efforts cranked out a wave of heat, one she could feel at her location. Though it had a working glow that illuminated the ground around it, it was overruled by the flickering tv nearby.

That smaller heater had burned her plenty of times. However as she stood there she couldn't appreciate the tools' radiant worth.

No other sources of life to uncover Simone stepped forward. Maneuvering around a pile of Jude's clothes she began her journey. This was her true field of monsters, within its fifteen-by-twenty-foot boundaries, lurked creatures both grotesque and unfeeling.

Their skin was not rough or jagged, like so many dinosaurs. No, he had camouflage that fooled most, but not her eyes. Its mouth didn't hold razor-sharp teeth for ripping her apart. Still, they could tear her flesh from her bones with a single word.

The worst of it all was that this unlikely creature, which skulked in the darkness, hated her. This beast had no discernible vulnerabilities, like daylight. No religious crosses could be held up to ward off any of its attacks.

Besides all this, it was likened to those unreal monsters of movies in one specific way. It seemed to relish the tears and cries of this little girl. Simone's woods in comparison, were the gateway to a dreamland. A place and land-scape that held at bay her monster. It was a protected realm where it would not follow. No one had domain over it, or what was better, they couldn't find her within it.

It had rules that would not be broken. Better yet, it had boundaries known only to her diligent pursuit. She could see and feel every step in there. Without exception, none of her missteps within its borders had sent her to the hospital with a shattered wrist. No slip or unfortunate fall had broken her collarbone and blamed it back on her.

Her mouth arid, an uncontrolled vibration spread as she continued her shuffle. Making things worse in the gloom, the nervous shake reached her shoulder and arms as it steadily grew. More aggressive was the twitch in her neck. Over her entire body now, the trembling even threw her balance off.

Luckily, there were no indicators that he was present. He was a heavy snorer. This was her biggest clue he was upstairs, probably passed out. It was a certainty, especially after a night of serious drinking. A few steps in, and Simone could hear none of it. Not the snort or gurgle of his congested nasal breathing. All of these were good signs for her friend to make the journey in. The true sign of his absence was that the television was muted. He would often do that before turning in and heading up to bed.

Given space for a soft pant, Simone was relieved. Following the slipped anxiety she could feel her shaking quickly subside. Though she couldn't see the front of the couch from her path behind it. Turning back, she couldn't yet go retrieve her friend.

Taking one last cautious glance up the stairs, Simone turned fully back for the kitchen. They could play in her room until morning. If she stayed till 12:30 pm, when her mommy came home from work, they could meet.

A small detour in her return route, she came to survey over the arm of the couch. Simone's nightmare began there. Jude came up like the monster he was. A rising threat from the grimmest of bogs. From a slouched position on the couch, he had found his prey.

Without a second to pass, his open hand smashed the girl. Its momentum was harsher than earlier; it took her off the floor just as she turned.

He had been sitting there, stewing in a bottle of darker drink. The passing ticks on his watch had lost measure of the liquor bottle's quantity.

"You think you can just run out of this fucking house? You got to be kidding me, you thick headed loser?" His vocabulary slurred and spat his baleful breath as drool. Stewing since she left, the anger needed recalibration on his part.

Up on his unsteady legs, he found her on the floor closest to the kitchen. A planted boot and foot landed close to her head before hunching over her. His annoyance twisted into a sinister grin. His other foot stepped on her hair to slow her escape. He drew pleasure from the sight of her shocked and shaken stare.

"I'm the one stuck watching you, and you think you have the fucking right." He knew his howls were spitting on her, but he wouldn't correct it.

A fallen deer under a hunter, Simone's entire nervous system needed to be rebooted. Under his heavy foot, she let rip some of her hair just to be free. Direction already shattered; Simone only had time to push up off the floor. Painful and rapidly as she could, she instantly lost her chance to crawl away.

Seizing her wrist, the disordered figure clamped down hard. His rage was just starting. Muscles in a tantrum and without consequence, he lost all control over limits. Viciously, she was lifted into the air. The fragile connections between joints and tissue in her arm were tested. Her powerless body in the air, her head dropped back.

Slipping out was a horrifically raw scream, Simone immediately began kicking. It would do little, but it was an involuntary struggle of a dying animal. Failing in her efforts to escape, she howled as he hurled her onto the couch.

"SHUT UP! No one cares, but I'm not going to stand for any of this. You hear me." His inner-ear balance taken for granted, a shored step turned him to find a needed focus.

"SHUT UP, I SAID!" His scream was louder than hers. The words spat more foulness over the couch. Jude's transformed anger intensified. Her wailing made his sneered lip flinch.

The small card table in front of the couch had the remains of his cheap whiskey. With a thirsty smile he grabbed at it as his other fingers pointed at her down on the couch.

Having lost the battle, Simone's reaction was instantaneous to ball up. Without seeing, Jude's intoxicated body came crashing down on the cushions beside her. Her frantic screams turned to heavier tears as she knew what was coming next.

"Just stop it already." His voice lowered vaguely, "I'm sorry." His character altered, leaning over her. "I didn't mean to yell like that." Jude's rotten breath came spitting down on Simone's tears as acid rain.

The wickedness in his eyes that would once again steal more from her than anyone could; Like no monster could; to take the one thing she would never get back for the rest of her life.

Chapter Twelve

Darkened Remains

Simone remained balled up tightly, naked, bruised, and bleeding in her bed. The light of day was flooding into her small bedroom window for hours. She hadn't moved since that wretched creature dropped her here last night. Her eyes, no longer able to shed any more tears, were red. A vacant stare was fixed on the white paint on the wall.

Expressionlessly, she hadn't even reacted to the chill biting at her all night. Simone hadn't fallen asleep, nor was she going to. As the hours had passed, she'd heard her mommy coming in from work. Later than most afternoons, the fight down there was instant.

She listened to the two yelling at each other. After an hour, though, it all became an unwelcome hiss that barely registered.

Floating somewhere far away in the peaceful forest, she imagined that her body hovered over the ground, she watched animals go about their lives. Looking upon them foraging, Simone heard the distraction first before seeing it. A wall of flames ripped through those woods. Instant and pushed by a furious wind the animals within those trees, after, lay burnt and dying. Each of their deformed bodies twitched as they called out for the relief of death.

Simone had heard her mom come up the stairs. Waiting with shallow breath, Simone listened as she failed to even pause at her door. It was the first at the top of the staircase and easily opened. Yet, without pause, she simply turned left and walked straight to her room at the end of the hallway.

There had been a second where she wanted to get up. It passed though. Simone even wanted to run to her, but she knew it always ended the same. Mommy never believed her nightmares, nor did she seem to care since she started this job at a small bar in town.

It was always the same–she'd push her tales away. The same words as always from mommy's lips. " No more of these lies, Simmy. Especially at this time of the morning." Simone's mom had no interest anymore, no energy to deal with what stories she had about Jude.

Unlike her mother's room, Simone's window was delegated to a small patch of the back yard. Beyond its four panes of glass was the back porch. Most of the view was swallowed by a half-dead but sizable apple tree.

An effort that took hours, Simone eventually sat up in the sun to check that porch. Probing the backyard, her last hope and her head sank. Gone was any sign of the girl. What was sadder, there probably had never been one to begin with.

Before slumping away from her window, she spied Jude. He was yelling at his dog in the backyard. No sooner found back there, Simone watched with a feverish hatred as he tossed a bowl of food down for the dog. Watching from the thin windowsill, she waited there. A hope that would never appear, she wished the tree would finally split. The hefty branches, in one swell sweep, could solve all her problems as it landed on them both.

The dog was older than dirt. It's been chained most of its life in a bare, tortured, corner of the yard. Rarely listened to or seen, the creature, like her, merely waited to die.

She'd worked it out in dream, and thought that the best it could hope for was dying the same time as 'him.' He cared for the dog more than her, and her mom, anyway. Exhausted by all her unheard wishes, Simone crumbled from the view. No longer interested in anything he did. Legs numb as her arms, she moved to the bed's edge. Sitting there, the floor still left a foot below her bare feet.

Lost there, Simone's weary gaze moved in slow turns. The room was half the size of mommies, and the search was over quickly. Every corner was the same, empty of what she truly was looking for. The piece of her heart was nowhere to be found. Scuff's patent and warm eyes were missing.

Any other time, Simone would be bawling for her furry friend. Today there was nothing. No tears would come even if she had the energy. Slouching with the physical and mental heartbreak, she could only wait.

"Maybe I left him on the porch or even in the woods?" It was a statement meant to protect her. She knew it was in the living room. Probably already in the trash. Try as she might to delude herself, the facts hurt her soul. He was a part of her, and now Scuff too was gone.

She was always alone.

She wanted to yell out. She thought of returning to the window and screaming out. Mostly to make sure that Jude's dog Pepper didn't get her most treasured possession. Likely, it had been tossed to the yard, a meaningless toy to be ripped apart by his pet. Her protest, even if she could open the window, would go unheard. It would only give that man reason to take even more from her. Besides, the window hurt her fingers whenever she'd tried to open it, all during the summer.

Wrenching forward from the substantial pain, she took another deep breath. It did little to help push through the agony, but the convulsions were mandated by her body. Arms wrapped across her frame, she remained seated on the edge. All purpose was lost, and her mind and cowering frame was unmoved.

The only thing carrying her spirit right now was the idea of finding both her friends again. Even if the girl hated her, she could only beg her to forgive. Not sure exactly where she came from, Simone could start where she met her first. She obviously didn't live in the woods, so her best guess was that she must live in the house next to the main street.

Peering through the room, there was nothing for her here anymore.

Scuff was all she had left; if she could only find him again, the losses wouldn't be so unbearable. A savage tremor reached every point in her hurt as she leaned to drop off the bed.

Sliding forward, she landed on weak legs. Blindly, she glanced over the room once more. The bedroom light was off. The sun filtering in left an active swirl of dust. Its dance was playful, but today the beam went unseen. Blind to the movement, Simone only recognized the emptiness. Eventually surrendering, she lowered to the hard-wood floors. Instead of resting there, she crawled under the simple single bed.

Her bare skin chilled by the floor's surface, yet it too went ignored. The space heater, now in the living room, had been in her room. Before the temperature dropped last month, it was hers alone. It was after the larger one downstairs broke that Jude decided he wanted hers.

He'd told mommy he would return it but never had. She dared to ask one particularly cold night, only to have one of his heavy boots strike her square in the chest. Simone could still hear that purposeful laughter. A sickening cackled breath, one that was anything but a laugh.

The sun's beam of light, positioned perfectly in the center of the room, illuminated the dark reach under her bed. Discovered, piled in the furthest corner, an old dust-cover dress. Missed or forgotten, Simone crawled over to it. Found in her depression, she drew it close, a substitute for a floppy-eared friend. Wrapping her arms tight about it, she imagined Scuff's fur caressing her skin. Against her freezing, exposed body, she lay there. Eyes lazy but open, she stared out. Hidden from nothing and protected by meaningless dreams, she wanted to stay there under the bed.

The green dress was easily a year-and-half sized too small for her. Yet her quivering flesh gave her little choice. No longer ignored, her chilled frame required protection from the bitter cold.

Working her legs then the rest of her small frame into the clothes, she cared less if it were a bath towel. It would give her the least bit of warmth.

Eventually Simone crawled out, only after the touch of the sun had been exhausted. Its journey across the floor ended as it let free the shadows. Slow, but determined, she was seated back on the edge of the mattress. Her needs all fought for recognition, but her mind was no fertile ground for any of them to take hold.

Unsure, there were two fighting within her: hunger and the need for sleep. Falling back across her bed, she pulled an odd, ragged, military blanket over. Covering most of her body, she brought her hand up to bury her face.

Chapter Thirteen

The Welcomed Darkness

Sitting in her mom's lap, Simone felt so warm and protected. These were feelings she missed from her mommy. Their absence hadn't gone unnoticed by Simone, but just how long they'd been out of attendance she couldn't remember. In her mommy's hands was a well-worn book. One she recalled loving to hear a thousand times. Simone buried her shoulders deeper into her mommy's arms as they cradled her from her pain.

The main character of the story was a girl, just like her. Intently Simone listened to the tale, the best part was coming next where she spoke just like the animals. It was her mom's voice that drew Simone further into the story. The calm, steady tone carried like a melody. She always brought new life to this book she'd heard oh so many times. One thing she loved most was how each character in the story was echoed with a different voice.

Treasuring the immersion, her mommy's voice somehow mingled with the tick of the rather large clock on the wall. With long silver hands that moved unobserved, the tick was internal. This dated model had no second hand to guide the minutes home, yet still it marched on.

Peeking out from her warm nest, Simone focused on the numbers. An aching, tickling, spasm in her neck muscles matched the sound. Eyes aimed clearly; she saw that something was wrong with them.

At first, they just looked backwards. This, oddly enough, wasn't the problem she had with it. There was simply something off, something more that she just couldn't discern.

They appeared to be out of place somehow, even obscured. Forced, her focus eventually corrected her misunderstanding. Eased lenses, she discovered they weren't even numbers under those eternal silver arms.

Slanting her head further, the surprise seemed amusing. How had she never noticed this before? The numbers were small pictures. Now curious to know their subject, Simone peered forward. The surprise was transformed into a weird, queasy feeling. Her new discovery– they were all contorted pictures. Yet further, they were all of her.

Each number had been replaced with a twisted image of her, they were troubling photos. Examining each, they were ones she didn't like seeing. Glancing back to mommy, Simone heard the clock ticking, getting louder and louder. Her lips were moving, but no animal story came out as before.

Above her mouth, mommy's eyes no longer had color. They were now just voids and under them was nothing. Dry and cracking, her mouth vibrated in a mechanical motion. A cyclical 'ticking,' echoed out of her moving lips.

Shuddering, Simone watched as her mom's gaping sockets drifted down to her. A vast expression of disappointment filled her features. Her arms, that had been keeping her warm, were now rough and heavy against her skin. Unnoticed before, her neck and torso began to grow and stretch upward.

Their shape bent and curved over her. Realizing this, Simone saw her mommy no longer held the animal book, either. In place of her story, was a syringe with a long needle attached to its ending.

The threatening tool rose slowly. Its angle now over Simone's head. What expression was needed on Simone's face was still undecided if not slighted. That hand above her hovered, ready for something malicious but Simone still waited paralyzed.

What had been her mother, waited, allowing the horror to build. At the terrifying apex of dread and under the threat of the steel point, all of Simone's world collapsed. A fierce jab came down. Although sharp and angry, the target of her mother was her own arm.

Violently, it plunged to the base of the needle. The depths unheard, it slowly exited upward again. Out of the flesh, a bead of dark red blood marked the brutality.

Before Simone could find her breath, the act was repeated. The arms trajectory aimed for the same spot but only managed the same area. The motion, like her clicking mouth, moved faster, stabbing her arm as an unsettling and terrifying moan began.

Contrary to the brutality, her mommy's body never flinched under the ruptured skin. Worse than the numb expression, she locked her absent eyeballs on Simone. A stop in the self-mutilation, the violent tip, drew closer to a new home.

Every hollow 'Tick,' drummed in her mouth. Its final shape curved over Simone, dark and uninvited. The needle's work, positioned above Simone, left a bloody trail of darkness pouring down on her. The slender mouth of the syringe rose higher. The barb would gain far greater speeds and force. Its direction was planned and understood as Simone fought to move even an inch. An arm moved as she started to regain control. Struggling frantically to get free, Simone discovered she was fighting against four arms. Their purpose was to keep her under the approach of the pointed blade. Full bodied, she fought against the hold and the weapon overhead.

The deafening noise was all around her, heavy and sharper than before. The thunder of the 'Tick,' now rebounded from every wall. The effect was growing more physical, as each of the surfaces wrestled and pushed inward. Each wall wanted to smother any life it found.

Panting uncontrollably, a scream roared out. The voice was hers, Simone jolted upright in her bed. Her eyes searched for the needle.

The room lay dark and empty. Though the nightmare had gone, it still drew a frantic breath. The horror fresh in her eye line, she continued her search, distressed about her mother.

Slow to leave her, the draining tempo of the dream had its own cost. Little to be thankful of, the emptiness surrounding her was the first.

Her heart rate was unwilling to calm, Simone became aware that the ticking sound was real. It had not vanished as easily as opening her eyes. A moment was needed before she admitted it had not left. It was not imaginary, and it continued to fill her room. She knew there had never been a clock on her walls, but the 'Tick' persevered.

She turned to inspect the floors. After looking at her bedroom door, she could tell the sound hadn't originated there. Over to the closet, it hadn't a door. Left in its place was a bottomless blackness on the distant wall. Though an uncertainty remained for that location, Simone hesitated to look deeper.

Under the scratchy blanket, Simone leaned farther forward in bed. Another tap and she finally narrowed in on the sound's creation. It came from the window in her small bedroom.

The overly painted casing hung at the end of the bed. Half above its reach and the other half past the limits of her mattress. Up and standing with her blanket, the shallow springs in her bed gave an aching sound. Towering on her bed, Simone lost the noise.

Its rhythm had ceased any measured tone and had fallen silent.

Simone's heart instantly skipped a beat. Although there wasn't a person there, a different prize was discovered. She swiftly shifted her weight to force the jarred window open. An explosive smile filled both her face and heart. Just on the opposite side of the dirty glass was an old treasure. A returned gift she hadn't expected to see again.

Sitting happily outside her second-floor window, balanced on the thin ledge, was Scuff.

The window opened up easier than expected, an uninvited blast of cold air rushed in on her. Not openly recognized by Simone, was the faint but corrupt tint on its boundaries.

Her hand reached open and slow, as if to calm a nervous pet. Simone's logic, already hazy after the frightful dream, was still fearful. Yet the childish reasons came down to nothing more than a fear the toy would run at her needy approach.

Taken from its perch outside, a joyful squeal escaped Simone's mouth. Its patted and dirty fur sped back to her and was instantly tucked tight against neck and chin. Eyes closed, she stood there. She wanted to extend the length of this joy. She needed to bathe in the pleasure of her love returned.

He was cold to her skin, nevertheless she quickly warmed it up with the powerful caress.

Willing to open her eyes once more, Simone's gaze foraged about the window ledge outside. The tapping had completely fled, but now she could hear the faint touch of winter's breeze.

Leaning out, she was receptive to the gusts as it moved up to the opening. Her face softened; Simone thought she had lost all her fear. Settling with her elbows on the sill, she searched the backyard more thoroughly.

Above her, clouds covered the late evening. The moon hadn't risen long ago, and it shed only a muted glow in the yard. Still, it was enough for her to see by. The yard was a mess. Jude's dog isolated in the far-left corner of the cluttered grounds. In the other corner an old blue truck sat rusting to nothing. Abandoned since the beginning of time, it had always been there as far as Simone knew. Car parts and piles of unknown shapes and purpose, collected near other wreckage. Littered metal chunks of engines dotted the area.

The only clear path where weeds held control, was directly away from the kitchen door below.

Simone, a bird on the wire, listened to the unrestrained winds. Cutting into that wide, 'L' shaped swath of overgrown weeds, was their fruit tree.

The breeze played there the most. Its fingers are driving through the apple tree's mostly naked branches. What insects might have been singing normally were all silent. Hiding in the night's chilled playground.

Possibly her friend was still around. Maybe she was the gift giver, and she was waiting outside to see if Simone had received Scuff. The girl might wait just beyond the border of the weeds, near the last feet of the yard. Perhaps in the forest, just beyond the cut where a fence once sat.

Lingering in the window frame, Simone watched the yard's distant edges. Although there was a bite in the air, she stayed. It wasn't enough, though harsher than the temperature in her room. She was happy in these seconds.

Sharply corrected, the gust caused a faster shake. Its warning snubbed; Simone hadn't stopped her hunt.

Obstinate, the bitter caress drew tears from the outer corners of her eyes. Simone loved this high perch, the view it afforded was only bested by her mommy's room. However tonight, in the scarce moonlight, her young vision was impractical and wanting.

Besides that weakness, she continued to stare. Plentiful tonight, a cumbersome abundance of shadows danced to confuse what she found. Yet Simone made a game of studying them. Like that of the stars, she could form shapes and moving figures of them. Her imagination worked as it sifted through those distant and murky trees. Her raised emotions cast each spot as a character. A band of players in the ever-changing play she made from the darkness.

Put on hold, Simone turned her gaze back downward. Closer to the house, and under her perch was the area in front of the kitchen door. Empty for now, something significant was nearby. Nothing she could point Scuff's attention to, but there was something askew.

Jude's dog Pepper had seen it too. He was out of his house and roaming the limits of his chain. Simone was able to see half of his worn-down path circling that pathetic doghouse. No sooner noticed, than the old dog barked in a spasm of ferocious blocks. After each, the creature turned back to pace the perimeter of his small domain.

Disappearing behind a pile of car parts, Simone could no longer see as he continued his protest. Pitying the cold, freezing mut, she listened. He seemed to be in a crazed state, unable to reach prey. His barks were half the volume of most dogs, especially Salty, her uncle Steve's dog.

Hearing a rather long pause, Simone jumped when a vicious wave of barks exploded out of the darkness. Leaning out further, she couldn't be sure, but the why's, she might guess. Could it be her new friend?

Mouth gaped open; she hoped that Pepper's louder volley would be ignored by others in the house. A pang of desperation made her want to call out. On cue, the kitchen door, broken as it was, slammed open violently. Hit against the siding, clad on the house's exterior, it was damaging. Behind it, a beast far more dangerous than any seventy-pound half-Pitbull mix.

Emerged into the night's air, Jude seemed to fight whatever hangover he had with a new bottle.

Having pulled back to the windowsill, Simone hid, but continued to watch. Eyes far enough up on the ledge, she heard the volley of profanity pouring out from below.

Pepper started a new rampage, even after the threats. A harsh vibration then shook the house as Jude returned back inside. The door closed again; he was gone. Fed up, Jude would just ignore the racket with the help of more drink.

Popping her head back up, Simone heard another pause in Pepper's alarm. Rested out on the window ledge, she searched the darkness.

Scuff, back under her protection, they both searched for her other friend. Though she felt her details, Simone's brain fell far short of recalling the girl's facial features. The memory was strangely unobtainable at the moment. The sketch of her, in her mind's eye, was absent. Only the events surrounding her discovery were clear.

Closing the window, the canine's fight outside, had more spaces between its angry calls. Sliding down onto her bed, Simone studied the recesses of her room. She could try to sleep, or she could get down.

Even without her bedroom light on, there was a fortunate ray of light entering. Her door had the widest gap underneath it. This slot allowed any light wandering; up from downstairs or further in the hall, to find a use in her room.

Collecting her blanket over her shoulders, Simone glanced at Scuff. His opinion was important to her. The conversation was entirely in her head, but the decision was the same. Plopping off the edge of the mattress, she repositioned the rough fabric better. The blanket dragged on the right side.

Standing firm on both bare feet, she picked at sore memories. Her attention scanned the room. There was nothing. Its sorrowful state was made painfully obvious, there was no one that cared.

If she disappeared like her friend's memory, there was nothing to even prove she had ever existed. The feeling made her want to run down the stairs. She would continue out the front door again and never stop.

"I should have never stopped running." Scuff's body was made to move as she said it. His head nodded up and down.

Over to the door, she leaned against it with her back to it. An ear against it she listened.

Beyond the slab of wood, Simone heard the television. Its drone was constant and that meant he was watching it. Likely drinking, he wouldn't stay awake for long, no matter the true time.

An hour passed and a broken moment came and went when she heard him shuffling around. He was down there and hadn't returned to her mommy's room. This was only a fact because there was no yelling or fighting taking place.

This was now just a waiting game. Simone had learned the rules of this game. The only loser was her but if she was smart, she could at least survive it.

Chapter Fourteen

The Path

Up and standing inside her bedroom door Simone was ready. The doorknob on this side still had a two-year-old sticker. She was determined as her hand landed over the worn animal picture.

Measured and slow, she pulled open the door. A slim crack opened between the frame and what path it meant. The weight on the door's hinges gave a building ache. One that might expose her escape. The whining would only get worse if she continued pulling.

Wincing as she shut the door again. She needed to silence the noise if she was to escape this captivity. Simone knew she'd have to take every precaution if she was to be successful in finding her friend again.

Closed just short of the doorknob latching, she released the handle to move over to the door's hinges. Though her room remained dark, the light leaching up from downstairs was enough. Leaning into the lowest hinge Simone gathered all the spit she had. With as much saliva as she could, her aim missed only the smallest amount. A glance up, she knew there was little hope for the other hinge. Unable to reach the top one, a prayer was tossed up to any noise that might have come from there.

Back on the handle, there was no need to turn it. Pulled, slow and even, she discovered to her benefit the door swung without much dispute.

Passing her first and smallest hurdle, she was not ignorant of the trials to come. Escaping this house, as easily as she did yesterday, had taken on new threats. Ones she was not willing to repeat.

The next barrier to jail her was a level-up in difficulty. In just four short steps, she stood at the precipice. A collection of twenty-one steps. Each of them has their own voice and weight requirement to make them sing. She knew the stairs were an unpredictable minefield of squeakiness and cracking, but it could be done.

Her best odds were simply hinged on whether Jude was asleep or passed out. Her preference for him was a liquor induced sleep. Simone knew even this had its problems. The amount needed was so great as to blind him to the world, but time was always a factor as well.

One fact was distressing as she glared downward. The low hum of words and commentary was coming from the tv. Yet the noise she'd hoped to hear was absent. Jude's degree of snoring was useful as a gauge helpful in knowing his level of intoxication. There was no sound of any suffering nasal breath downstairs. Not a peep was heard from him.

She would regret it; she was sure of it as she took the first drop.

Simone would have preferred shoes on. However, bare feet were better for feeling the pains in the tired rungs of the steps. Heels high and atop the balls of each foot, she descended.

Her speed sedated; Simone needed to shift most of her weight onto nimble toes. Every step was different in the approach, and she needed to keep them silent. Her weight fortified by hands leaned on the wall and she proceeded cautiously.

Halfway point reached; she saw clearly into the living room. Sliding over to her left she took hold of the railing. The thin spindles allowed her the best view, but these were best avoided for their noise.

The room below was frozen in a flickering glow. Happily, there appeared to be no monster standing guard. The breath of the creature was still unnoticed. A sneaky thing she wanted to find before reaching the last step.

She continued on her plotted course for the remaining steps. The front door could give her freedom. Its spot on the raised landing was her first thought. It was the fastest way out but the lock there was much harder to navigate. The kitchen door, even though it was further, gave her the best odds.

Even with her dainty poundage, Simone was able to find notes in some of the treads. A groan or cracking sound seemed to roar from under the lower steps. Where in actuality the sounds were minor, the noise to her keen ears screamed 'look at me.'

Stopping short, two steps from the bottom, she again scanned for teeth. The noise Simone had hoped for earlier perked her ears up. Though she couldn't see Jude, a snort reaffirmed he was indeed down here. The first breaching noise was seconded by a steadier wheezing. Not yet snoring, but it was an offering to her that there was a possible road out of here. Two more steps remained, her feet flat now, she waited. Eventually, Jude's snoring gained its more rhythmic course.

The sign was given. Simone would wait no more.

Looking curiously beyond one of the missing spindles a new surprise was witnessed through the last of the railing. Her gaze found Pepper, Jude's dog, was inside. Though laying content beside the couch, he was staring intently back at her.

The dog was never inside. However, tonight he was lying on the floor, his head the only lively part.

Reaching the landing before the living room's level, Simone now watched him. This was no game and she didn't want him to think it was.

A palm out, Simone's hand spoke only to 'stay.' He wouldn't be a problem if he listened. Older than her, he wasn't known to her as energetic, but this wasn't the night to discover a wild streak. He continued to watch from under droopy eyelids. Better, he looked utterly uninterested in following her.

Simone came round the baluster and looked to her left, toward the kitchen. Those lights remained off, but that was no problem. Her path was clear. She needed only to cross the last yardage and she could start the search for her friend.

Holding the post, she looked down to the living room floor. This was where the difficulty was maxed out. It seemed simple enough, but she was sure there was something to expose her. There had to be something that would give her location away, in turn, alert the creature slumbering at the gate.

Weekend routines were fraught with him smashing her. Sometimes, while seated on the floor watching cartoons and eating breakfast, his eruptions were too often. The couch, as his bedroom now, had sadly and forever ended cartoons for Simone.

Lowered from the last post, Simone wanted to cross the minefield quickly. Short as the distance appeared, it was dangerous all the same.

The floor downstairs was not carpeted, but thankfully a rectangular rug laid under the couch. Much of its shape was in front of the couch.

Nevertheless, a small section of it, less than a foot, reached out from behind. Simone loved that section only the more. On cold mornings, she would jump from the last step to avoid the gritty floor. They'd found the bash and brown rug over a year ago, but even then, it was worn. Under bare feet, it felt wonderful. Rolling between her toes, the fabric would cushion the coarse wood planks below. This night, Simone needed it to mitigate the planks' noises. The only problem she foresaw was that she would need to hold the back of the couch. Only for balance, but it was required to span it distance nearer the kitchen entry.

Thinking a second before she descended. The noisy floor, or her hand atop the couch? That much closer to Jude was a risk, likely asleep, there was real fear always. Sinking her toes in the dusty texture, her fingers delicately took hold. The top of the high back couch was firm. The tips of her fingers and her nails dug in as little of the fabric as she dared.

Balance there on her first foot Simone gave a concerned look back to Pepper. Beside the couch, nearer the front of the house, his interest seemed to be growing. Now seated upright he watched the peculiar dance still unsure of its purpose. On tippy toes Simone's nose then her eyes following cast a nervous glance over the top. She saw that the man on the other side was lying dead to the world. Face down his head was crammed into the cushions. The familiar collection of aimless beer cans and two liquor bottles lay discarded on the floor and tray-table.

She was able to pass through both the living room and kitchen without episode. Simone was grateful. In the kitchen she was quick to the door. Gritting her teeth as she spun the nob, and a small push from the same shoulder the door moved outward. Acceptably, the heavy frame only let out a low whine. It was okay and Simone had expected as much. Nonetheless, he wouldn't catch her now. She'd be outside, and that was her world if he woke unexpectedly.

Hand and left shoulder pushed against the solid door. The previous one that once swung here had a window. Not this one Simone had watched the brothers as they did their best to replace it. A much heavier door, she knew from the first time she'd opened it, the door was just wrong.

To Simone's great dismay the wind outside was much stronger than she anticipated. The opening she'd made gave the exterior gust a foot hold.

Stolen from her soft grip, the wind took hold of the door's weight and size. Swiftly it filled the solid door and moved it at speed. Yanked fully open the flat surface sped over the small porch.

In the seconds before the hefty mass slid free of her fingers, Simone's fight to hold on, tipped her balance. The grip she'd had lasted long enough to pull her outward. All security lost; the door disappeared, and she fell into the chilled air. The significant momentum of the hardened core slammed against the siding. The impact was violent and loud, sending out a shockwave throughout the frame of the house. A noise and reverberation that none would have missed.

Quickly pulling her legs back under her, Simone staggered for a moment. She was at the edge of the drop off. The makeshift porch, never meant to last this long, was without railing of any kind. The step off was onto a cinder block step. Over a foot lower, it had always been a mismatched drop for Simone's shorter legs.

Already fighting for balance in the moonlight, she dropped down. The slightly rotted board resting atop the cinder block shifted only a bit. Miscalculated, a harsh twist of the ankle sent her off the right side of the step.

Fumbling, she rolled back beside the porch. Her hands though found the speed needed to save her from a savage head strike. Lost in the accident, the blanket once wrapped around her shoulders flew away.

On her hands and knees Simone made a quick check of her legs and body. Surprisingly unhurt, she rose back up. Checking Scuff's health, he was good. A hand passing over her knee, she felt only a scrape on the leg that had slipped.

Having to turn back to the deck, her attention was immediately met. The two-foot-high porch came even with her stomach, and on top of it she came face to face with a curious gaze. She wasn't alone. Startled, she took a double gasp. Then with a relaxed tilt back of the head the fear diminished. Two pitched, and unblinking eyes were level with hers.

Had she had anything other than Scuff, she would have hurled it defensively. Furious, she scolded Pepper for scaring her half to death. "Get back inside Pepper. Please go lay down, don't you dare bark." An arm out, she pointed with her stiffened finger.

Her tone was as hard as she could make it without the danger of raising her volume. He just stood there, more interested in her movement than any command. Risking the level, she let a tempered shout out. "GO!"

She couldn't imagine the dog was the only one alerted by the door's clamor. The other hairy beast was next, she was certain of it. He would lumber out, bottle in hand and an angry fist, ready to do battle against a defenseless girl.

This slipping moment of opportunity, flashed in her mind. If he did appear, he'd have to catch her first. Spinning in an about-face turn, she would run. Alas, even as her choice was made, her legs were unqualified to lean into the escape. Her found dress was now being stretched behind her as it stopped her. Pulled back on bare heels, all thoughts and plans for freedom were halted.

The greatest fear possible, now realized. It was a large hand and she was sure of it. Soon, a second would come across to lift her from the ground violently. Heartlessly inflicting more damage, for nothing. A reactive scream of pain formed its shape forward in her brain. She pictured the entire beating, which was soon to unfold.

She was measuring her world, to that of the unknown and it was painful to have so little knowledge and less guidance. Guidance that she knew other kids might already have by her age.

Hard fought lessons were the only ones she'd learned to survive by. Tricks and cowering were the rule, to be hidden was her mantra and to run when given the chance, was the lesson missed tonight.

"I'm sorry, pleeeeease." Her volume now matched the emotion.

Her apologies fell needlessly on the dog's careless ears. Unable to turn around in her struggle, Simone thought of fighting harder. To fight against the hand holding her back. However, what was found was not anger or spite. Forced to release her pull she was finally able to look back. Jude wasn't there, nor was his drunken hairy face. The porch hadn't any other population, just her fears and the same curious mut. Pepper's head even misunderstood the howl she had given him.

Simone discovered the entire error was located inches away. Her dress had snagged on the porch and one of the hastily placed nails. Its curved and rusted finger jetted off the side of Jude's shoddy workmanship. Abashed, this new fact was openly welcomed with a nervous smile. Staring back at Pepper,

Simone let go a fleeting laugh.

Still, she knew this was no more than a respite. No promises made or traded, everything was already at risk. Her fingers grabbed eagerly at the section of clothes. Her weight pulling equally in her desperation, she found the nail gave no ground. Leaning backwards and tugging forcefully, she felt a small give. Then before readjusting, a patch in her clothes ripped away, and she was freed.

On a sore knee she stood back up triumphant. Facing the distant woods, Simone heard the first low rumble behind her. It was one of few in Pepper's vocabulary. A growl that purely offered warning to any of his owners. He was not happy with what he saw. A fearful turn to him, Simone's flesh, was too close to defend against any bite. Without time to understand his warning, her reaction was to move Scuff to the center of her chest.

Wide eyed, she immediately observed a mouth full of teeth. His lips trembled dangerously as they drew up and away from the older daggers. Although stained and missing a tip on one of the lower fangs, he was every bit of danger. His stance had also lowered in a rigid threat that spoke of his decision.

Even the hairs on his back rose as his growl increased. At some limit, the angry dog exploded into vicious barks. The posture left no doubt of his intent to defend against her. Saliva doubled as his teeth snarled and another barrage of howls began.

An unprovoked attack was far beyond what Simone thought the dog capable of. Stumbling backward, she only just averted falling. His dirty claws came to the very edge of the porch. Dumbfounded, his teeth looked larger than she'd known.

"Stop Pepper!" All concerns of being heard evaporated as she screamed. She could drop and ball up against his imminent attack. She could turn and run, but that was foolish. Even on his leash, in his corner of the yard, she hated to feed him. When Pepper wanted, even the ten-foot of chain wouldn't offer her room to escape any of his rushes.

A surrender was hated, but she collapsed to a seated position on the weed patch below. It was here in the dirt that Simone noticed his true aim. It hadn't been her flesh he was barking at. Some unseen form, past her location, was Pepper's focus.

Her mind flashed to the brutality this dog's noise was going to cause to crash down on her. Frantically, she tried again. "Please stop. Please. Pepper please? Be quiet, please." Hard as she tried, the words went unheeded. The enraged beast would have none of it, and no longer even saw her existence.

All diversion worthless, Simone's begging ended when a rumbling call out from within the house. Her spinal cord spasmed from the awoken mountain. The need for flight was the only response surfacing in her animal brain. Jude was no longer unconscious, and she was guaranteed to find him standing in the doorway immediately.

"SHUT THE FUCK UP PEPPER!" Jude's vote was brutal. Loud and growing closer, he would have a pound of flesh for being woken from a painful stupor. "LAY DOWN, YOU STUPID ASS DOG!" This fevered irritation wafted from inside the bounds of the kitchen. Its path was obvious as the sounds of collision crashed against some unseen clutter and him.

Panicked, Simone had to run. She needed to get to the woods. There she could hide and later return to her room unseen.

Lapsing any of these thoughts and choices, Pepper changed the narrative. Its anger unquenched, the dog took an unexpected and deliberate leap off the porch. Clearing both drop-off and the unsuspecting girl, the beast was on the hunt.

The mongrel bolted straight for the woods. Fixated on what it viewed as a threat there was no changing its mind. Without any hesitation, the old pup crossed the yard, avoiding small piles of car parts and the old truck rusting away. The riled canine crossed over the last inches of their yard, before plunging into the woodland border.

A befuddled spectator to the entire event, Simone fought to understand both what had happened and what to do. Idling there, she had somehow forgotten that the real beast had arisen. However distraught she might be, Simone's faculties returned, even if late. Her focus followed the confusion. Up and running Simone was after Jude's crazed dog.

She knew her stepfather would just kill her, if his prized mutt got hurt in any way. The punishment would be especially harsh since she had left the back door open. Pepper was always a flight risk, and Jude made many rules when the dog was off leash.

Just as she had worried, past the apple tree and halfway through the last of the weeds, she heard the drifting door slam again. Harder than her hand's mishap, this event shattered some siding.

A bare foot fell over the tree line. Simone heard words firing behind her like shotgun blasts. Her stepfather was already at the edge of the unbalanced deck.

"What's going on?" First at the door, then Jude's red eyes crossed the yard. "You little bitch, what in the hell'd you do!?" Every decibel was ratcheting up. His attention at a distance, saw the girl's shape vanish into the shadows.

Jude's footing, misjudged at the close perimeter. Under him, the platform unfinished and offering no railing to speak of, he continued with another step. An inch too far and the drop took hold. Between the disparity of a dampened stability and unmeasured rage he was lost.

Hurled to the ground in disorder, Jude smashed unprotected. Hands slow to act, his face took most of the brunt. Gravel and dirt-mix, in some forgotten path around the yard, his reward. Open mouthed, even his teeth hurt from the unforeseen meeting.

Pounding the earth in a furious fit, Jude glared out and howled. "IF YOU DON'T FIND PEPPER, DON'T BOTHER COMING BACK! EVER!" Cradling his wounds, he needed a pause. He would have to take a moment before he was able to stand again.

Chapter Fifteen

The Friend

Stumbling in the thicker sections of the woods, Simone scarcely caught sight of Pepper. Forced to jump over piles of branches, she was getting turned around. Through darkened clusters of undergrowth, the dog was speeding away from her.

"Come on, Pepper, please stop." The rally was for no one. "I can't keep up." Simone's call, slowing, but her feet taking the brunt of the effort. "Pepper! PEPPER!" The scream had an emotional toll, as it fractured in her throat. A tear already formed.

She was forced to repeatedly pull herself back up from the cold ground. Running through the tangled woods was limited to a small section. Everywhere else, obstacles hindered and fought back against the small girl's endeavors.

Entering a substantial grove of thickets, Simone was blind to the first thorns to rip and cut. Jerking at the touch, the souls of her feet were not immune to the plant's coverage. Jumping back, but that direction was not better. At every turn she was deeper into other competitor's territory.

In the distance there was another volley of barking. Gritting against the pain, she pushed through the newest thorns. The pricks and punctures were small against her chilled skin. Simone's feet were numb, and she couldn't feel the pain of the thorns as she went.

Freedom was short-lived after the cluster of trees; another patch of vines came round. Higher than the last, Simone was forced to sacrifice her forearms. A small price to protect her face– she moved forward. She never traversed the woods here. The very reason she flinched is why this corner was off limits to play. Fighting the agony of the fiery pricks, her ears waited for more information. The dog was on the trail of something, and she now wondered if she'd ever catch him.

Passing the worst of the thorns, she lost all direction. Stopped, Simone felt some of the wounds running along her arms. In the sparse moonlight they would have to go unchecked. The comparatively trivial dress had left most of her legs exposed. Although it was the worst, these woodland guardians could inflict nothing more than the physical. Scratches, easily ignored, in comparison to mental damage. These weren't monsters attacking her, they were defensive means by which the woods survived.

Searching out the face of the moon, she knew it fought to see through clouds. Thicker covering than the nights before, Simone felt defeated. The trees here had little to none of the summer's growth. What remained was the shape of twisted branches, like arms of some great god weaved above her.

Under foot, layers of dead leaves piled high. Some of the foliage, whipped up by her passing, clung to her legs. Held in place by weeping scars, heavy with her own blood.

Simone found her breath floating up. Its momentary life was short, before racing away from some flurries. The chill was bittersweet, but it gave a deceived pleasure. As the breeze slowed, it closed in around her revealed flesh.

The dog she chased had either gone too far, or she had gone in the wrong direction. It had always been easy to get turned around in her woods. Doubly so since she wasn't following her treasured path.

Simone's mind wandered. A sensation of calm was thicker here. Though meaningless to her, it was against the losing hunt for a dog that didn't want to be found. The lull gave her an opportunity to frame her thoughts as pictures in a paused moment.

Beautiful as the view was, she presently was lost. Mixed up in a twisting canopy above and all around her.

These stresses were still not fixated upon; Simone felt familiar tones, bringing her back to the day before. Similarly, the woods had misplaced its characteristic chorus, like now. The normal waves of animal and insect songs, all of them shut out of the area. Only the fractured moon above seemed to hum, though its voice was nothing more than waves of light.

Over Simone, were other darker forces, firmly they seemed to loosen the forest's grip. Their own threat was invisible to her eyes.

Simone, absent from all the changes swirling about, stood wishing.

The dog's escape was no longer important. Loitering in her sorrow, Simone wanted to forget what was expected, what waited back at her house, the endless fears.

Her gaze, locked upward, strolled the skies above her. A better under-standing needed focus. Beyond her control, she returned to one sense. Oddly, the stings and fire that were her wounds, gave her power. Disconnected from physical pain, a tear rolled away from her raised-up face. Its trail, falling as different as the emotion. Coming around her ears the tear rolled through thick hair and off the back of her neck. The sensation was novel, as a tingle lifted tiny hairs on her arms and legs. A perfect silence surrounded her.

Its summons, if the same, crystallized the fact she now remembered. Simone waited up there in the night sky, comfortable that what visited was dear, if not a gifted dream. Calm, she was not alone.

"Why do you cry?" The whisper caressed Simone's ear. The unnatural tongue so close as to kiss her brain.

Her view of the heavens stayed a moment. Her lips happy again, she smiled. An uncontrolled one with strings to her heart. This time Simone heard a flavor to her accent. A curve in her syllables, even the carriage of letters and spaces was different. It was as if the question was not a question, but Simone was happy again.

The friend's voice lingered, unknown, whether it floated above her or in her.

Simone's thought patterns tapered, narrowing to a single probe. "What's your name?"

On toes, Simone let her own voice pose the question to the sky. Turning round and round, she wasn't revisited. It was okay though; the silence had not left her. She felt as if she was wearing the muted woods, likened to skin. A layer that was protecting her somehow.

The search for Pepper was long erased from her concerns.

The dance on worn toes ended and Simone again stood flat-footed in the now damp leaves. The sensation of spinning still lived under her gaze. Her stare dropping level with her surroundings, she searched. What she would find, she left up to the woods. Scanning any of the inky blobs hiding, she wanted to just see the girl.

Simone's sweet voice embraced her lost friend. "What's your name?"

Longing to place shape to sight and words, her feet drifted dizzy.

Her heart was pounding for any reunion. Insistent, she widened her legs to keep aloft. Regardless of an eventual fall, she turned numb. Though the question reached out into the blanketed still, there was only silence to fill the gap.

Patient Simone lived in that void. Her eyes and heart extended into the darkness. With the emptiness building, her footsteps came to a halt. A sigh, Simone knew she couldn't push the hope, it had to come to her.

"Crischa, is my given." The air bent with the dark whisper.

Simone refilled her own lungs. The explosion of a name spilled, as if it were a hushed song. She'd less often heard such a beautiful name like this murmured.

It was a tone of revenant phantoms. After its spoken form passed over the area, silence came back from the shadows.

A beaming grin that belonged to girls far away, in happier homes, warmed Simone's cheeks. She had a name for her friend. "Crischa." She would never let it escape, never let it fall in anger or regret.

Simone gave no rushed reply. Her unbalanced system was still off center, but her spring had returned. She wanted to run to her friend, yet she would treat it as if 'this' was a timid companion. She knew she'd most likely lost considerable amounts of trust yesterday. If she wanted to see her eyes, her face, Simone had to apologize for what had happened.

"Your name is so beautiful." Simone stopped looking for her friend. The hush was still close, and this was everything. Not meaning to, the spin in her brain sent her a foot forward. The misstep turned into two, then three steps. Forward, Simone made the next smaller and slower. Simply out for a walk with a friend, she knew the girl walked with her. Unseen or not, she could feel that body nearby. Her friend was shy, and time would mend.

"Crischa, I wish I had a name like that. My name is so plain." Simone knew from a story told by mommy; her name was from a singer she'd loved. However, it had never been explained more than that.

Walking in blind directions, the shadows crawled along with her. Her path was only led by an incalculable belief; her friend lay just ahead. Simone's search was put on an eternal hold. She simply walked.

"Was that you who found Scuff?" Simone needed to ask forgiveness, but she was unsure how to explain her stepfather. The last thing she wanted was to scare her away from being a sister.

Continuing with her verbal offerings, the woods listened in. "He's my best friend, you know?" Taking the dog from its protected home, Simone rubbed Scuff's head and scratched his ear. "He's quiet right now, but he is a good listener, like you are."

Simone held him up in the air. It wasn't an offering to be taken, only to greet the abstract girl.

No answer. Simone wanted to step faster. "Crischa? Are you still there?" The innocent query broke softly midway. Holding back any sign of defeat, she looked again for movement anywhere.

Harsh and cutting, a blast of wind ran through the trees above. Dipping down through the larger limbs, it hit Simone and pushed her hair wild around her cold shoulders. A need to defend against it forced her to turn away. Also broken by the touch, was her stroll. Next, the calm peace she'd followed thinned out around her. The feeling of being left alone in the darkness returned. The cold breeze grew bleak.

The air abrupt, the temperature flattened; more closely representing the winter she was used to, it once more had powers. More worrisome, the blustering weather was heard combing through the treetops.

Gradually, the trees felt to be growing, as the wind's pressures gave them sway. Steadily the winds pushed harder in this dark forest.

The silence that had walked close to Simone, now evaporated. One after the next, the forest's chorus came to repopulate. From every corner, unseen and distant the voices returned grateful to be free of what held them at a distance.

Anxious, she stood motionless, looking about. "Hello? Crischa." Simone no longer felt the covering that protected. "Are you still there?"

Her opportunity to apologize was lost. A quiver in her lips, and she now hated herself for it. It was too late, and she knew it.

"Crischa! Please! Please don't go, I'm sorry, just don't leave." Her anguish called out, hoping, pleading. Simone didn't want to be left alone.

She was always alone.

The space surrounding Simone felt heavier. It was no longer occupied by the friend she thought she had found again. Eyes cold now, fell downward as her head did the same. Her fears and pain had always given her a dread of things to come. This was different. Arms dropping low, the spell from earlier was spinning again. The burden, this time, was more physical. Accompanying the odd sensation was draining. A core loss that saw what energy she did have, leaving her.

Her arms felt drawn downward, pulled. Her gaze close to her feet saw nothing, no hands, no weights, just gloom. It was all just an intangible rationale, one that she attempted to rub away, to wipe off her flesh like dirt.

Mournfully she watched as Scuff fell from his home. The laboring soreness grew sharper and burning. Her hand seeking out reason, passed over her arms to discover thorns. Further, her fingers found broken-off thorns embedded in her flesh. Her gaze needed, she searched for its shape on her naked arm. Gasping: an inward turned gaze saw half her dress soaked. Darkened and gruesome, warm waters spread wide across it. Without the benefit of color, it couldn't be red, but she watched as her head began to spin.

She felt a little pain. Trying to focus, but her inner core pounded faster. Her logic was first to go, as her feet staggered off beat. The ground had begun to lean heavily to the right. Simone didn't understand the cause.

Stranger yet, she thought to see the trees all bend one way, then turned to the other. The leaves that cover the ground now joined the confusion. Their dying stems, once connected to branches, all moved like Spring caterpillars.

A last heave of her head to correct her balance, the entire world immediately launched into a spinning blur. Weaving and swirling, the shadows and muted moon merged. Their gray-and-black, bubbling together as the colorless river flooded inward.

"Mommy?" The surrender was for a woman that once rubbed her head when she slept. Yet in these last seconds of consciousness, she needed some comfort. More congruent to her life, the plead was unheard.

Her gaze, then her body submerged. Failing in her attempt to compensate, the ground rose. Its surface quickly cemented her exit, and equally, any escape she thought she might have had.

Seated atop an ever-expanding mountain range, Simone watched huge black birds. Each with unnatural scales and sharply curved beaks. Their large wings flapped as they drifted, circling. Their null eyes, moving in a baleful search. Each looking hungrier than the other, nevertheless none of them rose nor dropped.

The sky beyond them had eddies of mixed lavender hues. All of it pleasing to Simone's eyes. She'd never seen such a sight.

The sensation of sliding was ignored. Centered in her view, she wanted nothing more than to reach her hand out for the beautiful colors. The ground under her was coarse as gravel and passed over legs and bare toes.

Resting here, a long, beautiful dress was on her. Delicately, it moved in the breeze, its shape was like so many characters of fantasy. Simone marveled at the intricate lacing in the fabric, its swirls of color and texture. Before she gave a pleasing smile, everything changed.

A scent that lingered on the floating breeze, offered her a transitory memory. Its shape and meaning she couldn't touch. However, the aroma was something she should know, even the feeling of longing mixed.

Struggling to place the perfume's contours, it changed too. This time, it mutated the very scene and sensation she wanted. Stronger than any shape, she felt dismay take form.

Ranker, the view corrupted under her touch, all within seconds. Lost were any happy emotions it had connected, and now the odor gave her a spasm of nausea.

Raising her hand to protect from the attack, she discovered Scuff. His roughened eyes yearned for her gaze. A welcoming emotion emerged to replace Simone's disgust.

Before anything was clarified, she noticed Pepper. He was in her other hand. Strange as it should have been, a feeling of normality was there. This dog of Jude's was also stuffed.

Pepper's eyes looked back at her. His gaze wasn't the same though; buttons looked back in place of his normal dark eyes.

Scuff, pulling for her attention, extended a happy bark. Following soon after, a wet lick to Simone's damaged cheek. The cheerful body and tail wiggled frantically as she gazed back merrily.

The stuffed animals were grand, but she needed to rise off the ground. The weight of her body caused her to collapse after each attempt.

On her last try, the expectation of the ground was shockingly absent. In place of leaves and soil, Simone felt her fall continue unchecked.

Flying downward, her muscles tensed. The expectation of a long fall could only end with a distant ground. A harder one, that she would inevitably strike if the fall lasted.

Instead, Simone never landed. She was met with a void of twisting shadows. Left to plummet backward, everything that's been folding away, disappeared. Like the falling leaves, she too was now gone.

Chapter Sixteen

A Mommy

A voice grew louder, reaching through the faded grays. "Wake up. Simone, will you wake up!" Each time the voice was no longer delicate. The gruff tone was uneven, but it was firm. "Open your eyes, girl." The man's voice showed the lingering effect of the previous night.

"Simone!" Jude's irritation was at its limit. Lucid the commands were going to plead with the girl any longer. He never had patience, today was no different and he wouldn't be ignored.

Without opening her eyes, Simone knew who was standing over her. Although she was unsure just where she was, one fact was clear. She hadn't escaped him.

Because there was no bed under her, she obviously wasn't in her room. The hope, in those last seconds, was to open her eyes and this dream would fade from her sleepy mind.

The ground under her had no leaves, rocks, or dirt. That negated the forest where she lay last in her memories. The temperature against her skin hadn't the harsh fingers of winter. So, it was true she was in the house.

If it'd been her room, or any other room in the house this still might be an issue. No, she could hear the hiss, off the gas space heater of hers. The flame inside it made a distinct sound. She knew it well, even welcomed it. The drone was one of the things she loved about the heater.

The noise would help her sleep, on those endless days locked away in her room. That wasn't a problem any more though. She was lying with her good cheek against the carpet. She was rather comfortable. Unwilling to move she listened but remained numb on the ground. Pretend or not, Jude would eventually stop if she hid her consciousness.

"Open your damn eyes already." Shaking her by the shoulder, Jude was leveling up and upset. "I know you're awake."

Reluctantly, Simone opened her eyes. Again, she'd hoped it would be a colored-filled sky. Maybe some of the lavender color would meet her, and Scuff too would be real. A happy tail still wagging for her to pet him. She begged the tops of the dirty carpet strands. Hoping that they would transform in the next seconds, but this was reality, and she was in hell. There was proof, inches from her head. The leather boots that Jude wore stormed nearby.

A step closer, his hand came down and flipped her the rest of the way over. Like a turtle on its back, she wanted to struggle to whine but he would yell, or worse.

Eyes, only slivers in the lit room. Watching through them she saw the distant ceiling. It was the living room ceiling. Twice as high as any other ceiling in the house, it took more to focus on the distant texture. Obviously, the blotch had been painted over but she could see it still. There was plenty of daylight coming into the room. The fact she'd lost the night and had drifted into the next day escaped her attention.

"What the fuck is wrong with your stupid kid?" Jude asked, but the question wasn't aimed down at Simone. The sound of a sloshing beer was standing over the still child. Jude pointed the responsibility of the child over to her mother.

There was the feeling that a large section of her memories were missing. Simone's senses hadn't fully recovered, but she believed there was another in the room. Even though she heard his voice and words, her understanding was as if she was underwater.

Her eyes defiantly and narrow slits shut again when she felt some of his beer land on her. Flipping her palm over to the rug's surface, she identified the strands. The thick carpet mingled between her fingers. Digging deep into its foundation, her fingernails filled with the dirt inside its depths.

An animated breath, Simone pulled her knees up. Her bare feet dragged flat against the top of the carpet. Before she spoke, there was something different about the feel of her clothes. Simone realized she was no longer wearing the small, ripped dress. This was different, maybe, possibly still a dream.

With her lids closed, she took account of the pieces she was wearing. It was one of her stretchy leggings and the warmer long sleeve shirt she'd had in the trash bag. It had to be a dream, Simone now was wearing some of the clothes lost days ago.

These pieces had dropped in the woods, ripped from her hands, and forgotten in the rush of her escape. Simone was sure of it. The entire bag had been torn apart and there was no way this could be real.

Moving near, to stand over Simone, was a different shape. Still wearing her work clothes, Mackenzie looked down, puzzled. Simone was alive on her back, but all what Jude had told her couldn't be true.

Without touching the ground, she bent down on weak knees. "What do you think you were doing out there? Why were you in the woods so late last night?" There was already irritation in her tone.

"Simmy, why are you doing this to me when you know I work all night?" There was the mingling of past accusations in her mother's concern. There was a stern correction coming, but the other adult in the room huffed at her words.

Burning, Mackenzie peered up to the man over them both. "And where the FUCK were you?"

"No, the question is, where did Pepper go?" Jude knifed into her sneer. Stepping back, he continued to hover beside them and the couch. Turning with no answer, he paced back toward the kitchen.

Simone's mother dropped back onto the couch. Glaring at Simone, her mom pulled out a cigarette and lit the end. She took a deep draw, and before she leaned back on the cushions, she saw the girl's jaw. Bending forward, one leg crossed, she looked at Simone's face.

Farther down, with the lit cigarette hand, she brushed the black hair away from her face and neck. The damage was new. Plopping fully back on the cushions, she sent the fierce accusation up to Jude's spot next to the kitchen entry.

"What the fuck, Mackenzie?" It was a deflect, and Jude had nothing to say better. A shrugged shoulder, and he looked away.

"The 'FUCK' is you. You damn inebriated idiot. What's that?" Mackenzie threw her cigarette at his stupid face. Grabbing a nearby empty, she threw that too. Her disgust for him was there long before she saw this. What boiled up now was somehow linked to other things.

"You freaking piss me off with this shit." A lighter in one hand, she pointed to Simone. "It can't all be her fault you shithead."

A glance around, calculated, all the cans and now two bottles of whiskey. Her head gave a negative nod downward. "You wasted the whole check already, didn't you?" Her anger rose to a crescendo. Hitting the piled blanket on the end of the couch, she launched off the furniture.

Nearly trampling the child on the floor, Mackenzie stormed over to his location. Standing a full nine inches shorter than Jude's five-ten, she was a threat.

Between them, he waved off an annoyed strike with his drink, but stood his ground. His face curled, as Jude's own temper accused back. "The bar closed at two last night–I called you know." He had planned his ambush entirely differently, but was now committed.

"What the fuck!" Indignant, she wanted to punch him in the mouth.

"You're the one to talk," Grabbing her arm, he twisted it over. His forceful effort exposed a new bruise, the sharp crimson track was evident in the folds of her arm. "Looks like our money isn't just going for beer." Whether he was jealous or upset, she hadn't included him, the anger was real. He knew he was two-faced coming at her.

"You said you'd stopped. You told me last week, the same bullshit when you didn't come home till Monday." Jude's meaning was explicit.

Her hand with a new unlit cigarette punched him in the rib. His gut large enough to feel nothing, she at least gained her arms freedom. Although Jude was the one fighting a hangover, she was the one stumbling back. A foot came down on the edge of Simone's shoulder and the wounded jaw. Her mom, off balance already, stumbled over her and crashed to the ground beside the tv.

Tripped by Simone, Mackenzie landed hard on her backside. Up quick, and ready for a fight, she grabbed more of the empty cans and anything else she could find. Slung out wildly, she hurled them in every direction.

"SHIT… You think so, you asshole?" Resentful, her attitude plummeted straight to violence. Face red and fist tightened, she was up. Back in Jude's face, a second swing glanced off his forearm.

Her strings easily yanked; Jude laughed that mocking laugh. Sharper than any knife it always pushed her buttons, in the middle of a fight. Even as he taunted more, he was defending one handed against her fist holding a lighter tucked inside. Blood pumping, Mackenzie knew what she was going to do to resolve this problem. "Okay," This was it, her hands fell away as she retreated around the back of the couch.

"We'll just see about all of this shit." Though her hand waved over the entire living room her eyes never left his contemptuous sneer.

Her having missed every punch; Jude felt superior. Although he had over sixty pounds over her, she was a firecracker and had always been one.

"Damn it Mackenzie!" Casting a loathsome glare down on Simone, he swiftly minused her out from his concerns. Following directly after Mackenzie, he was nothing if not equally upset. Joining her upstairs, one door after the next slammed shut.

Having flipped over and balled up on the floor Simone noted the stillness around her. Her defenses relaxed, she opened her gaze. Sitting up, she rubbed the same sore area around her neck and now shoulder. What had been powerful forces, dragging her balance off-center in the forest, were absent here. Here on the floor in front of a tv was a second of peace. Peculiar as it was, the tv was off and the carpet wasn't a threat to her. Though denied comfort in her mind, her aching body was warmed by it.

Her back resting against the couch, the old nausea moved back into her chest. A slow blink that grew longer with every close. A minute more and she wouldn't be able to stop vomit from coming up. Covering her mouth, both hands left the ground. The sickening feeling was a tidal wave. Its approach pulled and swelled in her head. Laying back down on the floor, her hair was matted but felt good under her head. Balled up once more, for health reasons, she hid in silence down here. Spiraling out of control, she slipped once more into the blackness.

Chapter Seventeen

To Play

Sitting up straight, Simone stared at her arms. The cuts from thorns, vines, and just falling, were so many. They weren't bleeding anymore but the scabs all could be picked at. Touching one of the smaller ones, she scratched it away. There was discomfort under the dry blood but with her nails, rubbing it felt so good.

A new bead of blood bubbled up as she moved on to others. The sensation of scratching the itch somehow proved that this was no dream. At most, the interplay between the ache and the pleasure that her dirty fingernails gave, was undeniable. The late day had escaped her. Out the smaller front living room window, she noticed it was dark outside already. Also noted, mommy and 'him,' had left her lying here the entire day.

Pulling at her clothes, Simone smiled down at the once lost outfit. These were for certain, the ones she'd dropped in the woods. Uncertain of a lot of things, could she have put them on? Maybe Jude had found them first, then her, and replaced her ripped ones? This thought wasn't out of the realm of possibilities but out of Jude's character.

A downtrodden frown gave Simone a deeper and much more serious groan. Arching, her entire frame felt as if she'd been dragged through hell. Laying sideways, she stared at the floor under her. There was no hiding it, she was in agony. Everywhere were cuts and gouges.

Even under the skin her neck throbbed. Other pains she hadn't yet located, were buried by more relevant soreness. Whimpering, her gaze drifted inches over the carpet's dull color. Though reluctant to do so, Simone sent a hand between her legs, her fingers returned with a bleak account.

Her eyes closing against the confusing facts, she wanted it all to leave her thoughts. How has any kid survived childhood in this world? The question had no bottom, and she wanted to cry. Opening her gaze back to the floor's texture, nothing came of consideration. There was no one around, no parent to comfort her even if she had asked.

She was always alone.

"Simone. Play with me." The message appeared out of the shadows. It was the same pasty whisper from the woods. However, tonight it came from much closer. Feet away from where Simone lay in the living room.

Still laying sideways with her back against the couch and her shoulder in the unwashed carpet, she turned her head. It was above her twisted location; from her angle it came from within the kitchen.

Before a hand pressured the ground to release her, Simone asked, "Crischa?"

Simone needed to be sure she had actually heard correctly. The angle was hard to clarify anything, she had to sit up. The desperate and heavy shadows that lived in the kitchen refused her. Waiting was the answer as her legs folded under her.

Her request to hear the words repeated was gone and still no sounds. Lights off in the dingy kitchen, she would have to get up. Though she was dressed, the bottom of her feet was naked and sore.

A better leveled eye, into the opening, Simone discovered a form. No edges or girl's shape, the void moved with the darkness. Unsure it was a welcome silhouette; the person was too tall to be Crischa. Yet with only an impression of occupancy, the shape disappeared as quickly as it had been found.

"Crischa?" She let the question be as simple as her mind knew. A bob of the head, the doubt asked of herself, 'did she want to go in the shadows?'

Her lips separate from her thoughts, "where did you go Crischa?" Simone's kitten tone asked for her friendship.

"I couldn't find you." Swallowing her discomforts, she wanted to be happy. Fixed and unmoving, her gaze stayed hardened on the last place an outline stood.

Watching from her minuscule protection in the living room, she knew she'd have to move. Exposed and coated, her feet build her weight atop the tender skin. Standing fully, Simone's head continued her search into the quiet. Ignoring the pins and needles on the floor, she headed toward the kitchen.

The clothes she wore, and the sleep carried behind her eyes, were alike. No matter the times she rubbed her lids, neither had left her. Another few steps and her focus wanted to see her friend take form.

"Crischa, will you play with me?" Her name was sweet on Simone's lips.

Stronger in spirit, Simone demanded of her feet. Off the limits of the carpet, she had one more step before the kitchen's chilled surface. Trivial in her thoughts was the temperature drop. In the short distance, a world of difference could be felt. Toes at the linoleum, she saw no movement.

Over the divide, Simone looked down to watch her first step inside the room. Search returned outward; her eyes missed what her ears heard. Whatever the figure, it moved. Fleeting an assumed laugh touched her at the kitchen opening.

The light switch was Simone's first and best option. Moving further into the pitch wasn't welcomed, but she had to know. Each step, her right hand rose to guide the journey to that goal. With the last uneventful foot, her hand landed perfectly on the doorknob. Not a thought conflicting with the action, she turned and pushed the door open.

Swinging open in the softer air outside, the door gently hit the distant wall. There was a calm night beyond. Overcast, still a moon had a view into the backyard. Exiting the house, Simone watched the sky drifting around the treetops.

Absent in her mind, was any need for warning. The dreary sensation of soreness was following her probe of the yard, but she could hold it off. She could power through if she knew somewhere was her friend.

"Crischa?" Again, her voice rose a bit higher than the times before. In comparison to her inner voice, the call was a muted mumble, yet she felt it loud enough. Begging was a miracle to form, a girl's shape to smile out of the weeds and play with her.

Waiting outside the open door frame was no one. "Where are you? Can I see you Crischa?" Simone's frame gave a full body shiver, under the encroaching cold. No answer came as she remained ready. Nothing inhabited here, standing on the porch, she played old games once more. The apple tree, a guard on her foreign shore, and the characters were the unmoving shadows further out.

Possibly Crischa was hiding. Seated behind some bushes or trees nearer the edge. Only focused eyes could see that far in the bleak. Out on the landing Simone would give her friend a chance, the opportunity she'd left her with a day ago.

Feet pressed together to retain any heat; Simone wanted to ask again. She wanted to apologize for everything. She wanted the opportunity to tell her 'She could play.' Her imagination pointed sharply at any of the piles of car parts and the darkness beyond. The only distraction to twist between the effort was her returned breath. With denser air expelled on each breath it didn't float away as fast as nights before.

Refocusing, Simone witnessed a shift in the grays out there. Unsure of any of it, she followed the first indication of motion. Then as she stared, the weeds nearest to the yards limit shuddered by an unseen form. Twitching more, something was there. Remaining with its foot in the gloom, a direction was finally chosen.

Scarcely able to believe it, Simone watched intently. Soon enough the dance was directed toward the house. Yards out, the weeds gave the impression that something unseen and low to the ground was coming near. She'd hoped it had been Crischa, but whatever the beast, it was too low in waist-high growth to be her. An inky form, the width of what approached seemed larger than any child crawling through grass. Still only a blur, the body moved faster toward the open door.

The yards dropped away as Simone's feet topped each other to make some friction. The entire time her eyes never ventured from whatever visitor came to find her. The moment when all would be revealed, the moon's rays fell behind thickening clouds. Any clarity in the night lost, Simone ventured a foot closer to the porches drop off. The girl's name on her lips, she would see her before another call.

Her breath trembling in the air was a constant stream of fog. The winds were absent, and every subsequent breath muddied her vision. Each puff of air confused who hunted for her. The weeds and grass weaved back and forth as the darkness cleared the limit of the apple tree. Its path had been seen to change, but now a straightened line was aimed at Simone.

Toes hanging over the two-foot cliff and cold ground below, she was hooked. Her eyes watched, as her head quickly curved around other breaths and chattering teeth. The distance was going to be close enough to finally see. Her lungs, making the effort to hold the next, Simone's eyes widened. With no Scuff to clutch, her forearms and hands pressed tight against her core. Simone leaned outward, her weight now precarious to a fall, she had to know the shape speeding up to her.

The last clump of overgrowth was just three feet from the bottom step. The shape ultimately hit its center. Just as fast as the weeds parted, the creature jetted under both straining eyes and porch. A blur meant to avoid the silence, it vanished into the unsealable below.

A fractured huff, Simone jerked her head forward, missing its details. Her balance shaky already, Simone fought off the fall. Dropping to bent knees she held onto her perch atop the porch. A lung full of air required she gasped in the freezing night. Teeth and shoulders competing for vibration, Simone came to sit on her shins. Her mind was wild, all the while wanting to know the lost visitor. Its location was now hidden in the darkest recesses of the area underneath her.

Try as she started to lean over, the reach was too far to clear. With an absent moon, her sight would require a closer approach. She would have to drop down to the ground to discover the visitor. Whatever the face down there, it seemed reluctant to emerge. There was time to wait for it, but Simone wanted to see. Her legs cold on the porches peeling paint, she stood back up. Though she could barely make out the first step down, her right foot made the best of it.

Toes pointed and her balance corrected she angled for its rough surface. Met atop the board, her other foot rubbed against skin to discover any missed heat.

"Hello?" She whispered before moving down to the last step. Predicted, there was no answer. There wasn't even the simplest of noise, to tell her the thing hidden there was friendly. Its nest, out of the grasp of her gaze.

Pure and immune to sight, the void under the porch had a mood. Whether hunger or longing, there was definitely something moving. Curiosity exploding, Simone's own need for a friend's touch, was powerful. Some similarity to the wood's silence seemed to call out to her, 'come closer.' Her last foot came alongside the porch, now in the unkempt yard.

Rotated toward that cradle down there, Simone adjusted her angle. Her pupils, no matter the strength of her night vision, were futile to break into its walled off darkness. Sharp pointed strands of dead grass poked at her flesh. Gently and crawling closer to the edge, Simone dropped down to hands and knees.

The obscurity felt to be looking at her. She knew it was waiting, opening her hand she motioned to it. If only she could get closer. Her forehead and eyes leading inward she scooted closer beside the steps. 'Maybe something wild was her visitor.' Simone's thoughts painted fanciful creatures that it could be. Possibly it was one of the birds, from her dreams in the woods.

It was too small to be her friend, nor the beloved deer of days gone past. No, all these things were colorful and slow. This being was playful, and she needed only draw it back into some moonlight to know its shape.

A keen idea maybe it had fur like the deer's antlers. What new and amazing thing could it offer her to smile about. The possibilities that might be were just inches away. She needed only to send her hand over that border.

Cluelessly Simone moved. If she entered the desolate den, her eyes could focus, she would see and discover. Simone smiled into the unknown.

Rather than crawling into the hole, she sent her hand above to the porch. She could then lean her head all the way in and get accustomed to the thicker dark. Squinting, she knew there was a body in there. Above her, far past the roof of the house, and miles beyond the clouds, hovered a moon again. The winter's flushed face allowed the moon's reappearance in a small opening. Its tinted glow struck the top of the landing in front of Simone.

Cracked spaces between boards that made up the porch allowed lines of light into the cave below.

Smiling heavy on her cheeks, Simone leaned further into the opening. Her free hand hung off the ground and moved ahead of her. Joined down here were the short lines of moonlight. Defined on the ground was the smallest of peculiarities to what moved.

Her thoughts building beyond reasonable creatures, Simone wanted magic from her mind. Hunger in her fingertips, she crept forward on both knees. Her other hand above her, supported the long stretched out body. Better yet, her focal point was a foot apart from fingertip. Cautiously they neared each other. Helped by the additional glow a silhouette matured. It was a four-legged visitor. She could no longer tell if it feared her reach or was still to be petted. Her bent extent was maxed out. Nonetheless she strained past logic to find the creature's texture.

Uninformed to the practical idea that what she was doing was dangerous, Simone let go her supporting hand. Meant to only give inches she dropped inward. Overreached she plummeted into the murk. All the while her floating hand dove forward.

The danger was greater than she understood, Simone fell farther into the creature's home than planned. Pulled back in the collapse, she grabbed for the ground first to stop a complete crash. Never off her goal, her scan saw no reaction from her animal friend. Motionless in the darkness, the mound sat awaiting her dirty hand. Room to sit, though bent over, Simone redeployed her anxious hand.

Faith of a child, Simone hadn't the hesitation best suited for what could be. Out again, her hand wanted to know its shape, its name, its texture. Possibly a wounded bird. Simone dropped her fingers into the shape tenderly. It was happily awaiting her touch.

A sensation, nervousness at the start, she pulled back from a first touch. The first impression was wet and cold. An ill-defined grin on Simone's face, she considered a call out to the beast. This time she would find it without her finger but use her palm open and flat. It hadn't moved and she was nervous, if she took too long to pet, it might run.

The creature's damp fur tickled, not like the antlers, just due to her tension. Slow but determined, she moved deeper into the animal's coat. Lively, what foreigner her hand thought to meet gave her a laugh.

Fingers closing around the creatures' main, Simone's hand emerged from the purgatory. No wild animal, the pet she came back was her own stuffed friend. Gazing at the small companion in the darkness, Scuff's fabric became familiar but wet and dirty. Hugging the wandering beast, she returned to a wide smile.

Crawling from under the porch, Simone stood with a stretch. Her attention was short at first, she knew who had returned the treasure. She was likely back out in the distant woods, wanting to play in the cold.

Tall, Simone piled on top all ten toes. Best she could, her loudest whisper was sent into those wilds. "Come inside. Come inside and play with me Crischa. Please?"

It was her present, meant to reciprocate for the twice returned pup.

Simone wanted to thank Crischa close up. She needed to look into her eyes and know her emotions better.

Chapter Eighteen

The Invitation of Hunger

Simone watched the extent of their yard. Standing atop the porch again the damp ragged toy was back under her protection.

She intently watched for movement in the grasses or near the apple tree. Whomever had returned Scuff, was nowhere near the porch any longer.

Nearer to the door, she could feel the warmer air from inside rolling out. She was cold but this minuscule amount was enough so that she could stay longer to wait. Her dog was wet, but this didn't matter as it rested tight in her chest. Her own heat transferred to the pet's fabric.

Simone's gaze, supported by a hazy moon locked on that distant stage. The backyard was still. No wind, no breeze, not a creature stirred in the shadows. As she marked time with each violent wave of shivers, Simone never ventured from the uncut tree line. Sadly, at night the shadows made the forest look unwelcoming, but she knew differently. The wicked lines of thick limbs and curving trunks twisted as she stared. Their hibernating mass was unchanging as she scanned for any person to return her calls.

Loud enough only for her ears, "Crischa?" Simone wanted to yell into the night, but she was probably back home already.

She blinked more with regularity, as hope was ending. It had been almost an hour standing here. Shoulders dropping, her sorrow was being repopulated by her body's old soreness.

Turning reluctantly to end her watch, a vibration was felt under her toes. A slight tremor easily missed by any other not so desperate for clues as her. Gazing wide again, she placed them back into the ink of the forest. New to this search, Simone saw movement. Something appeared to create waves through the treetops. There continued to be no wind near her. Yet out there, a storm that seemed angry, moved the silhouettes with vigor. A creature a hundred feet tall played with the tiny thousand-year-old oaks.

Both troubled and mystified, Simone felt to be a witness to something. Peering directly into it, she let her vibrating nerves heat the fibers of her chilled skin. The game of making shapes of the shadows, now strangely gone awry.

Looking higher than any man could stand, Simone was profoundly surprised. Pleasantly shocked when out of that gloom, a delicate creature pierced the tree line. What emerged was an adult, yet as it moved nearer it was an illusion. The explanation, easily blamed on a moon's habit of hiding over and again in darker clouds. The profile brought with it, a stature anything but benign.

A step back, Simone's nerves warned. They didn't like the shape she was seeing. Yet without it getting closer, she couldn't identify what approached her. No different than a nightmare, she was prepared to run inside and wake herself.

Then, as her mouth tightened, and her lids narrowed to protect, she saw it. Following the darkness, a small, familiar girl. Her head down and shy, she walked with only the slightest hesitation. Simone could see above the weeds, she looked sad. Her angled expression appeared drawn. Simone had thought that it was Crischa's parent, that was walking her here. The second Simone returned her attention to where the shape led, there was nothing. An adjustment of her thoughts, Simone instantly erased the fear of talking with Crischa's parents.

Walking free, Crischa's head left the path she followed. Looking up she found the waiting child. Stopped under the apple tree her gaze looked in the direction of where Jude's dog normally lived. Passed in a breath, the figure glanced back at Simone. Her eager eyes smiled, to see her nearby.

Nodding her head 'yes' frantically, Simone's apprehension had morphed into a beam of joy. Jubilation flooded her cold body, and she could hardly contain herself.

Stepping from the last patch of yard growth the murky figure of Crischa stood at the foot of the porch. Had she been a foot closer Simone would have leaped atop her, a panicked puppy in need of love.

"You came." Both question and statement. Simone's grin widened, with the arrival of her friend.

Motioning with a free hand, Simone wanted her to join her. Before she turned fully into the diminished warmth of the kitchen, Simone waved faster.

Crischa started up, as Simone looked down to measure the room she might need. Stepping back from the opening, she felt to give her more room. Her exuberance held at bay; she would gesture for Crischa to enter first. Up one step then the next, the girl rose as if no bent knee was used. Reaching the peak of the landing, the girl's face watched Simone. Tapering downward, she saw her hungry feet, both moving up and down in her excitement.

Unable to resist the opportunity, Simone lurched forward. She couldn't keep her enthusiasm bottled any more. As Crischa came to pass in front of her, she swung out to embrace her. Wet dog in one hand and greedy fingers for her other. A stumble in the moonlight and Simone's shock brain found no one. Where the girl had been a flash before, Simone found her hug empty. In a blinking eye, her friend had already passed by and was now inside the house.

Crischa was oddly positioned in the center of their living room. Looming as if lifeless, her bare feet were planted in front of the couch. Her back to the flickering glow of the tv.

Simone, standing now at the two rooms divide, looked at her friend. She could see her more clearly than any time before. "You're fast. How did you do that?" Innocent, Simone was amazed by her friend. "Can you teach me? You know, to move like you do." The trick was grand, and her understanding was as simple.

Studying her, Simone soaked it all in. Misunderstood before, she had dark iridescent blond hair. Its length too had been disguised as it now cascaded over shoulders and back, almost to her waist.

Simone's soul tingled as she carved it all into her memories. Never again would she be wanting for her picture. Joyful to see her, her gaze hadn't yet found everything. Her imagination had been wrong about a few other things too. Her skin shimmered under the blue, white, and yellow flashes of the television program. Whatever was on tv, bounced about the room and added its own flavor to her details. Her face, carved of pure alabaster, was beyond beauty.

Her eyes seemed to watch the staircase or the front door. Simone, finally given to motion, stepped closer to the side of the couch. Her approach oddly gave her friend no need to turn. Simone discovered she was no taller than her.

The child positioned static in the living area was the same height as the back of the couch.

Nearer yet, she examined the girl's clothes. It wasn't the same as the nights before. She was wearing some of Simone's clothes from the woods.

The round eyes that had been unmoved now shifted as if on rails. Slowly, and with purpose they came over to Simone. The happy face lingering at the arm of the couch met with an explosion of joy.

Eyes, though more natural, still lacked the percentage of white any other could know. These orbs, overpowering and fixed, had something within. An emotion that bore darker thoughts. Around each pupil, a glimmer of radiance circled her eyes.

Lips closed, Crischa's ribs and chest looked absent of motion. The young female profile was perfect. What was lacking was the nervous animation of either a child or character of true soul.

One hand holding Scuff, Simone's other deviant hand, rose off the arm of the couch. She wanted physical clarification. Some more proof to what her eyes told her, was the truth. What sections of her brain continued to question the site moved her arm. The girl standing there was a wonderful living doll. Not unlike so many Simone had seen in girls' hands on tv. Fearful of waking at any moment, she didn't want to miss this opportunity. She might prove it all reality, with the simplest of touch.

Crischa's perfect eyes blinked, slowly studying the approach of Simone's hand. The pale covering of its face was expressionless. Her reaction didn't flinch, as Simone's hand caressed first her chin.

"You are so pretty; I wish I looked like you." For once, a lonely teardrop rolled from Simone's right eye. Its reason was neither pain nor loss, this time. The distant idea of a lost Christmas visited Simone's mind.

She was sitting alone in front of the tv. A bright morning sun outside. She sat as she always did on the floor. A bowl of cereal in hand and cartoons played happily before her. A commercial played and in it were three girls, all around her age. Two of them sat on the floor and tore apart gifts from under a brilliant tree. Simone, placing a bite of the cereal in her mouth, watched only one of those girls.

Seated to the far right, almost out of frame, alone, the third girl. Her hair like hers, she seemed to be forced to wait. Then, before the end both her sisters ran to her and threw their arms around each other.

The evocation was a blurry one but there was a fulfillment she hadn't remembered, till now.

Simone's fingers were slow to trace along her features. Watching the point of contact, Simone wanted to find more. A twisted strand of the girl's hair slid close, and she took it in-between thumb and two fingers.

It was, as she had thought, lovely and Simone envied the texture.

"Crischa…" her name rolled from the tongue so caringly. It would always be new to Simone's ears and brain.

Novel and a first, the curious child watched Simone. Around them both the air was far warmer than outside. Deliberately and gradually, Crischa's chest rose to fill. Its purpose, not life. Capturing a remarkable volume of the house's scent, the effort was held as Simone merely looked at her hair.

The expression, if not immense pleasure, hid a darker rapture unknown to the child standing inches from her. Unlike any smile proceeding it, her porcelain skin pulled back what lips lived there. This mask was erased after Simone's hand fell away. Glancing tenderly back to Simone's wanting eyes, the girl's lingering gaze widened. A promising hunt crossed her inscrutable countenance.

"We can play hide and seek." No childhood accent bracketed Crischa's statement. Yet its utterance was a world of hope for the friend she had made.

"Yeah, that's a great idea. I'll hide first. That's okay, right?" Simone ran for the bottom of the stairs before finishing her last question. A hand on the newel post at the bottom, Simone turned unsure. "You won't leave again?" The heaviness was felt in the air. Simone stared at her friend. Finding the girl, she wasn't looking back. Her eyes unmoved, they seemed to glare forward into the kitchen. "You will play, won't you?" The question was pitiful, but Simone needed reassurance.

Unexpectedly, random sparkling flashes came from the television program. Colors meant to force drama, washed over the room, amplifying the lone figure outlined in front of it.

Finally, as calm returned behind Crischa, she turned fully to the bottom of the staircase. Perched on the waiting expression of an entire childhood, her eyes blinked slowly for her reply.

Arms laying close to her side, even her hair seemed locked to her frame.

Motionless, the gaze was centered on Simone. Her lips parted to speak, but only her previous breath seemed to exit.

Without a sound said, Simone heard her friend's answer. "Ok, great." Carrying a bounce, she climbed the staircase on all fours, confident of Crischa's offer to play.

Chapter Nineteen

Hide and Seek

Hidden inside her bedroom closet, Simone tried to keep an ear out for the door. All around her were some of the discarded boxes. Some with old books, but the largest was full of dishes from Jude's mother. Pushing into the tight space between them, she was perfect. Aside from no door, the shadows here were the deepest in the room. She knew this spot wasn't hard to find, but Simone wanted Crischa to find her easily.

The shelves above her, mostly empty, hung low as she sat under its edge.

The door that once swung in the frame was now meaningless. It had been removed and now leaned on the wall to the right of the bedroom door.

Staring out of her nest, Simone looked at it outside the closet. From where she sat it gave the impression the room had two doors out of it. Disappointingly, it had been there for over a year-and-a-half, but she hadn't even thought about it till just now.

Beside the door to nowhere, was the real room's door and it was closed. There was no overhead light on, yet she looked at that painted door closely. Unable to stop smiling, Simone felt ready. She had a small space behind her, one she could still pull back farther into if needed. It would at least give her a moment more after Crischa entered. If she didn't turn the light on immediately, she would have to navigate her room to find her. Her lifelong friend Scuff, tucked tight under her arm, was waiting in his normal position. Squeezed under her arm he watched the door with her.

Just in the short period here, she'd heard her parents shouting. Thankfully, there was at the very least, their closets between the two rooms. Simone wanted to be anywhere but here when they fought. Their room at the end of the hallway felt like it was only separated by paper walls when they started yelling. She could cover her ears, and that would block out some of the fight. However, if she did, Crischa might sneak in unheard. If their battles traveled out of the room, she knew they'd stop her fun.

A fool's wish, Simone shook the focus before putting it back on the door.

With the lights off and only the faintest of glow from the moon's passing, she grinned. She was happy with the protection of her hiding spot.

Eyes fixated on the doorknob, she remained motionless. Her skin, no longer aware of the lighter chill up here. She put her hands on the larger box and rested her nose just behind. Eyes attuned to darkness, she could still feel the nervous bumps rising on her arms. This game had a level of fear she liked.

Ears attuned to the aches of the door; she had time once it spoke. Evenly, Simone had to lower the noise even her breath made. She was sure she heard the floor outside first.

Counting her breathing, Simone wanted the game to speed up, she wanted this dark corner over. A minute felt like hours. Unsure if Crischa had even come up the stairs, she thought to go check. Shifting her weight, she started to exit the closet. At the very second, a shudder to her bedroom door knob came. It was a hand on the outside moving the tarnished gold plating.

Dropping back down, Simone returned her gaze outward again.

The two stickers, held tight to the inside handle, began a slow turn. Offering a yielding creek, the knob started to turn to the right. Its direction firm, the round knob, released its hold of the frame. Her heart rate increased, Simone's pupils widened, and a rush of chills raced round her body. Added to the excitement, whether good or bad, she heard nothing from the other room.

Though mostly dark, a spattering of light from downstairs continued to pass under the door. Raising her head to see that knife's edge, she looked for the shadow of a figure standing outside it. There on the floor, her friend's shadow shifted as the handle stopped moving.

Why had she not opened the door completely? Simone wanted to squeal, her nerves were killing her to stay quiet so long. The light outside her safety flickered. Maybe the tv was turned off, she thought. It had been just enough to warn her night eyes, but now it was gone. Watching, the door was still closed, but it was no longer latched. Her friend needed only to push, and she could enter.

Tense behind the cardboard box, Simone heard nothing anymore. No parents fighting, no movement in the other room. She'd never heard the girl come up the stairs, and worse, her own heartbeat was drumming in her ears. The silence was growing, and it seemed to hang here in the room. Sitting in some unseen corner as if needing to breathe her oxygen. Some essence watched her, from under the bed, up in the pitch of each corner on the ceiling, and deep within any space that had shadow. They all seemed to have eyes. Eyes that were staring at her from each location. This feeling even included behind the unused door leaning close to her.

Simone's eyes darted to each of these spots as if she knew she could catch the spirit hunting her. Every time she moved from one to the next, her skin jumped. Her heart and breath skipped in their beat.

Away from her doorknob, a floorboard squeaked. Speeding back to the long-suffering door, it hadn't moved. The noise sounded close, but it couldn't have been in the room. Waiting for it to swing inward, she desperately wanted to look around the room one last time to make sure.

Her breath was no longer quiet. Ragged and straining she could not stop her lungs from needing so much. Added without notice, she was gripping the box more desperately.

Though the room was cold, she was surprised to feel hot, even perspiration. What little light came in from outside her window now played tricks on her eyes. Under the bed, was at the limits of her sight line and there felt to be movement there. A twitch, she checked, but nothing was there. Before turning back to the door, a shuffling sound came from above her. Then another from beside her. Crouching lower she hid deeper in her panic. Returning over white knuckles she searched for the crack in the door. Late to any movement, she knew she'd missed something; darkness had moved there.

The door was not yet opened, then the hinges spoke. Its tension aching and nagging, the door fought effort. As if only a breeze pushed against it, the labored pace was unnerving. Slowly moving, the door gave inward only a sliver before halting once more. Stalled with barely enough room to fit her small fingers in, it stayed. Silent now, it sat a torture to watch, but Simone could no more look away than stop the thunder under her ribs.

Adjusting her head, could she get up and go look? Simone wanted to but something told her to stay. To pull back into that empty space, she had left behind her. A call was given inside her worry, to use the place reserved for safety. That same voice in the corner of her brain screamed, but it was no request for playful games. It was a panic that lived unconscious from day thoughts.

The sensation of pain in her digits told her to release the box. She'd been holding it stiff so long now that she had to shake the numb out of them. Resting them back atop the edge, she sought a better view. The door still hadn't opened enough. Simone leaned up to put her head above the box. She would need to push it aside to exit. The debate raged on but fixed on the splintered opening to her room, no figure had entered. Pushing free the box, she slid forward. Her knees under her, Simone edged to the closest lip.

Once more, the hushed creek echoed, Simone froze. Gazing from behind burning flesh, she allowed only her eyes to search, to the right of the closet first. A pile of broken-down and unused boxes. To the left, a window, and the bed. The thin springs of her bed moaned, as if some weight was placed there. A stifled gasp was held down in Simone's throat. Was someone in her room? Each muscle in her body needed command to simply turn her head.

A shaking hand migrated beyond the threshold of the closet. Flat on the wood floor Simone was unsure, yet softly a slow laughter raced from outside her bedroom door. Her eyes hurt, and she'd dare not blink once since the door moved what little it had. She needed her gaze wider, but there was no more to give.

The dusty floor might have been felt under her palm, but all that registered was growing fear. Again, the dark corners all blinked but were too quick to catch. Her head moved once more, so she darted to each, but nothing continued to live there. Her back crumbling, she thought to find protection anywhere she could. Maybe under the bed or then again, she thought to pull back. Refusing both choices, her other hand came out of the closet to match the first.

With frayed nerves Simone rose above her feet. One foot flat, the other dragged out of the closet to give her a weak stance. Swallowing with nothing to dampen her throat, Simone stared at the door. She wanted to go get her friend outside its frame. Her empty arm stretched out to take the doorknob. Three feet from it, she needed to push herself closer. On its surface, she felt a quivering shape moved on the other side. Its efforts followed by a shuffled foot in the hallway. Working to turn the handle even though it was no longer latched, a prickly touch landed on Simone's other arm. The foreign sensation sent her ill-prepared nerves into spasm. Piercing the dark, Simone squealed. Fallen away from it, she turned to protect.

Her fears were real, she turned and discovered the small girl's rigid form behind her. Crischa stood in a dim spirit inside her room. Standing over Simone on the floor, her face stayed buried in the ink. A tilt on her face, she peered down at the terror she'd created. Whether uncomfortable, the head atop her frame, straightened. The pits, where eyes lived, came out of the deeper shadow to wait for Simone's words.

Simone gawked up at her friend, a struck deer in headlights. She had to gather what remained of her flesh before she was given the freedom to move again. A hand over her mouth in embarrassment.

"Wow! You scared the HELL out of me." Simone now smiled. A laugh, hard to start she could only just breathe again.

Simone had learned every bad word, but always felt pangs in her stomach to use them. 'Hell,' was a flexible word she was a bit more comfortable using. Slipping it in many times, even when talking with mommy seemed almost a game.

Off the floor, Simone came to lean against the bed. "You can go hide now." It was Crischa's turn, and the opportunity to hide how bad she'd been scared seemed important.

"You go hide. Ok?" Simone verified the game was still going. A moment needed she then looked at her friend. "I'll count to…" She wasn't sure how high Crischa had counted. Peering down to Scuff, she used his happy face to brave the fright Crischa had given her. Undecided in the girl's stare, Simone just seized on the first number to come into her head.

"How about thirty?" Turning into the bed, Simone leaned face-down. Waiting for a second before the count, she peeked behind her for her friend. The amount of time she needed, if it were more, Simone was unsure if Crischa would speak up. Surprised as each time before, she found her search unneeded. The girl's last location in the room was empty. Simone smiled as her heartbeat had slowed and some comfort had returned.

"K, one, two, three, four…" Simone's counting was slow and intentional. Her friend would have no idea where to hide. Simone knew she needed to give her plenty of time, even more than she'd said.

Scuff cuddled under her arm; Simone walked from the room ready to find Crischa. Still a bit tense, she gave a cautious look to the right. Her glance toward mommy's door found it. Closed, there remained silence behind the larger door. Twisting toward the stairs ahead of her, she pushed any trepidation away. For now, it would be forced back into the corners with any of her other fears.

Standing above the top step, Simone recognized it wasn't a matter of hearing her friend. She was already confident in what would be her first choice. The closet downstairs would be her friend's spot. With little effort in hiding her descent on the steps, Simone walked heavy footed. Confidence bolstered, she thought she saw a shadow run, then heard a door close in the living room. Thought off, the tv was definitely still on.

Halfway down she watched the mood from the room change randomly. Under the control of the dancing lights was a quiet box. Simone moved to a position where she could finally see into that room. The action that moved the shadows over all the walls was oddly enough a black and white show. Cars raced by as several people could be seen fighting in the streets.

Simone waited for a cheat. Any sound that could spoil her friend's location, wasn't really cheating. The wait was fruitless though. Down to the last four steps Simone lingered there. A glance over at the lamp, left of the front door, Simone considered turning it on.

Before she decided, she heard what she'd been waiting for. A shuffling sound escaped up from below. Not the noise she'd hoped for, its shape was of something being dragged over dirty floors. The clue stopping, Simone pondered the thought it might be Jude.

This game was turning out to be a bust. Calling Crischa to return to her room was probably the smartest idea. They could sit and talk till morning, and she could discover more about her friend.

Sitting on the step, she hesitated a second too long. Prior to sliding down to the next rung, Simone was treated to a harsh clambering upstairs. Focused up there, her gaze hated what she knew would be next.

A fleeting moment to act, she turned her head to look round the area nearest the tv. She could rush down, turn the light on and grab Crischa from wherever she hid. She'd have to get to the lamp first, though her fingers were weaker than Jude's, Simone knew the trick for turning it on.

Barefooted still, she let slide down a foot to touch the next rougher plank. Her time expiring, she rushed down the last of the steps. The noise upstairs was increasing, and she had no more time to waste.

In the living room she heard a soft rustling nearby. It wasn't from the closet though, but it could only be her friend hiding. Moving from one location to the next, Simone found vacancies in each of them. One after the other, occupied with household stuff, dust, and spider webs.

Each notion was a failure. Simone had no clue Crischa could be so good. The woods should have been her greatest guide, that this girl was quite formidable. This was becoming vexing, as Simone's last, best, and even secretive hiding spots down here, proved a ruin.

The dimly lit room, possibly at fault, continued to be controlled by a single source. It no longer mattered if her parents came down, she was now determined as she sought to correct it. In a click from the lamp, the room was flooded. Yellow and powerful the single bulb flashed to life.

"Crischa?" She needed to shorten the game, maybe find a different one to play. It was a choice she had to make, alas it wasn't fair in that same notion, but she would apologize later. Rubbing one of her abundant cuts covering her arms, she tensed. Standing under the landing to the front door she couldn't understand the answer.

Scuff, centered in her chest, received most of her nervous attention. Hand petting him, her eyes hastened the search. Begging her memories, they offered up only the same hiding spots she'd plundered twice already.

Clutter in the living room, likely lent to the promising hides, but where? Simone was frustrated. Attention and time ticked away, and the noise upstairs had increased. Foiled by her friend, Simone returned to the closet under the stairs. She was more than positive, she'd been thorough in its interiors, had it been enough?

Though brighter than her bedroom by miles, the lamp still sent sharp angled shadows outward. It was within one of them, off the corner of her vision, a tapered blur moved.

However, this fleeting figure had run behind her. It had passed by the front door. The direction was unwelcome though some hope in it. Spinning round, Simone hadn't a doubt that Crischa disappeared up the staircase.

At its base, her head curved nervously up each of the rungs. A shiver rolled down her spinal cord. Crischa had returned upstairs, but Simone guessed she didn't know the boundaries. There hadn't yet been time to warn her of the end of the hallway.

Panicked, Crischa might open a door up there she should never enter.

"Crischa, I don't want to play this anymore!" It was a yell, but admittedly nowhere loud enough.

An unknown crash echoed down from that second floor. Its shape and villosity are anything but good. The sounds that followed were numerous and louder as the pounding seemed to travel.

Unwilling to run up there, Simone heard mommy's door open and then slam shut again. There was little explanation needed, other than what she'd feared. A foot came up one step then another. Her eyes watched that turn at the top of the steps to the left. It was dark, but who would she see first rounding it in the hallway?

Fearful, yet her climb continued up. "Crischa? Are you there?" The volume was hesitant.

Three steps short of the top, Simone was abruptly greeted. Pounding down the hall, her mother rounded the corner heading down.

"Fuck you then!" Her aim was toward their bedroom.

Another crash, as the door smashed back inward. Screaming from the doorway was Simone's stepfather, sending a volley of objects down the hall. "Don't let the door hit you in the ass!" He was fuming, but he punctuated everything with a forced if not fake laugh.

Bewildered, Simone was smashed against the wall. Heart lurching forward as she watched her mommy hammering down the stairs. She could see the clothes she wore were slightly torn and visibly uneven.

"Mommy." Whether she meant to get her attention or call for her help, Simone's voice fell far short.

"Get out the damn way Simone." Knocking the undersized girl hard against the wall on the stairs. She was on her own mission. With little concern for her child's presence, Mackenzie's face was red and her short hair wild and untamed.

Mackenzie pressed down the staircase headed for the closet.

At the bottom, Mackenzie swung around the end post. The hard left circled about to the closet underneath. The door almost ripped from its hinges, she began a crazed plunder. Rashly grabbing more articles of clothes, she shoved a thick jacket under her arm.

Much of the rummaging was pointless because of her anger. Fuming, she was still fighting with Jude, and he remained upstairs. Whatever she had deemed important, was likely missed, or looked over. Pushing what she'd found in an old carry bag she finished.

Out of the closet, she left it open and was immediately at the front door.

"Just stay out of his fucking way Simone. I'll see you in a few days, I promise. Stay out of fucking trouble." Her face was snarled, but it wasn't meant for Simone.

Though her mommy looked up the stairs, Simone felt the glare. Slumped on the step, she knew her mom's words had no heart. The tell tale signature, she hadn't called her Simmy. No hesitation bordered Mackenzie's escape. Door striking the wall she never closed it, and she was off to unknown worlds.

A quiver of the chin, Simone's entire body sank. Even the game she'd been playing was abandoned. She hated their fights, but what she hated the most was the outcome. Although the fight was between Jude and mommy, Simone knew who would suffer. Inside her, tears and screaming filled her skull. The hurt was immense, and she could do no more than head back to her lonely room.

This wasn't the first promise; still, it had to do with her mom's words. The ones Simone knew best not to believe.

At the top of the steps, Simone turned her head left. She saw clearly into mommy's open door at the end.

The battle wasn't over there, by any stretch of the imagination. Objects were continuing to fly. Smashing sounds and mumbling words of hate and murder could be heard. Violently, larger objects were being tossed against the walls. Things Simone knew were both precious and common, were being destroyed.

Jude's hate was occasionally spaced between short calm. However short she knew it was only because he was drinking. Standing in the dark hall was suicide and Simone knew when to hide. She remained watching from her cold spot, a space in front of her own door. Staring, she could only see a sliver of their bed as it was on the right-side of the room. Also in the opening, was half the window on the far wall.

A cease-fire lingered in his battle of one. Simone should have run to her room. The warnings were loud in her skull, but she remained a second more. Another brutal installment wasn't far behind but if he looked down the hall, things might escalate.

Stepping into view, Jude had a nightstand in hand. Before he tossed it, and out of the corner of his gaze, he spotted Simone watching.

As if fire she was burned. The threat was instantaneous, and Simone plunged into her room. She just knew he saw her staring and that was enough. Crawling far under her bed, she felt the fear reach the bone. Cold was everywhere as her shaking spilled out like blood onto the floor.

There was now a drunk monster lurking in the halls of this house. The gagged teeth were hungry for flesh and the only food was hers. This creature wouldn't stop, nor could it be swayed with any number of words or pleading. This monster above all others, had a special place in her 'list of fears.' It didn't need provocation from her; merely the sight of her. Though 'payday,' was number one on her list, she carried this 'Jude,' separate and far above any simple list.

Mad, there was no intoxication needed to power its spiteful claws or teeth to bite. It was an apex predator. His actions and brain were willing to forgo the laws of nature. Clutching her knees tighter, her tremors were uncontrollable. Back pressing inexorably harder against the corner, she could dig no deeper into the shadows. There wasn't a hole or closet deep enough. She could only wait and hide. Bathroom, starving, even bleeding, there was no reason good enough to move. The problem she knew to consider different tonight was just how long she had to cower from Jude.

She was always alone

Swollen eyes watched that door. Abandoned in the corner, the house was swallowed by silence. Prolonged and dangerous, she imagined the horrors outside her closed door.

Using her lowest whisper, "Crischa, are you in here?" She had forgotten the game. Wanting her to join her, Simone knew her friend's best chance was to go home.

Only now did she consider that she could have already walked out of the house.

A selfish thought came, maybe her stepfather wouldn't do anything. He might hesitate if there was somebody he didn't know around.

Holding Scuff, she corrected the idea. It was an error to believe him capable of kindness. If there had been a time, she hadn't memories of it, nor experience with his mercy.

Inspecting what she dared to look at, the only spot dark enough to hide her friend was the closet.

"Crischa, are you in here?" Each word choked under the bed.

Not sure she wanted an answer, she closed her eyes. Her head was already heavy, it slowly came against the floor. Struggling with it, Simone finally closed her mind. Forced by exhaustion and fatigue, she drifted to sleep.

Alone again. Fortunately, the only creature to take her tonight was slumber.

Chapter Twenty

Awake

Peeking about, Simone wanted a better idea of where she was. Waking in different places seemed to be the norm lately.

Stretching her legs out, her muscles ached, but they would rebound. A sharp twinge in her neck, the pain was less but still definitely not gone. Palms down, she crawled from under the bed. Emerging into the same murk as before, Simone faltered. Leaning her back against the bed, she worked on standing straight.

She was alone, and it was still night. Simone came over to the wall beside her bedroom door. However small, she continued a shiver. She was chilly, but this wasn't a concern. There were darker threats outside the door, and she needed caution.

Placing a nervous hand on the doorknob, she paused before turning. The last thing she ran from was an angry and vengeful man. Though he hadn't left mommy's room after seeing her, all this likely had changed.

For all she knew, he lurked on the other side of the door. Plotting her punishment for simply existing. A second then her hand fell away from the chilled metal.

Leaning against the door on her less tender side, Simone positioned. Ear squared off; she pressed it firmly on the painted wood of the door. Behind the barrier for this ten-by-ten room, she listened for footsteps out in the hallway. There was no movement she could discern, and the stairwell was also quiet.

Outside her door to the right was a dark passage. Out there, there were three doors. There was hers at the top of the steps, a bathroom on the left, and then at the far end, an entrance to mommy's and Jude's room.

The halls twelve feet were a smaller minefield for Simone. Each time she went to the restroom, there was a risk. Each time Simone searched for her mother, an unpredictable hazard might pop out of any shadow.

It wasn't a hollow corridor she might merely play in. It had been the smallest of toys, forgotten out there that had been the provocation to hurt her. A gaze, turned inward to her room, measured the result of that mistake, an empty room.

On the surface of the door, she pressed her ear harder this time. Under her head, even Scuff's floppy ears matched her examination. It was dark in her room still, or had it been longer. Unsure, Simone hadn't an idea if she'd slept only a few minutes, or hours. It was possible she'd slept all the way through to the next night. Curious, but none of it could be answered standing here and she knew it. The quiet graveyard beyond her door was the only one with the key.

If only she could hear the monster's breath. Living up or down in the house, she could open the door. Though she must, walking out would tempt its hunger. If not outside her door, possibly he remained standing in mommy's room, looking to see her exit.

"Hello, are you still mad?" Simone called.

There was light entering from under her door. It wasn't a soft flicker of a tv reflecting off walls and traveling. No, this light was stronger. Its yellowish color and mood were steady and even. More than this, it originated from closer than the living room. Not the hall light, Simone recalled sadly that one had burned out some time ago.

Briefed with these facts and no reply, her choice was made for her. Without a notable command, her hand grabbed the handle over her perch. Collecting an ounce of confidence, she closed her eyes and acted.

Tonight, even though the hinges spoke clearly, Simone didn't hear their echoing squeal.

Pulled inward, the door opened as her sight was returned. The shadows of her room were tinted with the light reaching down the full length of the twelve-foot hallway. The ink of night was absent from its start.

Switching to the handle on the other side of the door, Simone put her weight on it. Her ears searched for warning. Finding none, she extended her gaze out of the frame.

She first saw the weak glint of the tv's effects on the stairwell. Overruled by another glowing source the tv had always been a constant sun to the creatures that lived here. Hard-pressed, her brain couldn't think of a time its glow hadn't burned in the living room. A foot cleared the threshold. Wincing as it landed, the only conclusion was that nothing inhumane had occurred, yet.

The ideas of before returned. Having no answer for the whereabouts of her friend, Simone poked into the length of the hall.

"Crischa, are you there?" The second barefoot, more cautious than the first tested the ground. It was possible the ground might still open up and take her.

Reluctantly, both her eyes and the question were sent to the end of the hallway. Venturing to every foot of the lit hall, only her eyes arrived at the doorway to her mommy's room. The bathroom door on the left wall was closed, but it almost always was.

Discouraging at first sight, Simone had hoped it was closed and a snoring beast lay behind it. Strained in place she wanted to turn away and head downstairs. Once there, she could again start her search for that girl. Standing here, there felt to be a purpose for that uncharacteristically open room.

There was light coming from their room, a lamp dumped on the floor. There was silence. A hushed curiosity she could not pull away from. The light source now defined; she saw half the shade was covered by some of mommy's clothes. Strewn madly around the area she could see; a storm had hit the room.

Her head aimed at the hall's conclusion; Simone pivoted on the balls of her tender feet. Coerced by some atypical need in her mind, she crept gradually to its edge. Past the bathroom, she now stood at the doorway. It loomed so much larger than she knew it to be. Its borders stretched as if they continued to grow larger due to her presence.

This was the window she loved. Yet without effort, her eyes refused to look across to it. On the opposite side of the room, the window was cracked open a few inches and chilled air was entering. Though it wasn't enough to affect her much, she noticed the temperature had been touched.

Listening there before entering, she discovered nothing she hadn't already known fifteen feet ago. This was stupid, and she was making it worse just being here.

This hush was wholly unlike the peace she'd uncovered in the woods. She feared this emptiness; it was a secret lie that was going to hurt her. There was no mistaking this truth.

The pounding in her chest was more than fear–it was the engine of her body preparing her for flight. "Leave, turn around." Her words, a loosened breath that escaped over worried lips.

Covering her mouth, in case she gave her presence away, she leaned in further. Two dressers on the left, but mommy's bed was to the right, next to the closet that separated the rooms upstairs.

Far as she bent to see, she stepped into the room fully. Warning bells were going off, but she hadn't heard them. There seemed to be another voice in her head leading her on. A voice that suggested meaning to her steps.

The half-muted lamp near the window lay sideways on the floor. Its downward blaze pointed out the room and down the hall. Still, its warmth in the dropping temperature illuminated some of the shadowy edges around her. The one thing it didn't do for Simone was indicate if dangerous creatures were living nearby. Turbulent piles of clothes, broken objects, and all-around chaos littered the floors. Simone had never seen her mommy's room clean, however, this violence was beyond all. Anger, even hatred, had turned the room into this depressing state.

The evidence was everywhere. Unheard of damage, a chair lost in one corner had a broken spine. All the drawers of one dresser piled everywhere and their wooden parts smashed. Draped hopelessly around the room in no discernible manner was every stitch of her mother's life.

Likened to the living room, Simone saw mixed piles of debris. Boxes, bottles, cans of all sorts and ages. Some new, others that had been there far longer were spread haphazardly but all near the bed.

Unapparent when she'd first entered, something with the likeness of 'him,' lay in the bed. She couldn't see clearly, but the bulge in the sheet was her clue. Simone knew he was stoned to the world. The monster appeared to be in its lair. Unclear, but he skulked, patient for prey to grow near unsuspectingly.

"Mr. Jude?" She wanted no answer or reaction if it was him up there in the bed.

This was the second largest room in the house. Other than the bathroom, Simone knew hers was the smallest. If this said something, she refused to ponder on it. In front of the window seat, she wanted to get up there and look out of it.

It was night after all, and this was the time to see Crischa's house lights. That light which had led her to find life here on earth. Facing the bed, Simone's attention drifted down. Another light burned tonight and unlike the long steel post theirs used to stand on, this one lay broken and left abandoned for too long. There was a thought around it. An idea that had never been before.

Simone's heart was not pounding right now. Yet as she breathed, she smelt the aroma sitting sick in the room. Heavy, the scent was disgusting but too familiar. Unseen, she knew it was vomit. Allowing it to be dispersed easier was the lighter fumes of various alcohols.

"You should go." The voice in her skull was Scuff, and he was adamant. Not the same happy melody she made most of the time. This tone was as if the pet knew there were other voices in her head that should never be.

There was an opportunity in the room, and she was being asked to involve herself in them.

Head and shoulders spinning the lines of danger she imagined on the floor, didn't exist tonight. She'd crossed the one at their door and she was being asked to cross another, but this one was in her mind.

For once Simone's voice was cold, "Are you okay, Mr. Jude?" She made sure to never rise above the threat she was playing with. There was no response.

Led to the foot of the bedside, Simone continued her scan. Nothing here on the left side of the bed except his nightstand. Even this close, nothing was definite for who lay in the bed. 'Maybe he's on the couch.' She thought briefly. Silent bare feet, she walked on piles of clothes. It was odd. This all felt familiar to the woods, and surrounding her the same stillness. The only thing absent were the thorns to blame. At her back was the same chilled breeze from the window.

Along the bedside, she grew further convinced. The previous impression was correct. The lump in the bed was the monster.

Not notice atop some of mommy's clothes, was an errant liquor bottle. Untamed, her foot kicked it.

Sent rolling under the bed, her spasmed nerves tightened as it screamed away. The noise multiplied as it met up in the darkness underneath. Its glass voice clanged as it echoed against more of its own kind. All of them discarded for months and even years.

Her flinching face, readied in its expression for the reaction she was expecting. Prepared, Simone waited for him to jump up and strike her. A verbal thrashing could be expected just as easily. Peeking from under her frightened eyelids, the assumed payment wasn't to be found. His inebriation was most likely at that sweet spot. Simone grew closer to the bedside. The revolting stench was far worse here. Its smothering thickness was also padded by the human material that was Jude's odor.

Pressed higher upon desperate toes, Simone looked into this landscape. What she found was the polluted bed. The view was slightly better; she witnessed all that lived atop the sheetless mattress was him.

At the head of the bed, her stepfather. Poured atop him, blankets, clothes of both his and mommy's. His face pointed up to the ceiling and his disgusting mouth opened. Strange enough, he was neither snoring nor offering that wheezing breath of his. Jetting out over the edge where she stood, part of his arm. Huge and with a tattoo of some faded act of rebellion in his long-forgotten youth.

Standing beside this, Simone once again winced. Under her toes, she felt a wet surface. The color and texture were ones that would only lead to a nauseating response if she looked at it. Venturing down anyway, she thankfully discovered more of that oblique drink, spilling from unseen bottles.

Something more was realized. Her muscles hadn't let her brain know she was holding the hefty lamp that she'd passed by earlier.

Away from the peculiarity, she glanced back forward. Unresponsive and dead to the world, Jude's body hadn't moved because of her presence. This sight gave her a deceptive sense of power.

Mommy's room was destroyed. Though not beyond days of cleaning, it still broke Simone's heart to see it this way. Most of her mom's belongings seemed to be located nearer the door. Hands beginning to shake, a vote was being made within her. One voice, small and tiny in her head screamed 'no.'

The other, darker, and louder had already formed a verdict. A sensation and intensity that spoke of broken thoughts was compromising her mind. Thoughts latent and not recognized, she was on automatic. This section of her subconscious had touched farthest from warmth, it mingled with reasoning she hated to think long about.

Wrapped around the steel shaft of the heavy brass lamp, her fingers tightened. She wasn't thinking, as a battle solidified the intent of her emotions. Fighting inside her skull, she didn't feel her hand rising.

There was hesitation, that slowed the speed, yet it rose higher. The thing in her hand, tighter, her small fingers choking down on the metal till all warmth had vanished from her knuckles.

A numbing pain that already existed in her jaw, neck, shoulder, head and now had spread into her brain. What battle was being waged, only fogged what actions were taking place. Looming in those shadows behind her pupils was a larger consideration. An inner beast wanted freedom and Simone was feeding it as she lifted the tool.

A dark furtive place, she'd been starving it all her life. Its words, now able to give action as it wanted autonomy. Simone stared at Jude. Asleep but not peaceful, numb but not kind, he was a monster waiting to hurt her again when he woke. The power that looked down from atop shaking toes, didn't recognize her own thoughts. What was looking back at Simone was not her. Still, she wanted to offer it a birth.

No higher could the implementation of its freedom rise. Towering at the bedside, Simone buried her gaze. That point was Jude's temple, and its shape slept before her. Staring at him, knuckles white, she no longer knew her thoughts. That careless monster that had so often broken her, was centered in her weapon's path.

The creature lay unmoved presently, but soon he would rise. Her chance was slender, and it wouldn't come again. Her opportunity was now. Hate, pain, fear, and loathing, they all rose higher in a screaming crescendo until their call needed action.

She was always alone.

Chapter Twenty-One

Illumination and Cost

Sensitive to the soft tears rolling on her cheek, Simone let go of Scuff from under her other arm as that hand joined above. Loathing his every breath and a torrent of agony bottled up no more, down came the lamp. The tool of her freedom diverted a meager inch. Slamming down, it's thud on the sheetless bed, a hair away from Jude's skull. Fruitless, and energy spent, the truth was realized. The child's soul within hadn't allowed the darkness to take hold.

Even though she wanted it, and needed to see all her misery end, it wasn't to be like this. Improbable as it might be, Simone felt stronger for the control. The monster had stolen much from her, but she would not be twisted to be like him. Jude had been freed from a deserved fate, and for as long as she lived, she would know his clemency was her choice, her control.

Hands holding the weapon still, they lay beside his thin curly hair. Then Simone heard a thin laugh. First thought to be the weaponized laugh of Jude. It wasn't long in the examination, to know it was a child's voice. It hadn't come from the bed 'no' Simone felt its location. It was nearer the doorway, across from the bed.

"Crischa!?" Begun as a shaking wave of guilt. Simone hadn't hurt Jude, but she madly wanted to.

Having dropped flat footed, she again rose on sore toes. Her gaze reached the room's entry, and there she found a hazy form standing there. Possibly Crischa had seen every sickening moment, and now hated her for being so terrible.

Casting a glance back to her stepfather, Simone discovered an open stare. Truly hateful red eyes, and in them was little confusion about who he saw. In that flashed instant, she knew what was to unfold. Matched against his angry glare, Simone let out a horrifying scream. Pushed from the bottom of her lungs, her echo split cells in the man's skull as it extended. Mouth wide, she was a picture of panic.

Jude's eyes, which had flashed open, now shut as if able to silence the scream with his will. Closed, he heard a strange combination of screams but also laughter. The mixture of drinks, flooded in his veins and saturating his brain, wouldn't allow him to separate the two. He knew only the scream had stopped but Simone continued to laugh at him.

Hands on both of his ears, his degree of anger and irritation became elevated.

"STOP IT!!!" In the frantic craze of this waking dream, he spun his legs around to lurch out of bed. Nimble for his state, he immediately ripped the lamp from her hold. What followed up, to his matured anger, he sent her weapon across the room.

A long cord whipped with it as it flew the full length of the room. Light shade gone from his rampage hours ago, the missile found the opposite wall from the bed. The light bulb hit its point, and it struck the wall violently with an explosion.

His eyes wide open, the ruptured bulb blinded him in a hail of sparks and tiny pieces of glass. Though the room descended instantly into a deep bottomless pit, he was none the wiser. Jude's second act was to swing out at the girl. His reaction was slow but with position and balance, he was able to land a glancing hit.

Her fleeing arm took the brunt of his loosened fist. Simone dropped away into the side of his bed. No longer time to run from Jude's wrath, there was only defense available. Although the flash hadn't blinded her, she felt herself to be the wreckage and the first victim to its equal. Crumbling fast to the bedside she instinctively balled up.

"YOU LITTLE BITCH. WHAT THE HELL YOU THINK YOU'RE PLAYING!?" Hitting an echelon never again to be matched, his volume was entirely driven by the second assault to his gaze. "Tried to hit me with a fucking lamp. Wait until I get my hands on you." While other influences distorted logic, his rage was pure and filled every thought in his skull.

"FUCK!" Head splitting as if he'd already been hit once. The entire house shuddered under the volume.

Four fingers on each hand rubbed the length of his head. Feeling for any wounds, he might not have immediately felt, they all came up empty. Only the undeniable aching, of his own undoing, haunted his every cell. A hangover larger than he would've ever agreed to held a home behind his forehead. The constricted blood vessels pounding with uncontrolled volumes of blood felt violent. Each of the millions of veins protested in his rudely waking skull.

"You're just like your damn druggy mom," rubbing one of his temples, the effects were proving pointless. "You're a fucking nut job, the both of you!" His animosity and resentment spewed out into the darkened room.

Feet on the ground, his posture matched his lack of energy. Nonetheless his hand whipped outward to grab blindly for Simone. Unable to recover from the brilliant flash, he knew it was vain to try. Mulish though, Jude's other arm, with wide open fingers joined in the wild swings.

He was unable to see that Simone had already dropped and rolled against the wall a foot away. Not out of his reach but her silence made her invisible below him.

Pushed off the bed, Jude stomped through the maelstrom he'd created. Hand grazing the wall he pulled it back feeling the painful ricochet. Returning it for support, he needed to allow his eyes time to erase the flashed spots, centered in his vision.

Time greedy, he was offered seconds before he heard the fetid little child taunting him. Simone's warped laughter was a new one to him. She was doing the same irritant that he'd so willfully used on others, now against him. Dejected, it was working only to raise his blood pressure and the baleful punishments to come.

Turning to her location, she was somewhere by the bedroom door. The laughter was deliberate, if not effective. Had he been clear minded, he might have known his mistake. The hiss of taunts was troubling for any to hear.

"You think so, do you?" The question was an acceptance of an offering to war. Lips narrowing over breathing teeth he wanted a hold of her now. No little waste of life was going to win. Jude knew he'd been more than good to the little bastard for long enough.

"I'll make you sorry you ever met me, you little fuck." Pulling up his unbuttoned pants, he searched for the loose belt hanging under his belly. It slightly tattered brown-leather found; it was whipped out into the darkness.

Folding it once, then twice over his bruised knuckles, the thought of violence gave a smile. Jude's cheek gave a twitch, she should be so lucky to simply get whipped. Sneering past his aching head he wrapped it one last time, buckle displayed outward.

Unable to close her ears, Simone recoiled under every one of his footsteps. All of them inches from stomping her, yet none did.

His fight was slow to strike her, and she couldn't imagine he didn't know her location. She was breathing so loud that his dog, wherever he was lost in the woods, could hear her. Convinced of it, Simone could only wait for his entire weight to come crashing down atop her.

She'd seen his boots scattered around the room earlier so it would be bare feet stomping and kicking her. Focusing, she knew the pain that was coming but what was new was no tears. An unnatural calm covered her on the floor. The silence of the forest wasn't here but Simone could hear Crischa. Her laughter was a bit off, but it was for her, she knew it. She was certain, an entirely different sensation worked to pacify her on the floor. It was a part of her, but to name it wasn't for now.

Laying there, an utterly unusual smirk inserted its presence over Simone's lips. Cracked wide, it almost made her laugh. The sensation didn't belong. She couldn't understand how it had even arrived, waiting for Jude's feet to stomp her.

Whether it was connected to her wishes, Simone heard a thundering crash. Jude had fallen hard in the darkness. His anger multiplied, but it was after he'd walked away from her huddled spot closer to the headboard and wall.

A wave of vertigo and a misplaced foot on one of the many bottles, calamity was the result. Already wet feet, one had caught the edge of a bottle and his hulking mass twisted sideways. Increasing the spin, he had been in mid-swing to find anything to guide him in the dark.

Sent rotating from the hip, his face was the first to land. "HELL!!!" The pain was augmented and far fiercer. It was the same damaged area he'd sustained after falling off the back porch a day ago. Repeated over again, his curses were spit out like acid splattering the floor and his arm pushing up. Teeth at maximum pressure his head had found greater limits of hurt. Pain in his back and jaw sent him further into the need for violence.

"I'll find you; you know that don't you? So just keep laughing, you little shit." On one knee he just knew he was bleeding.

No sooner than him pulling himself up, than his balance was stolen feet from the door. This time, even with his arms out, Jude landed hard on the open-door frame. Bad luck, his face again took the brunt of his rushed move.

Head dipped, he leaned against the frame, the house was taking up Simone's fight and he wasn't winning. That would change when he found her, still he was being denied any prize. The whiff of a girl, so long under his fist, now only a vacant figure. Mocking him as he struggled in the murky entrance, he'd change her luck.

He hadn't dropped off his feet this time. All his weight against the doorway, he looked up then down the length of the hallway. She was just there. A silhouette in the middle of the hall. Standing there, she was backlit by the faint light of the tv. Its dim glow, just an impression as it came up bouncing off-white walls.

Her laughing had stopped but its effect continued in his head. "You can laugh all you want shithole. No one loves you." It was a frustrated venom, yet it flew out around the revolting spit of blood. Dripping now on the bottom lip, he ignored it and focused on the girl. Blood was mixing in his mouth, the taste raw, salty, and even metallic. It was his turn to laugh.

"Your mother doesn't even want you. You know this, don't you, you little fuck." The knife worked before, and his fogged brain was just fighting to return his equilibrium.

Forcing a dishonest laugh of his own, Jude couldn't get over his nerves. She'd tried to kill him. How was this possible? The blood was boiling up and he wouldn't make this mistake again. Gagging on the taste, he still licked the brew from his lip and swallowed. There was a lining here, he hadn't lost his weapon. Around his dominant right fist, he tightened the weaponized belt.

Nodding at the frozen child in the hall, she just watched as he stood straight in the doorway. Jude couldn't believe she was measuring up against him. Six feet away and halfway down the hall, she wasn't near enough to her room or the stairs, to outrun him.

Bare feet, she hadn't a chance and he stormed the hall for her. Her black shape turned and ran.

"You stupid girl, how can you make it so easy?" Jude's laugh was real now. She thought of escaping him by running into her room. Big mistake and now he could start making her pay for it. A crooked expression replaced his tired laugh. At a slower pace, Jude coiled into Simone's bedroom.

The burned spots in his pupils, comfortably adjusted. With the added reflection of moonlight entering, he could see better here. Scanning her room, predictably his gaze caught the familiar pants and legs retreating under the bed.

They were pink pants. Covered in random glittery stars they'd been one of the few things he had given Simone. His brother had given him a large bag of clothes from his grown children. Still, Jude had been loved for a time for the thoughtful gift. What was more, he took the praise greedily.

Short-lived, the feeling visited only the back of his memories. He wasn't here to make up or be friends. Crawling under the bed the legs hid. Pulled back into the farthest corner, Jude grinned once more. Disappointed in that chasm, it would not save her. This just meant he could take his time. Swaggering across the short distance he worked out the game. His needs changed only slightly. No fast punishment, he wanted to draw out the damage he would inflict.

Half a step away from the bedside he spun round to sit on its edge. Here he would first weigh his options on just how to extract her from under the bed. His gaze drifted about the room, he did feel a bit of sadness for a kid's playroom to be so empty.

Returning to this game, his first instinct had been to rip the bed from the floor. Sending it against the distant wall, he would've exposed the rat underneath in a dramatic way.

He relished the image. Her gaze would be a fearful one, sockets wide and mouth dropped open. He'd find Simone huddled in that stupid corner as the bed vanished. She wouldn't be laughing anymore, his prey cornered and under his might. 'No,' he rejected this one as too quick. He desired to parcel out 'its' fear.

A substituted notion sitting on the bed. He might have reached down along the wall behind her, but this idea was abandoned as well. Giving a small bounce of the noisy spring, he loved the gnawing anticipation. As he worked out her punishment in excruciating detail, he came upon the game. Halting his bobbing, the room was awash in silence. It was here that her laughter trickled up to him from that pathetic hiding spot.

The sound was grading and pure as it found his unreceptive ears. It sliced a tender opening in his brain and burrowed deep as its unnatural lilt. Its power echoing even against the walls, the reach was unnerving. Her unseen face was arrogant, testing him and his fury. Hitting the mark, Jude felt the gnawing anger explode.

Dropping to the ground in a tantrum, Jude swiped under the full extent of the bed. Fingernails scraping the far wall, he found only an empty address. A notion of trepidation froze him there for a second. Re-evaluating his move, he couldn't fathom her missing body.

"What the fuck!?" The words dropped as another bead of blood fell from his lips. Eyes dulled still; a frantic push was in his brain to understand. Though murky, his continued search under her small bed returned the same.

A hand wiped the drops from his mouth. Before resurfacing, he spied her upright legs. They were standing in the corner of his view.

Firmly positioned outside the end of the bed, they stood, lit by moonlight entering her room. She was actually watching his foolish attempt to catch her. This was a bridge too far for Jude. A threat readied on his tongue he was too slow.

Just as quickly, her naked and dirty feet turned and ran. However quick she might have thought herself, Jude watched them run into the sadder closet. Trailing her all the while, she dropped a burst of mocking laughter. Its reverberation was far more damaging than any he could muster right now. Disoriented by the stupid child, it was fuel poured on his rage. A bonfire ignited; it sent him higher. Back and his hands ruptured under the bed frame and hurled its entirety. Flipped over, he pushed it to almost cover the only window in the room.

"Really? Hah!" Insulted, he hid the idea that her laughter affected him at any level. Focusing on it, Jude rushed closer to the closet. She thought herself smart enough to attempt an escape, but there was only pain where she ran to.

"You're alone." Another wipe of his mouth, he looked at his hand, but the darkness only gave a black stain across it. "You will always be alone." He stabbed her mind.

"You will always be Alone." He needed her to give back some sort of an answer. He fed off the proof that he could reach out, even without his fist, and hurt her.

"You–are–alone." Each word spread out; he weaved the taunt. Yet somehow it even gave him a subtle chill.

"Why didn't you just run into a corner dumb ass?" After a pause, he worked out a twitch on his back and neck. The diversion would make Simone wait a bit longer.

Taking an annoyed breath, Jude learned much of the alcohol still coursed through his system. Bending backward to stretch other muscles, he regained his upright balance. Yet still a nauseating wave accompanied by dizziness appeared to linger no matter what he did.

Looking at his hand, he examined the blood covering it. "Looks like I owe you one." Said casually, he nodded his regards.

The room entered a hushed pause, where neither combatant laughed nor threatened.

After a small groan of correction, Jude stood back tall. His sight locked deep in the void. This closet backed to his room, and there couldn't be more than four feet of depth to it. Yet he couldn't see any further than the doorway. Its bordering white paint offered nothing as his view ventured inward. Premeditated, Jude took those last few steps up to his victim's hideaway.

Blocking the exit entirely, he watched the darkness for any movement. The child was inside, and this was a fact. Looming, he wanted her to beg for mercy, to plead for a losing side. He was going to force the fear out of her sad eyes.

Standing there only a moment longer. The light from outside dimmed. A thick and impenetrable darkness covered the world outside. Looking at the window, Jude also sensed any glow traveling up the stairs dissipated to nothing.

Sent into another inky abyss of night, Jude felt the chill run his spine. The feeling was odd, but his brain could only explain it as a presence. Looking toward the bedroom door, boards were heard aching on the staircase.

Creatures, possibly bigger than the one monster standing in front of Simone's closet, moved.

Chapter Twenty-Two

Home

Enraged, Jude charged headlong into the closet. Blind to its interior, he thrashed and kicked. Each blow found nothing. His foot knocked holes in the walls, even as his hands grabbed and tore at the shelves. He wanted her throat–even a bruised and whimpering mass would suffice. Jude knew she would take advantage of the pitch, so he continued; sure, he'd make contact eventually.

Finally, he staggered, when one of his wider swings smashed into the solid door frame. Off-center and twisting with his heel caught in a box, he was delivered face-first into the back wall. Grabbing for new balance, he pulled up near straight. Baffled, his anger was stumped by the empty closet. Confusion reigned in the darkness. She'd been there, Jude's thoughts had been sure of it. Yanking the last of the shelves free, Jude sent them flying back into the room behind him.

After a pause, he placed flattened fingers against one side of his pounding temple. Turning around, he used his hand with the belt covered fist to stabilize. Leading him out into the bleak, he was forced to trace along the right wall. At the bedroom's exit, he punched at the light switch with his weaponized fist. Unsure if he'd missed, nothing happened. Fingers opening atop it, he discovered there was no power to the switch.

He shook his head, disappointed. A sigh, Jude knew Mackenzie kept a flashlight in the bathroom, and with that, he would have that little girl's neck. Drifting into the hallway, he could see that the entire house lay in the same sinister murk.

Plotting back toward his room, the bathroom would be on the left. His elbow found the corner of the bathroom door. It was closed, but he pushed it in with a simple twist of the handle. The flashlight was in one of four possible drawers at the side of the sink. Tub to the left and sink to the immediate right his search was quick. Some luck, he quickly worked through the first two before finding what he came for.

"Let there be light." He pronounced the victory with a flick of the switch. A wave in the air of the shameful kid's flashlight, Jude sent the beam of light to the ceiling first.

Attention turned to the mirror; he saw blood. Smeared about his face, it looked like a mass murder. The troubling effect was intensified as the light arched close under his chin. A fitting grin was opened as his mouth spread wide, his bloody teeth to greater impact.

Two heavy blows to his scalp and Jude's forehead had a channel of blood running on both sides of his face. Bad as it looked, he knew he'd smeared it to look worse. Dispatching another latent and evil smile, he placed the flashlight ominously under his chin one last time. Exposing his face's many natural flaws, the dark red elixir drew out his inner demons.

"Okay Simone, let's play then, little girl." He dropped his profile to an angle, his gaze stealing a quick glance out into the hallway.

Now bent forward over the sink he turned the water on. Placing down the flashlight, upright, and balanced on the shelf under the mirror, he let the water run over his waiting hand. One handed; he splashed water over his face. Washing away a majority of the blood, he glared back to the mirror.

"Shit, what the hell did you do to me, woman?" Jude's question was meant for Mackenzie. He'd soon give her a taste of his wrath.

Staring into the reflection, he didn't move for a moment. Locked on the remaining spots, where diluted blood continued to hold to his face, his thoughts ran awry. Dark ideas, a sense that there were corrupted cells in his mind, and he might go too far tonight was a reality.

Swaying back and forth, and unwatched, his fingertips lingered for warm water to reach them. Filled to the overflow, the sink faucet was turned off. A raised chin and a curve of the face, his inner monologue was a sickening laughter. It was a horrid blend of the girl's tease, and his purely sarcastic taunt.

An entire hand wading to-and-fro in the lukewarm pool, he noted he still felt a bit dizzy. Without looking into the blending waters below, his ears heard the dripping blood. Persistent, his draining life fell around his cheeks, through a week-old beard, and fell to the sink below. The white porcelain holding the brew was a swirling froth of tainted water, and his hand continued to stir it.

The trance, ultimately broken, Jude lowered and with both hands, he scrubbed better. Before grabbing at the place where a towel should've been, he spit darker blood into the water. Hand jabbed into the wall under the empty towel bar, the frustrations of tonight continued. Sadly detouring, he pulled at his own shirt. Adjusting some of it from under his belly, Jude pulled harder to reach his face and dried it.

The shirt already soaked from a sloppy bath, it did little to help his disappointment. Moving on from these annoyances, he heard the belt fall from the edge of the sink counter. Although a simple latch-over buckle it was of heavy steel construction, and it hit the tile loud at his bare feet.

A huff, he braced on the sink's edge with one hand and bent to retrieve this night's weapon. Clutched in-between fingertips, he moaned as he pushed back up straight. A moment of reflection, his gaze drifted back up to the mirror over the ruined water. Slow to focus, he centered back on his image portrayed over the glass.

A jump and shaken shoulders, he braced at the sight. A second face watched from behind him. Obscured by liquor and blood in his eyes, the figure loomed taller than him. Eyeballs black and skin drenched in wickedness, it cast a reflection only for a second.

Deadly as the shape flashed, Jude accidentally knocked his flashlight off its perch. Heart rate wild, and his actions stumbled, he'd confused his mind. Both reaching down for the means of sight and defending against a threat mixed in his frantic twist.

Pounding in his head, his hangover was an erupting wave of violence.

Late and underpowered, he sent an unruly swing. Built with panic, his fist came round and tangled with the tub's curtains. Twisting violently, Jude discovered Mackenzie's harmless robe hung from the rod behind him.

The entire mistake rushed in his mind. Stupid and childish, he now knew the error was a trick of the light. Unsure of the time needed to slow his beating heart, he leaned again on the counter. Breath slowing, his head was a thunderstorm of blood.

Thankful for the returning quiet, he slouched heavily over the sink. Avoiding the mirror, this time he waited as the storm drifted away. All the while on his elbows, he continued to fight off that creepy chill, covering his skin.

Shaking free of those phantoms of a hindered childhood, Jude worked his twisted back to reach down. Slapping at the floor, he retrieved the flashlight before heading out of the bathroom.

"Well, then." He wanted time, but there was work to be done. "Guess it's time for round two, Simone." Out the door, he first looked left into his room.

The flashlight strained after its jarring fall; its diminished power was proof it was nothing more than a toy.

Jaws tense from the continuous grinding, Jude jerked around when he heard feet moving. The pattering toes of bare feet ran behind him. Baffled once more, it gave him the impression the child had escaped from the bathroom with him.

Focusing his confusion down the hallway, he listened for her getaway. Heard clearly, she trailed past him and was leading him toward the stairwell. Flashlight slowed through the darkness; it caught hold of a pink blur.

The girl's frame hadn't turned right for the stairs. Shaking his head, Jude couldn't understand her stupidity. Had she run out of the house again, her flesh would've had a chance. The reality was far stranger, Simone had instead returned into her own room.

Annoyed by the unchallenged effort, Jude once more stood at Simone's open door. With no better hiding spots, this game was quickly coming to its conclusion. A weak flashlight, but more than adequate to discover her next hiding place, in a cleared-out room. A step in, and Jude's jaw widened with shock. Beyond reason, he froze at the sight. Struck dumb by the bizarre twist to this chase, he glared unprepared and unable to act fast.

Seconds passed, as he couldn't help but marvel at Simone's resourcefulness. Somehow, this helpless little girl had got the recessed attic-ladder down. A damp shirt and puzzled expression, this turn of events seemed impossible.

How'd she easily clear the nine-foot height of the ceiling? That answer waiting, he couldn't even reach the recessed knob of the hatch to open it without a ladder. Continuing in his confusion, Jude placed an unmeasured step to the side of the riddle.

The unfolded ladder's length stretched down into the room and landed almost perfectly in the center of the floor. Narrow and dirty, the aroma of the attic could now be smelt. The ranker smell was airing off the throwback.

"Hell no, I don't think so." Jude's plans and mood were being constantly tested. This brat seemed to lead him round and round.

This new turn of events pissed him off. There was nothing worse than the hated attic. He'd made great efforts in most things but avoiding the attic and everything up there, topped them. What went up there was condemned to a forgotten oblivion, and as far as he was concerned, unneeded. Cringing, he didn't relish the idea of chasing her, and the last place he wanted to follow was up there. Despite its ability to return him to some murky corner of his childhood, it was dangerous. Though it had a floor in it, the lights never worked, and it was covered with spiderwebs, and dead critters starved of light.

He knew he'd find her cornered up there, but he would have to do everything to shorten the visit. Correcting the notion, he needed to do all he could, to retrieve her, without stepping up there.

Tugging at his crotch, he adjusted. Putting a foot on the first step, he gave a disheartened sigh. Thin and restricted slats, the base of the unfolded ladder was anything but firm.

Plainly fake, a cheerful tone reached up into the darkness beyond. "Just come down out of the attic. Simone, come down here and we can get this all over with as little pain as possible." Holding the belt behind his back.

Looking up the ladder, his gaze and tone wavered from the angle of his neck. Waiting was his first stab at the girl's stubbornness. The endeavor had little hope of success, yet it tested his own patience.

Half his skull burned from the physical, the other half tormented by such tiny feelings as a dark attic. A near crushing pressure was building on the surface of the flashlight.

He was at his limits and exposed, his mouth smacked of other obligations. The thought that tonight had already proved to be shitty, and now with a homicidal girl and her infuriating games, it was all wasted time.

What became obvious, lingering at the foot of the ladder, was the needs of his system. His brain had retreated to a deprived posture. He was exceedingly parched. The replenishing need for drink was becoming a problem to him and of utmost concern.

The signs were unquestionable, his body was in full revolt as his cotton-mouth worsened.

Adjusting that foot on the first step, he called again. "Simone, get down here now!" The defiant brat just needed an authoritative tone. "This is your last warning."

Fighting every inclination to curse, he growled. "I promise we're just going to talk about this. Just come out of the damn attic." Both hands occupied, his grip of the ladder was going to be tricky. The best he could, on the sadly vintage ladder, was a shared grip with the flashlight. Skyward, the ascent would be tenuous to say nothing of his efforts to come back down with a fighting child in tow.

Employing more deceit against the seven-year-old, "Mommy left you some dinner, come down and I'll warm it up for you." All of it, fat lies. He knew it easily shattered, however, anything to shorten her stay and keep him out of the attic.

The idea of food was silly, but it was likely a product of his own hunger. Besides, as he thought, it wasn't like Mackenzie to think ahead. She had been working that bar job their entire relationship. At least when the courting was new, she worked days. It was going on close to three years since she'd switched to an a.m. shift.

His patience for this disobedience was an ever-shrinking commodity. Forced, his foot took a rung higher. Setting aside the girl's irritating rejection of his authority, Jude thought of starving her up there. The words were there, though unsaid. 'I don't want to go in the fucking attic.' He knew it was a weakness, but it was ingrained in some lost experience.

The flashlight's yellow-white shimmer pushed up. A far cry from any real light, Jude hesitated to bring his other foot onto the ladder. The glow was barely enough to reach the ceiling, much less be helpful. Its batteries were small, and it did little against the dense foe, holding at the opening above. Jude wanted his brand-new flashlight; the one he'd bought a few weeks earlier. Simmering on the rung of the ladder, he was annoyed because he knew who had it. Mackenzie, the asshole that she was, had taken it and likely it sat useless on the floor of her car.

The indignity felt fresh. Jude wanted to throw the shitty toy light as his other foot took him up another rung. Without other options, his belted hand took hold of the other side of the ladder.

Constant and chilled air dropped over him from the hole in the girl's bedroom ceiling. Though he had no intentions of heating her room, the air falling on him gave pause to a third step.

"Come out of there." Desperation was peaking, and he wanted her out. "Or--- I'll, so help me, I'll lock you up there!" The threat was adjusted, as his hands hated the feel of the grimy wood and the smell, he was drowning in. "No food or water either, I swear I'll leave you up here." The threat hadn't been planned, but he needed it to be understood, he was beyond mad.

The odor crashing over him was putrid. Probably a dead rat, maybe even mold, it was a mixture that had no defined shape and it turned his already queasy hangover.

"I know you hear me!" Voice cracking, he lifted to the next placement. Sharper, his thirst for alcohol was growing with anger and his advancing foothold of the steps.

The angle of the risers, so steep, they touched his knees as he stood there. Pushed up another two steps, Jude's head was now under that murky frontier. The perception of rushing air was less here but the smell hung on him as if it'd had teeth. His warnings had all gone unheeded, and he'd already climbed farther than ever planned.

How could he be more charitable, his nose snarled as his lips could close no tighter. The option or choice wasn't his any longer and he'd promised himself. Jude wanted payment for it now. He'd sworn he wouldn't go up here. This was a blazing mistake, and his skull was killing him.

The lecture played out behind the pain, thrusting on red eyeballs. The idea that he wasn't nervous, and it was just all anxiety, did little to calm his jitters. The shaking in his muscles around the shoulders was a clue it hadn't worked.

A pathetic man of forty-nine, and he was hesitant to push upward. He stood a mere step before his head would cross that attic boundary and he was talking to himself.

Painting a lie on his face, Jude's eye line progressed to the level of the thick floor planks. His gums felt the chilled air as he grimaced. Frigid and dusty, the air-dried his already sore eyes.

Though his gaze refused to blink, the narrow search expanded in the scene. Nothing had shape up here, and without the flashlight above the lip, it sat in dark emptiness. The first seconds, everything was under his scrutiny. His mind was wondering just how the girl could see anything.

Reluctant to release the problematic ladder with either hand, he had to. His hand with the belt would have to linger below, and this was painful. The other, with the flashlight tight in his grip, rose slowly. Dull at the start, its teasing radiance peered straight up. Useless to the search, he was cautious to discover anything near his head.

Striking the numerous rafters above, the batteries inside his flashlight allowed for a soft dimming. Although it caused a flinch in Jude's nerves, he gave it a swift shake.

Even angled impractically, the toy had found a clue. A positive impression that there was a cowering child moving up here. Somewhere adjacent to his gaze, something small ran to find a better cover.

Headstrong, and with a willful need to rise higher, Jude continued his advance. Above the floor line, his entire head was clear, and he might now find Simone's face terrified he had her cornered.

The beam turned quickly. Its glow pushed into the longer stretch of the house's attic. The space seemed to span the full length of the rooms below. Joylessly, and against his harder wishes, the light could only touch a tiny fraction of its span.

What Jude had found, as he waved the beam, was a trickle of dust falling nearby. The path of the disturbance was odd, but she was somewhere beyond. A few feet at best, he thought.

Laying his hand and the light on the thick dust of a plank, he listened. Concentrating harder, he accurately found her nervous breathing–a soft moan of dread. It was gratifying to hear the worry in her lungs.

A quivering ache lived there in her sad concealment. Squinting into the deeper ink of the attic, Jude would increase that uneasiness. He was going to make her pay for the effort to catch her.

Considering he had to hand it to her, the attic was a good spot to hide. A place never thought of, and had she had a different way to enter, he would have never found or cornered her.

Walking down the hall, Simone could hear her stepfather yelling at her. The one thing she couldn't understand was why he was asking her to come down from an attic. Even though the house was drowning under the murky shadows of night, this was a mystery.

Slow steps in the dark, she was out of their room and had a hand on the wall. Confident in the ink she moved further into the hallway to find her room and Jude's calls.

To Simone's astonishment, the growls for obedience had and were continuing to come from her room. At her doorway, she stopped cold. A moment needed to center; she saw nothing at first. Curiosity quickly followed the noise to its source. Up and onto an odd ladder she had never seen.

She'd lived in this room forever, and however it was; this was new to her. She hadn't had a clue that what had lay beyond the square shape on her ceiling was an escape hatch of sorts.

The two-inch-long string and ball on its surface had always been a curiosity. To her surprise, it was the marker for a handle she didn't know about. The attic door had few trace details other than this. It had never suggested to her that a secret room lay beyond.

Standing atop some of the highest steps, was Simone's monster.

"Mr. Jude?" Oddly, her voice was absent of fear. Upon the utterance of his name, a pinpoint of light descended. Its meaning and reason lost above, yet it now was used to confuse Simone's night eyes even more.

Striking a path directly into her up turned gaze, she defended with a hand. Close, and in front of her face, Scuff was the shield she used to stop the floodlight. Simone needed it for a short time, before shifting it aside. That light, pointed still at her, was certainly dazzling in the surrounding bleakness. Squinting now at it, she waited.

"What the hell!" Jude's thoughts were disoriented. His blurt emotion came from a place lacking even the smallest touch of his previous anger. Head inside that darkness, his facial expression was trimmed with that same horror and fear. The same statement Simone's face would often be endowed with by him.

A probing terror swallowed all of Jude's logic. What reasoning he'd had seconds prior, quickly vanished as something else took hold of him.

In that fractured and failing instant, he couldn't fathom how Simone had gotten to the doorway. How had she done that? There was simply no way she could've passed him on the same ladder and escaped the attic. No way she could have survived the drop and now watched him from below.

There were other things to prove this was impossible. Atop those last few steps and his vulnerable head remaining in the pitch of the attic, he could hear her breathing. The lungs he'd thought fearful and hiding up here, were now hovering closer around his exposed head. His brain flooded in panic, he only now realized the sound wasn't fear, nor cowardice. It was hunger. Before Jude could choose flight, that same callous laughter circled him from the obscurity crushing down on him.

Simone watched uncaringly as some unseen thing in that restricted room took Jude. Too dark for her to notice any aggressive act, the full-grown man left her sight and the ladder under him. The room below was confused as the flashlight flipped upward ascending through the attic. Hitting the floor up there, its light rolled.

Asking at a loss, "Mr. Jude?" A tone flat if not puzzled, Simone could only wonder why he wasn't answering.

The square opening, fixed to her ceiling, now had gray shadows and shapes shifting about. Watching, she waited with the tiniest tilt of her head.

The new roar of some rushing gust was replacing the moving effect of the flashlight. Then once again, as so often had followed Simone, a stillness controlled the space far above.

Continuing with her curiosity, Simone heard the roll and remained patient. Possibly sent out by Mr. Jude, Simone saw the flashlight tumble out of the attic. Flipped off the ledge of the floor above, it hit the top step. Skipping the next three, it hit others to land on the ground. Rolling to a stop at her feet, she could tell the plastic light was the one she'd gotten from mommy's friend.

Pleased to be reunited, she picked up the lost gift. Unaware of any conflict, Simone turned and headed downstairs. Her gaze never seeing the elongated arm reach out to pull the ladder up and close all secrets.

Chapter Twenty-Three

Another Day

Sitting on the mattress on the floor, this new morning was still cold. Clutching Scuff with one arm, Simone neither smiled nor cried. She didn't even wonder why her bed frame was lying separated from her bed. The night had passed with little more than a bird tweeting outside. A moment was needed as it finally reached her ears.

Simone, hearing the bird's voice, bridged to a tune she'd heard time and again from mommy. The words were not important, but she had the melody pure. If not happy, it was at least a marker that had long ago locked her into the feelings of mommy.

The song's tone felt sad, yet it was nice. It was also simple, it gave a pulse that connected something inside her heart and chest. Humming in its peaks and valleys, her eyes followed the visible signs of her breath. A soft floating cloud in the air, she played her game of shapes.

Without shoes, Simone's toes wiggled in the bitter morning. Drifting off several times in her head, her outline never laid back. She released a sigh, she finally straightened on the disheveled bed. Her brown eyes staying wide, they'd fully broken free of her brain's numb pattern. Another sigh, she decided to get off the bed.

Prior to standing off the mattress, the same question from last night resurfaced. A rabbit from a distant hole, the query simply wanted a clue. 'Why had Jude not returned?' Drifting away from those tired thoughts, she didn't want to ponder the reasons, but it was just a curious thing. Any forgetful meaning, Simone gave a quick glance up to the closed and once more hidden entrance.

It was possible that it'd all been a dream. Thankfully a tangent took hold, 'what time is it?'

All of Simone's considerations turned to a meal. She couldn't recall her last morsel of food. Had she even eaten for days? Her stomach hurt and the time lost no longer mattered. She needed something and now. Up once more and on the floor, her concerns headed her downstairs. Simone's thoughts were singular as she walked from her bedroom.

She'd left her door open last night. Walking out, the hall and the entire house felt flooded. Every window was full, they were sharp and bright. Stepping into the hallway, it echoed the rising sun perfectly. The blades of sunlight reached through mommy's window and down the length of this passageway. Cutting a path in the very center, it gave Simone's toes the first touch of a warm surface this morning.

Her journey to the kitchen wasn't plagued by frayed nerves. Fear of the local monster, absent from her waking thoughts. Without worrying about what could be lurking in the corners or on the couch, she walked. Her head never veered, nor had it hesitated from the set mission and her stomach's intent.

Stopped abruptly, Simone stood uncertain of her eyes. At the entrance to the kitchen, she gawked. The confusion was hers and she needed to know if the oddity, that had never been, was real. Piled on the island and other counters, was a spectacle she'd not believed. Both of her eyes failed to focus adequately.

Situated in peculiar heaps, were lopsided pyramids of cans, breads, fruit, and tons of snacks. All of it sprinkled liberally around the open spaces in the kitchen. Most of the shapes and labels were things she'd seen little of in this house. No grocery bags were lying about. No boxes discarded on the floor or crates tossed aside.

Mouth gaping wide, she scanned it all. The bounty was overwhelming as it appeared to all be dumped there from an army of hands. Though it was slow, a smile worked into her cheeks. Pulling over one of the three mismatched chairs, Simone watched the food. The other two chairs hemor-rhaging under car parts Jude had brought in.

Wrestling the stool into place, Simone climbed atop. Eyes already saucers, she rose to the island's surface. Her happy gaze met the banquet. Her hands as hungry as her eyes stared, she felt nervous to reach out and take the first thing.

Stationed atop the stool, she glared at the glorious treasure. Examining the bounty, she was dumbfounded as to what this was, why, where did it come from? Grabbing the closest item, she saw all the cans appeared different. Some of them were vegetables, others fruit, and even some cans of spam were scattered within.

Simone had no idea where a can-opener could be, so she decided that cans were out of the question. It didn't take but a moment before her hands wrapped tight around a bag of chocolate treats. Another tucked under her arm, had white frosting, and looked like cupcakes. A quick rip and her hands were covered in the sticky brown goo. Her mouth hungrily devoured the treats, she hadn't finished the first before she was back finding another of the like.

Collapsing on the couch, she laughed for hours at one cartoon after another. Her every concern and thought glazed over. The day would change little from morning to late afternoon as she repeated the path between stool and couch.

After making the largest of dents in the pile, Simone settled in for the coming night. Her face covered with her exploits, and now a cheerful glowing box, she was set. Two blankets on her and the heater cranked up to its highest, she swore not to move again till morning returned.

The day fell away, and evening greedily took the sun's lazy arching path. Outside, the heavy clouds had returned, and a deeper chill hung over the windows. The front window, with its inside face barely covered, had a hazy film as well as beads of dew rolling down the surface. Under its shut frame a slight whining of air from outside, getting in.

Laying on her side, Simone stared at the tv. Her thoughts no longer followed along with whatever show was on. Scuff, warm and happy with Simone, laid quiet. Even he'd eaten some of the food, or as indicated by marks of chocolate around his sewn shut mouth.

Surrounded by empty wrappers and half-finished bags of various food, Simone wiggled. Her stomach uncomfortable, she gave a soft moan on the couch.

No longer facing the television, her coarse blanket was the last one to remain hold of her. All the others were no longer needed in the raised temperature of the living room. Tucked under her feet, mostly unused, she drifted off into a fitful dreamscape.

Waking harshly to a thunderous pounding, Simone pushed up lost.

Having forgotten her adventures, the location she'd been woken to, looked foreign. The angle before her was the wall of couch cushions, and her sleepy eyes unable to see over.

Forced to focus, she re-positioned with her back correctly, and feet pointed to the tv. Rubbing the sleep from her small eyes, she recognized the tv if not the program on its blaring face.

Glad to see this night and the last day, hadn't been a transitory dream. Simone comforted her confused mind and wondered what exactly had made the racket.

There was no sun, so one fact was checked off her list, it was night once more. Although life from the television sparkled and jumped, she was the only one watching. It was the light by which many lived in this house and tonight wasn't different.

"JUDE!" A pounding and deep voice echoed from the other side of the living room door. Rigid and frustrated, the name was repeated. "JUDE!"

The male voice barked outside the locked door. "ANSWER THE DAMN DOOR, YOU BUM!" A breath for pause. "I know you're in there."

Simone was familiar with the drawl and unique off-tempo speech of Jude's brother. It was Steve, and she was alone. She loved only one fact about him when he came over to get Jude, that meant they would be out for the day. However, it was night and Simone wasn't sure why her stepfather hadn't returned to begin with.

Wishing he would just go away; she closed her mouth tight and buried the noise of her own breathing. Yet no matter how hard she tried, she flinched with every hammering strike of his fist.

"Simmy?" The puzzled tone was now asked through a pane of glass. Peering in through the window beside the door, Steve covered his brow to hopefully see through the condensation on the inside.

He called her 'Simmy,' Simone hated it when anyone, but her mom called her that. Stepfather always called her Simone, and it was exactly what she wanted, but his brother had a knack. He seemed to purposely go out of his way to piss people off.

Her mom disliked him just as much, if not more. When he came over on her days off, he could say the meanest things. Simone was unfortunately witness to them all. Worst, Simone knew that Jude would add on, to make things even more hellish. Inevitably trouble would start, and for the next few days, fights, and arguments. Simone knew it was because of this very fact, and the brothers working together more often, that her mother had changed to nights.

"Simmy, I can see you there. Open the damn door girly." Leaning on the porch rail, just the top of his head could be seen glaring inward.

The living room's only protection was a bed sheet. Pressed into service, it was their curtain for at least a year. Hampered by haze, dirt, and the glare of the tv, Steve wiped the outside surface before pressing a stare back on the glass. Adjusting up and down he was positive he found his brother's puny stepdaughter on the couch.

Beating on the glass, he wouldn't be ignored by her, as it was thwarting any calm he might have had. It took him over twenty-five minutes to get here, and no little girl would send him away for some tv show she was watching.

"Open the door, Simmy." Returning to it, a hand rested on the door. Feeling slightly defeated, his head dropped. He couldn't believe he was being forced to wait. He knew she was determined not to look away from the tv and over at the door.

Of equal height to his five-years older brother, Steve's clean shaved face was curled in a pout as he waited. Though it was straighter, he had the same brown hair as his sibling. Lacking the curl but not the thinned hairline, wasn't the only difference. Steve's body weight was leaner than his brothers', as he'd put on at least thirty pounds over the last decade.

Having always pity Simone, Steve lingered longer than he liked. One truth he admitted was that he'd never spent more than a few hours in total with the girl. This included Jude and Mackenzie's wedding, when Simone was already two years old.

Steve's sympathy was partly because of Simone's unfortunate fate. Never having liked Jude's choice of a wife, he'd always called her 'a drunken bitch,' even to his brother's face. Discounting his own sloshed marriage of youth, Steve returned to beat on the door.

He'd already raised his own kids, and Jude, now raising a child like Simone, was simply messed up in his opinion. Having been raised alongside Jude, he knew him to be a malcontent asshole himself. A fun drinking partner, but a father he was never. Even though Steve loved his brother, it was what he thought the hard truth to be.

Irate with her disregard, Steve pummeled the center of the door. "Simmy! Open the door!"

All the wishing and mumbled pleads, Simone tensed, as she buried her back into the cushions. She could cover her ears, and hope he'd not seen her hiding there in plain view. The need for him to just leave crumbled away. Surrendering, she dropped her legs over the edge and finally slid off the couch. Her demeanor sunken, she headed to the door to let him in. Brooding, Simone used the last moments. A hand on the doorknob, the lock was above it. Faltering before she put her fingers around the lock, she tried.

"Mr. Shears, my stepfather isn't here." She could hope that would turn him away. She could hear an aggravated huff outside the door. Putting her back to it, Simone waited in the space left open. Against the odds, he was still silent. Possibly, she thought the next sound would be a door slamming. Maybe then his truck started up, and then Steve would drive away.

"Simmy! Simone, I told you to call me Uncle Steve." The man paused for a second. Whether he was reaching out with kindness or preparing to kick the door in, Simone wouldn't know.

"Just open the door, Simmy." Jiggling the knob, he continued to find no change. "I know he's here. His truck is out here." It was logical, against a child, but the door was stronger than his shoulder.

"He has to be here, because I know Kenzie is at the bar right now." A fact he wasn't sure the kid already knew.

Steve's temper grew hotter with each passing second. Leaning with his shoulder on the door his annoyed gaze drifted upwards. "So, unless he freakin walked somewhere, and my brother NEVER walks anywhere, he's in this shithole house, somewhere." These were relevant certainties, but he feared they hadn't worked on the silence inside.

Thumb, and bent finger on the lock, she continued her fight. Simone paced her inhale, biting the side of her lip. Struggling to think of any other argument, she only groaned and gave up. Unable to disobey longer, she turned the latch. The click was loud as it unlocked the door.

Instantly following the metallic clack, Steve barged in. Indignantly he slammed the door in, leaving it fully open. Prepared but taking two steps more, he stiffened.

"Where's that asshole?" Steve hadn't yet looked down for Simone. A restrictive gaze, it sped upstairs then to the kitchen. "Hangover's my guess." The sarcasm was dry but respective of his brother.

Standing her uncle, yet a bully all the same, Steve ignored the sad face below him. Placing a booted foot on the first step, his inspections wanted answers. Prior to moving up, he scanned over the couch again, then deeper into the distant hush of the kitchen. Both locations giving him only disappointment, he passed over Simone. Her heavy head low, she closed the door as he focused back up the stairs.

"I waited all damn day. Had to get the fucking neighbor to help me. That was its own shit-show." Steve was droning on, as if another adult was near or interested in his woes.

"Sorry Mr. Shears." Simone held Scuff close as she avoided his words and jeers.

"No damn call, nothing. Freakin 'jerk told me he'd be there too. Should have known better I guess?" The banter was in his head as the girl hid behind him.

Gripping the banister, Steve leaned against his own weight and pulled. Annoyed to be here with the child alone, Steve took the first two steps in one reach. Pausing as his other step was planned, he gave a motion of the head toward the couch. A step more and he would have missed the kid's visitor sitting still in the glow of some show.

Eyes speeding in the direction of the couch, Simone flushed.

"Who's your little friend there?" His question wasn't offered directly to Simone. Its willingness to wait was lost as quickly as it was asked. Not even a break in his search, he turned away instantly weary of the seven year old. Receiving only an odd giggle for his niece's answer, "Yeah, okay, whatever. Where is Jude, drunk, passed out in bed again?" Stomping up the remainder of the stairs, he left the events of the living room unchecked.

Staring from the doorway, Simone wanted to laugh, she wanted to ask what Mr. Shears meant by, 'her friend.' The little she could see, she hoped, was the top of Crischa's head. Too low to see over the back of the couch, the girl was unmoving.

Deferring her joy, Simone heard Steve's dog. It had started barking outside, probably sitting inside his truck. She hated his dog, Salty. The name was a play off Jude's dog's name. Salty and Pepper, though they played rough with each other, Steve's dog was anything but friendly.

Stepping into the living room, the world seemed favorable once more. Circling the end of the couch, Simone was able to finally see who sat there.

A pleasant gasp. "Crischa?" Simone loved saying her name.

Seated on the side closest to the kitchen, her friend was motionless. Hands crossed in her lap she looked at all the details of a doll. Beautiful lines, and hair that cover one of Simone's shirts. Crischa merely glared at the moving pictures on the other wall.

Simone could hear Steve's pounding boots. They were upstairs echoing his search, but she didn't care. There was only one concern at the moment, and it had to do with her apologizing to Crischa. Instead of a statement of regret, Simone was silenced by the turn of Crischa's head. Leisurely, it came to center on her as she rested on the far end of the couch.

Met for a second, Simone worried she was mad at her. With puppy eyes, Simone looked to the right. Her arms holding Scuff with more force, she would have to work up to the apology. Calculated as it was unnatural, a smile peeled across Crischa's ashen skin. The visit was a game she seemed ready to start. "We can play hide and seek?" There was no laughter, no joy, nothing said a child had asked.

Though her interest in playing with Crischa tonight was high, 'hide and seek' wasn't at the top. Hiding the small strain, she came back to her new friend's smile. "We can sit and watch tv?" Simone's eyes pleaded but she'd do whatever her friend wanted.

"There's cartoons on," but Simone didn't receive any facial reaction. Was her friend scared? She seemed occupied, with a further turn of the head Crischa tried looking to the stairs without her body. A pang of trepidation entered Simone's chest. If she refused, Simone feared her friend might go home again. If she did, there was no telling how long it'd be before they played again.

Reciting the request, "we can play hide and seek." Crischa's intonations never appeared to fluctuate. Its address to Simone was a monotone manifesto. The almost absent whites of her eyes lay hidden behind a growing deep. Two staring orbs had returned to Simone, but they looked through her.

Stomach aching from all the sweets, Simone leaned forward and came off the cushion. The sharp pain moving a bit, caused her to place a hand over the spot. Concerned with keeping her friend interested, she ultimately agreed.

Up on her feet, Simone created an enthusiasm and a painted smile was used to disguise her discomfort.

"I'll go hide upstairs again." She shook Scuff as if he'd said the words. Waiting a moment, Simone looked to receive her friend's acceptance. A shuffle in Simone's feet waited but soon decided it was unneeded. Voted against the wait, Simone painted the smile back on her face. "Okay, you count then. Alright?"

In spite of her tenderness, Simone hurried up the stairs. Each step a warning to slow as the pain increased. The thought was odd, but she wondered if her wounds didn't hurt less for the diversion. Nearer the top step Simone could hear Steve continuing his rummaging. There were only three rooms up there, and she didn't understand what was taking her stepfather's brother so long.

Cautious, the last step was dark, and she feared Jude had finally returned with Mr. Shears.

Around the hall corner, Steve came stomping. His temper carried in his heavy boots; he'd obviously not found any information about where Jude had gone. Simone considered pointing out her room, and that secret door far above. However, she was in a game right now and she could tell him later.

At the drop off to the staircase, Steve stopped short in front of Jude's ward. A twitch in his expression, he said nothing but presented the peculiar girl with another annoyed glance. Plotting down each step, Steve thought of other locations. He might be walking his dog. The very idea was laughable. He'd passed Simone but his attention was lost. Considering a turnaround, he might ask about the wrecked bedrooms. He took another step down and he simply let it go.

Steve knew he was avoiding what would most likely be a lengthy story from the girl. Irksome if not an annoying voice, Simone howled from some-where upstairs. It was simply a clarification for Steve, of the chatterbox child.

"Count slow! I need some more time to hide! Okay!?" Yelling, Simone needed to make sure her friend didn't prematurely walk up and find her.

A questioning hand on the end post, Steve curved around into the living room. Since there was nothing in the living room he advanced to the kitchen. A few minutes passed after he exited into the backyard. The still in the house broke, as he returned, slamming the back door closed several times to keep it shut.

"Shit it's cold out there." Steve pouted, having left his coat in the truck with his dog.

He'd wasted the day, the drive out here, and now was going to leave empty-handed. Standing with a hand on the island, he puzzled at the food piled about. Mackenzie was crazy he thought, just why his brother put up with her he couldn't for the life of him understand.

His wife, Dee, had a best friend. Time and again, he'd tried to get her to steal his brother away from Kenzie. Today was just another reason he was going to force it again. The deceitful concept, though good, vanished as a tune wafted from the tv in the other room.

Although Steve's patience had thinned out, the show's jingle was familiar. Tapping a finger, he recalled the sound from his own teen years. Nonetheless, trying as he did, the name of the show escaped his memory. It'd bug him all night if he left without at least knowing that.

Out of the kitchen, Steve came to lean against the back of the couch. His eyes focused on the show, yet he continued to think of where else to search. It wasn't but a moment before his attention was taken in by nostalgia. Glaring at the television, his purpose and mindset had easily wandered. Letting a small chuckle slip, he was grinning in the same.

"I used to watch this shit when I was your age, well maybe a bit older." His comment was a lark, as he leaned on elbows now. His head all the way over the girl, he gave a brief pass over Simone's friend.

Seated under him was something altogether different than whom he'd first thought. There was no seven- or eight-year-old kid resting in front of him. Steve felt the foolishness redden his face.

The astonishment was jarring. Lingering over her, he admired how well-endowed the teen was. He had truly missed this, the first seconds in the house. Staying just far enough back to not be caught by her eyes, Steve stared.

A twist of her head, the girl cast a small fleeting glance up to him. A warning, he was unsure, but an unwanted embarrassment radiated on his cheeks.

The relaxed bend in his back straightened, and he rose off his elbows. In the same turn he attempted to hide what he could of his undue gut. Forcing its errant mass to shift tighter, he knew little of the fat obeyed. A concealed moment and he combed fingers through his thin hair. Pushing it back several times, he wanted to correct what mess a hat had covered earlier.

"I'm sorry," A slight stammer was brought through all his words. "I swear, I thought you were a silly girl." He could see she'd turned back to the tv. Yet even at his newer angle, she had a grin.

"No, I meant you aren't a kid…" there wasn't any swagger in his vomited words. It was almost uncontrolled as he wanted to circumnavigate from the back of the couch.

In one adept move, he rounded to the far end of the furniture, while sliding a well-worn wedding ring from his finger.

"I haven't seen you over here before." Steve noted she was smiling a bit bigger now. "You're a friend of Jude and Kenzie, or…?" His control was tentative, but he was starting to feel confident. A practiced nod he watched her fixed expression.

A second before he invited himself to sit, the woman seated squarely on the couch pivoted her legs toward him.

Ebony eyes and long hair, she seemed happy by his approach. Offering no more than the right side of her face, she teased his carnal gaze. A smile sinful and growing, she peered out the edge of her lids. This was a game, and his move was next.

In an upward tilt of her chin, she displayed the corner of her hungry lips. Her gaze back on the tv, Crischa pulled around an alluring smile as she waited. Her eyelids tightened, the view was his to take. The bait wasn't easily given, as it was made to need taking.

Like detected scents of animals, she called for the man to join, to move closer to her on the couch.

Chapter Twenty-Four

A Game

Sliding down the arm of the couch, all two-hundred and twenty-three pounds of Steve sunk into the worn cushions. A drawn declaration on his lips, he looked at the tv. An adjustment of his weight he wanted to look over but held back for the moment. Concealing any unsightly nerves, he peeked on the edge of sight. Her legs were on the couch between, but her direction was on the show playing out.

A dizzying amount of air was being called for, and unsure just how fast to take it, he would need more. Wetting his lips, he felt her scoot closer. She was young, alive, and better than he knew he deserved. The slim hope was how dangerous she was. Steve had already decided he would take it farther than any vow would permit. She was like the girls he knew in his youth. Those days of unabandoned fun, he desperately wished to relive.

Under the thick shirt he knew his chest rose and fell at a max that told of his nerves. A steady turn, he wanted to give the impression of being aloof. Yet not so much that she mistook his willingness.

The blinding flashes of the tv were starting to encumber his efforts to measure her interest. Recklessly, he turned further, but he was rewarded.

She was no longer subtle about looking at him. A leg and knee under one of her holding arms, her body sat ready to pounce on him. Her stare was all his and she had a crazed look of recklessness. From the bottom of her eyebrows, she was fixed on him.

The playful smile was there, but it had evolved to a wickedness that spoke volumes. Already pounding, this sent Steve's blood pressure spiking. A light chuckle, Steve knew she was ready to push the bounds of decency. A trailing mimic to his laugh, he heard her low tiger moan. Its reverberation was deep and almost unheard as she transformed it into a barely audible laugh.

Cocked toward her without the entirety of his expression, Steve watched. She was now up on all fours on the couch. A game he had little problem playing along with.

One hand, then the next she approached. Any noise she made, drowned out by the tv. A back raised in the air she moved closer to her prey. Lips and flesh smiled as he sat there waiting. Motionless and wanting her to climb on him, Steve didn't budge.

He felt his muscles flex as he stared forward, meant to ignore her, and drive the expectations higher.

The animal beside him was now at his door. That same chuckle as before, he was about to burst. The anticipation ended and he felt the soft touch of her breath. First it found his ear. In the warm room it was still a wave of heat. Her lips hovered by the flesh of his ears, teasing. The slight touch was nerving but he would let her play. A lung full of air pulled through his nostrils as he remained her plaything. Without shifting his head, he sensed her hand. She was a bad girl, and Steve would make her pay for her sins. He would punish this young woman even as she was taking control.

The tender trail her hand was tracing, moved over his nearest leg. The breath that had felt so hot was now a tingle on his earlobe.

Beating wildly, Steve's adrenalin and libido were harder to contain. Those lips of hers, slow to make full contact arrived. Lightly, to tickle his nervous system they followed the shape of his ear. Drifting in the area they moved to his neck then back again. Her hand, like a cautious snake, slid across the top of his pants.

Focused on that area below his belly, the breath in his ear was chased by a whisper.

"We can play hide and--seek?" The utterance pulled at his manhood.

Whatever the game she was playing, made a meal out of him as he smiled larger than any before. The murmur and her wet lips cover the side of his earlobe. It was anything but hot, yet to Steve she held lava in her mouth. The act matured with a soft suck and her teeth pulled only a bit on the skin.

There was an increasing pain about it, but Steve was tantalized by the turn. The reaction caused his blood to race in anticipation of sin.

The lips and teeth left; no mark permanent as she released. Drifting to the neck once more her widening mouth repeated the tease. This time she seemed to suck at his flesh, working his temperature higher.

A shaking breath, Steve had experienced nothing like this before. Dee, his wife, was older than him and when they married it was because she was pregnant. It had seemed they skipped all the dirty couple sex he thought of as young love. Quickly pushed from his mind the last thing Steve wanted to destroy this fling was the thought of his old bat of a wife.

Almost impossible to hold his hands back from her body, his eyes closed, and his head turned skyward. The moment here, her hand ventured over much more incendiary areas.

The living room had a space heater, off the sidewall, yet a sudden chill filled the air. The deviant grin on his face was now wider as he felt the unbearable temperature under his skin begin to soar. His body in full fever, her body came to lean against him. Colder than he'd imagined, he had to ignore her chill. His skin ignited; the mix was numbing to his mind. Her body was frosty, still he knew her mouth and teeth, on his neck, burned deep inside.

Held back no more, Steve sent his left hand out to her. Head remaining up, he flinched every time her nibbling grew sharp or more painful. His prize for putting up with the kink, his hand and greedy fingers rested over her ample breast. Shapely as she was, Steve established she couldn't be any older than seventeen, hopefully at least eighteen. The idea of an underage girl was the furthest now, as she had her other hand on him.

The real fear was Simone. He prayed Simmy would stay hidden upstairs long enough. He wanted to take full advantage of this glorious opportunity. There was a fleeting thought to moving this affair up to his brother's bed. However, they might get there, they could then lock a door.

Rejected quickly, his veins were pounding under his flesh, and she was not stopping. Breathing the pleasure deeper, he wanted to rip her clothes off. His appetite expanding, there was no stopping them on the couch. Modesty had flown out the window the instant this stranger ripped open his shirt. No sooner had the buttons landed elsewhere, her hands raced under and over his hairy chest.

Excited beyond any rational consideration, Steve's body heaved under her full weight. "Yah!" The howl was profound and loud. Steve's manhood was more than set and ready.

With both hands over her clothes and feeling the throbbing body, he reached to undress the uncontrolled girl.

Before he'd closed his eyes, a cork of thought remembered the clothes she wore. Not understanding why? He'd noticed earlier that they were oddly familiar. Super tight on her curves they were far too small for her teenage body.

"OW! That shit hurts!" The identified path of pain was no longer a mistaken avenue to any more pleasure. Steve's gaze pointing upward, quickly flashed open.

That pricked point, midway between his neck and collarbone, screamed in his nervous system. Instantly, a rising danger wave removed any enjoyment for Steve. This was no longer a kick or pain-for-pleasure.

"What the hell was that!?" Steve discovered she wouldn't let him drop his head even with hers.

The tv was dimmer than before as some late-night shows meandered in darker rooms. The sounds even felt subdued as Steve's gaze focused on the ceiling. High above them both, was a darkened shadow. What had been nothing more than a high ceiling, now the shape moved above them both.

"Stop for a second!" He wanted to get her to look at the movement. "What the hell. Let me go!" Steve couldn't stop, or even remove the vicious lust attacking his neck. Panic, pushed by thundering veins, shuttled massive amounts of blood to where the girl was still biting him. Her hold of him was unbreakable. Hands sliding from her ripped shirt, he felt her skin and chest, but Steve wasn't a man anymore. He was prey, and the fight his hands were looking for, was freedom. Trying, he was able to shift one hand to her shoulder and his muscles strained.

Wary and prepared, Crischa sank into him deeper.

"STOP, PLEASE!" There was a gargle to his plea. Muscles that were stronger than someone so small punched. Fingers and hands now devolved to clawing and scratching to remove the feast around his upper chest.

Unwilling to close his eyes, the ceiling was alive. There were sinister shapes nearing him as death's teeth sat on him. Her figure seated atop him; he felt the unnatural legs mounting tighter around his waist. Her thrust remained wicked but quickly tightened on his lap. Her hands moved quicker about him, and he realized they weren't cold as before. They were damaging him as they pulled closer with claws that cut.

This thing, that was no more than eighty pounds, was ripping into the sides of his ribs.

In the storm of her crushing attack, other things were registered. From the limits above them, his sight watched darkness dropping from the corners of the ceiling. The overwriting terror was erasing any certainty in his thoughts. Even as escape was the foremost need, he felt other hands find him on the couch.

Other shapes, never heard or seen, had joined the carnage.

Opening his hollow maw, Steve's scream of pain fought to be free. The air that had remained in his lungs, now pushed up through a bleeding throat. Weaker than dizzy, he was unsure a sound had exited as a call at all. Lips and mouth pumping up to the ceiling, not a word or cry developed.

His gaze continued to rest on the ceiling, he watched the flashing effects of the tv. The dinghy paint seemed to move in jerking patterns, all the while colors changed and merged with the shadows. The sight was his last bit of control, as expanding eyelids matched the yawning silence swallowing the couch.

The hurt was pushing him into the trembling lights he watched. Colorful tidal waves, all of them taking him out to sea. Not forced to witness his own death, Steve wanted the glowing flashes to take him.

Teeth unseen, longer, and sharper, they moved heavier around him. Their punctured touch, tracking as far back as the nape of his neck and throat.

His body no longer his, jerked up and back from undetected slaughter. At last, his eyes closed, and his ears listened to a droning tv show. It sounded as if from far away, and Steve was gone before the noise filled back the room.

"Crischa," Simone walked off the last step. Her hand landed on the side of the couch. "You said it was my turn to hide. Where are you?" Coming around the corner of the couch, Simone saw that Crischa was gone.

The couch was empty, and the TV continued to flicker without its audience. A heartbroken moan crossed her lips before she sat back on the cushion. Body slouched, Simone pulled the closest blanket and settled in. Another sigh, she wasn't hungry and the tv had only adult subjects playing. The feeling she'd messed up again, was there. She wanted to say 'sorry' every time she saw Crischa but now, as before, it was too late.

Bored but unable to sleep anymore, Simone stared at the programing without thought. A sad pain, she leaned over to rest her head, even if sleep wouldn't come. Rolling over, she faced the back cushions.

What time had passed; she hadn't measured. Her eyes were wary and the waves of light, from behind her, danced on the back cushions. It was there, as she watched them, that a new shadow was found.

Without immediately flipping over, she felt those same pair of eyes on her. Hopeful, Simone only turned her head to find Crischa standing there.

In the TV's warmth, she could see her clothes were ripped. The worst of the damage was across her thin chest. The sleeves as well, torn and falling off her shoulders.

Empathetic to it all, Simone offered a patient smile; she knew that fallen stare all too well.

"It's ok. I know how you feel." Simone had no one after, but Crischa would.

Off the couch, "Come with me. My mommy has a needle and a bunch of thread in the bathroom. I can at least fix your clothes."

Taken without objection, Simone took Crischa's waiting hand.

Her skin was warmer than any time before. Simone smiled at the sensation. Looking at her clothes, she again consoled Crischa's gaze. Seeing the bloody marks on her friend's torn fabric, she just nodded.

The apology she'd wanted to say before was no longer needed and she felt it. "Don't worry about the blood. I'll help you wash it out." Simone led them upstairs. Any hesitation in Crischa's hand relaxed, as she followed after her.

Chapter Twenty-Five

Faster Moves

Resting softly in Crischa's lap, Simone had drifted off to sleep. Her body was here in the house she lived in. Her vision and soul were running in open fields of a colorful fantasy. The sounds of laughter, peeking from behind darker shapes, yet there wasn't fear.

The night's chill continued to be held at bay, by a heater pumping out steady waves of warmth. The TV that had been unchanged in its picture was static. Its volume maintained a low hum in the living room.

Simone was the happiest she'd been in this house. Unmeasured and abstract, her joyful dreams had no equal for as far back as her sad history traveled. To her childish eyes all this, the gift of friendship was her birthday, Christmas, and glorious holidays all mixed.

Her slumber wouldn't be haunted by the reality of her waking nightmares, till morning.

Crischa, seated with her entire shape nestled against the back cushion, seemed calm. A numb expression stared at the steady snow of the tv. Patient to the shape resting below her; she had newly patched clothing. The oblivious flesh under her doll eyes twitched time and again, but no movement treated it.

Outside the house morning choruses had begun. Birds, and insects weak in their winter coats were slow to build but determined they rose. The tiresome white noise of the tv had faded as some dog barked nearby. Easily after, the house was handed back the same silence.

The room had gained peace as only one figure lay on the couch now. The sun outside, woken by nature, started a path through the living room window. A journey that would take hours, its slanted angle looked for life.

A stretched yawn, Simone's dreams faded until another time. Pushed back into quiet corners, she wished to return to them if she could tonight. The first voice she heard was her stomach. Not hunger pains but a slightly twisted knot. They were aches she'd tried to mend with candy and treats consumed so late last night.

Rubbing the crusty sleep away from the corners, Simone felt rested for once. Flirting with her vision, her eyes turned to Scuff. He was with her and after all the times he'd been lost, his face still smiled at her. A new morning and he seemed joyful, more so this morning than any the ones before. Simone was simply happy. Glancing around, she saw she was alone. Every corner finished, the count was the same, just her and Scuff but it was okay.

"Did Crischa go back home this morning?" Simone made her dog shake his head 'yes.' With an honest smile she simply nodded back at him. Though a bit sad, her expression remained unchanged.

Out from under the three blankets, Simone slid onto the carpet and stretched again. Pulling her gray blanket from the others she walked to the kitchen. All that was on her mind this morning was if there were still sweets that remained undiscovered.

Sitting atop the lone stool, she clutched the rougher fabric around her shoulders and the search began. Out of treats, her hands grabbed one of the loaves of bread. After a short struggle to open the wrapping, she eventually was able to pluck at the unsliced bread.

Mouth packed; she pushed in more pieces, feeling the soft fluff of the bread roll over her tongue. It was a great sensation; one she'd done a few times. However, with the abundance of food she had the chance to indulge.

Resting Scuff next to her on the counter Simone pretended to feed him. "Don't eat too much." It was hard to laugh or talk with a full mouth. "Your stomach will hurt like mine does, and trust me, you don't want that." The grin was not enough, she let slip free a fun giggle.

The smile on Scuff's face agreed as she helped him to eat a fist of soft interior bread.

The kitchen had no lights on, but she didn't need them. A healthy amount of sunlight was pouring in. Not direct but it was warm and bright from the exterior. Under a protective hand, Simone stood from one of the stool's foot supports. Her gaze curious, she let it speed out of the window over the kitchen sink.

Though she couldn't see it directly, the sun's power was authenticated. It wasn't morning like she'd thought. The orb in the blue sky had already traveled most of the day, and its journey was late afternoon. Even though this had been the best day she felt blue as she realized it might come to an end.

Back on her seat, another wad of bread replaced the swallowed one. Bare feet hanging, she felt a touch of air entering the kitchen. Scanning about, she saw the back door was open. Only by a slender crack, but it was allowing winter to find her peace. It wasn't the oddest thing, as the door was no longer latching completely. The reason is obvious from all the abuse it's sustained just over the past few days.

Pulling the last best piece from the bread's interior, she watched the door shift. Its movement was not so much as to swing open, but one that needed attention from her. Chilled by the cold bite, her blanket wasn't enough. The worthless door was letting too much of the winter's cold pluck inside.

Tugging free some of her cover, from under her seat, Simone gave a sigh. Her blanket wasn't the best, and with this breeze it wasn't affording her much warmth. Fighting the touch, any decision to ignore it wasn't working anymore.

Off her stool, she needed to close it. A glance around the island she repeatedly pulled at her blanket. Most of it was needed around her shoulders but with one hand holding Scuff she struggled.

The fabric in the dark-gray wool was old and a bit stiff. Against any other blanket, its touch was a comforting sensation that none could match. The feeling had been locked into her brain as a welcomed and familiar texture. Where any other child would have protested, she longed for the feeling it gave her.

Walking on raised toes, Simone carried her frame over to the escaping heat of the back door. Nearer it, she heard the low whistling of weather entering. Unlike the other night, this was thankfully a gentle breeze pushing on the door in the evening glow.

Reaching out for the handle the door swung as if a hand moved it from the other side. Slow but shifting out over the empty porch, it swung away.

Doorknob missed; her hand stayed in the air where it'd been. The view offered by its absence was better. Eyes still happy, Simone gazed out over the backyard.

As cluttered and misused as it was, the colors were all brilliant and dancing in the rising flurry. The scene was welcoming even as it pushed loose leaves and some pieces of discarded trash. The apple tree, sad as it appeared, caressed oranges and reds of the day's ending tint.

Her attention focused on the few brown leaves holding fast to some branches. Added to the experience Simone heard that same distant bark. It was somewhere far out in the cold, but it didn't sound like Jude's dog Pepper.

Standing a moment more before she stepped out, she watched the weeds. Some of the patches between all the piles had grown higher than others, but a clear trail formed there. Having never been mowed, the browned covering of the backyard swayed gently.

Like some placid lake's surface, she felt mesmerized. Spaced out, there were small gusts that pushed the ragged fields. Again, Simone heard the distant howl. However, different from Pepper, the dog was closer than she thought before.

The gust increased evenly over the backyard. Casting a glance at the area where Pepper was normally chained, she felt a pang of guilt. The dog hadn't returned, and it was her fault for leaving the back door open. It was a possibility that Jude hadn't returned because he was out looking for Pepper.

A hug went out to Scuff, loitering in that playful opening, Simone let the rhythm soothe her culpability. Though it was a bit cold out here, she liked the peace. It was nice. Up to the right and west, she could see that the sun was nearing the tops of the trees.

Harshly, but somewhere left of her, a single bark was out there in the woods. Its call was definitely closer than the last.

Simone's first furrowed brow of the day, she scanned the entire perimeter of the yard for Pepper. Her happiness had drifted like the door. Swallowing a mouthful of bread, she had been mashing on, Simone doubled her focus.

Unlike most winter choirs this sound had been misplaced. The howl had been desperate if not angry. Gone in her scrutiny, she'd missed the chance to truly narrow-in on its location. The pause, over, Simone turned her attention back to the wild door. Reaching out she had a tentative hold with only her fingertips. Slipping from her nails, she needed an inch more. It remained just out over the limits of the porch.

Slamming against the outside wall, it caused her to jump from the blow. Acknowledging the ease with which she'd been startled, she demanded that the internal alarm be turned off. Staring about for a witness, she saw there were no eyes to comfort her. The lone pair that watched her came from under her chin and they were hazy plastic ones.

Increasing, the winds began to populate the area. Their buildup pulled more of the loose leaves from the branches. Door striking with a rumble, Simone searched back within the doorway for her monster. There too, no faces glared at her. Inside were shadows, as the lowering sun changed the voice within the kitchen.

The growing mood of stress had started to speed-up any effects. Again, the yipping was approaching her location. A turning-point in this play had changed. A line she might have missed, had somehow been stepped over. Even with the protection of her blanket, some yet unseen force, bit harder.

A full-body shiver achieved what other messages seemed to have missed.

Toes planted over the ledge to the small porch; Simone aimed her left arm out for the wandering door handle. Disobedient and wayward, any hold of the handle continued to be an inch away from her grip. The distance seemed too great even as her fingertips repeatedly found the metal. On raised and chilled toes, she attempted to add the reach she sorely required. One finger then the next, she almost had control over the shape. Before she found full success, the corner of her blanket whipped round her view.

In this forced darkness, her gaze fought against the wrapped fabric. Peering into that confusion came a cluster of mad barks and they were the closest she'd known. Turned slightly by the gray, the blanket whipped like a sail in the wind. Fingers holding both Scuff and the last corner, Simone strained to defeat nature's attempt. Frustrated by it, she struggled against the wild swings before turning in her direction.

Finally, a lull in the gust, she pulled the rogue fabric from her face. A glance down to her feet, she'd almost fallen from her perch nearer the drop-off. Simone made sure to take a breath to calm down as she sent her attention back to the errant doorknob.

Found in her gaze, blurred at first, something moved fast. Not close but its shape came toward her from the distant corner of the house. Broad and horrified, this discovery answered Simone's question about the dog barking.

Already in full charge, Uncle Steve's dog Salty, was running for her on the porch. The rather large creature had apparently circled around the house and now was on a mission. The idea that Mr. Shears had left and dropped off his dog was a troubling one to Simone.

Its bulky legs tore at the ground even as its frantic expression ran at top speed. Its mouth, foaming and dropped open, was carrying it directly towards her. Wide and desperate, its eyes had a hunger that said the beast was focused. The only distraction that slowed him was having to circle discarded piles blocking any straight line.

Beyond these things, Simone simply saw one thing. Teeth, sharp and pointed, they were looking for her, and they were not slowing as he ran.

Panic-stricken, Simone fell off her toes and flat to the soles of her feet. A rejection of what she was truly witnessing, her head gave a nod back and forth. A step back was all she started with.

Another rushed if not staggered pace back was the follow-up. Every cell in her body screamed for her to get the door and move inside. Nonetheless the handle was abandoned, and she turned to run.

Simone's aim was the kitchen. Unfortunately, her loose blanket, possessed by some conscious wind, wrapped up her fleeing legs. Maddening, the fabric clung to any escape as she was sent careening over the threshold in a twisted confusion.

Horror had returned to the house in force. Steve's dog, in some abandoned frenzy, leaped onto the porch. Its speed was too fast for any traction and long nails, as it overshot the length. Past both Simone and the door, it had quickly exceeded the size of the porch.

Sliding, the dog gave a lawless snap of its jaws. Salty had missed Simone's feet as half its struggle fell over the other side of the back door's landing. Twisted with its hind legs over the drop-off, the short haired creature fought to correct. Filling into the time here, vicious barks rang out.

Sending out a shrill scream, Simone wrestled with her own dilemma. Hands in desperation, they fought against the tangle around her and her legs. She needed to break free of the blanket.

Finding that freedom, she worried she'd be too late. Her fears could hear the dog's aggressive scratching, and any second, she'd see him again. He'd be back in the doorway before she could rise and run away.

Rear paws fighting to win out against the bottomless ledge, the barks and hungry yips multiplied. Finally successful with one of its legs, the beast pulled his hind section atop the porch.

Erased, seemed to be any sign of domestication. Steve's hellhound leaped without hesitation for the house's entrance. Its ravenous teeth, and eyes back on the hunt, a scarred nose came in search of Simone's scent. The dog's speed had slowed as it came deliberately. Walking up to the open doorway the beast stood unsure of the direction it needed to take.

Head lowered and a tremor to its upper lip the animal lurked inward. Its fixation once more found, the dog snarled as she struggled on the floor. Ready for its pound of flesh and clear of the prior mistake, its jaws thrashed out into empty air. The threat was for her, as she pulled the blanket away.

The noise of its unclipped claws tapped on the aluminum threshold. The rumble was deep and growing as the muscles on its back arched. Eyes locked on Simone, its need for contact was inescapable. What control it had was uneven and the adrenaline coursing in the animal's veins was now measured in waves.

Another slipped front paw and the dog's assault lashed out to a missed bite. Undeterred by it, the beast hadn't slowed and repeatedly snapped out to reach any meaty flesh. A possessed glare, the animal looked to bite at the child's closest foot. A lunge forward and it only collected a mouth full of tattered blanket. Though small, the fabric in his teeth was held tight as its neck jerked violently to both sides.

Never calculated before, but Simone hated the dog. It had never been nice to her, even when Steve had it on a leash. Every time he brought the dog over it snipped at her, and was just all around agitated. This time was far beyond any previous visit. Besides all that, she didn't understand why it was unleashed and out for her flesh.

Scrambling backwards atop the linoleum floor, her feet kept slipping in the dirty grime. Fast on sore palms, Simone had to get her feet back under her. The moment was short, but while the dog continued ripping at the blanket, an opportunity. Flipping over and clambering to her feet, she caught a fleeting glimpse back as she ran.

Front paws holding the gray cover down, it had proceeded to shred the entirety of her beloved blanket. Quick work of the already old fabric, Steve's brute froze again to find her scent. Pulling through to its lungs, the nose found the clues he searched for. An odor he was crazed by.

The taste back, the dog seemed further infuriated by it. Ears and nose perked, Salty's head rose to see. Locating what plagued its hunger, the lips again sneered at Simone and her escape. The last shattered piece of Simone's blanket dropped from the dog's mouth. A rabid snarl let go of drooling saliva as the dog's visible teeth opened.

Speeding across the living room, Simone ran past the couch without looking back. Skin on wood floors carried her faster than shoes ever could. Past the post of the stairs she was headed for the front door, but instead slammed hard against it.

As she crumbled to the ground, she was sure the beast would be on top of her. One hand in front of her face she searched through fingers to discover the creature wasn't yet at her. Her life was being measured out in seconds, and she couldn't waste any of them. A glance up to the locked door then the stairwell.

Unexpectedly and for unknown reasons, the dog had jumped up onto the couch. His attention for the moment wasn't on her. Angrily the beast bit the couch cushions where Crischa and she had sat last night.

Simone could see he was crazy. Snarling and biting the fabric as if it hurt his brain. Those seconds she needed were wasted watching the spectacle but immediately she snapped out of it. Pushing off the wall, she was up and headed in a mad dash. Her room at the top of the very long staircase was the thought. Reaching the first set of steps, Simone heard its claws land some-where on the wood floors. Not yet at her, it was still in front of the couch and looking.

The girl's scent flooded back into its nasal passages; hungry once more the beast moved. Ripping at the floors its ferocious needs were running faster than the floor allowed. Salty was no longer distracted by other odors as he focused again for Simone.

Amending his slippage and with paws firmly under him, he aimed around to the stairs. Its temporary halt, over, hungry jowls now we're ready to stop her from escaping up the steps.

Just past midway, Simone like the dog was on all fours. Each of her limbs climbed as fast as her muscles allowed. Ascended in a mad dash, her burning lungs shrieked loud and long. Frantic and in overdrive, her control was clumsy but there was a finish line.

Missing several steps at the top, her crazed work never slowed and even increased. One obstacle down, she had to reach her open bedroom door before the beast behind her won. Panting excessively, the struggle behind Simone was faring only a step better. Nonetheless, the dog had more experience sinking front and back legs to drive his teeth forward.

Falling behind, Salty saw that the girl had reached the top. Its quickening drive decided to make up for lost ground. The teeth and brain ravenous, and only midway, it launched up with every muscle for one last chance.

Simone's very life was racing away from her as she balanced back up on shaky legs. The door was right there, and she had to get in and close it before tragedy hit. Blind to what was in the air behind her, her foot had the traction to reach that entrance.

Twice her weight and larger than her, Salty came crashing into Simone. The force sent her back to the ground. Her body was half in the room, half in the hall. A tie for the finish line but she was not the winner. Simone had lost and the beast was on top of her.

Howling and afraid that his next bite would hurt, Simone fought to turn over. With no carpet on the hall floor the dog was at the disadvantage when she flipped.

Although he'd managed to stop her from getting away, its claws slipped once more on the floors.

Screaming cries ignited as she remained under the violent snaps of the dog. Simone's panic flat on her back, she was sure the dog was faster.

Legs only now began to kick, as the creature's gluttonous teeth angled better. The first few stopped by her jabbing feet. She was almost in the room but there was little chance she'd get the door closed before the dog took pieces of her.

All her time and options had vanished, on one elbow and a flat palm she might only surrender to her fate. The dog was too fast, and she was too small to help herself. Time slowed as she saw the greedy fangs deciding where to strike.

She felt the reality of what was coming. She could not be more alone.

Growling, its intent was ferocious. A dog made for the fight; this thing was a threat to her. Shown far more prominent, were its teeth, wider and open to brutalize the girl before it.

Her feet in the air, she wouldn't be able to fend the creature off for long.

Obvious to it, instead of biting the kicks, Salty jumped over her defense. Stronger leg muscles were instantly stop her trivial frame. Nipping with starved jaws, the dog found more limbs protecting her fight. With weight and speed on its side, the girl's luck wouldn't last.

Her feet under its wide chest, Simone kicked randomly. The mass was heavier than she could push off of her. Connecting one foot between ribs and front leg, she temporarily stopped the thrusted maw of daggers. At a momentary impasse, the pet shook with a full-bodied effort. Its hope was to drop closer to Simone's face but couldn't. Instinct and habit had taught the creature a fight was the only answer.

Again, it attempted to leap over the problem. It knew what it wanted, and her legs weren't to deny it.

Off center the attacker was pushed up on hind legs. Simone had postponed the inevitable but a defensive hand to-close and she felt the teeth she avoided till now.

Its teeth hadn't got a hold, but a quick slash on the left arm. Fiery pain was there, however Simone's mind blocked the damage for now. Pushing harder with her foot, she was able to send the unsure beast twisting into the length of the hall.

Mad and redirected, its splintering bites came in faster head weaves. All four paws returned to the ground, it repositioned and aimed around her flailing bare feet. Its body in the blind side left of her doorway, Salty had only now gained the advantage. An opportunity was opened, and the beast lunged for the thickest parts of her legs.

Her kicks were no longer valid, as the creature ultimately got hold of soft flesh. Catching hold of just enough clothes and skin, its mind locked down. It wouldn't soon be willing to let go.

A shriek reserved for the most horrific moments shook even the dog's ears. Keeping hold, the dog refused the distraction at first. Meanwhile small fists desperately beat on its head.

The anger inside wanted more, as Salty shook both neck and shoulders. The hold began to crumble away, the fangs attempted to sink deeper. A fast jerk forward, it managed only more of her stretchy leggings. Reaching out for the last vulnerability in this attacker's armor, Simone scratched at his opened eye.

The first distressed yip was heard. The dog relaxed its hold as it struggled to find a firmer mouth hold. In that instinctual effort, the dog prematurely released its clamped bite.

Fabric ripping open and the taste of blood moved away from her fingernails. Both eyes closed tight to protect, the setback released the girl. A damaged vision, the dog realized its mistake. Bleeding from the right eye, it used the other to double its endeavors.

With enough time Simone managed to get her freedom. Away from snapping jaws she pushed her bleeding leg and body back into her room. The moment made of opportunity, she twisted her pain behind the bedroom door and leaned hard against it.

"CLOSE!" On the inside, she screamed as all her weight was needed to close the door.

Late in moving, the latch couldn't find a home in the painted-over strike plate. Smashing ruthlessly against the other side of the door was a dog's wrath. Its weight far greater than that of a small seven-year-old it would sooner win.

Resolute in its need to enter, Salty refused Simone's wish to close the door. On hind legs it pushed on the surface with scratching nails. Eager, the plague on the other side, scarred and dug into the door surface. It would no sooner stop than push its weight back to her.

Pieces of paint flaked away, as the short-haired beast began to win against the swing. Moving the door inward and further away from closing, its continued fight was winning. The cavernous gouges on the door's exterior were growing and fatigue wasn't going to stop it.

Dripping off of Simone's lower thigh and opposite arm, her wounds leaked. Their contribution to this fight was to cover the floor under her. Each attempt to gain footing or control was being taken from her. Pushed further and further from hope, she was losing the door, and soon the dog would have his meal.

Again her foot slid in the warm spill. A complete failure was seconds away as the weight moved her inward. Under burden from the beast, she couldn't hold anymore against him.

"No, please stop." Her cries were for the darkness. "Help me! Someone!"

Her howls stole even more of her energy.

Filtered beyond, frightened tears, was the heat of the blood pouring onto the ground. Its texture was thick and soaked with a fact that she wouldn't escape. Her thoughts were only for closing the door, but she felt a dizzy wave cresting in her mind.

Weakened, Simone's hands slid out from under her. That collapse allowed the door to open a bit faster.

Still on its hind limbs, the dog's clawing efforts became mismatched. What had been a firm surface, slipped, just enough that the beast slid off toward the hinge side of the door.

All the pressure gone for a split second, Simone's smaller weight returned. A single shoulder against the wood, she fell back onto the vacated force.

One last push, the door slammed shut. Echoing as thunder, that small latching sound was gleefully welcomed by Simone's ears.

Furious on the outside, a thirsty barrage of barking ensued. Testing the security of the door's connection, Salty once more scratched at the paint. Its moment passed; the dog was slow before eventually its old fight subsided.

Though uncontrolled in her tears, not a sound was made to accompany it. Simone was far beyond spent as she now lay flat on her back, exhausted. With the door firmly closed, most of her fears of attack took a recess.

Mind shaking, her arms lay deep in the spilled life under her. Dropping her hand and fingers flat into the warming pool beneath, she felt to spin.

Abated, any further barks, no matter angry or hungry, stopped their report. Yet even with the pause in hostility, an unforgiving search moved outside the door. Ill kept claws continued their tapping noise outside, to-and-fro they moved on the floor in the hallway.

In the lull, Simone heard the dog return downstairs. The growing blur over her vision stealing more of her thoughts. Awake and still alive she pulled her knees in, and simply stared vacantly.

Chapter Twenty-Six

A Stranger

A headache, Jude recognized the sharp pain. He'd woken to the aftermath of his stupider night-self, since he was fifteen. This day seemed an especially rough one, though. The likelihood he'd mixed wine in the rotation, now seemed a plausible misstep. Uneasy to open, and fearful of being blinded by an afternoon's sun, he stayed in his safe thoughts. The discomfort was a rhythmic pounding behind his eyes but there was more to this hangover. A section of his brain, that had been numb, was slow to report other alarms that he needed to be worried about.

All thoughts focused on the aching; he'd neglected the physical. That portion of his consideration felt like it was in a fog. A space that seemed unwilling to announce its presence still waited.

Spatial awareness was impaired. Reluctantly he squeezed his eyes tighter, afraid of his reality and having to get out of bed. 'Bed,' slow to the sensation of its touch, he thought it just odd. Not yet a concern, he moved on to his breathing. Though he smoked, he couldn't recall problems, if any, that might affect him from last night.

Motionless, his mind had no reference for time. Lost were clues to the time of day.

Normally, when he was in bed, the morning sun would have already flooded into the bedroom. This was not the case, possibly he'd passed out, and night had returned. Not beyond consideration, he didn't want to think about the consequences.

The thing that would clarify, both time and location, would be Mackenzie home from work yelling at him. Her endless nagging was a pointed and sharp knife for anyone drinking all night. This hazy picture of his previous night said little of what he could expect this morning. Mackenzie was great at dishing it out, but she never aimed that power back on her own sloth.

However, she was a pro at hitting his every button.

A new vein of hurt was screaming to be heard, but Jude wanted, not, to focus on it. Fighting the pain in his head, the topic of her faults remained. He could count on one thing from his wife. That 'thing,' was her constant onslaught of, 'Why this…? Why that…? Why can't you be like…?'

The real question he knew was, 'Why can't you just shut the fuck up…?'

The throbbing in his head wasn't quarantined. It had friends and they were hungry to be heard. Leaching down through his spine to his lower back, pressure was building. Something masked by either liquor or something more drastic, he didn't yet know. He was pressed for the missing knowledge he needed to widen his thoughts. Fighting against the disguised and substantial fog in his brain, he considered other things.

Whether a mistake or panic taking hold, sharp points of agony were quickly multiplying around his body. Acutely aware of their uncomfortable numbers, Jude's lungs wince at a set of new pricks.

There was information breaking through the barrier and he felt even more tension built. Eyes stubbornly closed; he was becoming aware of some tilted facts. Ones that didn't fit with his last memories.

The mattress they had in the bedroom was uncomfortable, yet there was something far different. The first real sensation was temperature. He wasn't sure, but as it eked into his nervous system a level of anxiety was forming.

'Cold,' it was a description his brain was positive of. This was progress, but Jude needed more, faster. The bed was not the bed, it was hard and flat. Maybe the floor, maybe the living room, the surface wasn't comfortable either way.

The collection of what he knew, what he thought, the flood of pains, and murk of his memories was overloading. His mind was under assault but try as he might, it refused any and all direct access. It sent through warnings, but nothing clear. Hazy inferences that he should fight, even struggle was building. It was growing to be a concern all its own.

Simple and basic, a feeling was washing ashore from all these sensations. However, instead of fearing, he heard excuses and exemptions. Jude had experiences, matching the growing sensation, and it was usually due to excessive amounts of wine. This result was sometimes the cost of the grape; however, the struggles wouldn't line up.

Disconcerting to him, the buzz inside was dressed-up as 'dread.' Try as he did, nothing, even his taste buds rebelled against the growing specter. There was something drastically wrong. Something he had no expertise with.

"Mackenzie?" The name was hard to get out. "Simone?" His effort was once more needed.

It was time to brave the consequences. Shock, worry, louder alarms rung behind the ache in his temples. One of those pains he'd been ignoring was his brutally swollen lids. The throbbing hurt had been there the entire time, but through the fog it'd been disregarded.

That feeling of 'dread,' couldn't be erased anymore.

Not all systems reported, but he had to see. Jude wanted to know even the worst of his predicament. Energy required; he drove the blood to push either lid open. Agony real and not dreamt, his right eye peeled open slowly and only offered a crack, into the darkness.

A pitched gloom was his first sight. No window, no bed, not even the bedroom. He was lost.

Echoing over him and all around, was just a blur. Doubling his labors, the span of his sight peeled wider. More information crowded into his confused brain.

There was the sound of some hushed wind. Jude listened as his eye continued its singular struggle. There wasn't silence, no, he found it was a dulled whining. It seemed to be some yet unseen and if not diminished, sound of wind. It seemed to be a stagnant signal that was pushed through something between. Yet his flattened floor suggested he wasn't outside, and it further frustrated him.

The murk holding nearest to him had been thought bleak. Nevertheless, as the minutes added, the dimness wasn't without the tiniest of radiance. Possibly reflected from a distance, the room was visible, if only barely.

Smell was the next visitor to Jude. Without clear sight or hearing, this was a disturbing problem that threw all other ideas into melancholy. Any description in his heavy mind felt corrupted as all other leads came back to the same shores, 'dread.'

There was so little to base his location from. Although some orientation was beginning to take hold, it lacked. Most of his surroundings were yet unseen, Jude narrowed his lids to focus on one thing. Everything else would come later.

Near him, on the same level, flat on the floor, were piled boxes. Without any discernible meaning, he hadn't yet a place, as his lone eye tried for more information. The needed details denied, Jude closed his lid. Waiting in darkness again, he had to let the sore wave of redness pass.

Trying once more, he pushed clear his throat. After a muted cough, "Come help me. Simone!?"

A larger mistake was only discovered after a breath was needed. Sucking filth and dust into his lungs, a fit of half sneezes and coughs erupted. After the spasm passed, and weirdly enough, it gave more clues. Jude realized the pressure of before was more considerable than thought. An attempt to move his arms, he found the sum of his exertions failed. Though the degree of strain given to the move was low, it was a discouraging one. His mind was running to darker corners, and he had to focus. He needed to turn his head, he could do that. His face positioned downward, he could at the very least lift the hangover off the rough surface. A groan in the back of his throat, his head moved. A fraction of the effort moved it, as it came back down in a soft thud.

This is when Jude's hearing noticed a change. A subtle one, the room's grating stillness moved. A low shuffle that was no more identifiable than precise for a location. His left cheek felt sore. Its contact against the thick dust on the floor, noted dry blood mixed on his skin. At least his open eye was the furthest from the filth. Throat parched and dry, the dust was working against any spit that might help.

Air at a premium, he made sure to breathe shallowly. Closing the one eye, a concerted attempt was repeated to lift an arm. Jude asked again for either arm to move. Anything that could give hope to the desperate state he found himself in. Pulling a shoulder close to his neck he started with his right arm.

Through mounting pain, the simple command came back with minimal success. Anxiety was beginning to rocket; something was obviously bound tightly over him. Both his arms had the same constraint and could shift only by flex.

Jude's mind at the edge of understanding, registered he was tied up. He was limited in movement by something he couldn't see, nor did he feel. The action of testing his restraints earned him a shrouded groan.

Somewhere beyond, a moaning of some strained boards. Its location was out of reach and still distant. The sound wasn't over immediately, as Jude froze to listen. Although it had shape, the noise grew Jude's understanding of one thing.

He was not alone.

Jude waited before trying to move again. With a modicum of touch returned to his fingertips, he tried there first. Though he couldn't as of yet move his arms, both his hands had noted the return of touch. They were piled tight against his body, and with this, Jude was given new news.

Despite the waking nerve endings, he rubbed with three of the fingers to discover he was without clothes. Quickly, other extremities reported the same facts. He had no shoes, no pants, no shirt, he was completely naked.

Attempting a kick of either leg, they refused any flexion. A diminishing volume of oxygen and he was feeling weaker at this point. The strength needed to break free of whatever had him, was terrible. He already needed rest for the small amount of exertion.

Looking through the swollen aperture of his eye, Jude searched for further clues. Exploring the strange environment, his solitary eye blinked fast to clear dust from his vision.

"Where the HELL am I?" Even as his anger erupted, Jude felt lost in the dirty and secluded landscape.

Voice fractured and breaking, he sucked more of the smell and grime inward. The stench was regrettably familiar as mice and rat excrement. The idea of taking in the fumes caused greater breath and coughing. Compounding the smell, Jude pulled in more of the filth.

A sharp pain in his neck arrested the fit and permitted him to hear a quick shuffling. This breach of the darkness was closer than any other.

"What the fuck!?" Jude wanted answers. More than this, he needed the pains that were growing sharper, to stop, to leave him be. Gaze fixed only in one straight line, his fight was useless to turn and see his threat

Jude's exposed fat and muscles lay rigid against the unfinished boards. Here, lost, and angry, he heard something yawning from an inaccessible corner. A newer sound, its faint rustling, woke in the inky recesses out of his sight. Surfacing into the stillness, a whisper, an unnatural sound of something godless, ached.

"Whoever that is, I can hear you." Meant as anger, a shattered vocal cord spit the words out. "You better let me THE FUCK Loose!" Jude's voice towered before it crashed to a wheeze.

The mysteries around him grew deeper, as the sound drifted to silence. Although he forced explanations that might answer some confusion, they helped him little. A muted hush took back the bleakness. Anxious and unnerved in the stillness, Jude's brain caused the race to broaden paths, both darker and unwanted.

"Ok! Is it you Steve? You had your laugh, now let me UP!" Shaking in the void, Jude's body fought the fear and chill equally.

Blood pumping, he felt a peak surge in his tissue, and it gave him power to move. Hoping to break free of his bonds, Jude fought with every muscle. None of this Jude found himself in, was beyond his brother. He'd taken jokes too far many times, and this had to be one of those times. Jude played it as a reasonable chance.

One of those unfortunate times and pranks leapt from his buried memory. Equally, as harsh as this, Jude recalled Steve playing a similar gag on him one hunting trip. Having fallen out after too much drink, he and Steve's friend cuffed him naked, to a deer feeder.

Jude recalled waking to the painful pricks of hundreds of ants covering his body. Even then, Steve had left him there all day to suffer.

Another coughing fit. After, Jude attempted and failed to turn his head away from the swollen cheek and still sealed eye. Passing through the worst of it, he settled in. Returning altogether were most of his tactile senses, and behind it was a painful reality. An unwanted fact of just how much agony he was truly in. It was arriving as if someone had removed the dull screen. All of it was a shock to him, just why he was still awake, or alive. Not able to accomplish much else, he worked on plans and schemes. On the cold floor, he knew most of them were beyond his state of control.

"Whoever you are, I'm going to stomp your head in. If this is all you're doing Steve, get ready to eat some dirt till you bust. You're such an asshole." The thought of beating his brother was real, if Steve did laugh from the darkness, it meant things would eventually stop. Miserably, no answer or clues. All the mumbles had accomplished was to suck in more of the dirt and rotting smell. As before, his fight and words drew some attention.

Another square of flooring, moaned, under some shifting mass. By its weight, Jude could estimate, and it had to be large. It wasn't Simone. Coughing even harder in the filth, he found one hand, his right one, able to pull away from his exposed body. Forcing his lone open eye through tears and dust, he focused. The closest thing was the box beside him. A degree of clarity, he finally made out what sat beside him. Jude was surprised but a flash in his brain reported it was his father's old trunk. On its side, it towered there, a clue that'd been there the entire time.

"WHY THE HELL AM I IN THE ATTIC?" He screamed at any that would listen. The very idea boiled in his mind.

He'd been on a ladder. The recollection was remaining fuzzy, and no more clarity of memory was entering. This consideration returned nothing more than the same sensation as before. The phantom, lingering in his mind's way, was purely a shape to warn him, but to warn him of what?

Working under only assumptions, Jude randomly created theories. The most prevalent idea started to gain some respect for Mackenzie.

"So, you plan on doing me in, huh? You're stupid if you don't think my brother won't find out." He knew she had to have something to do with all of this. She'd threatened as much, a hundred times, but never was one to follow through.

"You're dead, and whoever your friend is, there has to be someone helping you. Him too."

Jude had spied on her at work in the bar several times. He knew she did more than flirt with people, though hadn't caught her. Even his brother would, from time to time, secretly spy for him. This all shoved to the back of his concerns, the idea she'd planned all this, now infuriated him.

A new appreciation for life jerked and tugged his arms. It was probably just tape or plastic holding him and if he fought hard enough, they'd break. Struggling desperately, for as long as he held his breath, Jude ended it with little to show. Although he couldn't see it, something stronger held his legs together.

Wheezing through clenched teeth, his muscles were all screaming at him for the effort. His exposed skin raw on the floor was chilled and sweating at the same time. Despite him now laying still, his entire body produced an uncontrolled wave of shivering.

"OK, I'm sorry!" Adrenaline pumped, but he had to calm down. "Please. Just let me sit up at least, okay, you jerk?" The distress in his voice filtered, if not diverted, from his fury.

Recognizing the naked vulnerability down here, Jude felt a sharp sting of regret. Whether forced on him or trying to protect himself, he believed himself humbled.

"Why are you doing this to me? I've been good to you, haven't I? I mean I– " He'd always felt crippled if not vaguely aware of his faults and actions.

"Come on! Said I'm sorry okay. This has gone far enough already, Mackenzie." He put what he thought was a rough point to his struggles.

Another meaningless and aggressive fight on the ground to be free, came and went. After a puff of dirt pushed from his mouth said it was all a failure.

Away from his body and searching for the ground nearest, was Jude's hand. The area immediately beside him wasn't an empty floor. Fingers slow to recognize, he'd found clothes. They were likely the ones he'd been wearing before all this.

"Fuck you then! Fuck you bitch and whoever is helping you! I hope you choke on your own spit!" The venom was dull, and he knew it. If someone stepped from the dark and began to stomp him, at least then, he could spit from the ground on them.

Fading as all the others had, his bout finished to nothing. Then, a real threat moved somewhere in the darkness. A subtle shift, movement that marked another's presence. Something hidden all the while, and it was no longer docile.

Jude noticed this one, it hadn't shifted from some dusty corner up here in the house's attic. This wasn't the floorboards, or dusty overhead rafters, nor was it someone shifting uncomfortably.

'Dread,' the sensation had dark images in Jude's head. There were plenty of horrifying ways to die and he only wanted to consider the fastest.

The sound that moved seemed wet. A crackle of unshapely and sickening aches were moving somewhere behind him. Out of the reach of his vision or lone eyeball, someone wanted him dead.

It was someone watching him, cloaked in shadow, he knew they happily stared. Aware and sated by his grotesque bare body, some hateful person's gaze watched him squirming in the dirt and rat covered filth.

He was sure they loved it all. Reveling in his dread, they probably drooled to see him fearing the end.

"Just do it then! You piece of shit, just do it already, you fuck!" This was a threat of his own, even if the knife fell, he'd go out fighting.

There was far more he wanted to say; however, each word brought the cost of thick and foul matter. The smell had not only inundated his nostrils but with the quantities of dust, Jude could taste the sewage.

Even while he was distracted with his curse, his hands frantically rummaged over his clothes. His pants pocket the goal of any reaching fingers.

Slipping from that darker incubus around him, a presence. The cold shape was one that had worked the fates of this house. Its form, a shadow covering the woodlands that surrounded the area, and now part of it moved closer to Jude. Muddy and low, the scant slurring noise came closer over nailed down flooring.

To Jude's ear the sound was a feral creature. A wanting mouth that possibly looked for revenge. He knew somewhere out there, the conspirator sounds were proof to him, as the prey he was on notice.

Tumbling from one obscure pile, another crash. Under cobweb covered rafters, a once still collection of boxes fell nearby.

Chapter Twenty-Seven

Hunter, Hunted

Stretching from one end of the house to the other, the area in the attic was expansive. Twisting in a long 'L' shape, the twelve-foot-high peak was dominated by a rafter forest of lumber. Dust thick from over three decades of abandonment, the smell covered everything.

Items placed and forgotten, spanned multiple occupant and lives. Thin vented louvers on each end allowed the faintest breath, of even the strongest sun outside. Above her the boards that held up the ages, and a rusting tin roof over it, carried age marks.

Leaks that had gone unattended and were slowly leaching into the bones of the house, dotted the space. The stench of hungry vermin and trails of sinister insects covered every inch of open space. Boxes with forgotten contents and furniture, all deemed old or useless, cramped every corner.

Resting flat and alone, Jude heard the clatter of a bumped box and knew his executioner was teasing his nerves. Whatever the contents of the container it struck the floorboards, but quickly became hushed. Rendered out of the darkness, the noise was still located further back into the unseen.

Every facial muscle stressed, matching the pain of his rib cage and shoulders. Tense, Jude was assured on the floor that none of this would end with a hearty laugh. None of it would be a story anyone would be sharing years down the road. It was a prank, but he knew it was one played with his life.

"Just let me go. Okay?" It was a fracture demand. A veiled plea to whomever it could reach.

Useless to bargain, Jude still took the route. "Alright, maybe I touched your kid," Recoiling in his own disdain, Jude let surface one of his greater sins.

Teeth grinding in regret, "That little slut wanted it anyways. What the hell do you care anyways? You leave her for days."

Sickened to hear his own admission he might only justify his lechery in bites. "And you think I don't know about you? You're out there sucking off every Tom, Dick, and Harry that drops you any Jersey breakfast." The words spit out like vomit that poisoned from inside his skull.

Far from innocent of his own abuses, Jude was still equipped for a critical reply. He was confident whoever was with Mackenzie had had enough. Possibly they were ready to get this entire murder done and over.

Straining against the mixture that his body was making from sweat, blood, and grime. Jude waited, listening although unhappy about any of it, he wanted his audience to say anything. Fearful of a booted foot to drop, he wanted those floorboards to warn again. Any retribution for his words or actions was called for.

Visiting him on the floor, only the same. If darkness could echo, it was here in the filth of the attic. Something, anything, was preferable to this heavy gravity. To Jude the stillness roared in his eardrums. Its shape was a threatening noise, made to drive him mad.

Pivoting his attention he heard a change. A feverish mind Jude knew this noise was different. It wasn't coming from behind or above. It was from him alone; this sound was his own body shuffling under him.

His dead weight was being tugged slowly but he was being dragged backwards. The ground below him was sliding, grinding against his hairy chest and legs. His face, feeling the swollen pain and indignity of being hauled to his death.

Provoked to fight against the deed, Jude could feel no discernible touch of a hand. There were no spiteful fingers choking down to finish him. There wasn't the sound of effort to move his two-hundred and fifty odd pounds.

Thrashing with all his neck muscles, he tried as best to look round behind him. Still, Jude failed in his attempt to discover his executioner.

"You're a pussy, you know that. Fuck you! Just look me in the eyes." He wanted to kick. He wanted even the smallest fight to be felt.

"Whatever she's paying you--I can double it! Just give me a chance." Unable to verbalize his panic, desperation was surfacing. Even as he converted his frustration, his lungs choked deeper in the dust and shifting air.

The movement was glacial, but it allowed him to discover other facts. Below him was trailing a muddied path of his own blood.

This was a reality he'd been ignoring. The pains he felt had more voice to his brain than he wanted known. Chin dragging back, he was forced to stare at what was left behind and the meaning for what was ahead.

All of it was horrific, Jude knew he needed help. A hopeless sense of how his life was about to be snuffed out. A sad realization, he couldn't refuse this end, no matter how obvious it looked.

Insurmountable now, that approaching wave of dread was here. It's cold waters began to wash over his nervous system. His legs, no longer being pulled straight back into darker places. They had changed their path; they presently had started into a measured, but upward turn.

He couldn't imagine the reason. The purpose he thought, if to hang him from the rafters was the result, he couldn't picture why. Over the roar of his body being dragged, another moan hovered nearby. A breath, if he were forced to give it a name. Slow, long, uneven inhalations of dirty air, were speaking for an unseen figure.

Bending his spine at an ever-growing painful angle, Jude fought against the pull. His back spasmed to be straight but it was refused as the pressure increased. His naked weight and inflexibility threaten to snap him in half.

Born of desperation and flaring agony, Jude thrust his shoulders down into the floor. A reactive wave echoing through his hefty frame and joints, finally managed to flip his entire drained body.

Slamming onto his back, Jude tried focusing up to his feet. Shaded in discolored sweat, dirt, and blood, it took a momentary pause to find them clear.

Squeezing them both shut, his one eye opened again. Cleaned temporarily, the sludge built around the corners. With that one window, he worked on what details he'd been given. Nonetheless, as he searched, contradictory logic had taken shape. There was no one standing over him.

Around him were dark growing angles, and all of them seemed to be impenetrable shadows. Large voids that any intelligent person knew were incapable of existing in any natural world. While he watched them, all of them pulled tighter around him. Each seemed to be alive as he ascended toward some place above the attic flooring.

Against the burn of his ears, blood pounded in his skull. Beside the agony and pressure, Jude felt the arrival of an eager groan. Not woman or man, it was a gnawing scratch from the bleakness.

Head able to turn faster, Jude searched for his enemy. Dejected by the darkness, everything his singular pupil sought out, avoided his path. Each shape in the shadows escaped his rocketing anxiety.

The last direction, before he might lose it, was straight up to the distant rafters of the roof. Narrowed by the location, more unfamiliar things, all murky and hungry, something lived there.

His pupil widened and almost entirely black, it grew to every limit. Desperation sent above him to the attic gloom, Jude fought to know what exactly he might be looking at.

His sight continued to struggle, he felt the pressure building on his legs. Hip squared off with the floor, he was moving skyward now. The burden of his own load had changed above his waist. The ultimate turning point, Jude wanted to see his threat and what it could be.

Though it was only a suggestion through the ink above him, something was inconceivably draped there. Gathering all these lies together, his brain failed in every way to understand the reason and logic.

"Wait! Wait! Wait a minute, no! NO! Someone help me. HELP!" Terror was rushing in, replacing where his rising body drained of blood. Most of his years of excess, paid for tonight. His torso and head flooded with their own pains and all this atop the existing aches.

Jude started to feel the drowning effects of too much blood rushing into his skull. Tears, even as he yelled, were pouring from bloated skin and eyes.

From some cold crevice of nighttime, a sleeping creature shuttered. Whatever the sequestered shape which inhabited the safety of the rafters, moved in small ticks. Its yawning mouth, no longer hidden behind stretching webs this far up.

More angles convulsed in its mass as it continued to stir. What was thought to be shadows lent to the transformation of its shape.

Unsettling a sight, some ghoulish head pulled clear of the blackened figure. Centered in that ink, two orbs opened and gave their attention to what approached.

Foul and seemingly wet, the beast peeled wider into the space. The noise gave way to an uncomfortable sweep of what could only suggest to Jude were arms. The smell lingering here was a pureed collection of decay and rot.

Almost a life on its own, its perfume came in retching waves at him.

Calculated to his rise, the head inside that bleak form conveyed back and forth. Its blinks watching, and almost studying its food. The hunger denied for long enough, it drank in all the scents of life that surrounded Jude's naked body.

An indefinable stare, it wandered little about the room. All else in the attic lay dead to it. Its full attention singular, the eyes cold and unfeeling were confined to his rising body. Returned from Jude's parts, the slow-moving gaze narrowed on the one open eye, not yet even with it.

His head the last to leave the ground, Jude looked back to his doom.

"HELP! SOMEONE PLEASE! HELP!" The walls gave no empathy. "HELP!" In covered corners unseen, spiders and worried rats all stayed silent. Every waiting creature in the dusty attic wore deaf ears to Jude's needs.

Boxes laid around, trunks of history, and lost memories, were the sum of things interesting to watch his fate. A worm on the line, Jude's cries were repeated as lingering echoes in a dead space above the living.

His head finally leaving the ground, he found it near to impossible to breathe. The calls for 'help' ended thereafter. Unable to stop it, Jude vomited as his body writhed in the prospect of a coming attack.

Enduring this hellish torment, Jude's tears poured out. His opened eye, witnessing the door to purgatory and famine staring at him.

Now mere inches away from him, something beastly and unholy stared at him.

Free of all contact from below, his body began a gentle spin. From the side of his flight, he was harshly stopped as a clawed limb reached out. In a singular motion, Jude was pulled toward it and his unknown fate. Mouth already gagging he plunged inward, making contact with his killer.

Chapter Twenty-Eight

Two Words

Minutes had become hours as she sat jailed in her room. The wound on her leg continued to spill out the rip in her pants. With no bandage to cover it, she couldn't do much except hold a hand over it. The slash on her left arm was ugly, but it had stopped weeping. With a sigh, Simone had moved away from the lake of red she'd made in front of the door.

Closed but unable to lock it, she continued to stare at it as if the dog's anger might open it. Salty hadn't scratched since it had closed, be that as it may, she'd heard his uneven claws, pace by. They clicked along the hallway and stairs, but they were gone for a while now.

Jude was mean to her, yet he'd always kept his brother's dog back. That connection returned her mind to him, and her being abandoned here. Where he remained was a mystery. The door above her was closed, so Simone knew he couldn't be up there. The idea he'd gotten onto the roof and left that way was her only option.

With the mattress beside her, Simone stayed on the cold floor. Her attention watched the night outside. Passing in between this journey, of window and door, she would pass over the closet.

As clouds darkened that view outside, she slowed over the midpoint. Spied now, was an odd glow. There was an aura, soft and covered in the closet's havoc. The scattered bits and boxes Jude had punished, now spoke up. Trampled and crushed, one of those boxes had something else, something she could see. There was definitely a glowing light coming from inside the closet.

Up with a moan, Simone felt the prick of pain but could still walk plainly. Bent inward to discover the green glow, she pulled a flattened storage box from the piles. Moving aside scraps of forgotten objects, she uncovered the light. An old Christmas glow stick had been mixed into a box of old shoes. Odd, but the reason was glazed over as she pulled the string attached.

Swinging out into the room, Simone pecked at the soft light.

Using its kindness, she checked the rest of the room. Back in the closet, she looked for others, but there weren't any.

Likely, Jude's feet had stomped it and its power had been there since. Slowly dying, the glow stick would last a few hours more.

Pulling more trash from the piles, Simone took a discarded rag and tied it around her cut leg. All else within the closet was spoiled. Interest in anything more was gone, so Simone cast her eyes back to the door. Weary of the dwindled light, the luminescent blaze was welcomed and friendly to her eyes.

Today's light had drifted with the hours, and with night revisited, Simone's breath sank. A different flavor to the colors of her room, the light moved as she turned. Its ability to affect the gloomy room was odd.

The blood staining the entrance had even changed its gruesome meaning.

Feeling the soft wave of dizziness, Simone took a seat back on her mattress. Staring into the chemical shine, the thought of darkness surfaced. She lived much of her life now, with the moon as her sun and its hold around her growing to be normal.

The idea that in most of her dreams, whether they were nightmare or fantasy, had one thing in common. The thought was deep, but she wondered about the light inside her dream world. She pondered about the light inside her dream world. The notion traveled out into her real world and how she lived much of this portion in the shadows.

A child of dark spirits, she looked around again. Pulling her arms in, there was a space empty inside. Not wanting reasons for any of these thoughts Simone noted a place where Scuff should have been. Tucking both her arms and the glow into the center of her chess, she lingered. Sad and always in pain, she wanted to sleep it away.

In the dreamscape of sleep, her soft friend could see her with real eyes and sometimes even talk. Imagining new adventures, she pulled the glow away.

Its touch reached out for other walls. Moving it around, Simone slowed to an area of her room where once sat a small girl's dresser. It used to be beautiful. Simone's grandmamma had gotten it for her. Though it was hard for her to bring the picture of it to mind, her memory continued.

Fondly, the soft yellow color of the dresser lived deep in her heart.

Depressed about it being gone, Simone knew her grandmamma was as well.

It had six drawers and atop its delicate edges, Simone had positioned her only collection. Ten dolls, and a few toys that her mom and grandmamma Lewis had gotten her. All the dolls used to sit there on top.

Cherished and loved, they were lined up neatly and seated happily. Simone had arranged them all around a discarded shoe box and had covered it with a red cloth. A table for them to eat and play at. She let a smile go, simply thinking about it.

Her favorite of all the dolls was Fanbee. A special one her grandmamma had told her stories about. The best part of her story, that Simone loved, was how the doll had lived in 'Dutch land'. Her father had given it to her, and she'd been happy to give it to Simone. It was one thing, among so few she'd had, that reminded her she even existed.

Slouched on the corner of the bed, Simone's sighs came out deeper. Her feet on the floor, she knew none of it mattered anymore. She'd loved that doll, carried it everywhere, ate every meal with her, and played outside every day with it. It was heartbreaking when 'he,' threw it away after stepping on it. Jude had twisted his ankle, or so he said. That had been all that was needed as the blame was hers. He hadn't needed any other reasons, nor did he give any.

The rest of her toys weren't long behind Fanbee. He had his own reasons, but Simone knew she should never have left the toy out, for him to step on. It was about the same time that mommy had started to work more and more.

Anger was warming her cold skin as she sat there thinking about it. With little else to vent her hatred, a clenched fist hit the bed. She wished she was already bigger. A plan already existed for then, she'd simply run, she'd start and never stop.

Any other night, a tear would have followed the reflection. Tonight, her face sat as a dry field, and a broken soul behind it.

The heavy smells of Grandmamma's rubs were a favorite of Simone, and this thought only came because there was an odd smell lingering in the room now. It was a strange odor and carried the sensation that made her want to sneeze. Unable to have the satisfaction of a good sneeze, Simone leaned back. Her arms clenched into her core. Feet still on the floor, her back on the bed, she stared upward.

Humming softly, she laid there. Without looking into the light of the glowstick, her eyes had again acclimated to the dim.

Pushing her gaze high above she found the ceiling and that secret door up there. Capturing her attention, Simone saw that the attic door was slightly open. Not so much she could see within but curious to her mind all the same. Tonight, the rope to pull both ladder and door open, was for once hanging lower than ever. A long thin string, it reached down into the space above all. This glowing green room watched it as it gave hope for her to open it herself.

'If only I had a chair,' Simone looked about, already assured there were none.

She found the glow stick in the closet, possibly there was hope for something else helpful in there. At the border of the doorless space, the efforts proved pointless.

Above those boxes, hanging to the outer edge of a twisted rod, were empty hangers. Once filled with some of her less used outfits, in the green hue they were meaningless.

Jumping up for one of those empty, twisted metals, she managed it on her first attempt. All the other hangers on the rod jingled as their departed mate left with Simone.

Pulling the hanger apart, she positioned herself directly under the attic string. She could see at its end a tempting loop. A small and welcoming noose she might reach with the end of an opened hanger.

Above that rope and loop was a ladder. Beyond the squared off door in her ceiling was a pitched room in the attic. All of this waited for her to investigate if she could just reach that small noose hanging over her head.

Balancing on desperate toes, Simone pictured the fun she might have up there. Even with the idea of finding another door up there, she might be able to reach the outside roof.

Out over her head, the wire swung one way, then the other. She discovered she was still far too short to clear the distance needed. Back flat on the ground, she hesitated. A quick look around her the mattress was not enough and the only other thing was crushed and destroyed boxes. These were useless for the distance she needed.

A new notion, but it wasn't without its detractors. She might jump. With sore feet and a cut leg, she knew she could still possibly do it, makeup that distance. Bandaged with the found cloth over her dog bite, the blood still hadn't stopped completely. Holding the glow close to the ragged covering, she saw it still wept. A thin trickle of blood even now, ran free of it. Giving the weak-knot a tightening tug, Simone looked up ready. A set of teeth on her lower lip, she gave her knees a bend and pushed up with her best jump.

She was close. On a second leap, she landed and crumbled to the ground, only just defeated. Forced to rest her hurt leg she was confident another shot would work. Wincing as a wave of knives worked through her leg muscles, Simone stood strong against it. An arm and the tool above her, she balanced against the sway. Springing up, the wire and her body were sent higher into the air this time.

Piercing the loop, her hooked hanger-rod found a home. Coming down hard, her leg muscles felt on fire as the tightened connection almost ripped the wire free of her grip.

Beaming under her one victory, Simone repositioned the wire so it couldn't slip further. Floating on only two toes on each foot she felt like a towering giant. Stretched out and long, she wrapped both hands over the wires ending. Fierce around it, she pulled slowly at first. Regrettably, she'd convinced herself that she might not have the weight to open it. At least not enough to free the large door.

Her pull worked as it creaked in the first seconds. Then a gentle shift of the frame, and the hatch far above the wire and girl opened wider. The hinges, somewhere beyond the covering, ached. Some balance released up there, the weight behind it shifted. A vibration followed each inch the door moved. Wider as she had the wire near her, its growing promise was continuing as she pulled.

Steadily, the entrance moved downward. In snapping moves the covering maxed out and a ladder lowered section after section. The final step, slamming to the ground at Simone's bare feet. The thud was loud and uncovered.

Startled, Simone bounced in the glorious accomplishment. Easily thought impossible, she always wanted to play on the roof, but it had always been beyond reason.

Staring at the length of the steeply angled ladder, she knew nothing of the adventure up there. There had to be ages of escape and creativity up there. Though she thought her imagination was limited, she would have this chance tonight to explore.

Placing a foot on the first thin slat of wood, she felt the hesitation arrive in her nerves. The voice in her skull knew this had to be forbidden. Setting aside what wrath could befall her for the defiant act, the punishments would have to be paid tomorrow.

Her other foot came beside the first and her empty hand moved even. Watching the darkness above her she moved again. The punishment for going up there was inconsequential. Perhaps she'd find a path out of this house.

Up to the next rung, her foot moved again without asking. This was to be the only argument she would accept. Both hands, one with the glow stick slid further as she hugged the precarious ladder.

Already halfway up, and she heard some remote suffering reach down from that hole. Defiant on the ladder, Simone paused in her climb.

The thought hadn't been there before, but she humored the idea. Somewhere in the attic might be a person hiding? It couldn't have been the doors' long springs, making the noise. She was unsure as she listened. It hadn't said a word, just an almost imperceptible notice, that she wasn't alone.

Concentrating on a follow-up to the whimper, Simone stood with both feet on the same slat. If a word followed, she was to make sure it wasn't Jude. Sneaky as he could be, was he waiting to strike her from those shadows?

Nothing repeated, and the emptiness hovering overhead told the pain in her leg, move up or down. She needed to decide if there was some presence waiting, or it was all her imagination.

Simone looked around the room below her, there was no one to see. "Anyone up here?" Yielded into the dark, her volume was trivial.

Raising a foot, she heaved all her weight to the next wooden support. The sharp angle tested her balance, as she was obligated to keep her hands locked.

Jude had gone up here earlier. Simone still debated this fact. 'It hadn't been a dream, surely?' Repeated in her battle of thoughts, 'what if he was up here?' Whenever mommy had brought up the subject of the attic, Jude would carry on. He hated putting anything up there. He'd then complain to no end about the dark and dusty space. This usually worked on mommy, and the reason Simone had never known of the door up at all.

Once more, to a higher step, she conjured up a different scenario. One situation, that maybe Jude had fallen up there and he was possibly hurt. She had only six more rungs, and she might see into that void.

Chilled toes halfway to the next, and a sharp thud reverberated out of the opening. Eyes and mouth spaced open; her nervous curiosity peaked but it also cautioned her to retreat down the ladder.

What words to say? Simone leaned her chest on the steps. Her hand and the light rose the highest.

A question on the tip of perched lips. She stared up.

Correcting her hold, before asking. "Mr. Jude, are you up here? Mr. Jude!" Counting each second, her breath was held greedily in her lungs.

Hanging on the steps and gloom, Simone smelt an aroma drop from above. Far thicker than expected, her nose turned as she didn't want to take in any of it. Lips closed against each other, she even squinted to stop the stink from covering her. Any future she'd imagined up there vanished, as Simone found her passion draining. Locked there, her head and foot stayed below the boundaries above her. She'd wait for 'his' voice to answer her back.

Instead of holding the ladder's sides, she placed an empty hand centered in front of her. The next plank up felt weird. With a cumbered sight she realized as her hand landed, that it was wet. The liquid now between her fingers felt thick. The color was black and sad under her torch. An annoyed glance and Simone merely wiped it away on her pants. Up, she moved again, over the last spot. Rested above her head, she found the next handhold had the same spill.

Pulling the hand back, she simply wiped it without a thought. In the haze of night, she could no more identify it than a spilled can of paint. To her nose it had no smell, at least any either bad or related. At last, she moved close under the edge of the framed entrance. Dripping from one side of the doorway, looked to be more of the same accident. Simone knew to avoid stepping in as much, when she came up.

"Hello?" She invited anyone hiding.

Before her light left the top step, she turned just so her head could see more.

A thick wall of darkness met her gaze.

The expectation of getting an angry foot to the head was not far fetched.

Jude could still be here. Head above the floor line, she waited. Her gaze was not totally denied, she found monolithic shapes. Shadowy outliers that all had hard edges and no detail without more light.

Thankfully, none of these fit the silhouette she was cautious of. Although the glow stick helped, she wished she still had the flashlight of the night before.

Centering her attention past what looked to be piles of boxes, she squinted. A few more pieces of furniture rested up here, but there was far more, she couldn't yet see. Patient, she stood as hard as stone. The inspection that traversed the expanse moved slowly. Her stepfather wouldn't surprise her again.

Everything seemed timeless and hollow of threat. Void of any life, Simone felt confident that Jude was not here. This idea recalled an entire month, when Jude was fired up about squirrels in the roof or attic. The damage he always went on about was never clear to her. However, the noise she'd heard must have come from missed critters still up here. Her footing remained as she cast her gaze with the rise of the glow stick. With only her shoulders above the line, the light stopped under her chin. Up on tippy toes again, she searched as far forward as the glow allowed.

The exploration slowed as she fought off the dust and smell. With only her head turning in circles, she discovered something tall behind her. Something she could neither identify, nor recall its shape being in the house.

Deeper than her light permitted, Simone's mind worked on the pitched shadow.

Her eyes looking for character in the furniture, her head drew back sharp. In that instant she was convinced the object had moved toward her.

A flood of panic came forward as the glowing light slipped out of her grasp. Its life falling downward to her bedroom floor. Simone, abashed with fear and a harsher hand that might come, she cowered on the steps.

The moment passed before she peeked round. "Mr. Jude, are you ok? I thought you had…"

Her sight of it was over a shoulder and her back aimed at the shift. Closer and lofty, the objects seemed to distort. Its true form hidden, in the bleak behind her, yet it had begun to advance on her.

Ahead of Simone's facilities, an aggressive hand wrapped tight around one of her ankles.

Tight and covering the full circumference of her shin, the unseen force pulled at her. The exertion needed to tip her from the precarious landing was small. That darkness which had been held at bay by her glow stick, now thickened and moved unwelcome toward the small girl.

Yanked from her footing, Simone instantly crumbled. First forward, she bounced on empty hands. After the strike, she was immediately sent down through the opening. In an uncontrolled descent, she was again without sight of what held her.

In Simone's fall, she hit her head as the edge of the opening passed. Her breath now a screaming howl as she surrendered any balance in a spinning tumble. The unforgiving bedroom floor was to be her next stop, and the pain she looked forward to, was going to be a dire one.

Hurdling unchecked, except for what held her, Simone hadn't the time to protect. Powerless to break the grip on her ankle, she would fall the full distance.

Abruptly, and before her final impact, Simone swung outward. Twisted and wild she passed beside the base of the ladder. With all her downward force mitigated, she continued to swing there for a moment. A doll in the hands of someone larger, she opened her tight eyes. Before any focus or understanding she was released. Landing in a pile, not the floor but her mattress, Simone still felt shocked if not hurt. Head recoiling, she missed the pair of murky legs now waiting for her acknowledgment.

The owner loomed tall over her, and at the moment a blur of a figure. Simone was sure it was going to be Steve. Possibly close to him would be his mean dog.

The shadowy figure quickly came down beside her. Alone, the person bent over her and a sparked-up flash of a cigarette lighter blinded Simone.

Chapter Twenty-Nine

Run

Simone was brutally made to stand. A handful of her hair in the hand of the figure above her.

The flame of a lighter in the other hand blinded Simone, as she looked up to see her assailant. Whoever was her attacker, she still didn't know. All her fears remained assumptions.

As the yellow flare moved to one side, the trepidation instantly vanished. Welcome was the face of her mother. After she stood, the rough hand released her mane. No sooner had she reached out and took Simone under her hurt arm.

"Little girl, what the hell!?" She wasn't at her best, and the slight audible slur said she'd been drinking most of her troubles today.

A firm hold on Simone, Mackenzie pulled her off the bed onto the floor and next to her. "Why's the power off?" This was the least of her concerns.

A glance up to the attic ladder then back to Simone. "Where the fuck is Jude? Why the hell are you in the attic?" There was anger in her tone, and she was confused by the situation she'd walked into.

Furthest from the bender she'd started, after leaving the house a day ago. Mackenzie was at the end of her buzz. The regret for returning and losing the sensation was washed away.

Switching the lighter to her other hand, she bent down for the end of the ladder. A grunt and she sent the entire assembly slamming back into the ceiling. Once again flush above, the hatch and string disappeared as the rebounding spring spoke.

"Mommy, please, I didn't do anything." Simone's excuses were always the same in Mackenzie's ears. Joy and caution mixed in her defense; she wanted to tell mommy all the things that had gone on. However, she knew her mom wasn't in the best mental state to understand.

The bleeding pains, in her arm and neck, spiked, as Simone's need to warn her about the dog dropped by the wayside.

Looking past her mother, she tensed to see the door. Her bedroom was wide open. The hallway was a gaping rectangle of darkness, where teeth could be waiting for them both.

A tremor started to grow as Simone's eyes couldn't look away from the space. The bandage on her leg continued to leak from the beast's last visit. She wanted to scream at her mommy to close the door but didn't.

Mackenzie didn't wait for more of the lies. Thoughtless she swung back and prepared, with a ringed slap. Whether just a threat or in her slightly foggy mind, she needed to force the girl's attention. Readied in the air, was her other hand with the lighter. Then it dropped to the level of Simone's face.

"I swear girl, if you've run him off, I promise I'll be harder than he is." Sending her hand back down without a strike. The words were enough for now, but the frustration was sinking in. Mackenzie sucked her teeth and nodded.

The darkness easily caused some balance issues and she wanted to lie down. More importantly, she hadn't said a thing about the stain of blood on the floor behind them.

Feeling the towering figure begin to pull away, Simone stretched out for her. The hand that moments ago would have hit, now pushed her back as she turned for the door to leave.

The mix in Simone's gut was now fear and desperation as she followed after. Her mom stumbled in the low light but stopped against the doorway. Her hand up, it was needed to support her miscalculation of the turn.

Pursuing her mom's leg was Simone. Terrified, she moved with her before exiting the room.

"What's fucking wrong with the lights NOW?" Her finger worked the switch off and on.

Remaining a step behind, Simone lingered as her mother exited. Afraid to follow, she hugged the door frame glaring into the bleak of the hall. Slowed, she was worried about exiting yet as her nervous gut howled for protection, her feet stepped out.

"Mommy, where's the dog?" The light in her mom's hand dropped away then stopped.

"Damit!" Mackenzie stopped as the light did. Her thumb repositioned; the flame returned with one pull.

Violently, Mackenzie felt an attack on her leg. Simone had latched on to her with a desperation she couldn't understand. "What the hell are you doing child?" More of an irritation she just wanted her to let go and leave her be. Let her at least have a sleep to clean the past few days off her mind and skin.

A stronger hand between her and her mother's leg, Simone fought the attempt to remove her.

"Stop it already! Jude will fix the breaker, but I just want to lay down first." Mackenzie attempted to walk again. The idea of laying her head down was the singular thought that gave her some peace. Holding the lighter higher, she could see the mess Jude had made. It was everywhere and lingering out into the hall. Her bedroom was, as she thought, in need of a bonfire to cleanse it.

One arm held tight around the inside of mother's leg. Simone's fears darted around the hall; her wide glazed eyes worried the four-legged beast hid close by. Throwing her mom's step off, Simone gave a nervous glance behind them.

Her own door and the stairs beyond appeared empty. Nonetheless, Simone knew better.

Try as she might, her mother couldn't remove that last grip inside her legs. Clinging to her was a frightened little girl, and Mackenzie was ready to strike. Provoked by the neediness, she swatted at her daughter with the back of her hand.

Yelling with a cough between, "Stop it I said. That's enough already and if I have to say it again." Instead of pushing her by her body, she took hold of her wrist. "They send me home early because of this kind of shit." Pissed about Jude's earlier fit more than her paranoid child, this neediness was working on her last nerve.

Eventually stripping Simone's frenzied finger, she wobbled for a moment. The flame continued burning hot by her thumb when a question she'd forgotten to ask surfaced.

"Why the fuck is Steve's truck here? And his driver window is busted out all over the ground." Her afterthought was connected to the blood found on the floor.

The pause was longer than her brain was willing to continue. Choking down a spasm of nausea she fought it as the touch ended in her throat. Whether it was the precursor to being sick or vomiting, it threw her inspections off.

"What the hell was I saying?" The idea she treated her girl like an older child wasn't lost on her, but it hadn't been any different for her when she was young.

Makenzie's thoughts no longer blocked; she recalled what's been said. 'It was about Steve's truck outside.'

A mouth open, she was about to rephrase the inquiry when she took another step past the bathroom. The habit of a closed door was hers. Looking into the deserted space, she was about to scold Simone for leaving the door open. It wouldn't be the first, no, it was the millionth time.

What became more obvious was that Simone had stopped her struggling hold. Looking back and down with her lighter, she found fixed eyeballs in the girl. An expression unfitting for her, especially in a simple dark hallway. Her gaze wasn't on her, and Mackenzie was about to ask why.

Following the glare, she saw a body moving in the deeper spaces of the bathroom. Fighting a thirsty swallow, Mackenzie came to its opening. "What the hell. Jude is that you?" Her tone fluctuated because of the competing emotions.

Stepping from the buried ink of the crowded restroom was Steve's dog. Its legs moved closer out of the confinement and into the light held in her hand. Her first impression was to be mad, but quickly bled away into concern. Staring at the dog, she needed to be fearful, she needed to step away.

Its head lowered and looked motionless as it walked deliberately toward her. Short hair and hungry eyes, it wasn't looking at her but who was behind her. He moved as if stalking some unwitting rabbit in the forest.

"What the hells the matter with him?" Mackenzie's question was a defensive one but piled on with nervous fear the dog would nip at her. Feeling Simone's absence behind her, she wanted to bring her eyes around.

The light, once felt to be a burning torch in the dark, now felt to be a tiny spot of protection. Its power was small, between her and the teeth, her hand caused it to flutter.

A low grumble escaped the dog's throat as it neared.

Stepping away from her bedroom and the snarling dog, Mackenzie pointed the flame in its face. "What's wrong with Steve's dog? Why is he…" It was clear to her the beast was staring behind her at Simone. Stomping her foot hard on the ground, she hoped to break its fierce glare. The dog snapped in the air.

"HELP!" Simone shrieked, horrified the beast would reach her.

Against the wall, Simone's mom came to wedge her there. Standing between her and the dog, she continued swinging the flame. All the while Simone pleaded for her defense, but the words came as nothing more than screams.

Its barking jabs came out fierce as the beast wanted the figure behind Mackenzie. Screaming, "GET OUT OF HERE!" Mackenzie had no weapons to back up her distress. Her hand was too close as the dog attempted to circle around her.

Vicious and fast, the teeth flashed out under the solid yellow flame. Its long canines found a home in her hand, they didn't keep it and immediately pulled away.

Developing her own ear-splitting howl, Mackenzie let the fire die. Soon pushing back to the wall, Simone behind her.

A regrettable pain filled her mind as the blackness swallowed everything. Before attempting to restart the lighter, she kicked out. Her own feet clad in heavy boots, the defensive attack hit somewhere in the dark. Automatic and powerful, she could hear the air leave the dog's body. Then a whine sent the beast toward the end of the hall and the stairs.

"Simmy get to the bedroom!" She yelled at Simone, yanking her from behind and pushing her ahead. The newly purchased lighter in her other hand flashed to life again.

Angled wrong, Mackenzie turned with her back to the bedroom and saw only hungry daggers at the end of the hall. Their purpose changed, they now stared at her. The snarling mouth was pointed, while Simone hid. Panic and fear pumping she thought to close the door if she could back up enough to reach the room.

Those same angry steps as before, Steve's dog wasn't deterred. Nothing was done and it wouldn't stop returning, until it had its prey. Closer it moved from deep shadow to reach the limits of her light. Only able to see her in the way, it moved to close the distance before she blocked it further.

An obstacle in front of him, Salty's jaws snapped repeatedly. The growls of discontent increased to spasm.

Flight instincts measured against hers, the ability to enter, then close the door, didn't add up favorably. If she turned to go into the room, then there was no time to close the door.

Time cut from her choices; the dog bolted forward before she was fully in the room.

Slipping on the cluttered floor, Mackenzie never let go of the light or its gas valve. Both hands hitting the ground were a surprise. One of the alcohol-soaked rags lit under the lighter's burn. A small flame but she hadn't the moment to react as the dog struck from behind.

A mouth full of teeth sunk into the back of her leg and then again on her ankle.

Up and kicking again Mackenzie heard Simone screaming from the far side of the bed. All the fight she had, was needed simply to stand. Used against the rows of teeth, they were gone long enough that she took two steps and jumped for that distant side, left of the bed.

On the other side, the flame on the ground forced Salty to step back. Its determination hadn't ended, it found her escape and the child was still screaming behind her. Furiously it continued barking, the beast readied its attack as its muscles now dumped full of adrenaline.

Crashing off the corner of the bed, Mackenzie landed almost on top of Simone. On the floor with her, she had different ideas than screaming. A hand frantic, she grabbed Simone from beside her and sent her violently into the corner.

Unstopped and with crazed teeth, the dog leapt, allowing its jaws to lead the way. There was drool falling from its mouth and was tainted with the taste of Mackenzie's blood. Yet still, its nose searched for only one target.

"Mommy, please!" Simone grabbed hard at her back. Horrified, she didn't know where the dog was.

In the few seconds before the madness took a life, Mackenzie acted immediately. Hand bleeding and frantic, she would counter the malevolent dog's design. She would stop the hunt. Jamming her hand between mattress and box spring, she searched for the gun she hoped was still there.

Successfully, her bleeding fingers pulled the loaded weapon free and aimed.

Already gone from the fiery spot near the doorway, the beast had jumped atop the far end of the bed. Its beady black gaze on Simone alone. However damned it might have been, those teeth had already started their run at her.

The first shot without consideration took a notch out of the dog's shoulder. Before a second shot the dog was in the air aimed as a missile at her face. All eighty pounds of muscle, sinew, and brawn coming down as a second shot rang out.

Off center and desperate, Mackenzie hadn't the angle any longer and the bullet was too wide. Across the room it is embedded in the door's metal hinge. Although it was meaningless to stop him, the dog came down on them.

Its flesh hit; all eighty pounds of momentum hadn't been halted. Full force, its weight slammed against the raised gun, hand, then her arm. All of them positioned forward of her head, they bent back and struck with force.

On her knees already, the collision sent all of them backward and violently into the wall. The concussion, ricocheting in volume and damage, Mackenzie's body piled on top of Simone.

Saved only from the dog's hit, Simone lay trapped under her mom. The havoc already done she feared the dog would now take its anger out on her.

The hottest pain in its flesh, Salty scrambled to its paw. Wounded badly; it pushed off both, turning to escape another shot even though Mackenzie lay knocked out. Without sight the dog was up and headed straight for an escape. Scared of another shot, the beast exited the room, vanishing down the hallway. All the while, it sent up yelping pain from the assault.

Hearing the dog's retreat, Simone looked from under her silent mother.

"Mommy, mommy are you alright?" Fear present but her volume a louder whisper.

Crawling from beneath, Simone peered out at the door. The flame, which had been burning on the floor, stalled as its fuel dwindled, then died.

A pounding heart that refused to slow, Simone jumped up and ran to the door. Trying to slam it, she discovered for some unknown reason, it wouldn't close all the way. Its doorknob was unwilling and couldn't be forced to latch.

The best she'd do in the moment was lean against it. While there, she hoped the dog wouldn't return before mommy woke.

240

Chapter Thirty

Three Words

Whirling air was entering around mommy's window. A gentle tickle separated Simone from her tenuous sleep. Under her and the blanket she pulled over them, was her mother. There wasn't joy or happiness for her, but she considered the warm side of her face. This was a welcome sensation, and nothing more. Unwilling, Simone refused her sore muscles movement even to find different comfort.

Simone wanted the warmth to cover her entirely, also she wanted her mommy to wake. The sky outside the window remained dark, and the moon seemed absent for hours. She could open her eyes, but it was still dark on this side of her mommy's bed. Awake, she lay there thinking.

Listening to the sounds around her, she heard the window's voice. A calm hum; it was peaceful even if it wasn't helping. On the floor, she slipped into everything she needed to fear. Simone felt a shift that hadn't been there seconds before.

The darkness that lived in this house was moving. She was a magnet and not wanting any more of it, she squeezed her eyelids tighter. If there was light nearing her, she didn't want to know. The noise she'd found peace with drifted away as silence found her once more. Just as she feared, its hand moved down from above and softly it landed on her back.

Whatever its meaning, she tightened her eyes even more. The weight of that hand could not be good for her, and she needed to protect mommy from the dog or even Jude. The hand, if it was one, lifted. Buried in her mommy's chest, Simone had to open her eyes. She'd have to know if it was her anxiety that had caused the feeling.

A deep breath, she counted to ten. At nine, Simone peeked with only a slit.

Her resting angle, pointed under the bed, and there she could see all the way to the door from beneath it.

A radioactive green gave everything in the room a sinister hue. Wicked and dreamlike, she feared all was lies, and a nightmare prepared to steal her.

Wider, her top eyelid opened to see more. There, at the end of the bed, she could see legs. Feet familiar and small waited there for her to sit up. Not with a frown, but the closest she could come to a smile, Simone rose. At least pleased to find her friend safe from the dog, she stood to greet Crischa.

"Did you go back home?" The story she might tell was not important, but she asked.

A faint nod in her head agreed with Simone's question. In Crischa's hand was the fallen glow stick from Simone's bedroom.

A sunless doll at the bed's end, Simone stared at the quiet girl. Her inflexible expression staring down at her mother. Seeing the look, she wanted to make up an excuse, but there wasn't one she knew to tell. The space dark between them, Simone watched her eyes as they left the body lying there and glared at her.

Again, the empty eyes only glared through her. Motionless she stood before Simone.

"We can play hide and seek?" The offer was aided this time, by a raised and open hand. Crischa's empty palm filled the space between them. Simone looked at her hand. It was the same color as her own in the glow. She was beautiful but like the monsters in cartoons, she was colored as a creature. Traveling up the arm, Simone cast her gaze back on her face.

Those cold eyes hadn't moved from hers; they seemed to offer friendship. A heaviness in Simone's chest forced her to look back at her mother. Questioningly, she wasn't sure about leaving her, worried about saying it, she looked at Crischa.

Although she'd never had an actual friend, was it always like this? Simone couldn't work out the complexity of the world, her question was still real in her head. Games were not often in this house and 'friends' more so in their rarity. Yet with everything that had happened just tonight alone, Simone was uncertain about playing. At the very least, she wanted to spend time with this friend.

"We can sit here and play in my mommy's room?" It was an option she hoped would be acceptable.

Past the girl, Simone saw the door was wide open. "There's a mean dog out there, and I just don't want to…" The statement was nothing more than a fact, and worth repeating to herself.

Watching Simone, her face gave no communication, no expression to the scared girl's words. She simply stood there as if nothing was said, those hollow eyes drinking from Simone's care.

"I don't really want to play that." Simone filled the awkward space, even if her admission to Crischa was weak, she studied her expression. The air around them was sickly, Simone wanted a friendly agreement, and any awareness of the pain she was dealing with.

Without movement, a stray lock of Crischa's hair rolled off her shoulder. This, the sole growth of her expression or outer shell. The phantom was shaped like innocence, kept her hand out to Simone, before the phrase repeated. "We can play hide and seek?"

Letting slip away what she hoped could be a smile, Simone felt some damage forming inside her brain. The needs of others were never kind to her, and now she felt like something was wrong here.

Conceding to the emotion, Simone felt her head dropping even as her hand rose. Its reach added to the dark space between, and she met Crischa's cold fingers. "Are you really my friend?"

Intensifying her deceptive emotion, Simone looked back to those sunless eyes. They'd never left.

"Friend." The word came from Crischa.

It didn't seem practiced, and where every other thing she'd ever said, this was separate. Simone saw a crack where there was none, but it was a river of hope she'd not had, till now. Her appearance never changed for Simone, there was a weakness from the wilted green creature standing there.

"Good," A delicate smile appeared as she closed her hand around Crischa's.

Firmly hers now, Simone took advantage of the opportunity that she knew to be rare. Pulled up from her frame, she came up to the stranger no longer. She let go of Crischa's hand. In that same action, Simone brought her friend deeper and hugged her tightly.

Unable to stop an outlying tear from escaping, Simone stayed there if Crischa would allow her. No smile nor other tears, just her sensation of the now.

As a crack opened between them, Simone immediately started with something else. "Crischa, I want to give you something. Alright?"

Left to right, Simone took her hand. Still with mommy's blanket over her shoulders, she placed half over Crischa's smaller frame.

Fingers mixed together; Simone guided the chilled hand. Leading her toward the door, she felt the cautionary spasm when she saw a wide-open door.

Over the wall, and even some of the dressers to her right, was a splattering of blood. Its black stain in the glow was disturbing. On the floor was a dripping rain of dog's blood, left from the shot mommy had hit the beast with.

Before they left the room, Simone snuck a troubled glance back. Able to see only her feet tucked to the left of the bed, they wouldn't be gone long. Admittedly, without her concerns finishing, she led Crischa out the door and hadn't attempted to close it.

Into the hall, the shine from her friend's hand filled the passage. Simone could see the contrast on the faded wood floors. A tramped path of darkened footprints. All these markers, black to her night vision.

She would have gladly welcomed color; green was the preferred. Then she might simply imagine the carnage was likened to cartoons.

Hard to pass it all by unaffected she stepped over footprints. Many of them were both mommy's and hers. Spotted in that same direction, headed out, were the dog's prints. Fresh and still glistening in the low light, it caused a shiver that always seemed to be there. She knew the dog had been hit, but how bad wasn't apparent. Heedful toes, she used the cleaner spots on the way back to her bedroom. The thought worked in her brain, 'just how much would a dog bleed, before it affected any ability to hurt her?'

An escaped glance came back to her friend. Holding the glow stick, she couldn't see her expression. Had she the same pains as hers? The feet under her path needed no patience as she walked through all the slaughter. Though Simone knew it was unclear, 'what was the walk to Crischa,' she wondered a second about her. The notion passed quickly, but she wouldn't tell her later of any misgivings.

Attention turned back forward; she was still uncomfortable. A twitched search, one good thing came of it, the dog's bloody path led to the stairs. Most likely, Salty had gone down there to hide for the time being.

Guiding Crischa past it all, she drew her through her doorway.

The dried pool of her own spill, just inside, she made sure to skirt it. Even in the dark glow, she saw the marks of her struggle on the floor against the door and the dog that had fought her. This time in her room, she had some semblance of comfort. The other set of five fingers clasped to hers was some grand force, inside her mind. Tied together, she was aware of the light pressure her friend's grip placed on hers. Each digit iced but without struggle, held hers. All the steps since they'd left mommy's room, took the warmth from hers as it bled over to Crischa skin.

Her friend's hand was chilled, but Simone was glad it never gave any sign of fear. She was sure Crischa feared much as she did, but she looked better at hiding any visible degree.

Leading her in, she had purpose. Beside the mattress on the floor, she stopped them both. Swallowing through a crumb of difficulty, Simone let her hand go. The dog foremost in her thoughts, Simone made sure to push hard on the door to receive a click.

Breathing a small sigh of relief, she let her fears subside before continuing. Dry lips and aware of the girl staring at her, "wait right there." The explanation from Simone was nothing more than a nod toward the closet.

Seeing her motionless, she decided it was her answer, and stepped away. Although the room was a disaster, it still accommodated Simone's smallest of treasures.

Walking to the closet, Simone recognized something. She felt a naked sensation, without Scuff's fur tucked against her chest there was a loss. 'Just where?' Had she dropped him troubled her, but it diminished as she entered the closet. Inside the inky nook of the room, she gave a quick twist, a step inside. Turned enough to reach up along the frame's inner wall, she searched for a stray nail. It hovered over the height of her head. Finally, her fingers found the home and resting on it was her gift.

"My stepfather took away all my toys and everything I've ever owned." Her statement was stark and sad, but Simone's face and meaning were elsewhere. "He told me I was leaving things all over and…Well–he didn't get this."

A beaming smile showed on Simone's shadowed face. The touch of the glow stick was enough to reach her but her fingers knew the details. Head back down, Simone left the closet but was instantly startled.

Right there at her first step, stood Crischa. A frightening figure that watched Simone's every move.

"Stop doing that." Her words were almost a giggle.

Taking the girl's hand, Simone placed the purpose of all this. In the center of Crischa's upturned hand, she let her see the gift.

"My grandmamma made it with me." The pride was shining. The glow stick in Crischa's hand helped Simone focus in with both of her hands. "We were best friends too, my grandmamma and me." The words convey too few happy moments. However, welcomed as they might be, the finality of that relationship lingered in it too. She'd died not long before Simone's birthday, and the pain was always present.

"Crischa, I want you to have this." Looking deep into the calm eyes, Simone knew she smiled. Even without any indication, there was emotion.

"It looks so pretty on you." Softly admiring the colorful string band, she finished tying the end of the beaded rope around the gray skin of her wrist.

Finished, Simone was interrupted by her own emotions. Sinking in her thoughts of what the present meant and the gift that Crischa's friendship meant to her. Before any words hid her reflection, tears rolled on both cheeks. The love her grandmamma had shared now lay on Crischa's wrist and in Simone's heart.

A slanted head, Crischa reposed her question from days lost. "Why do you cry?" The collection of words arrived on Simone all the same, emotion-less. Wider pupils glared at Simone, without a single blink.

"You asked me that before." Thinking hard to answer it, "I don't know why. I guess--I'm happy?" Quickly wiping away the tears, she looked down. The word 'happy' wasn't the reason before.

That moment was far sadder than any she wanted to remember. Simone didn't want to talk about it. It didn't matter what had happened then, she held up Crischa's hand and shared a new smile.

"I've never seen you cry. Are your parents as nice as you?" Simone's push felt selfish as she let her gaze fall to the floor. She wanted to cry more, but not in front of Crischa to any further extent.

"Why don't you talk much?" Innocently asked, there was no answer. Simone kept her grin before looking around them.

"Friend," Crischa's uncharacteristic inflection was new. Though her face gave little change, she stepped back from Simone. Her empty hand rose between them. Crischa stared. "Friend." Repeated with another dimension to its meaning.

The space between her brows shrank. Simone heard the change but didn't quite understand. The meaning was there, but it was a scent on the surface of some confused emotion. Absent of better shape, she still took the hand offered to her.

This time just fingertips on both sides curled, one above one below the other.

The two sets of eyes worked in a conversation. The two girls moved away from the closet. The diminished shine of the green, guiding them away. One set, headed backward toward the door: Simone's feet following.

The cold fingers under her hold never grew tight. Their curved edges felt fragile and wary of breaking the hold. Softly they tugged at Simone to keep following.

After walking through her door frame, Simone anticipated more words from Crischa. Somehow, she was going to explain, to say or ask something other than the words she'd said so far.

Down the steps, her friend had turned and merely escorted her. At the bottom, Simone's panic returned. The hesitation she showed now traveled the distance to slow her playmate. A glance around the quiet room below, Simone worried it wasn't an empty living room.

"We can't go in there." The objection didn't stop Crischa as the fingers curled only a bit tighter.

"The dog!" Simone pulled back without letting go. The effort to draw her attention was successful.

Crischa, looking back into the deer-eyes, her momentum continued to pull softly in hopes of moving Simone's legs. The uncommon reach of Crischa's smile, furnished enough answers to restart their journey.

Her trepidations soothed; it was temporary. Simone cleared the living room, only to worry about the kitchen. No matter her search, when she returned to those eyes, she followed in their radiance. As if possessed by their powerful glow, Simone focused, locked onto the strange effect.

Deep in those orbs, she forgot all her fears of the dog. Simone's wariness hadn't fully returned until she stood outside the back door. Below her feet, dropped off to the yard and the forest further beyond.

Revisited and wholly separate, from the warmer interiors, was winter. Unnerving and a splash of reality, it was the alarm Simone needed to stop. Halted at the line between danger and safety, Simone let go of the link.

"Crischa, I don't want to go out here." A demur, heard only by the silent insects in the yard. Looking at her friend, she was already standing on the ground and moving backwards.

Away from her frail shape, Simone's eyes sped to the thousands of spots where a wounded dog might be hiding. Hurt or not, those unquenched teeth waited to launch out at her. They were fangs, that she saw in her mind's-eye so clearly. They had already tasted her blood and seemed crazed to have another bite.

"The dog can be anywhere, though." Focusing down on her darkened shape, the glow stick was gone. Only that familiar pitch of her body traveled deeper across the weeds. "I'm still scared of him." Searching around her, the moon helped little in-between drifting clouds.

"No, wait I…" Simone knew the loss would be something physical, if she allowed her to disappear completely. Harder to breathe, Simone looked on as the girl's hand beckoned her to follow.

Seeming to float effortlessly, Crischa was nearer the forest edge.

Toeing the dry wood edge of the drop, Simone stalled as her arm started to reach out. The distance, its own obstacle.

"Friend," Crischa's elastic tones crossed the hushed yard back to Simone.

Old panic took hold in Simone; her concerns were distant from a dangerous dog, she didn't want her friend to leave her alone.

She was always alone.

Simone wanted to move, she wanted to get outside of her mind. The feelings she shared with her new friend were too strong to let escape. Now just a suspended shadow, the gray trees behind her held the last of her waving arm. Finally, submitting to the call, she jumped down off the porch and ran to it. Her every fear wanted her to search the shadows for danger. Alas, she cut them out before they took hold.

The ground was real, and it was the only thing that had detail for now. She let nothing else divert that attention. Breaking that border between the house and her kingdom always offered peace. Nearer her forest, her eyes betrayed. An odd shadowy form stood tall around Crischa as she approached her.

The vision appeared real, yet before her feet and eyes came to her, Crischa was all that stood waiting.

"Where are we going?" Simone stared.

The figure never answered, only motioned to follow.

Around them both the woods held on to their fading life. Grays and blacks that had no color watched the two figures move deeper under the neglectful moon. Behind them out of sight, a thin confusion fought to stay low on the ground. Pushed away from where one led the other, all sounds under foot and body moved with them.

"Are we going to your house?" Simone asked. "Are your mommy and father nice?" Her tone ached to have Crischa soothe her. She desired a picture of the outside world, anything different from the one she lived in. She wanted to know all things out there were nice, soft, if only with a touch.

Each step was a journey, to where no one beat down the fragile. A destination that Simone might hold in her heart. An idea that when she was older, and free of all this, she wouldn't be running the same everywhere.

Chapter Thirty-One
The Real World

Simone's feet were battered and blistered; she said nothing to Crischa. Her escort filled the emptiness with no more conversation than her hand waving to follow faster. Deviating little, the two maintained a straight course for the house nearer the street. Exiting from under a thicker clutch of the woods Simone saw their goal. A sizable two-story house loomed on the other side of an overgrown field.

Completely overrun with decades worth of weeds and uncut bushes, it almost qualified as its own forest. The space between them had no path or notable trail. Scattered here and there among higher grass were the remnants of cars and trucks. Rusted roofs and hoods, most of the vehicles looked parked there and never moved again.

From their approach, Simone could see there was no logic to the scattered mess. Some of the trucks nearer where they exited the woods even had larger branches, if not small trees growing out of them. With their varying years, styles, and makes she knew most were older than her.

Although the relevance to her was missed, the vehicles were parked haphazardly further away from the house. She wanted to ask, but after exiting into the grass, the bottoms of her feet began to hurt worse.

Stopping abruptly, past a small, rounded truck, Simone marveled at what she could see of the house. Despite its position, further back from the main road, she knew it would be beautiful inside. Having never seen it up close, she didn't know what she expected.

The thought of meeting her parents wasn't the most comfortable idea, yet she would do it for Crischa. Winded by her friend's brisk pace, she took advantage of the pause. Her eyes healthier than her muscles, she scanned the nearby woods. Dark still, tonight she sensed a difference from the woods behind her house.

The shadows here were not still. They seemed to move even without the wind. All the trees here were evergreens and she noted the darker places lined everything.

This was not her forest. Its voice even felt odd to her. The insects that lived here seemed unwilling to speak close up. The occasional cricket could be heard from the distant ends of this domain. Simone was able to slow her breathing but continued to shake from the chill. The blanket she'd taken from mommy's room helped.

Standing straight, she saw better the full measure of Crischa's home. Besides all the invasive ivy crawling wild over its bones, it was humongous.

Still a hundred feet from it, the building sat surrounded by large and overhanging trees. All of them hid portions of the mansion. Their arms were all substantial, but in winter's cold breath, these trees had no leaves. Likened to protective skeletons, Simone didn't like the feeling they gave her.

A nervous sensation that couldn't be shaken off. Her sight in the thicker clouds was limited but from here the house appeared in relative health. Looking twice the age of their house, she imagined a family totally foreign to anything she was comfortable with.

Walking again she hesitated to ask about her parents, even though she needed any warning she might need. Some clue on how to act around them would help.

The closer they got; she realized the enormity of the structure. Soaring high above the land around it were the roofs. Mystifying, they jetted above the green clad sides like towering mountains, all of them different sizes and heights.

Thousands of questions burst to be asked. "How long has your family lived here? Mr. Jude always says he never sees anyone." Simone's drought ended.

Behind her pale friend, she saw that there was no trail she was following. The weeds all seemed virgin to passersby. Every car and truck passed; the ground had no wear to it. All of them had been dropped into the natural land-scape it seemed.

Unstopped the torrent poured out of her. "But at night, we can see the lights out here. Or at least, I used to be able to see." Simone felt the babbling but couldn't help it. They'd been quiet for so long. The sprinkle of moonlight oddly gave her the sense to open up.

Halfway across the weeds and grass of the opening, the quantity and density of cars', thinned to almost nothing.

Flinching from sharper blades of grass, Simone checked the bottom of her foot. On her hand returned to her night eyes, were the signs of blood. Checking the other foot, the same address was found.

She knew they'd had pain, but this was troubling. Looking up, she'd lost Crischa for a moment.

The stillness that seemed to follow her friend so close, opened slightly.

Behind her, deep in the weeds, a moan. Then beside a crumbled old tree, something else. In the darker shadow behind the last car, things unseen ached to move out. In all these places, creatures seem to look for her and move closer. Grinding noises, no longer hushed, moved under the taller grass.

The sensation was unnerving, as Simone spun to each new voice. Each hungrier than the last. Wrapping the longer blanket tighter she was being watched. There were hopeless eyes staring at her and they could smell the blood and with every turn she made to catch them.

"Crischa? I'm a little scared." The anxiety was building, and she still couldn't find her friend.

Another turn and a subsequent spin were completed. There, four feet in front of her, the colorless skin gleamed in the opening from above. Eyes and face pointed at Simone. Crischa said nothing as always.

Raised from her side, an open hand came up to find Simone's fear. Hovering in the air, Crischa waited for the breathing to slow. An ability that Simone envied; the girl's attention was enough to return calm.

"Can't we come in the day, when everyone is awake?" She didn't want to sound scared. She was never afraid of the dark, but these shadows had greedier needs she didn't understand.

"Do your parents work during the day? Can't I see them then?" Simone's words couldn't pacify, but still, she knew the sound of inner alarms.

The offered hand taken, Crischa pulled the child deeper into her lands. Further than Simone was comfortable with, but there were reasons. With a head turned over her shoulder, she led the child. Gesturing with the other, she let the girl know everything was fine. Every step the two strangers in the night made the house grow larger, taller. Exiting the fields, they neared the expanding footprint of the structure. A guest here, Simone again drifted over the details of the house.

Behind it was the widened façade. Above its gloomy shape, the moon disappeared once more as the furthest creatures in the forest sang. On the house's face, windows all looked down on them. Grayed openings, they collectively frowned on the movement around its structure. Eyes that watched and followed, yet they all were sheltered entirely from within.

To Simone they created pricks and bumps underneath her clothes and none of them were welcomed.

Crischa stopped abruptly two yards from the back of the house. Without the connection between them, Simone would have crashed into her. No longer ushered along, Simone wondered what was next.

It was obvious to her; they weren't at the front door. This was anything but. It looked to her, as if it were an old attachment to the larger mass.

The only similarity to her own house was clutter everywhere. Heaping piles of unknown things dotted the area around them. However, any search by Simone merely found weeds and ivy covering most of them.

Closer to the house, she saw the untended growth here too. Covering every inch of ground skirting the house, this section was undeniably the rear of Crischa's home. Dotted about, countless bushes, taking over almost all of the walls.

Her attention closeup, Simone's eyes passed the larger shrubbery. Discouraged, she found no porch. There was no landing to rise up on and enter by. More troublesome than this, there wasn't even a back door to speak of. If Crischa was taking her in, Simone knew they'd have to go round to a more obvious door.

Questioning eyes on her friend, she was jolted to discover Crischa square off with her again. What Simone knew once to be blue eyes now lay sheltered and colorless. Waiting and fastened on her, she'd had a reason for stopping. A subtle wobble of the head, Simone worriedly asked. "What?"

There was a notion, and one she'd pushed too deep and forgotten about. Steve's dog. Did Crischa see him? Was she warning her of the beast? Simone tensed as she started to turn to look around.

Unrecognized till now, Crischa's linked fingers halted the search and kept Simone's gaze.

The grip between them was firm. There was something more happening here, and Simone couldn't guess it. Was she asking something of her? If so, what she hadn't any idea at the moment.

"I don't know what you want." Another doubt surfaced was she about to ask the same of her, that she'd asked of Crischa. Was she going to ask her to wait here? To stand in this strange darkness, while she told her parents of her visit, this late at night.

No different than the breeze around them, her question was a whisper and Crischa gave no answer. Her body stood fixed in the shin high grass. The girl's lips hadn't a smile and Simone was already scared. If she left her out here and didn't return as she had?

Had Simone been a spectator to the two, she would have questioned the trust needed between them. Her friend hadn't let go of her hand, surely that was trust. The muscles in Simone's neck twitch, not pain, nor any soreness. It was an internal battle played out over her fears.

Those numb eyes were saying nothing she could answer. The tightness of her fingers was not transferring information she could decipher in the darkness.

"I don't understand what you want." The plea was erased as Simone received a slight parting shift in her friend's lips. It was as close a smile she ever gave but tonight it was the world.

The act was more than curious to Simone. Crischa, stone in the receding light of the moon, gestured with her other hand.

Out in front of her she asked the same of Simone. Her body is leaning toward her one molecule at a time.

Taking Simone's hand, this hold was dissimilar from the other. Crischa took it not by the fingers or palm. Collected under her chilled touch, was Simone's wrist. Straight once again, the girl stepped closer.

Unblinking, the pearls that were her vision darkened. The buried color of her eyes stared into the girl from across the forest. The border separating their houses, a world of difference. Peering silently into the nervous face and an uneven peace, Crischa seemed to inhale the air around her friend.

So close but there was no discomfort. The unrest of all the questions Simone needed answered were lost. Listening to the breath she let the girl take her hand by the wrist back to her body. Carried tenderly as a bird's broken wing, Crischa took it and placed her palm flat over her heart. Placing the warm hand against her cold flesh, she then rested her hand atop Simone's heat.

Covering what heart she had, Simone's fingertips inched near her throat. Looking for the reason, she understood little. It meant something, she was being told without words. The misunderstanding was either because Simone was so young, or because her brain wouldn't hear words that had unbelievable meaning.

A patient gaze, Simone searched back over her expression. Rooted somewhere in those widened pupils she was telling her a story. There were no words identified, yet Simone had everything she needed in the offering.

Nodding her head, Simone was speechless. She had no answer but gave her friend a truly delighted smile for the act. The steady hand holding hers, covered with an icy touch but this was just temperature.

Simone could feel it and her own pulse, but no other movement reported from the contact. This lasting embrace wrote clues. A message she thought to mean a connection. Yet somewhere in it there was no heart pounding under her fingertips.

A haze was in her thoughts, yet somehow the fact was both confronted and comfortable to Simone. Her understanding of just what any of it meant was limited. Nonetheless the truth Simone needed had already been given an answer.

Simone always felt at peace around Crischa, and this truth was more important. It was a bond she neither understood nor cared to pick apart. She felt happy right now and she could thank Crischa for that, and that's all that mattered.

Dropped away, the last connection was their other hands. Simone still felt eyes watching but she was safe. Crischa turned toward this side of the house. Pulled through some of the thicker bushes, she was leading quickly. On the other side, in heavier shadow a boarded-up cellar window met them.

Simone took a cautious breath, as Crischa plucked the board away. Uncovered beneath, she could barely see an opening. Dark and bleak within, she should have been fearful. At peace holding that hand, she wasn't.

Before any query could be posted, her companion entered with her in line. Passed quickly, they dropped into a voided abyss.

Chapter Thirty-Two

A Handhold of Trust

Immediately they came to stand on the ground of Crischa's family's cellar. Simone's first impression was the sense that she'd made a mistake. The safety she'd felt with Crischa was now a clasped hand in the darkness.

Skilled as Simone's eyes might have been, her art of seeing in the deepest gloom was broken here. Whatever the size, depth, or meaning for the rooms she hadn't a clue. Without her friend, she would be lost in this ink.

A quiet yet troubling breath couldn't understand how Crischa found any passage here. The murk was in every direction. Even as she looked to where they'd accessed there was nothing. Pulled up by her useless gaze, Simone's connected hand lived in the same pure pitch. The sensation was further disoriented when a tug to her hand started walking.

Simone had two contacts. One force pulling her along and the other anguishing feet walking on unknown ground. Thus was the total of her reports, and she couldn't know for sure if this was or wasn't some nightmare tricking her.

The touch that was her friend's hand had grown tighter. It was a warning in Simone's mind. One that said not to slow. Regrettably, she wished Crischa would say anything to alleviate the rising panic. A word to make this a game, or at least some reason to reach her friend's room. What little she knew of the floors seemed to change within a few feet. It gave her odd clues. From landing here, to every maturing second, she was in unknown territory.

In her own home, she knew where fear fit, and protection could be found. In this dark forest, there could be beasts, creatures looming over them with every step. She hadn't a clear guide, only the touch of a chilled hand pulling her blindly. Simone worried, but there was hope this wasn't a new scarier game.

The floor felt anything but firm. It was able to shift softly under her pressure. The surface didn't clearly move, still it wasn't hard like the floors of her house. Mommy's house hadn't a basement, so the entirety of this experience could merely be the norm.

There was no sound of water, and her toes could feel no mud. Even so, the impression was anything but dry ground. No matter the hurt and throbbing in her toes and heals, it was the oddest thrill. Maybe fear but it was not pounding a beat in her chest.

A revelation, Simone noticed the temperature. Unlike all the wood planks and linoleum in her home, these floors were warm, almost like walking on hardened flesh.

"Where…?" Simone's question was cut short. Fast and out of the darkness ahead of her was Crischa's finger to her lips. What had been meant to be a sentence, was abruptly suspended.

Her friend's rigid finger remained, as she then felt lips pressed to her ears. Wicked and low, a hushed whisper shushed any further interruption. Patience was needed in the stillness they moved in. Crischa's disquieting touch was instant, and away as fast.

Obeying with no other choice, Simone further regretted coming this far. The center of the woods, between her house and Crischa's, had always been the line to never cross. The idea she was beyond any protection was sadly present in her thoughts.

Crischa's escort restarted as they moved in the elusive surroundings. Their path was not straight. Weaving, they turned almost round. It started to feel like they rose in areas, only to descend time and again.

Unseen objects buried in the grave blackness, felt to move but Simone's eyes could prove none of this. From one area to the next, an anomalous sound increased. Its droning hum had let Simone know it was present and not just an echoing wind.

The disturbance rose and fell like so many engines. Nevertheless, she hadn't heard anything like it. Any similarities she could imagine fell far short of describing the rising wail. Muddied in her strained ears, Simone thought to ask, miserably worried about upsetting Crischa once more. In the end, Simone trembled to picture as if it was some thunderous thing. A framed caution seemed more real as her guide slowed. Her hold tightened once more in Simone's left hand.

Jude was terrible with snoring, and Simone knew even her mommy would sound as bad. Somber in the lack of sight, this couldn't be that she thought.

Baffled by many things, Simone took in the air around them. Expected to be colder, it was like the floors, damp and warmer than believed. It had weight, possessing a similar effect to a hot bathroom. These clues further tossed Simone into uncertainty. No jacket, but remaining was the blanket, hanging off one of her shoulders. Discomfort not new, she was already beginning to sweat.

Oddly enough, her heart rate had remained a steady drumbeat. Unchanged during the entire endeavor, Simone was shocked by it. Taking smaller steps, she imagined it would be interesting to return during the day. To see and discover what she'd missed walking without sight.

What fear was absent, she knew was filled with an aching. This distance, from what was her entire life, was stressful. She'd been running for years. Running to leave that house but never reaching further than the safety of those woods.

Now away from them, she oddly wanted to go back to hide under her bed. The sensation was compounded by the sense that they were being watched from the darkness.

Unevenness was in the air, the newest obstacle was arriving in stronger and stronger waves. Pulled in through her nose, it caused a frenzied twitch of her head and chin. Grimacing away from the odor, Simone found no safe angle to escape it.

No matter how hard she fought, the world surrounding them smelled of rotten food. A stink so harsh and putrid that Simone could no more breathe, using her nose, than vomit her reaction.

It was here that the ground's texture changed in parallel. Noted as well, Crischa had slowed considerably. Though the temperature fluctuated slightly, Simone felt yet another deviation as they walked.

Sickened to her stomach, she still marveled at Crischa's skill to see. Even to have a hint of bearings was struggling in Simone's brain. Hopeful for a word of reason to any of it, Simone listened when Crischa came to a momentary stop. Her hand was the only sweaty one, she needed to swap. Cautious to say, Simone prepared to ask another question. Slipping from her friend's hold, Simone wanted first to change to her right hand.

In that instant, Simone unconsciously added the smallest of steps backward. Equaled only by dream, Crischa was lost even as she reached out for her friend. Her foot, having taken the space of a shoe, found all touch of the ground gone. The speed was boundless as her thoughts matched in the confusion. Her entire balance trailed behind as the direction was a descent into the darkness. A nothingness behind her, she was already over.

Drifting fast with empty hands, Simone thought she lingered in midair. Her mind, in pursuit of some rising ground, knew she'd soon hit hard. The discovery was a misplaced floor. Thick into the void, the following sensation was the oddest feeling. Baring no sight, Simone's every cell imagined floating free of anything.

Unfortunately for Simone's small wounded frame, the moment was fleeting.

Brutally and violent, her back smashed down. Head following in the collision, the darkness was substituted with a brilliant flash of exploding dots of light. Filling every corner of her vision the light was dazzling but short.

Struck hard, reality and gravity had found Simone in some deeper location. All the air in her lungs, though soured and sickened by the air, rushed out. Vacated by the impact, it also increased the effect of her mind's spin.

As air flooded back into her system Simone let free a scream. Painted on that picture in her skull was fear. Dread was in her thoughts now. Lost when her hand broke from Crischa, was any sliver of safety she'd been leading her by.

"Crischa?" It was a question, as well as an accusation. Its dimensions were bouncing off the tightened walls she'd fallen into. A desire to return to some sort of familiarity ached over Simone's lips. "Mommy. Please help me." It was just a breath, as the shadows around her gained weight.

Drowned, or buried under physical darkness her breathing became labored. Along with the feeling, her thoughts spun faster. Seeing only darkness holding her, panic was taking hold. Finding a small morsel of strength, Simone rolled from her back. Pulling her legs to her body, the wound that was her entire shape, curled up tight. Burying her head in between her knees, Simone's lungs resisted the air needed. This feeling was familiar, as her fearful spine balled-up.

Of all the questions she'd wanted to ask, a frightening one formed. 'Why had Crischa brought her here?' Her thoughts as delicate as glass, she drifted into darker places in her mind. Miserably there too, Simone was unprotected and alone.

She was always alone.

Warm, Simone sat on a lap. Circling above the dream was her grand-mamma. The face she wore was stressed as she said something to her. However fast they moved she strained to reach her in some corner.

Turning from that corner, Simone stretched a hand out to hers. The only thing found out there was the absent ground. Its missing shape focused her body smaller. Opening and closing her eyes she felt like she was flying among tree branches.

The wiry limbs came closer, each of them snapping against her skin. Painfully they scratched at her but before twisting away the view narrowed. She watched as her lone body landed and then started running.

This sensation jagged, she needed to escape from something. Simone knew she had to run faster from danger as its overwhelming touch wanted her skin. The panic was so strong, and she thought she could taste the effects of it in her mouth. Already a frightful nightmare, Simone turned to find Crischa looming tall beside her. The feeling of peace or friendship was tenuous at best.

With Simone's legs tucked tight against Crischa, there was something dissimilar about both her face and height. Arms, limbs, even her neck rose high above her small body. The eyes she knew to be blue, now shimmering orbs of gray.

Watching her unprotected, and alone the eyes didn't leave her again. Crischa's hair moved as a storm of curled blades floated nearer her shoulders. Simone hid her stare, afraid of other skulking figures within this grave. All of them, influenced by the gloom surrounding her, still rose then fell away.

Staring through a hole in this dreamscape, Simone found only one more piece of the confusion.

Lips ruined and unfamiliar to her, they moved in a soft sway. Behind them, no longer hidden, were two ivory daggers. Moving over them a summoned word came to Simone's spin. "We can play hide and seek."

The words gave Simone ease, as darkness swallowed again. The last sensation was her feet. Floating in the air, this was reality as an unseen shape and ground moved away.

Chapter Thirty-Three

The Last Fall

With a splitting headache, Simone knew the strike to the back of her head was bad. Deeper thoughts slowly emerged as she let the air surrounding her be felt. It wasn't chilled, and it wasn't hot. There was no more smell of heavy rot shaping her every breath. Where was she now?

Simone didn't like this game. It was always a place she'd hadn't expected.

Unsure whether she wanted to escape from her world of dreams or the reality of pain. Had she been reinstated to reality? A fingertip found the ground, and it wasn't her bed, it wasn't the living room floor, and neither was it the woods.

Although her brain was slow her memories couldn't fill the last few hours. The edges of all her discomfort had been from a fall. Focused inside her mind, the level of hurt fell second to where this unfamiliar location might be. Was she comfortable? It took a second longer to make sure it was true. She took a breath and counting to three she opened her gaze.

Above her thick rafters. Flat and long, they supported an unfamiliar roof. This purged her mind of any of her choices to where she thought she might have been.

The pair of eyes moved back and forth to measure better where she lay. On her back, there wasn't an immediate feeling of safety. Even if she'd woken with Jude standing over her, it had a level of comfort for her.

What punishment was she to find here?

With a slow turn of her head she discovered a sizable room. Easily twice the size of the largest one in her house, this room was foreign.

Though agonizing, she pushed with elbows then hands to sit up. It wasn't cold but an unwelcome shiver traversed her body.

The room was big, a size she'd not expected to wake in. Seated on the ground, she tucked her legs in. Searching from behind folded arms, she noticed that the room was filled. Not with debris like her house. There were no piles of car parts like her backyard, or even their kitchen.

Here it was busting, floor to ceiling with wooden crates. Boxes of all sizes filled all around her.

They looked similar to a large box Jude had gotten shipped to him. It was a large wooden crate, he had to bust apart to enter. These were somewhat the same. Although there wasn't one the same as the last, all of them had dimensions larger than her.

Dotted about, bundles of candles burned. Placed as if just for her benefit, they hadn't been burning long.

Spreading wide the curiosity as well as her gaping confusion, Simone didn't understand the connection to Crischa. Pivoting in her tuck, she found her friend.

Skipping a breath, Simone's every muscle tightened. Happy to see at least one welcome sight, among the avalanche of strange. The long black curled hair was Crischa's. She was several feet away but looking at something Simone couldn't see.

Watching, she wanted her to come beside her again. Possibly to hold her hand, it would at least soothe the panic building under her flesh. It had taken a second before she felt better. She now saw that fear lived in Crischa's house also.

Pushing her attention to stay on her friend, she saw her arms digging. She was searching through one of the larger shipping crates set flat on the floor. Dirty as the other boxes, Simone noted that everything around her was covered in layers of dust, webs and simply neglect.

Not unlike the blue truck that sat abandoned for ages in the backyard. Having played in it once, she knew one of the windows was busted out. Its interior was coated with years, if not decades of dirt and debris just like here. Equal, it was not, but this area was covered by a closed roof.

Tranquil here, the chamber did have distant walls. Two of them she could see. They were both aged and covered in the same neglect. Moreover, she found through the growing odor, there were several braced but hefty garage doors. She was in Crischa's garage.

Pulled away from those doors, the smell she thought missing was here.

How'd she somehow avoided it in her waking brain, she wasn't sure. It still lingered, but for unknown reasons, it seemed to stay at a comfortable distance from her cowering spot.

Pulling a knee down, Simone wanted to stand. She thought of walking over to her friend, but sharp and stabbing pains cautioned. She needed a little longer to rest. A prickly gasp radiated out from her back, and she was forced to listen.

If she was in her room she could lie down, she could hide under the bed. Another intense pain spoke, but it wasn't physical.

Scuff was missing from her hold. He listened better than any, even better than her new friend. The idea was sad, and she could cry, but only if she'd let it. There had already been so many tears, and scared as she might be, she didn't want any more of it.

Held back, Simone continued to watch her friend. Crischa's size was odd. Because of the head strike, Simone explained it away as her brain's confusion. Forcing a deep, shaky breath, Simone closed her eyes in defense. The temporary shutdown allowed the wave of discomfort to pass. Slumped over in her ball, the idea of asking to go home was becoming a necessity. Inside her arms, Simone wanted the worn fur of her little friend. There was little else that mattered.

Before her head rose to check on Crischa, there was movement. Without direction or much warning, feet neared as a yielding section of Crischa's hair swung down. Brushing against Simone, it was followed by her icy touch.

Heeding the shock, Simone's head rose quickly. The room was still lit with yellow flames. Possibly twenty candles in all, but still their color was flickering a life of shadows. In need of swift focus, Simone's gaze discovered cloudy figures, further out disappearing. After this, an ache continued to live in her head trauma, Simone saw the room was only hers and the girl.

Kneeling in front of her chilled toes was Crischa.

She was back from the box she'd been searching through. A worn but focused expression on her face. Those emotionless eyes had returned to stare through her.

Adjusting her seat, Simone straightened her spine to return a look. No smile, but having her nearer, had cut the alarms in half. First to do so she decided to offer her friend an artificial smile. Starting to speak, she was stopped by Crischa scooting closer.

"Friend," Crischa's lips looked dried. The hushed word was protected from traveling too far, and a hand once again came out to rest on Simone's crossed arms.

"What happened to me? I think I fell." Simone was asking, yet she still saw a space, one that glared willfully ignorant of the pains she had.

The touch on her arm wasn't seen until Simone felt her knees push up to her toes. She was closer than most times and she knew that had meaning. A glance back to her eyes she discovered a smile living there. It was Crischa's only answer but it was volumes.

The two sat in the connection, then Crischa flipped her hand over to ask with her upturned palm.

A slightly frustrated nod, Simone unlocked her arms and surrendered her right hand.

Crischa's turned back over and took Simone's hand from the top of her wrist. A tender hold pulled toward her and was flipped over to expose Simone's closed fist.

Kindly, Crischa let go of her wrist and came over top of her closed hand. Dirty and blood-stained, Simone's hand and eyes didn't understand what the girl wanted from her.

Dropping her hand she asked if Simone's palm might open. Petting her fingers, Crischa watched her fluctuation in emotion and confused expression.

Unwilling to reject the touch and what she wanted, Simone opened slowly to what might happen. This was a game she was almost sure of and if it hurt her, she would go. At least she would ask Crischa to allow her to leave.

 Lips parted and a concerned tightness in her forehead, Simone watched it all apprehensively. Her touch was soft and bare, as it passed over once, then again. Desperate to ask, Simone giggled as the touch felt nice a third time.

Unseen on the fourth stroke of her palm, an object fell into the center of her open hand. Colder than the opposing figure's skin, the thing had weight to it. Simone saw it for a short-lived moment before Crischa lifted it with her other hand.

Simone's one leg dropped as did the other arm. Leaning into the mystery, she let Crischa keep hold of her upturned hand. Closer. Her head drifted, she wanted to see what game she was playing. Begging, her ogling eyes examined with frozen breath. Simone was impatient and wanted sorely to know what was happening.

A briskly turned head, Crischa's hair blocked all clues. Both her hands crawling over Simone's wrist, they worked something unseen. Whatever the object she held, she moved it tighter over Simone's darkened wrist.

Swallowing deep, she wanted to know. Simone continued to hold her breath as the friend finished up. She'd placed something close around her flesh, and a moment later she moved away.

All that Simone knew was that something was left behind. Something heavy now hung on that place where she'd toiled. Around them both, golden candlelight flickered under the high ceilings. Their breath and touch, dancing all around the room. At the center of its effect were the two girls, and a gift.

Bouncing off countless facets, Simone's wrist was ablaze. Where it had been naked and dirty seconds ago, sparkling beams of light flooded outward now. The gift was far more stunning than she'd ever seen in her entire life.

A beautiful bracelet, barely wider than her wrist. Possibly meant for younger hands, but with Simone's smaller size, it was perfect. Its luminescent edges clung round her flesh and sent waves of reflective light outward.

"Oh my god, this is so pretty. Did you make this?" Simone glowed. Astonished by the present, she wanted to stare and never look away. The concern was, if she stopped, it might be some dream's tease.

Carefully she twisted the beauty under her gleeful smile. If she moved it too fast, it may evaporate like so many shiny bubbles. Round and round, she rolled her wrist. Her eyes were mesmerized by the dancing lights of color. So easily they moved inside the endless faces.

Mommy hadn't anything even close to these stones. Simone had tried on all the few things she had, long ago, and nothing compared to this. Her other fingers were slow to touch its form. It had to be toy jewelry, she thought.

"Is this really for me?" Hard to look away, she gave Crischa a loving expression.

A smile so large, a soft laugh exited the corner of Simone's cheeks. She wanted to leap out and drown her in heavy hugs. The shake in her nerves was wonderful, and if her aches or Crischa would allow the hug, she would.

There was no precedence for this level of happiness, and Simone couldn't decide if tears would be okay. This past Christmas had been her worst. They hadn't even the smallest of trees. The only gift she had gotten was an oversized jacket her Aunt Dee, Steve's wife, had absently brought over for her.

"Are these diamonds?" Simone was unable to stop the inside corner of her eye. Escaping, the tear rolled down untouched. Her friend stared, and if she waited for a certain word, Simone would give it to her.

Unable to stop looking back at her wrist, she knew they couldn't be real, because of their size. Several of the stones must be glass or plastic she thought, they were reds, and blues. She'd never heard of a diamond that had different colors.

Having studied mommy's ring endlessly, before she sold it, its single stone was a hundred times smaller. She knew real diamonds were small, but none of this mattered at all to her. "I don't care. Crischa, this is the most beautiful gift I've ever gotten."Up on one knee and one foot, Simone tried again to obtain an embrace from her.

Standing away from Simone, Crischa merely backed another step.

Up in front of her, Simone swung the spectacle out. Looking for the gift, she'd given Crischa. She aligned their arms beside each other. Another laugh trickled out, as a matching tear found Simone's other eye.

"We are sisters now. You and I are friends forever." Proudly, she twisted it in the light around her.

Level with the girl, Crischa lifted Simone's hand. Both hands and bracelets came up, then rested softly on Simone's chest. "Friend."

The moment dissolved almost immediately when a chilled and unknown breeze came through the garage. Each candle, one by one flickered. Their heat and strength drained as they ceded their power, to some darker force.

Oblivious to any change, Simone's view lay narrowed on her new treasure. Powerful medicine, even her collection of cuts, blisters, and gouges hadn't returned to her thoughts.

Shaken free of the charm, Simone sensed something different to Crischa's lighter expression. The room had darkened, and she still saw no electric lights on the wall or ceiling.

"How long have you been without electricity?" Splashed on her lips and mind, the question had just surfaced. It was an experience Simone was familiar with. Gazing past her friend, she looked for any ceiling lights further back.

The search and question found a subject of much larger hesitation and it was moving in the shadows. A lofty figure loomed among the piles of boxes, drifting on the boundary. The person was walking deeper in the shadows. Its stride and form approached with some possible objection to what was happening. Heart rate increasing and lack of air, Simone turned her gaze downward. Arms against her core, she slid closer to her friend.

"I think one of your parents is awake." Where there remained tears on her face, she wiped them away. "Crischa what should I do?" Her volume dropped lower as did her demeanor.

Guilt or regret, the feeling wrung loud in her bones. Able to be no nearer her friend, she concealed her size there. Hiding her newly adorned wrist, deep within her heart, just her eyes came up to Crischa's expression. Buried but not out of view, Simone noticed the shape behind her was advancing.

Panic was bubbling up, and with it twitches and shivers she'd had earlier, multiplied. Her jaw clenched painfully; Simone felt her throat closing. Unable to close her eyes, she needed Crischa to say something, anything to assure her.

Facing Simone, the expression on Crischa's face was nothing if not some form of fear.

Within the mysterious corners of Simone's gray matter, she was happy to see this emotion. 'Fear' was something she'd never been able to hide. She'd always been jealous of Crischa for this. Having thought her somehow capable of concealing her feelings and their effects was troubling.

That jealousy ended here, as Crischa's face changed. Her eyes told a story as well. At this moment, Simone knew she was no longer alone. The dread of anybody's father wasn't hers alone to bear. Simone's gaze stayed there. Witnessing Crischa's cheeks and lips, as they shifted unevenly. Somewhere inside of there, was a discomfort for her to turn round.

The entire mood in the room changed for the worse. As if capable of turning summer into winter in a flash, Simone felt it. Like needles over her skin, the air grew heavier. Some worry, that lived in the corners of her house, felt to move in on them.

From around Crischa's back, Simone saw one of her friend's parents cross the barrier. The line formed by the crates fell away as a pending fate was approaching for Crischa. She knew, whether it was her mother or father, she was in trouble. The difference in this house was if it might spill over to a guest, under Crischa's protection.

Whirling away from her, Simone stayed fixed as the girl rotated on stiff heels. She was around and looking to meet some punishment.

The thing that was front and center in Simone's thoughts was Crischa's gift to her. Fearfully confident that her parents wouldn't approve, she still concealed it under her other hand. Giving her such a beautiful piece of jewelry was anything if not wrong.

Cowering lower behind Crischa, the girl's arms came back to her. Surrounding Simone, they felt protective. Collecting her close to her, they both backed away from the darkness.

Whether embarrassment or behavior, Simone never looked up to any gaze. Avoiding the taller outline, she waited for the harsh words. What she did see up from the ground was that the room had lost over half its illumination.

Looking close to Crischa's hand, Simone struggled to clarify the sight. It was not the same, it had darkened. The smaller fingers that had once taken her hand and walked with her now appeared as long slender digits.

Avoiding her need to fully look up, there was an agitation in her brain that said Crischa's height had changed equally. Not dissimilar to the fall in Crischa's cellar, the room surrounding them dimmed. What had been healthy yellow flames flickered and struggled to stay alive.

"No!" The protest was a howl as Simone's eyes closed unyielding. All hopes of cleansing the corruption, was not as important as waking. She knew this was all a nightmare and it had fooled her for so long. Why, when could she hope to sit up in her bed, covered in dread?

As dictated by all her fears, she dropped low on the ground. Balled up, she immediately sent her hands to cover her ears. Rising around her, was a storm. Meanwhile she tried, she continued to hear judgment begin to thunder over her.

Screamed in her head, 'why,' why did anything good turn into horror? Why hadn't she a moment's rest from such dark fates?

She wished to open her eyes again and have it all gone away. Even if the cost of such a plea meant the gift was a figment too.

Flipping over to her back by unseen hands, Simone fought to turn. Though she was now located against one of those distant boxes, she needed her eyes again. Crawling around the large wooden box, she kept her gaze locked on the inches needed to move forward. Fiery pricks of panic buzzed in her eardrums, but she wouldn't venture a view outward.

Desperate to get away, she heard the detonation of vile screeching. The howling of unnatural creatures generated volumes higher than she wanted to look. There was only escape in her mind.

At a terrific volume, unknown things echoed through the dirt and filth below her. Rapidly the wicked shrieks rose and fell. Each of them attempted to burrow into her skull as she scrambled along the floor.

Finding what she'd thought was escape, she passed through a nearby door. Simone was instantly sent back into more of the pitched abyss.

Ageless and all consuming, she felt it had trailed her here and was forever after her.

Chapter Thirty-Four

The Long Move

Ahead of Simone a convoluted maze of black. The first hike through it had ended badly, what chance had she alone? Alone, lost, broken, wounded, forgotten, there were a hundred more. Hopeless, seemed a more relevant word she thought.

Passing through something that resembled a doorway was just an opening toward doom. No source of light, not even the weak candles of the garage. Demented by the ink, she crawled on what filth she could feel between her fingers.

Behind her a furious struggle could be heard. It wasn't vile words nor a parent punishing a child. The confusion she heard, were wild things, dangerous and soon would be looking for her again.

Her hands unnerved, they trembled uncontrollably, even so they pulled her along the floor. The sounds had briefly dwindled behind her. Their confusion about her direction drifted to nothing, as she moved forward.

The path she took, she worried it descended into some unseen ambush. While her brain swirled with rushing blood, thinking wasn't as straightforward as anyone might have hoped.

On the ground, she was as simple as any animal, running on instinct. That impulse was to escape. She'd tried balling up and the violence had found her.

Further forward, a wall came to block her. Hands searching, she would have to stand in order to circle it faster. It all led nowhere. If she slowed, the noises left back there would find her.

She'd walked in her own home countless nights. More than she could count, where the ones after their electricity had been cut. Frantic in this darkness, she told herself this was no different.

What was profoundly separate, she hadn't a map of this forest. She'd never even seen where they'd entered Crischa's house. Only a small window and a passing view of a larger house was her reference. Standing in it, what lay before her was a bleak game.

Wholly ill-equipped and broken, she searched madly for any kind of exit. Staggering on her feet she feared another fall. Possibly one so deep she'd never land.

Although her feet gave little objection to further abuse, they found no promise where she headed. Anything to lead her, the plea couldn't help but if repeated it might. The chaos had returned somewhere in the distance. Its buffered shape grew louder, but it was different from the start.

In front of her, nothing, just a fleeting hope of escape. Freedom was a beast all its own, and Simone knew she chased it like that sleeping deer so long ago. Confusing her hunger to find an exit, the evolving cacophony seemed to follow her. Each time she stumbled; it tried encircling her dropped body.

This forest had no paths, no thorns to stop one direction over the next. Simone wanted to stop it all. Yet repeatedly she was up, moving again. She begged the darkness, but her hand out found yet another corner. Leading deeper, she sensed her eyes began to burn.

Painful tears now rolled over paths of wiped away happiness. Simone could stop, she could let her body fall to the ground and ball up in the filth.

Brutal to her thoughts, a swelling river of stench found her. Its pressure like some unbreathable weather she either moved through or drowned. Weakened by the fog, her ability to fight the ranker affected her lungs and eyes.

"Let me go. Please! I want to go home, just let me go." She shrank in her defense.

Arms before her she stepped without reason. Try as she might, she began choking with no more air to scream. Carried forward by her staggering heals her body was blind.

Dropped to her knees, Simone was unable to take a life's breath. So small and she was faced with a dark fact. She was going to die here, on her bleeding knees. She thought herself isolated, cut off from any safety, the weight of the horrors around her too heavy to continue.

Even without air her hands returned over her ears.

Around her, wave upon wave of mêlées crashed, their roars peeling through her defending finger. Simone was sure the house would soon pour down upon her. Its confused timbers, burying her finally in a grave naked without her sight. She was waiting for that touch, any moment she would feel the end.

In the center of this maelstrom, she consigned her flesh to the peace this ending would offer. Her tightening fingers and palm were useless, they finally dropped to her sides. She would now yield. She'd allow fate its welcome, and in it give up her dull pain and the tortures of fear. Death could have it all, only if it were swift. She was ready.

Rested on firm knees, Simone straightened into this hell. Her first breath found here, it powered her blind gaze and found a difference in the void. A hazy spot at first, its shape opened to her existence in the darkness. Simone wasn't alone as a glowing halo circled around the light.

As if drawn in the shadows, the ring centered her thoughts as it met her tear-filled eyes.

Streaming from some battle-touched corner, something was offered to her. Living as a slender ray of radiance, it was daylight reaching out to her in her own tomb.

However undefined, what filtered it, the light was pure and powerful. The ink that held tight against her moved away as she fought to get closer.

A hand down, she pushed off to stand, weak-kneed and burning lungs. Her heart thundering, brain unsure of the light, Simone moved closer still. The idea of home wasn't safety, it was an agreement. No matter the pain, this feeling she understood, wanted to return there quickly.

The ground gave no objection as she stepped under the spring. Forward to whatever wall grew the blur in her vision, now a narrowed tunnel of hope. The distance she needed to cross vanished, as Simone slammed into a door.

The source of the light was massive. A keyhole was the fountain and a home, for the shaft of daylight. The thick portal standing between, Simone thought heavy and massive as her fingers spread across it. Violently shaking as her hands moved wider, both searched feverishly. The limits of where she stood had shadowy edges and seemed to have no handle.

"Help!" The panic and frustration slammed a balled-up fist.

Life had returned to what crumbled depression had knelt in the bleak.

She wanted freedom to run, to escape the things howling behind her.

No sooner asked than one of her strayed hands landed. Found, was an ornamented, metal handle, its surface felt damp and coated. The doorknob curved and long, it seemed just as neglected as the house around it. Its layers of rust told of unwelcome, but here and now it was Simone's entire world. With both hands wrapped tight around it she closed her eyes and pulled hard.

High above her shoulders, there wasn't a clear lock to be considered. With every remaining ounce, Simone worked, possessed to open it quickly.

Begging the door, it offered none of it back as hope. Refusing her first attempt, it looked as if it might keep her under the blanket of this tomb. Smashing her already agonized fist on the solid wood, she puffed. Body and shoulders tugging; her foot came up against the edge of the frame.

Spreading from top to bottom, a long echoing crack appeared. Stretched upward, left of the handle and aged door it didn't want to grow any larger. A blazing wound, what it touched, extended out from the door and deep into the gloom behind Simone.

Tied to the glistening fingers somehow, the storm that had been raging instantly fell silent. It all vanished with the white line, hurt, and anguished.

In the expanded space was left a vacancy. The calm she heard, Simone knew, was a lie. Screaming behind her grimace, she never slowed in her efforts. She leaned away from the frame, foot pushing harder, hands tight on the hardware. Concealed in the pitch of the house, a new growing rumble hissed. Low and vibrating, the sound shook the ground, and was moving as it built.

Pulling beyond her ability, Simone was paid-out in a sorrowful defeat. The door would move no further, no matter the force she gave. Like so many things, Simone watched as what was given, was taken away. The opening between frame and door lost its blinding edge. Closed up, the shimmering line disappeared.

A river of dread filled the available void and Simone was left with her depleted will. Sliding from the anchor, she began to sink toward the floor. Dropping fast, she was to revisit the despair she'd earned.

Her body, likened to the effects she'd seen in Jude and mommy, Simone now staggered on sore feet. The door cold once more, the keyhole and its source began to shrink as she watched.

Kicking the villain, Simone needed violence to heat what was falling away. One hand hit with a lackluster strike, then the other. Again, the next was harder, and another came to land painfully against what would not open.

The impenetrable wood, tall and unfeeling tendered back only more agony. Slowing as she felt flesh rip, Simone's unfocused energy was lost.

Dimmed even further, the remaining light threatened to disappear altogether. As the last particles of light stopped, a baleful force landed flat above her on the door. Far over her head, she felt trapped. Whoever it was, they'd decided her choice and here was where she was to stay.

A blast of cold air pushed Simone's hair back. The shock was hers, the person, tall and threatening, was helping her. The door was opening once more.

Fingers worried about being crushed between door and frame, Simone waited until it grew just large enough. Wider than her chest, there was a new fear. If she hesitated too long, the exit would close for a final time.

The monolith beside and above her, Simone saw the problem shift to give her space. The room to escape this gloom was hers now.

Her hand first, she needed to test this charity. Scared and thankful in the same emotion, she decided it was real. Quickly, Simone poured her frame in. First her legs and hips, she was made to push the rest of her body between unforgiving hardwood. Screaming, her chest ached as it scraped out.

Heard behind it all that rising thunder wanted to stop her release. It came for her and her escape, but she was almost free.

Pushing through, some skin would be sacrificed. This wasn't the thought; however, the fear was if the door snapped shut while passing. Her head was the last to squeeze as the door had begun to close.

She felt trapped for a second with her ears and hair being the difference in thickness. A fighting push and she'd be free. Simone could taste the daylight behind her.

Her head, the last through the gateway, she felt hair ripping from her scalp. Fearful, every second she lingered, the door tightened and soon would slam shut.

The fear was her fuel, Simone pulled as more hair ripped away. Ears folded and bleeding, she fell free of the newest mouth to bite at her.

On the ground, a moment was needed to check all her parts. Simone was out and only superficial scars to live by.

Beyond the doorway a collapsed archway and past this, a liberation. Despite the blinding sight of a breaking sun, she was away. The morning sat slanted on the horizon, Simone didn't care if it was falling or had just risen she wouldn't look back.

Carelessly above the escape, groups of clouds played in the blue sky.

Chapter Thirty-Five

A Path in the Kingdom

Birds were singing cheerful melodies. Their dominant sounds weaved into the bitter morning. Pushing through the forest around Simone was a gentle breeze. Its chilled breath shakes many of the remaining brown leaves from their stubborn branches.

The evergreens where she now walked in the woods had thinned in their cover. All around her now lay a coating of frosted dew on the ground. Each patch, Simone could feel clinging to the fabric of her pants.

Wobbling slightly, she hadn't run since she crossed the open area around Crischa's house. Behind her those horrors were out of sight, she swore she'd never revisit it, ever. She wanted to tell mommy, she wanted help even understanding what was back there.

Her friend had turned out to be something of a nightmare, even a threat. It pained Simone to believe something so bad about her. A defense had begun in her head, but it went nowhere. A sharp jab from a stick on the ground brought her back to the here and now.

Simone had made a large assumption when she'd escaped the front door of that house. The direction she ran was instinct and she could only hope it was the correct one.

Peering back through her blazed trail, she heard only the waking forest. There wasn't the silence she associated with her friend, and whether this good or bad the loss was being felt.

The carefree voice around her was familiar. She'd come to the woods many times to simply sit, and listen. This morning was 'not' one of those days.

The placid surface around her could easily be the wings of another nightmare. The lore that would allow her to drop her defenses. The sun rising was only a warning to her fears. A sunny day had fooled her many times before.

Waiting before she moved on, Simone dropped further into the cold damp. She needed better rest even if she was chilled on the wet leaves.

This feeling of shaking discomfort was something she recognized as real. A clue to the waking world, she decided this was all real. Unfortunately, this link into her thoughts also meant what she'd seen back there was real. Real monsters, although Jude held the dominant title, they too must be feared.

Automatic to collect her hands inward, she found only the empty space. Scuff was still missing.

Tough as it was to swallow, she measured each inhalation. Felt each blink of her eyelids. She sensed the gentle breeze cutting through every stitch of clothing.

Though there was pain, and wounds they could be lies. Holding tight, a long-drawn breath, Simone got to one foot, then another.

Her eyes were ever vigilant, they turned to look for anyone spying on her. Looking round she gave another glance behind her. The only thing there was the trailing foot path she'd made.

The ground was covered under a pretty white powder and tracking through it was her straight line. What was not safe about it, were either of those tall figures she'd left back there. They could simply run down the path she'd made and find her waiting.

Scolding herself, she thought, 'This was enough, she needed to move, to go home.'

She required her muscles to obey, no matter how bad she felt. A determined step and she made the judgment as she pushed into a thinner brush. Dotting the sides of her new line were more of the sinister thorns she hated.

The sky was clear, and the sun's abundant touch spread wider as she walked. Her pace was dictated by the wounds on the bottom of her feet. An uncomfortable march, but one she needed to continue, if she wanted to find her home. That thin film of white had quickly vanished even as the cold clung to her and the ground.

Every step, Simone wanted a familiar tree, or marker. Anything that might give her hope, something telling her indeed she was on the way to her house. Unsure of the return angle, she hadn't hit a road or area that said her nose pointed in the correct direction.

These woods had been the recipient of so much of her time. Eyes on the ground, she struggled to know why or how she could be lost.

Jerking away, there were more pokes under the bare flesh of her feet. Simone didn't stop this time as she tried to ignore the tenderness. The cold was helping, but the pain was working harder.

A vacant glance up, and Simone's small wish was answered.

Wickedly twisted and old, a deformed looking tree trunk appeared on the edge of her sight. Simone immediately headed for it. This character of the forest was one she'd visited less often in the last few months. This was known to be a friendly face to her.

Larger than any around it, the tree had a blackened portion all-round the base and a long chard streak up the other side. Though it wasn't an evergreen, it still had over half its foliage fluttering in a soft breeze.

This area had been forgotten. It had been some time since her last visit. What paths there might have been were unused and nearly gone today.

Small, but Simone took some of the welcomed peace into her heart. She had a clear direction home now because she'd been here before.

Back in the brush, Simone hunted for a moment. Disguised by time, the corridor home was nothing more than a rabbit's trail.

Twisting between dry branches, Simone's alarm was set to full. Firstly, she wanted to avoid the sneaky thorns mixed within some of the under-growth. Largely, Simone's eyes continuously darted wide in the limits of her sight. She wasn't alone in these woods, no matter the comfort she thought to have.

Each time she felt peace or ease, the warnings were back to remind. A snap or some uneven area in the woods, would speak. They all seemed to watch and trail after her. All of them were things that could be hunting her.

This was supposed to be her kingdom, but it had been taken by a deceitful friend. One that was likely after her even now.

Simone jumped each time a voice different from the woodland creatures spoke. Most of them came up harmless, yet she feared the ones that hadn't been explained. A majority of the offenders, merely birds hopping around dead leaves and brush.

Her momentum impossible to rush, Simone's mind worried about one particular sound. It hadn't yet been explained, and it continued to repeat.

An innocuous shifting sound, somewhere in her background, was following. Although at present it seemed to hold its distance, she was growing more and more cautious of its meaning.

Ears adjusted; she was apprised of that noise. No longer satisfied with the outskirts of the woods, it had begun to come closer.

Any slower and Simone would be stopped completely. Nonetheless, she was stressing about the size and demeanor of what was looking for her. Pressing delicately on the foliage under her, her feet measured each step as she listened.

A louder snap, told of something heavier than any bird was able to make. Though it felt further in the distance it was following almost parallel with her line. She could no more be sure than see it.

The noise wasn't consistent footsteps, but as it tracked her remotely, it knew she was here. Her breath and heartbeat loud, she stopped her next step to hear better.

Repeating its location once more, Simone knew the evidence was all true. No more listening, she had to move doubly fast. Something was pursuing her and whomever or whatever it was, nothing good could come of it.

Threading with a light warming touch, the sun contributed little. Neither hiding her nor did it elate Simone's dread.

Her own feet now the loudest echo in the forest as she ran. Confident that her house would appear any moment she held back none of her dwindling resources. Simone left nothing in reserve, as she marched faster.

Sadly, and equal to her efforts the distant form was continuing to pursue.

Sliding sideways from atop a substantial log, Simone finally caught a glimpse of the trailing marauder. Devastating to her expanding anxiety, it had black and brown fur. On a low and obstructed path, the beast hunting her was Uncle Steve's crazy dog.

No sooner was it found, than it turned back through the underbrush. It disappeared again. Simone knew if it didn't have sight of her, it soon would.

The perch she found herself on was both an advantage, and a curse. She had seen the dog at a distance, but it could have seen her in return. Heartbeat already ramped up; she felt her lungs begin to struggle.

She could stay atop the fallen log and have a semblance of safety. Yet recalling the ease in which Salty leaped on mommy's bed, it wouldn't hold him off.

Swallowing multiple lumps of fear, she nearly choked to decide on the obvious. She needed to run, fast and without one more stop.

Mind twisting, she imagined the blood-soaked teeth snarling. His angry eyes locked on her flesh as before and just before sinking deep into it, those furious claws pushing her down.

It had already taken too much from her and she wasn't waiting around to offer another piece.

Glancing down, her feet stretched out, sliding off the moss-covered bark. Under her landing, her barefoot pressured a hidden stick. Covered under a layer of browned leaves, the branch detonated in her eardrums. However dull the snap actually was, its defiant volume was deafening and telling to her escape.

Frozen beside the log, she searched for any consequences. With too many seconds passing by, she was convinced. Without proof, she knew the dog had narrowed in on her location.

Having to force oxygen in and out, she straightened her direction. With panic blanketing her every nerve, she sprinted forward. Racing through the slight trail, she cut off any turns or meandering edges.

Whether headed straight to her house or the general area, she had a goal. One hope, and that was to gain enough ground before the beast would reacquire her. In answer to the challenge, she heard a howl. Although it felt distant, the creature had speed and at the very least three good legs. Simone knew mommy had shot it once, but the effects weren't yet known.

Her own feet were bloodied beating the ground in a fury. She was now moving in a painless abandon. Rocketing around a small bend in the woodland terrain, Simone tumbled forward. Franticly back up, and beginning to move, she realized her true predicament.

A tiny opening ahead of her, it was a place she'd stopped at before. A good place to play in the warm sun. A few old broken toys, covered by some dirt and random leaves, lay strewn about the flat area.

It was the location that troubled her the most. From here, she knew the house was still too far. The distance home, with a mad dog in some blood lust following was impossible. She could no more outrun him than avoid raindrops in a hurricane.

Looking about, the trees here weren't of any help either. She'd thought of climbing a tree when running, but the consideration was useless here. Unfortunately, the tree trunks around her were all exceedingly straight with few to no limbs to help climb.

She'd been trapped in her bedroom from this beast. The very idea of being trapped in a cold tree, for who knew how long, wasn't an appealing choice.

Edging into these concerns were the awful shadows Simone had witnessed in Crischa's house. It was another reason not to be stuck out here. Whatever the plate of horrors there, night was not the time to identify them.

A frantic search back, Simone hadn't a choice anyways. Forward was all she had, and now pressing barks came at her from somewhere to the left. The paralleling pursuer hadn't been slowed, even if not in sight.

Simone returned to the trail, she heard the dog's campaign barking nearer. Whatever the gap she'd built, it was cut in half. Whenever the paws came, Salty's teeth would soon be at her heels. Stomach empty and lungs bursting, she continued the push. Driving through the knives of agony, her legs carried her inches from the brink of total collapse. Somewhere still unseen as the monster of these woods was behind Simone. Snapping teeth brought the dog through vines and branches.

Fighting back tears to conserve energy, Simone struggled to not howl her own fears out. If they had begun, their cries wouldn't be stopped nor be denied for long. Over another smaller log in the way, Simone felt the last moments of life were slipping. The fact was that her determination was dwindling with each footstep.

Plunging through small bushes, she witnessed the flash of fur. Its shoulder and front leg limping, it still ran. Black and gross, his shoulder was wounded and covered in dirt and debris. Off to her left, that mouth she was worried about, now yawned wide. Panting heavily, a blurred face of teeth and hunger had spotted her directly. The creature turned for her, and it was the picture of fury and demon. Crossing the few bits of underbrush, in the forest floor, it had one last obstacle.

In its rush, his angry legs leapt. Crossing a murk covered stream, he was in the air. From one high bank to the next, it jumped, already sure of the landing on the other side. Any inward concern absent, the dog came down on what it had thought, a bank of leaves.

Short of the true edge of the winter's stream, it splashed into the seemingly bottomless waters. Instantly, its weight and complete lack of swimming skills sent it under. A carpet of dead leaves on the surface was sent back as a wave, concealing the unsuspecting victim.

Breaking the tension of the water and leaves, the dog surfaced. It was there for a moment's freedom, before it plunged down once more. Watching from that other shore, Simone was shocked and scared by the sight.

Again, the beast erupted. This time it was further from either shore, its desperate claws splashed atop the waters. Opaque and evil, the water seemed reluctant to free the beast. Head, half-covered with fractured ice and decayed leaves, its front paws fought to find any firm ground nearby.

Ridiculous, Simone stood watching. Fixed on the dog's struggle, she saw it clawing miserably to keep its gaping mouth above the surface. Bobbing over and over again, the beast submerged, only to resurface more frantic than the last. Thought to love most animals, Simone was torn by the sight, mixed about what she wanted for this creature.

Denied any exit on her side of the water, the dog was forced to turn back for the far bank.

Simone could see this as a gift. It had given her only the slightest chance and she couldn't squander it. Before it was out of her sight, she'd spotted the dog. He'd already reached the distant side. The beast would have to circle along the waters to reach her.

Damaged legs and clothes ripped through vines. Simone's efforts were showed to be miraculous. She almost traveled in the woods past her house. A second almost missed, she spotted her house to the right, just in the distance. Huffing as she staggered over the softened rot of a fallen tree trunk, Simone looked round. Her discovery was at full force, using even the limping paw.

The dog had escaped its grave and was seconds behind her.

Moving quickly, she couldn't feel. Saplings closer to the house thrashed at her face as she ran. There was no need to add it up, there was just no way for her to make up the distance home. Somewhere in the last yards of the woods, she searched for any tree to climb.

All of them were saplings. There was no rescue from the teeth charging up from behind her.

Had she been closer, the apple tree could have saved her. Nevertheless, she was still too far. Every last option she might think of had vanished.

The hellhound bouncing over the tallest brush had cut the gap to nothing.

The outer edge of her backyard would be the best she'd ever do. These were the last steps she could take before that dog would take its revenge.

At the perimeter of the cluttered yard, Simone was tackled by the rushing force behind her.

Both bodies were lost in the collision. Simone forced straight down instantly fell flat. The dog, higher and faster, tumbled further into the yard.

With no time for Simone to even curl up, the dark fury turned back for her. Its pulsing eyes quickly lay upon her again. Though the violent clash had taken its momentum away, Salty had found its legs under it almost instantly.

Off center and between Simone and the house, he corrected his angle. Never moving its stare, the girl was now trapped. Pressed with her back to the nothingness of the woods, his growling canines stood tall. No door or obstacle would stop it this time.

Almost invisible whiskers trembled as Salty's lips drew back and teeth again were displayed. Its lower jaw snapped upward, its brain already tasting the flesh it hunted. He was still five feet away, but this would change. The morning's sun was against its eyes, but whether blind or not it would sink its teeth for sure.

A step to the side, the dog stood in the only path available to Simone. The singular trail in the high grass and piles for her to reach the back door.

Unnatural was this rage, some curse hanging over the house and all animals. Salty wanted her dead, it craved the girl's flesh to be ruined and erased.

As the creature's muscles spasmed, blood, not yet hardened, continued to darken its right shoulder. Legs squared off; the beast cared little for the pain it was in. Its mouth continued to chomp; the time was now.

Two motions, the hind legs snapped forward, then the front. The dog almost instantly leaped into the air. Its head turned sideways after, and its mouth flew open. It wouldn't be denied her throat.

Her screams were no longer concealed, Simone's life poured out in seconds. The teeth were off the ground and her back was against the dead grass. This was a flash of the same moment upstairs in her house. The difference, Simone had no chance to escape, no door to hide behind.

Thrashing in her last moments of life, Simone sent her arms up. She was offering it to the violence yet to land on her. Behind it, in her head, Simone was where death had found her final resting plot. An echoing scream was to be her last word.

High above the child, the dog's mouth was ready to accept the meat. Soon it would take all the defense in its jaws.

Chapter Thirty-Six

Blood

It swung unrestrained as the siding was hit hard, and the door echoed. Its already warped shape, further damaged as it opened to the backyard.

Mackenzie staggered out the kitchen door. Her face and body were spent; trauma was there long before she'd come to stand in the opening. Blood covered her face, hands and even much of her shirt. Leaning on the door frame her right arm rose up. Her left hand, wrapped loosely against her chest, had barely white cloth any longer. It was dripping and strained heavily with crimson.

Engaged and aiming with the raised hand, she struggled to breathe. A second passed and her last bullet rang out. Exploding out of the gun, the shot came with a flamed ball of fire. Spreading across the yard the hot metal found a permanent home. The thud carried behind it had with it all the momentum.

Her brother-in-law's dog was struck in the path. Her aim was dead on, if not almost late to the play running its course. The impact and its force sent the beast flipping. Although his teeth were already around Simone's arm, it hadn't even landed fully. Jerked from its clamping hold, Mackenzie's child screamed louder.

Instantly the creature had expired and tumbled into taller grasses further out. Through the growth, its leg gave a last twitch before the beast lay in its final defeat.

Sitting up, Simone grabbed at her newest wound. Unsure how she'd been saved, she needed to just breathe again.

 The eager gulps of air never slowed. To her right, Salty. He didn't move. Simone could see the wounded, but there wasn't a reason he'd fallen over dead. Her own screaming had probably hidden any reason.

The wind had stopped, and she felt the warmth of a winter's sun. When it struck her face, she liked it, but this was not her concern.

Toward the house she saw the back door was open.

"Mommy?" The initial emotion was happiness. Yet there was far more she'd missed. A misplaced laugh vibrated through her throat. On that cold ground, more facts filtered in about what she saw. The whole gamut of emotions overwhelmed Simone as she stood to see better.

Her back against the door frame, Mackenzie slumped off her legs. What breathing there was, labored and struggled to fight against her injuries. Her fight wasn't fatigue or fear, it was a fractured and bleeding body.

"Mommy, what's wrong?" A step toward the porch. Her tone wasn't quiet, as her concerns rose harshly.

Mackenzie starred out. Her position outside the kitchen door was limited but holding against the doorway she searched for her daughter. She'd saved her but at what cost?

The gun's usefulness was spent as she let it spill from her hand. Striking the wood planks under her, it tumbled off the porch and into the weeds all-round the ground.

She watched her child walking over. Her eyes couldn't accept what she was seeing. Wanting to speak, she opened her mouth yet all that exited was a gurgling breath of slurred sounds. Her vision fading, all that held her seated here was crumbling away.

Limping closer, Simone wanted anything from her mom's stare. Her gaze was nowhere but on her, yet any motion had left. Walking, she made it over to the side of the porch where her mommy leaned. Slowing in her movement, Simone for once wanted her to yell. To scold her for playing in the woods.

Frozen to the ground, Simone waited. Numb behind her eyes, she felt the nervous twitch in her cheek. Reluctant to the sight, Simone came closer. Rolling off her mother's lap, the bandaged arm dropped. Its lifeless shape landed beside her, then slipped over the edge to hang there.

Gazing at her mom's face, she saw that she'd been crying. There was more to the reason, but Simone waited for her to speak.

Confused, she reached out to shake her blank stare. "What's wrong? Mommy? Mommy can you hear me?" They shrunk away to broken whispers. Only now did she focus on some of her clothing.

Her body had been brutalized. Some of the wounds weren't isolated to her hands but there was so much more. In the shimmer of a late morning sun she had no glow to her expression. Simone could see she was absent, passed out with her eyes open. Over her slumped body she saw more of the signs of a fight.

Cuts could be seen everywhere.

Gasping as her head looked away. What had been witnessed, she would never unsee. Worse than any cut, these scars left her flesh opened. The deepest injury, a gaping wound stretching the length of her chest, all the way to her throat.

Hands over her eyes, Simone didn't want to face it nor know any more.

"Mommy what's going on?" It was a question that would never be answered. Her gaze was into covered hands. She heard things moving around them, but it wasn't her mother.

"You killed the dog before it hurt me." She couldn't face what lay before her, on the porch. She didn't want to see the death around her. The hate and darkness dropped here, was in the light of day.

Mackenzie's body slipped further, laying silent on the blood-stained deck. Rolling out beside her a useless flashlight was now freed.

Standing on the side of the porch, she was upside down to her abandoned mother. Her feet in the weeds, Simone collapsed over her mother's face. Her inner beat, a steady thud. The tears had begun, and nothing was to stop them as she hugged her head.

Simone's knees gave way as she crumbled to the dirt below. A hand remained above, its fingers refusing to release. Connected to the touch of her mother, she stayed there broken even further.

The tears led her to a shrill scream of pain. The newest form of anguish, this one, had different effects. Its shape was something she'd never felt before, till now.

Simone had wished death on Jude a thousand times. Nevertheless, however many times she wished for it and begged the heavens, it never found him. This thought broke her even more as her hand fell away. She had nothing, staring into the shadows below the deck.

The sun above mother and daughter was pure. Brilliant and clear, but all it allowed for Simone was a dark sight. She was seeing the life of her mother, and it was in the shape of a dripping ebb. Her life, pouring through cracks and falling into the dirt below.

The air around Simone fell quiet. Even distant birds' songs disappeared from their branches. The voices of winter life in the backyard vanished. Below the level of the porch, Simone continued her weeping as more within the house moved.

Beside Simone's kneeling pain, she found the discarded gun. The same mommy had saved her in the bedroom with. A revolver she'd watched Jude shooting bottles in the yard with it. All she had to do was pull the hammer back and she could use it.

Tucking the heavy steel into the back of her pants, Simone would stop the death. She would see the monsters and she would find them no matter where they hid.

Gathering herself on the ground, she wanted to stand and say goodbye to her mother. She would close her eyes and kiss her one last time.

Above the platform Simone rose to see horror.

What was witnessed was her mother's hands dragged into the darkness of the kitchen. An unseen form had taken her body. Pulled away from her, before a word could be shared. The shock was total, but too much to let go. Simone pried herself up onto the porch, and back atop her feet. There her rest ended. Her mother was gone. She didn't lie in the doorway nor in the kitchen. A path of gore spread on the floor and all through the house.

Standing a sorrowful figure, her gaze followed the tragedy. Unsure if her eyes would give shape to the darkness in the kitchen, "Hello." There was a voided tone in her reach. She was alone. Instinct merely wanted to run, but her broken muscles wouldn't allow it. Standing with nothing more to lose, she towered at the open door.

Heat rolled out around her legs, but her inner chill wouldn't let her feel.

The darkness within the house was not normal. It was deeper than any day the sun had shown. It felt to be a lie, but she could see little of the detail. The gore that covered the floors led into that bleakness. They were all bread-crumbs to a game left unfinished.

Kicked was the flashlight her mother had dropped. Eyes red and all systems teetering on pain, Simone looked down. Picking the torch up, she recognized it as the one her parents had fought about.

Without thought to turn and run away, Simone was home. There was nowhere else to escape. There were no friends in this world to run to. No places to hide from sinister shapes.

It wasn't that she was always alone, it was simpler than that. There had never been anyone.

Simone took the step in. A sense arrived with that wet floor under her skin. There was no worst pain to feel, no more darkness could take from her than what had already been taken.

Walking into the separation between rooms, Simone was offering that beast, herself now.

In the doorway, she gave a moment as her eyes cooled to the gloom. Hanging limp from her left hand, the long flashlight, still off.

Gazing past the couch, there was only silence. The tv was off and no one sat on the couch.

The living room was warmer than the kitchen, but here Simone felt none of it. The numbness was the sensation under her skin, in her head, and over any emotion.

Leisurely she followed the horrific trail to the base of the stairs. Although its path moved through this dangerous forest, it turned and headed upstairs. This kingdom was filthy with creatures to harm her, but she no longer cared. Her mother would be at the end of the trail. At that ending, things would be finished. Her thoughts went no further as her feet stumbled to an abrupt stop.

Seated midway on the stairs, a friend sat.

Simone's eyes missed the emotion the friend meant to her. The plastic and scratched up eyes stared at her asking why. The sown-on smile said he was still happy, but Simone wasn't. Taking what steps up, her empty hand took him by the leg. Any security it once offered, now useless. The toy was hers again, alas it hung at her side. Dangled by the end of his paw, she never looked at him.

Simone moved flat footed. Feeling every ounce of the blood under her feet, she climbed. Traversed, the worn planks all fell behind her. Each of them plainly spoke of her approach.

Over the last one, she gave not a thought of worry to the chorus. Her tears gone, she continued to hold Scuff limp at her side.

Each step had been a countdown. One after the next, they'd been ticking off the seconds and footprints in the gore. It was an ending for her and soon the last parting sight.

At the staircase's apex, she stopped. Somehow, all of the upstairs was dark as night. None of the late morning's sunlight had power here.

The hall lay in a profound pitch, thick enough to cause Simone to struggle in it. Stubborn, her eyes carved at the shadows, for her broken heart had no other path.

Till now, she hadn't noticed every window had been blackened. They'd been painted with the same red that was everywhere.

Somewhere down the hall, she could hear a sickening sound. Something of death waited for her there, and she would see it. What was wanted, Simone felt cold about. Without knowing its reasons, she would watch its fingers work to finish the game.

Every fiber in her shape screamed to turn, to leave this place and never return. This was the entirety of her body, save one, that which was behind her eyes. Turning into the length of the hallway she couldn't leave, nor would she scream.

Heart pumping, her brain used the volumes. Veins pulled each of her footsteps toward the noise. Something feasted in her mother's room. Beast, monster, even ravens from her nightmares, the sound was ravenous.

There was nowhere else for her; she was a child of what was here. A thought to worry if it were more hungry dogs she knew little of her mind and what she'd do. She could clearly hear the terror that was taking place. Looking sightless into darkened floors, Simone saw only mixed shadows. All of it framed in a stillness that gave the familiar history to her.

Ripping and slashing, the violence ahead grew even more brutal. The stone that had formed in her skull was weakened but still another footstep. Her toes deep in the heat of spilled life, Simone was further along the path.

If only she could be depressed. Sad in the moment, but somehow, she'd always felt it. Her entire life, it had been here, even before her birth.

The racket that had been steadily growing, crashed down to an ultimate silence. Her presence had been noticed. All movement within the creature's den froze.

"We can play hide and seek?" From behind Simone, Crischa's suggestion was small. It was unchanged, even as from the first time she'd spoken to Simone. Oddly enough, it was not the same.

"Crischa?" The disbelief was peppered with understanding. The essence of Crischa's words had been searching for her. Simone's mental capacity slowed as her brain failed to fill in any other facts. Prepared to turn around she listened.

Scuff remained hanging low at her side, her fingers loosened. There was something else she would replace the toy with. Deep in her chest, Simone had wanted a friend.

"Why have you done all this?" Her voice was corrupted as she tried to understand Crischa. Somewhere behind her was a small girl or maybe a towering creature. A taller thing that a child's shape concealed. Simone knew she'd hidden it to take advantage of her.

With the noise gone from her mother's room, Simone went back a step.

The hush was waiting, listening to each heartbeat of hers in the hallway. Larger and clearly hungry, the threat was watching the damaged girl as she thought of all the deceitful lies.

A slight turn, Simone stepped back and found some edge of the hallway's wall. The familiar silence was holding everything away, and she no longer liked it. Her head sinking, she peeked back to where the stairs and her room should be.

A hushed glow played there. Standing close to her questioning eyes was the voided shape. Just before her bedroom door was the thing, calling herself Crischa.

Before Simone pushed off the wall, she sensed it move. Not away as she'd hoped, but up to her.

There was no time to construct the fear Simone needed. Her head rose to know better just what was walking up to her. Her night eyes failing in detail, still the cutout silhouette of a fragile sister came to her.

"Why me?" It was an emotion that asked. Not enough strength to push away, Simone let the girl stand before her in the hallway. Both of them were fixated on the blood under them.

Her shape and chill, inches from Simone. Those gazing eyes within, rested upon her flesh and internal suffering, but said so little. She was a shadow in darkness.

Crischa was unmovable, curious about the girl's words. Staring deeper her next word was for Simone. "Friend."

"Why did you kill my family?" A ripple in Simone's determination. Her spirit cracked and some lone tears rolled free.

Even prepared for her damnation, Simone was caged against the wall, as she shook her head 'no' to the girl. She was not real; she was a liar, a fake, a monster. There was no friend behind those eyes in front of her. The entirety of this play was for her.

"You killed mommy," Hollow, a swelling was beneath Simone's skull. There was that pain she knew as unfamiliar. A spot inside that said dark things. There was a pinprick growing, one that now told her to pervert what she knew to be right and wrong.

Beside them both, Scuff finally slipped from her fingers. His innocence part of hers, the fire inside had been snuffed out.

Crischa drew her wrist between them, up to the worried eyes glaring at her in the darkness. Exposed to her stare, she showed the simple string and bead band given to her. "Friend."

The word was a lie, a wolf in sheep's clothing. Scuff was gone and her hand moved to the found tool. In her other hand she felt the weight of the flashlight. The entire time she'd had the flashlight and never turned it on.

"You are not a girl. Are you?" The statement was beyond her understanding. It was all too large for her to know just how right she was. All senses within her screamed of the towering threat that glared at her.

Knowing she would not answer her question, Simone flicked her thumb over the power button.

Brought to life, the beam of light shot between them. Sent straight up to the hallway's ceiling, the brilliant flash was like lightning in the small space.

Found by the intensity, there was another form nearby. It was far more than the small child lurking before Simone.

Worlds of suffering exploded in that moment. Violence crashed in over the flare of light as a force sent Simone flying into the air. Her body was sent toward where her bedroom door lay. The force was not constrained to brutality as emotion howled outward.

Crashing to the ground, Simone knew only the confused picture inside her pupils.

The flashlight being the center of the upheaval, it was sent sailing wild above all. The spinning strobe offered a small glimpse of the carnage. All of it had been started by her.

Blasted up to the ceiling, it struck there before bouncing to the opposite wall. Coming to land nearer her mother's bedroom, the beam aimed into the room. Found there was the ravaged carcass of Simone's mother.

Seeing by its light, Simone regretted its power. The vial remains were murderous, and she quickly turned away. Larger to the story was what slipped in that instant. Between there and her, something raged in the hallway.

Not a lone girl, but in her place, two colossal monsters were engaged in battle.

Buried on the floor Simone had instinctually balled up to hide both body and eyes. As her thought and purpose returned, she fought to open in the fog. Anything but a flower, she could no longer retreat or surrender to her pain.

The hall felt like it was filled with a similar struggle, as from Crischa's house. Yet looking now, Simone was upended by the size of one of them.

Outlined by the recessed flashlight, this other form was not the same. Angry and larger, it wasn't what she'd witnessed last night, this was not the same creature. The confusion was also accompanied by an unnatural fear and hate.

On the wrist of the smaller creature, Simone spied the glossed reflection. It was one of the ten beads of her gifted bracelet. The thing was Crischa, and it was fighting a monster twice its size.

Before a word could be shouted, the superior size beast ripped and cut the former girl down. Crischa, cast to the floor, lay vanquished and now motionless.

Simone, unsure of her confused mind, was standing again. What had been her friend for days, still lived on the edge of her heart. Losing her was not as easily erased as Simone had decided. She wasn't unimportant, even as she mourned for the fallen body. Although not the same small child as then, what lay presently had been her first friend.

Hard to breathe, Simone knew this feeling hurt just as bad. What was the lie, she didn't want any of this darkness. This loss was bleeding inside of her, and she couldn't separate the emotion. She had her mother's gun, but she let it fall to the ground. Her hand had been willing, but not her heart.

Hands both empty, she could feel the second figure standing taller over her friend.

Glaring, Simone could only watch. She was alone as she stared at the larger creature paused over what had been Crischa. The slumped-over creature on the floor never moved.

Hovering nearer the fallen, the beast surveyed its prey.

A new panic made itself known to Simone's soul. It had been an outlier before, but she now heard the low crackling laugh as it grew louder. Heart dropping lower than could be imagined, Simone was back in those mine fields she hated.

Her friend was dead, but not by the hands of her own kind. What stood over her was a real monster, but it was hers. The resolution in the darkened hall was useless, yet there was no need for a flashlight to illuminate this creature for her.

Hate filled where sadness and regret had lived. Simone watched as the victor turned to her.

"NO!" She screeched against the truth standing there. Yet denial wouldn't change the facts.

"I see you have been a bad little girl." The rumbling voice had a familiarity behind it. "I have tried and tried with you, but you just don't fucking listen, do you, Simone?"

Every muscle, joint, and bones shook, her mind knew the hell she'd expected.

"You little bitch." Jude's tone smiled at the powers he now possessed. The control was new, but he was the one to wield death and grew stronger by its taste. Blood fresh over his face and hands, he continued his mocking laughter. Its power was a thousand times eviler than dreamt.

Any of this was unbelievable still Simone couldn't look away. Each step brought him over to her. The floorboards straining to hold against his weight, bent and ached under him.

"You thought your little vampire, bitch, friend, could kill Me?" Sharp wicked eyes narrowed on Makenzie's child. She wasn't his blood, and he wanted to taste if it were as lovely as her mother's.

A glance back to the felled creature in the hall. "I cut her friend open. Thought I was going to die up there…" The crowing laugh returned. "Never thought this would come in handy" Flipping the knife he'd retrieved from the discarded clothes in the attic.

The blade was small in his clawed hand, still it was drenched and glistening in the dull glow of the hallway. Unrecognizable, a divisive smile ran along the length of his face. Knife to his lips, Jude slid his tongue along the thirsty blade.

His clawed fingers in sight, he threw down the knife. Its usefulness, overshadowed by his own might. Curved and evil on his face, a twitch under his skin called for more blood, more to eat.

"It's your turn now Simone. Mommy can't help you anymore." His laugh changed. Its form came as a sucking cackle, drowned in mockery. It was as if Jude had new powers. Able to reach inside Simone and shape her darkest nightmare, from deep inside her brain.

She was forced to stand there and watch as he soon would inflict his last wishes. He'd stolen everything. 'What more could he do,' Simone thought. Taking her life was so small now and she didn't truly fear that.

She could reach down and grab the gun back up. He, it, the beast looming tall over her, deserved to die.

Seeing her stare, Jude followed it to the ground beside her. There, resting a foot away from Scuff was a revolver. Covered in blood and sorrow, Jude smiled then a laugh came.

"Your mother already tried that." This fun was given to a chuckle. Stepping back, he widened his arms. "Your turn you little shit." He spread his chest for her to shoot. Just to the right of center an already closed wound that Mackenzie had hoped for was deadly.

Jude backed up another step. Mocking the child, he took a knee to even the angle for her.

Unexpectedly, Jude felt a strange and sharp pressure as it wrapped around one of his legs. Having to turn for the slowed claw, he discovered Crischa was still fighting.

"Still alive, I see." Jude hadn't lost his grin. "I think we need to rectify that little mistake."

Kicking his leg back, Jude centered on the rising attempt of the creature. "I'm going to do for you what your pal in the attic got, for fucking with a beautiful bastard like me." Drawing back and with all his newfound might, an open hand slashed out. Savage and brutal, the swing took Crischa's head clean off.

Flying up, it hit the wall, and rolled into his bedroom. Through the open doorway, Jude jumped back atop his bare feet.

"Goal!" Primping his oversized body, he laughed about the severed head. Carrying the sarcasm higher, he pounded his chest, feeling every bit of satisfaction. "Maybe next time."

Interdicting any turn for Simone, a blazing fire ran through Jude's skull. Blades sharper than his claws, they ignited and felt like they were ripping his mind and skull apart.

Screaming in pain, Jude was sure the child had shot him from behind. Clawed hands immediately came to cover the agony around his head. A fiery vein ignited, a wave of torment grew in his skull. Anger unable to be filtered, he hurled a clenched fist straight through the closest walls.

Some heated craving, under his flesh, wasn't satisfied. Its thirst awakened, he realized the sensation was far from sated. Mackenzie's blood and flesh had only started his growing necessity. There was now a raw and possibly uncontrollable river of thirst. One that Jude would now be responsible for.

Chapter Thirty-Seven

The Fall of Atlantis

Jude's volatile rage was Simone's greatest opportunity. Her heart had sunk, but she'd heard Crischa's words. The same had been asked numerous times, and it was so fitting now. 'Hide and seek,' her life had been a game, and this was her final turn.

There was, in that insight, a thought that she'd welcomed back. Crischa might not have been the villain she'd accused her of being. Regrets were tied to that thought. However important, escaping and hiding from the thing Jude had became, was first.

Taking advantage of the fleeting opportunity, Simone left the gun and scrambled for the stairs.

Behind her, Jude was continuing to rip through walls. His cries of agony and pain echoed in his arms as he fought against unseen foes.

Dropping down the steps on her backside, she slipped down faster and safer than her feet would have let her. The volume of pain in the hallway grew louder even as she continued to drop away. The front door was visible as she thud from one step to the next. Sorrow found Simone as her thoughts drifted to the one she'd abandoned.

Forsaken in her misery, Scuff was under the feet of Jude as he howled and tore through walls. He was a piece of her heart but there was no turning back.

Matching the horror of her regret, the room was darkened with a red haze. One that muted the front window as well as the one over the kitchen sink. Nearer the foot of the staircase, Simone knew the sunlight was just past the front door. From the steps, she noted it to be locked.

The torture upstairs had stopped. There were no more screams or sounds of falling walls. Jude wouldn't be long, and she knew it.

Sliding against the door with her momentum, Simone grabbed for the bottom lock. Immediately, she discovered a problem. The handle wasn't the same, it had been crushed. He'd thought of her escaping and damaged it to the point it wouldn't turn.

Simone slammed a fist.

His approach was missed, and Simone's world exploded. Jude had jumped down the entire twenty-one steps.

Violence his master a deformed hand sped behind Simone. It was too late for her to try, and escape into the living room. The full stretch of his palm and clawed hand made contact. Hard and without mercy, she was carried along with the force.

A doll to his crushing power, Simone's forty pounds, was sent flying. Her speed was unchecked as she hurled through the air, striking the top of the couch. All her weight was a rag. Simone's body, arms, and legs went limp as it spun across the last of the living room.

Even as her legs felt shattered, her body smashed down. Its speed and collision were violent against the space heater. The remains of her momentum crashing into piles.

Already manipulated and old, the kerosene heater ruptured dangerously. An escape flame jetting out over collections of trash and debris nearer the shelves. Added to this was the heater's spilled fuel.

The effect was intensified by a spray of compressed hot liquid. All of it ignited and spread to more of the room. Like a jet engine, the blue flame spit out over a five-foot area. Spinning round on the floor, it added to its fire line, growing even faster.

Everything in the living room was fuel and a wildfire started. Fed quicker by a full tank, the sequence was a fuse, linking separate shelves and finally the wall.

The wall and all the corners between kitchen and living room were engulfed. Whipped upward, the flames looked to crawl, like some living, and growing beast. Its mind was its own, the fire had with it a malice of thought.

Leaping over the banister, Jude crashed down behind the couch. His weight and mass splitting boards as one foot was sent through the floor itself. A rage inside his soul had taken any logic or reserve. First his arm crushed down to break the couch's spine, then in the same pull flipped it over. It was sent just as easily toward the front door in pieces.

Some of the flames trailed with the shattered furniture, all of it spreading further the bonfire. Where the burn landed it clung to everything.

One foot pinched under the wrecked flooring; Jude grew his rage. Howled out was his hungry mouth and fury. An insane wrath let loose, he sent back his head and a more terrifying screech poured high above all the fire.

His breath a growing huff, he turned his focus back for the missing runaway. He was dizzied only slightly by the blaze increasing in front of him. Gnawing at his savage anger, there was one pathetic prize he wanted. Small and cowardly, he wouldn't stop till he had Simone's blood.

A craving both freakish and uncontrolled, he had no other thoughts. "SIMONE!" He called out.

Yet another distraction needed his attention. Twisted claw-like fingers slashed at the planks, holding his one leg trapped. In between the struggle he snapped back and forth. His gaze searched for her.

Where he'd expected to find her was a disappointment. The tv and all the cabinets along the wall, swirled with expanding flames, but she wasn't there.

Powering it all, a tank of kerosene hissed. Its body sitting in fire, it was threatening to explode under the burn.

The girl was missing from where he'd sent her.

Jude pulled harder at his foot. Using the strength he had, he could hear beams under the floor breaking. He desperately needed to free himself. Glaring into the kitchen, Jude discovered the inferno had profited greatly there. If she was there, she was cooked, and better off.

Around behind him, was where the flames had been slow to reach. Not separate from it was the closet under the stairs. Its door opened; the depths were still undiscovered. Simone was hiding in there he knew it.

Washed away was the concern for the blaze crowding in on him. The rising heat and temperature were nothing more than an annoyance to Jude.

His might, significantly stronger, yet such a small hindrance was his ability to free one leg. Now sunk deeper in between the floorboards, he couldn't reach the closet to find Simone.

Hotter on his back and skull, were the hungry flames. As he ripped wood from the floor, he allowed the wave of burning debris to encircle him.

Jude's only alarm was the feverish throb of his blood lust. As his skin began to blacken and blister, he'd decided that small child was his cure. A fevered mind, he felt none of the blinding scourge. More fire dripping down from the crumbling ceiling and walls was ignored. An unknown desire was feeding Jude's lost humanity.

One thing he hadn't been exposed to yet was the burning touch of daylight. The sun's face high above the house, soon would breach the flame and billowing smoke.

Hate ripped at the floor and now broke supporting beams holding everything above ground. Crashing deep as the other foot, Jude's free leg sank equally into burning timbers. His efforts were having the opposite effect. He was finding it fruitless in both his search and getting out of the crumbling floor.

Another echoing cry, Jude's skin wasn't simply being seared, it was actively on fire.

Pushed back further inside the closet, Simone hid from Jude. The shower of flames was only secondary to his reach. The wall behind her was solid and there was no escape from this house any more. Part of the door frame already burning she tucked harder.

Outside the open door, white-hot jets of anger consumed the living room. Looking past the opening she saw only the side of Jude, while further, shelves and entire sections of the wall peeled away. Sooner then she could run, the house would fracture and tumble inward.

One of her legs felt broken. She wasn't running away from this.

Resilient, she sat up. Her back to the closet's recesses, Simone left her eyes wide and alert. Suffocating smoke was beginning to fill the room above her head. Under her, Simone felt something greater, a yawning quake.

Instantly the troubling vibration exploded. The result was unseen floor-beams shattering somewhere below her.

The living room erupted in some violent cataclysm. Floors warped and shifted in rebound. Every wall and stud, supporting half the structure above, moved away before collapsing inward.

Simone was still at her place. She watched out there as a cavernous rip opened under everything. Swallowed, she fell into darkness. It was a short drop before she teetered in the collapse.

The hole seemed to breathe in flame as she landed, some feet below a new roof. It was the living room floor above her, and she waited for it to crush down. Even here at the bottom of hell, Simone's body began slipping in the wrong direction.

There were deeper spots down here. Holes, caves that seemed hungry to take her.

Greater than the first explosion, a louder blast took half the house. It was the remains of the kerosene tank detonating. Snapped wider, the flooring collapsed, and her sight was erased.

Motion was gone, and her ears heard the last of what remained. This was the noise of hell falling on her before she died.

Body, blood, wood, and flames all descended into the cavernous hole. Simone only sensed the world collapse. The heat and glow mixed around her blind eyes. Doom was once more here.

Chapter Thirty-Eight

To Escape

Time slowed. All around her vibrant colors fluttered and washed into Simone's mind. With the pressure and heat traveling away, she knew she was being held in someone's arms.

Cold fingers, and chilled flesh she was being cradled in the blackness.

Simone heard fewer things. The world was rumbling but it was drifting farther, faster, and away from her senses. She could see nothing, but Simone wasn't even sure her eyes were open. They felt sore and dry but there was no feeling of the fire burning them.

The only true signature was the aroma of earth, damp if not moldy. It was dirt, and somehow the smell was sweet in her nose. Her brain knew it as decay but would not report it as natural or foul. She continued to have pain and it was real no matter what dream or reality. However, it wouldn't be the thing to snap her back to what moved around her.

Side to side, she was moving. The arms holding her, had protected her. Possibly they were keeping her from what she didn't want to know.

In her thoughts, Jude had been there seconds ago. The fire had been there too, but after it started to burn her flesh, there was an escape. All of it had drifted away from her, and her skin. Wherever she was now was cold. Still moving, she recognized a temperature change. Not dry heat but that same smell and warmth Crischa's home had introduced to her.

It was welcoming this time. Simone understood little of why but she wouldn't fight the sensation.

The rigid arms were boney and without a degree of warmth, but they tightened as they moved. What connection she could feel from it was painless.

Opening one able eyelid, she witnessed the thick void, but there was dirt filtering down around her. Muscles refusing her movement, she stayed.

Closing her sightless view, Simone wouldn't know if she slept or lingered in nothingness.

Both eyelids opened, she heard a distant noise rumbling. It was nearing as she recalled the sound. It had to be that dark cellar, the smell, the heat. Then that same rotten smell washed over her, foul and corrupt.

Again, Simone wanted to wretch yet equally a sense of safety came over her.

It was Crischa's home and someone had brought her here. Saved, whether temporary or not, Simone hadn't decided if this time would be different. What was important to this location was that monsters lived and hunted her back there.

"We're in your house, aren't we?" Simone's lips felt blistered as they pressed the words out. The thought of her dead friend lived in the emotion of being here.

The question left unanswered. "Are you… her parents?" She didn't know, but there was another moving form beside the one holding her. No proof, but she could feel it.

Any response offered was foreign to Simone, but something she'd done or said caused a hesitation. The figure turned with her. Not a direction but it seemed to search behind them. Back to move over land it saw with whatever eyes might see in this inky black.

The sensation that he or she had stopped was firm. Simone wanted to ask more, than she heard it. The reason the person had paused.

Swollen eyes, they were forced open and into use. Simone could feel there was something building. A distant gray was approaching. If there were direction in the upside down, it spoke. It was nothing more than a feeling she lived in. This thing, nearing them, was following her.

Somewhere a light source was growing closer. Unlike the unnatural tint of her lost glow stick, this shiny haze was warm.

Multiplying faster its power was raging. As something fought the darkness behind her, it grew sharper in the void. Simone knew, before seeing what the spark was.

It was flames. A moving body that rippled with fire as part of something angry and spiteful.

Having to wait seconds, the glow erupted up through constraints. Out of some distant hole in the darkness it fought. A volcano of blazing flesh and flame, a massive body was the core of the lava.

Simone was sickened to see the sight. Jude's entire body was ablaze, like so many flames. He witnessed flesh and skin grotesque as it boiled and burned. Under the flames that held tight to him, Simone could see he searched still.

What hunger he'd destroyed was still after her. Still mad to sink teeth and claws into her soft flesh.

If tears fell from her eyes, Simone couldn't know. The silhouetted shape that held her no sooner turned and fled.

Those last seconds of sight had shown her a battle had begun. The space she'd entered through hadn't remained benign to the intrusion. The ground, wet and alive, there'd been movement. A sprawling cave of sorts, it all began to rise. An unknown number of forms fill the negative shadows. Their rippling intensity angered by Jude's violent appearance.

Whatever the nest she'd observed, it had awoken.

His skin was flaking away with each step. Its tortured flesh continued to blaze, being sent out like burning rain. All around Jude's arms, he slashed out to stop what threat he posed.

Centered in the fight, Jude towered over the others. His blistering flesh used as his armor. As he killed and fought to reach her, he spread havoc. His fire hungry as him, it clung mercilessly to everything he passed.

Away from the deep, the expanse of that cave dropped away. Simone was raised up, and she felt a house around her now. Her savior had escaped with her. Up into the timber shapes of neglected halls and rooms, they now stalled for a moment.

The sole light up here, rose from the stairwell they'd used. Moving once more, Simone was alert to the dim rooms they passed by. They all looked old, used, but vacant for a living soul. Wherever the person was taking her, she didn't know.

Toward some other hallway, the chilled hold stopped in its march. After a deliberate search, the shape seemed to stress. Simone's eyes soon found the reason.

Under them, the aged planks began showing some unwanted glow. From between many of the long strips of flooring, light. Heat and flames were starting to penetrate upward from below.

From that sunken den below, an inferno was pushing upward. Smoke poured through larger gaps as burning embers worked through.

Suddenly, a wave of savage thuds rocked the floors to escape. That beast from under them was fighting to reach Simone.

Though steps unsure, her protector wavered in a direction to move.

Wood flooring shattered, while a hole was being ripped open in the hall. Jude's hand came up to pull further boards down. With him, the hungry fires spread. His fury greater, he came with it.

Those desperate hands were looking for one thing. Until he found it, he pulled up through the opening.

"NO, STOP! Leave me be!" Simone cried out. He would never stop, till she was dead.

Flames were growing on every surface, red, blue, and an unnatural furnace was being made. Bubbling off Jude's opened and blackened skin, a howl called back for Simone.

"You can't run from me!" Howling as if a harbinger to his fever, other creatures below him fought to pull him back down.

Stairs found, the arms carrying Simone moved up. Another flight and they might escape.

Almost at the top of these steps, Simone felt the idea of escape was lost. Jude's rage was faster, and he was behind them. The shapeless legs, under Simone's champion, dropped. Their fight was now with the monster following one person.

Thrown wider than it, Simone tumbled deeper into a curved corridor. Illuminated for the first time in decades, Simone saw several doors. It was a much thinner hallway on this floor. Regardless of this fact, all that lay before her were closed doors.

Desperate even more, Simone was on her belly. Her arms, her own again, she crawled for the limits of the hall. Ignoring the rooms, she headed for the end.

Another, much leaner set of stairs could be seen. These steps, barely her width, rose high into this house. Left here, her mind was numb to what she'd find. There was only the need to escape Jude.

Simone had given multiple attempts to use her legs. After the last, she knew they wouldn't allow her weight.

"They can't stop me forever. I'll have my pound of flesh, I promise!" Jude's roar wasn't disguising the pain. Hate was pushing him even as claws cut at him from all around.

There was a fight taking place behind Simone, even as she reached those steps. Close to the ground, she was choking on the smoke flooding this stairwell. Ahead of her, she could feel each step heated up. By the top, they would all become super-heated. Worried, Simone knew what was more likely they'd be red with growing embers below.

A snarl of skin folded between Simone's eyes. Her nostrils flared to breathe; her fingernails dug to climb each step. She had nothing in her muscles yet her brain would never surrender again. She could lose her feet, her legs, even half her body and she would continue the fight.

Near the top of an inward curving spiral, she found a lonely but closed door. Screaming through bloody hands and excruciating pain, she reached up to the handle.

Opening it, she slammed her head against it to push it inward.

Light, brilliant light poured over her from windows of colorful glass. Stain glass of ornamented beauty was washing into the circular room. Only five feet in width, it was mismatched to what had been below.

Her subconscious was the only place where she saw the magnificent birth. Simone flipped her legs into the space as fire had already reached the middle of the stairs. Thick and choking smoke had also followed. She needed to close the door before all the air was spoiled.

Matched in the sounds of a horrid inferno, was the raging thunder of other creatures. Screams both fierce and deadly called out to kill and survive.

Crazed in sadism, Simone shuffled over the lava that was the floor under her. Her gaze spinning as it searched, she looked at the collection of five windows. Through tears, smoke, and glass, a rainbow of light pointed to the only window that would open.

Whether she ever understood the nightmarish landscape, Simone pushed up. Her struggles, now fought against wounded bone to reach the latch. It would have been simple on feet and stretched arm, but Simone couldn't cover the distance.

Her fingers were short by everything, the space between was too great.

"No, no, no." She couldn't be defeated by this. Again, she buried the pain, and she unfolded those legs under her. Clawing, she took back those inches.

Pounding on the door to her small room, she heard the beast knocking. Simone was hanging from the window latch. This was determination and not fear as she jerked hard at the handle.

Splitting the door in half, a sickening and charred arm pushed inward for her.

Under her arm, Simone had pulled up onto the window's ledge. She could feel the winter's embrace. Behind, her legs were hanging heavily. On the sill, the balance of weight telling her she hadn't the strength to pull any more.

Crashing below those toes, the floor opened and fell away. Swirling up, to singe every bit of exposed flesh, was a hellfire.

Harder the door was brutalized by the anger kept from her. Through the fracturing wood, Jude's head came to see what he needed. Eyes, both pitch orbs of fever, he saw only Simone and not the opening under him.

Not far enough, Simone watched as he came for her. She wasn't deaf to the fierce screeches of his violence. Over the burning abyss he reached out to take her back. A desperate craving, he would parish before letting up.

Hands and arms slipping from the sill, her legs were dragging her down. She was unfortunately headed back into the fire and a missing floor. Simone began screaming, fearing she'd fall even before her monster might kill her.

Something was clear to her as she drifted further backwards. She could let go. It would be her choice. The fall would end worlds of pain and agony. The best part, he would follow. Jude would kill himself.

All restrictions behind him, Jude leapt from the door and the last step. Off the floor his body would have every inch of hers. Once in the air, Jude felt his power stolen.

Something behind him had taken most of his force. Though he'd pushed from the steps, there was no way he'd completely clear the distance.

Thought enough, his aim was short, and he hit Simone. Her body was higher than his, she was sent out and over the lip of the window.

Jude saw his own fall. Down into the inferno he'd created. The walls that had held for countless decades all of them followed him downward.

Although cruel and unkind, Simone was thrown from a full height. Against a steep roof, she hit the adjacent angle peak. Tumbling downward, she was lost for any kind of control. Violent and rough, her body spun against the last incline and dropped to the thicker brush further out.

The afternoon sun floated above. Spiraling in her sight, the day wasn't over. Her surviving body burned and bleeding she was alive. Simone was free of both flame and her monster.

She had descended inside her own home. Running from hate and vile, down into hell. There she was buried under crumbling wood and flame, only to be plucked up. From that descent, she was brought up into the darkness. Lifted in a home she thought a friendship had grown.

On each floor in Crischa's house, she had risen in a futile chase for freedom. Only when she'd seen the rainbow of glass had there been a chance.

Was any of this a gift given to her, for all the suffering she survived? Turning her head, Simone felt the heat. It was a growing inferno. The entire house was beautiful, a single, blazing flame that watched her, free.

From under all corners and cracks, black billowing smoke begged for the sky. Towering high enough to touch the sun it rose. It was searching for the same freedom as her.

Simone wanted to smile, but instead, she closed her eyes and listened to the music.

A howling echo, the piercing roar had life all its own. The torrent of flame and smoke pushed and popped. Inevitably every surface of the house joined the rising chorus. Burning strong, the flames stretched into the sky, competing for height with black rivers of smoke.

Once and finally, Simone was alone.

Chapter Thirty-Nine

A New Start

"Rise and shine, sleepy head." The upbeat nurse slid the curtains back. Clean and perfect, the double window allowed tons of the crisp morning sun in. Flooding the room, it was brilliant to open eyes.

A job to do, the woman tended to several things about the sterile room before heading over to the bed.

The room, longer than it was wide, was sparsely decorated. A thin stiff couch sat under the window and several sparse pieces dotted the room. By the door inside, was a dry erase board. On it were scribbles, of times and words that didn't look like real words.

Simone was drowsy and just understanding her waking confusion, stared at the odd woman. Her demeanor was bouncy and it seemed happier than needed. Her clothes drew her attention.

She wore a light blue shirt that matched her pants. Both looked like pajamas, yet Simone knew they weren't.

Constantly moving, Simone spied her clothes had a small name tag.

Hanging straight on the left side of her chest, 'Alice Jonston.' The hard white plastic stood out against her light blue dressing. Tucked beside her stamped name, a tiny sticker of a colorful Easter egg sat in the corner.

Werry of the shine from the windows, Simone blinked fast until she saw better. Her stare moved away from the woman and tested everything around her.

The room was completely foreign to her. She had the sense inside her chest that she needed to panic. Yet as she looked the feeling never matured. Although she didn't know just where this was, Simone was sure this dream was leading her somewhere.

Things began to change quickly. Voices that had been distant all started to filter into her small room and her ears. Watching them, they continued filling her room. Figures dressed similar to the first, all of them unknown to Simone.

Loitering about, they remained backed away from the central bed. However, out of the way, they carried on in low whispers. Unconcerned by her staring eyes, their tones changed little as they one-by-one became still.

The air was tinted with a subtle chemical flavor, but Simone was indifferent as she lay almost flat in the large bed. Casting her curiosity over the bed, she saw soft white sheets covering her.

The edges smoothed out; they were so clean. Rounded over every side, she could feel she was tucked in tightly. A growing stress returned to visit as she looked at the sides of her bed.

The perimeter of the mattress was blocked, guarding rails sat in place on both sides. If she wanted to get out of bed, she'd have to climb over them.

In the center of one guardrail, Simone saw colorful buttons and symbols she didn't recognize.

This entire dream was becoming a bit much. Her brain, not fully awake, was refusing her even the simplest of answers. Was she in some sort of daydream, or could it all be some sinister game?

Pushing up on one elbow, Simone tried to gain some perspective. Instantly, waves of pain found her as she suffered in the attempt to sit up.

Her struggle was immediately corrected by that first blue clothed woman. She'd been hovering near her bed the entire time the room had been filling.

"Hold on sweetie, I'll raise that for you. You definitely need some of the morning's sun." Her hand came over the railing and pressed one of the sectioned off buttons.

With a genuine smile poured on her, Alice reached over the railing. Over her, she brushed short hairs from Simone's face. Fluffing the pillows behind her, she helped her incline. The smile wide and steady, Simone watched as it never shrank.

Afterwards, the pretty woman grabbed a controller hanging from the bedside. "I'll turn this on for you too." Pointing with a remote in hand, there was a small tv mounted along the ceiling. "We'll keep the volume down, for now though. Later, we can find some cartoons if you want?"

With her eyes wide, Simone pulled away slightly from the hand. Simone could identify the feelings; they were out of place to all the kindness but the reasons escaped her.

The upper half of the bed continued moving.

A nervous fear lived deep, out of sight, but Simone waited to act on it. An innate sense told her that something bad was to follow. She didn't recognize anyone here, and the uncomfortable feeling was persistent.

This puzzling emotion, even as the mistrust was registered, Simone couldn't define memories to frame it.

The confusion on her face was only cultivated as other faces watched hers. They all looked at her patiently, happy even, to just see her open eyes.

To that sunken itch, they all appeared false. Offering her smiles of differing intensity, one on the next returned to hidden conversation.

Before Simone might ask the lady a question, a taller woman entered. Her head was buried in a clipboard she'd carried between a pen and her other hand.

Simone noticed her presence gave the others pause. She had in an instant pulled everyone's attention from her in the bed. What was more, the other adults standing about started to quickly filter out. Only the closest, remain nearer the end of the bed.

Dissimilar from the rest of the people, she wore a darker blue shirt. Covering it was a long white thin jacket, with pockets. Around her neck was the odd-looking tube instrument. Simone recognized it but had forgotten the name.

Simone shrank as she rounded the bed alone.

She didn't smile at her either. Standing there, she continued to study something in the paperwork she brought in with her. Only after flipping a few pages, did she even look at her. Opposite to the smiling woman in all blue, this lady was hesitant to even connect with Simone's gaze.

Before once looking at her body, she took her wrist between her fingers.

A shaking had started inside Simone. She wanted to take her hand back, but the lady's pinch stopped her. Eventually ending, the woman handed the clipboard over to Alice.

"We're extremely happy to see you finally awake this morning. You've been asleep for quite a while now. Have to say, you had us a bit worried for some time." She offered a smirk, but never more.

"You had a bad time of it, I can see." Her tone ebbed away, as she turned her attention to devices wired to Simone. "Let's bump her up to sixteen mill on the hour." An order aimed at Alice she tapped at a bag hanging above the bedside.

"We have a couple really hard things to talk about," The lady only gradually returned to the sad girl. "But for now, we're just going to try and answer a few easy questions." She finished fidgeting elsewhere to stare fixed into Simone's eyes. Skeptical of her words having been understood, she peered closer.

Waiting a few seconds, she turned to the nurse.

"Where am I?" Simone's fractured throat and words were almost impossible to push out. No more than a whisper she started to repeat. Stopping her, a deep, and painful cough erupted. Sharp and horrid, the discomfort traveled out from inside her lungs and chest.

"Take it easy, don't talk." The doctor placed her hand on Simone's shoulder. Her pressure prevented the girl from sitting up any further forward than required.

A hand over the coughing fit, Simone discovered much of her face and head were bandaged. The dread had been real. A wave of panic was causing her to shake. Looking over to her other arm, she found it was also wrapped thoroughly.

"You need to work with us, ok?" The woman offered a clinical smile.

Before the doctor could continue, Alice was alarmed by a loud ruckus announced in the hallway. It was a loud protest, coming from two people just outside her doorway. The figures, desperate, seemed to argue with some of the standing nurses. They obviously wanted to enter Simone's room.

"I don't give a bloody hell who you think you are!" A drawn British accent clear in his rebuttal. Behind that voice, a female voice repeated the objection, to them being stopped. Both their superior tones powered past all obstacles and any of the blue clothing.

"Move, I say, before I have you all arrested." The woman, nearest to entering, now pushed some of the techs and nurses out of her way. Of measured success she entered the room.

In that insistent struggle, the nurses were only able to block the doorway. Then with a wave of the doctor's hand, "Let them in, it's okay."

Their stronger accent echoing, "We want to see her now, and there is nothing you…" The man and woman had their emotions checked just inside the doorway. Finally gained access, the shocking sight worked to silence both of them. A clear view to her bed they instantly felt the small girl's hurt.

The well-dressed lady stood five inches shorter than him. Both working through their profound breathing, only he was able to paint a happy smile to cover the feeling welling up.

Laying in that bed, attached to countless leashes and instruments. All of them meant to bring her back from some dire ending. They'd helped to pull her lingering body back. Saving her from some dark cliff she'd persisted in for over a month now.

Although new bandages covered a good portion of her body, their numbers were fewer today than when she'd arrived in the hospital. The entire sight was in itself, traumatic.

"Hello Mr. and Mrs. Ruggells, we talked on the phone." The doctor moved to head off the distressed faces. "I'm Dr. Lorna Cutter."

Without a word to the doctor, Mrs. Ruggell's sorrow and panic turned away. Smothering her face within the comforting embrace of her husband, she stayed, as he shook the doctor's hand.

Simone studied it all, a feeling of distress washed over her about the entire demonstration. Watching the three of them, she was more than puzzled by the crying. None of the other people looked so distraught, why them?

The tall man never looked away from her. She could see brows narrowing as he fought off deeper emotions. Connecting with his eyes, she watched him devote the best smile he had. His spine even grew taller as he looked at her in the bed. If it were pride revisiting, he continued, exposed was some lost aching pain he'd suffered.

Together the three moved over to the bedside. The two, holding each other, came between the bright window and her bed. A glow behind them made them glisten in Simone's eyes.

The two couldn't stop staring, holding each other as if they would fall if they didn't. Their faces were tight and carrying some unknown longing. Neither were able to speak as some unknown passion worked their tongues into knots.

Pulling them aside, Dr. Cutter began whispering in a hushed caution.

"I told you before;" A stern and corrected tone, "she is out of sorts. It may take a few more days. Give it a short while for her memories to return.”

Simone heard little of the message. Yet she did hear the hesitant break before the lady continued lower still.

“She may never,”

Simone didn't appreciate the conversation being about her. What little she understood had to be about her in this bed. Albeit disconcerting, it was just all so strange to her.

The man and woman quickly pushed past the doctor. Alone this time, they stood back at her bedside. Her hands came to rest over the railing. Nervous to reach out but wanting to.

Simone could feel their faces wanted so much of her. She didn't know what was desired to help their trouble, but she could only watch this play out. All the questions she had let build up, had to be set aside. There was time and until they left, she'd wait.

“If only you could remember us.” Her hand came off the guardrail and she moved to pet the damaged girl. “Ducky. I'm sorry you've suffered.” There was a story behind the name, but the woman's tears fell heavy as her husband stopped her short of touch.

“I don't think she knows that name anymore.” He placed his hand and hers back on the rail. His other arm pulled her tighter. A tear rolling from him, “she was so young then.”

Simone wanted to help them. The name ‘Ducky’ was meaningless to her, but she wanted to say yes. She wanted to ease these nice people's worries. Even if she could talk it felt far from her abilities.

She didn't know who they were, much less any other. Watching intently, something, anything. “I…” Simone's brain gave no help. Her throat closed before more was available. The effort was painful, not only to her flesh but her own blank life she was reaching to explain.

There was a hole inside, a gaping loss. In her brain a fractured feeling of victory, yet in her heart Simone was missing things. She was laying here without an anchor, and she felt hollow.

“It's okay.” The woman leaned into study what was lost for so long. Soft and loving, she whispered as Simone turned away from them both. “It's fine Ducky. It'll all be better from here on out, I promise you this.”

Looking at her husband then down again. “You just rest. We're not leaving you."

Turned away by her husband, the woman covered her mouth as every emotion amplified. Walking from the room the two were immediately followed through the door into the hallway by the doctor.

"Take her home…" The doctor's conversation drifted off as they exited Simone's reach.

The last of these distractions, Simone couldn't hear anything after that. She didn't know why the idea of 'home,' gave her a knot in the stomach. It was such an objective word to cause such physical pain. Yet laying here, Simone hadn't the framework to know for sure, just why it did.

If anything justified the feeling, it continued to linger in the darker corners of her brain. With no real fears in her memory, to call forward, she just felt bad.

Try as she might, frustrated and hazy already, she looked inward. Still, there was no house, no room to recall, no toys. There was simply nothing that called to her, as her own.

The room cleared except her nurse in blue, and a second face joined her. Laying with her face away and tightened, Simone listened.

Approaching the bedside, a second younger girl joined Alice. Together they both looked at her cheerfully. Their expressions were similar as they adjusted one of the spotless white bandages on Simone's leg.

Smiling wider at her, "You're so lucky they found you sweetie." The comment was meant as nothing more than a statement of fact.

Simone wanted more; she wanted to know what was going on. Where did she come from? How did she get here? How long had she been there? Then there was the most important question: why could she remember nothing?

"If it hadn't been for 'this,' they would have never been able to identify you, tiny angel." Finishing up, she brushed her frayed hair back. Lifting Simone's unbandaged wrist, the nurse placed it back closer to Simone's heart.

Simone looked to the women as they cleaned up and then removed the older wrappings. Unsure of the implication of 'this,' in her comment.

Looking at her scratched-up palm, then the healed-up spots on the back of her hand. There was nothing of interest to answer her. Moved along, Simone found the focus of both the ladies.

Light streamed into the window and warmed her home in the bed. Yet the greatest effect was the shimmering fire on her wrist. Beautiful and studded in what looked to be endless sparkles, was her bracelet. Having drifted low on her forearm, its countless facets twinkled like stars in the sunlight.

For the moment, she forgot her confusions, as the child inside studied the wonderful jewels. What to think she was at a loss. Saying nothing, Simone allowed the younger lady to brush through her hair unchecked.

"You still don't remember a thing, do you, you poor sweet thing?" The older nurse worked a few tubes around before rechecking some instruments on her bedside. Giving a tender pat, she smiled even larger at Simone.

"Don't worry my tiny angel, your family is here now. I promise they won't let you slip away ever again."

It wasn't the worst thing she could have said. Simone looked away from them both. Her words had no facts to sink up in Simone's head. She put the facts together with what little she knew.

Could the two that had left with the white coated woman, truly be her mother and father? They look striking, even pretty. The thought was fun if nothing else, still it did bring a smile to her face.

Set up to let her sleep, Alice gave a last check. "Soon you'll be leaving me and going back to England. You'll love it I'm sure, not stuck in this dreary room anymore, you lucky thing." With her last words the two walked out.

The idea came to Simone as she lay, 'I think I'm happy.' She couldn't bring forward the emotion, but everyone seemed happy for her. The world was a hazy, unlabeled, and blurry place, but sitting here, Simone realized something new. Her mind wasn't even sure of her own name.

Walking out of the room, the tech slowed Alice, "Sorry, I just came back from a short leave. Who is that little girl?"

A smirk checked the question as they headed for the counter on the floor of the hospital.

"I only knew of her, because my brother used to live in London. That is, about four, five years back I mean." Going round sitting behind one of the computers, she pulled out some procrastinated work.

"Yah, what's that got to do with the girl, what happened? She got in an accident here?" The younger tech wanted the gossip Alice was famous for.

Leaning over the top of the counter, she was invested in Alice's story.

A troubled expression filled her face, disappointed in the younger woman's smile. "It's far worse than just an accident." She felt her own demeanor narrow to a lower volume. "Her parents, some Richie Rich type in England. Well, they were murdered just so horribly a few years back. Well, their baby, one or two-years-old at the time. She was thought kidnapped and killed; they didn't know."

The feeling was becoming morbid, but Alice continued seeing the eyes fixed on her. "Everyone believed her dead, drowned or something in some river somewhere. Then." She stopped glaring at the shocked face above her.

"Providence, divine intervention, who knows. A month ago, she was dropped here, square out of a fiery hell. They found her up there in Summerville. Some backwoods section, near where all those old mills are."

Struggling to take it all in, the tech leaned in further, "But how'd they figure it was the same baby?"

"That's the thing, they found her burned and cut up to no end, but God be saved, she still had that bracelet still. Miracle, if you ask me."

"Craaaazy."

"Firefighters found her on death's door, mumbling her name they said. Been here since, unconscious till today."Alice shrugged as the young tech looked back toward the girl's room, at the end of the hall.

"Who were those two?" She turned back, "you said the parents were killed?" thinking possibly Alice might be kidding.

"Aunt and uncle is what I heard." Alice said absently.

"It's a pretty name though."

The nurse glanced back with an open smile. "Crischa. Yah, can't say I've ever heard of it either." Handing the tech, a paper list of her orders for the day, "At least she's not alone anymore."

Chapter Forty

Back Home

THREE YEARS AFTER

6 Sadlers Wells, Bunbury UK

Waking to a tapping sound, Simone sat up.

Stacked all around on her bed, stuffed animals. The variety spans all genres and stretches into fantasy. There was a tender chill in her room, but it was only because she refused to have her window shut tight. Winter, summer, or rain there was always a cracked space to let the night's air in.

Rubbing the sleep from her eyes she looked round. She thought it odd the dream hadn't anyone knocking. Yet the noise felt so real. If it had been someone at her bedroom door, it wouldn't be silent still.

Reluctant to rise out from under the fluff of warm sheets and blankets, she searched the distant corners of her room. Her clutter was everywhere. The dressing desk on the far side had a mirror facing her bed and she could see herself sitting in the canopy bed. Curtains, frilly and draped high above she waved at herself.

A sigh, she swung her legs over and slipped to the floor. She'd at least check her door. Then she'd return to slumber.

Stumbling sleepily, she tugged at her cheek. The room was never so dark that she couldn't see the overtly pink walls and furniture her aunt and uncle had spoiled her with.

Click, the door swung in, and her head came through the opened space. Leaning with the handle in the left hand she searched the long hallway outside.

Empty. The corridor wasn't dark either. One way then the other, there was no one out here.

Prepared to run back to her bed, her head retreated within. Out of habit, a hand went to one of the numerous healed burns. She had plenty, but the scars on her shoulder always tingle at night.

Louder this time. Four clear taps called for someone to hear. The sound was coming from downstairs.

Pulled wide open, she stood in the doorway in her nightclothes.

"Hello? Aunty Beth is that you?" The test came back with silence. Darkness wasn't the problem, she hadn't the least problem with it. Yet tonight, something was speaking to her.

A step then the next, her clothes made a swishing sound as she walked. Her feet bare, she refused to wear socks or slippers in the house. This fact is her own, even as her aunt had pleaded a thousand times.

The hall was lit only by the bathroom on this floor. Its light remained on, always. Toward the other end of the spacious hall, there was a cloaked hush. Not so much she couldn't see in it. However tonight it felt heavier than the norm.

The house lay tranquil, even as the dull sound of her pajama pants continued. Like someone shushing another they melted into the back of her thoughts. Nearer the steps down to the ground floor, she wondered. Curious, if the knocking would return while she waited.

Passing the last door before the drop, she stopped to listen. Again, she wanted to call out.

Wide stone runners dropped to the entryway. Slightly narrower than the steps, a dark green carpet led down the staircase. The wall along the outside of the steps curved to the left. Dotted on the way down, two different sculptures sat recessed in the wall.

Her eyes traveling the length of the stairs, she dropped them to the round entry table. Topped with an audacious flower arrangement, there was no one standing by it playing a joke on her. The lights down there were off, and she felt something again.

Centered in front of the table, two towering doors sat locked and quiet.

Still, she felt that eerie notion of familiarity. It was anything but clear to her as toes led downward. Sleep was the obvious reason for the feeling, but it carried a necessity. There were missing pieces in her memory for years but never a need like this.

A yawn escaped as the end of the flight approached. "It has to be a piece of my dream." She wanted the air filled with something to rid the feeling.

Marching off the last step, she stood ready at the front doors.

Standing there, she watched the door as if willing the knocking to arrive as she had.

Silence and darkness played tricks. Obviously, a mistake, yet she thought to see movement to her left. Her imagination, sluggish, but it was leading her into the darkness. Nodding, she gave a defeated sigh and turned to head back for her comfortable bed.

With a hand on the railing's ornate stone newel, she heard it again. Not a knock on the wooden door, this sound was tapping. This time it begged to follow from other rooms to the left of the front doors.

Cocked back, her face turned toward the door. Her gaze over the shoulder, she considered simply ignoring it and running to bed. Her warm bed called and this game of 'find me' was working into an alarm.

Centering her attention upstairs, if she ran, she could hide under covers and would never know.

Then she nodded 'no.' She didn't have to get close; she could just discover where it originated.

The first minute expanded to two.

The reoccurring tap hadn't spawned to tease, not while she waited listening. It wasn't coming from the entrance and she'd heard it closer to the dining room, maybe the kitchen.

Rotating on heels, she forced her ears to listen. First, she searched through the dining room. Empty. As the hall and the front door had been.

Outside the wind had picked up and the sound of light rain was echoing its effects.

In the kitchen, counters lay clean and still. The glow of a digital clock on the distant wall was the best light to see. Beside the oven in front of her was the walk-in pantry. Past it was a door, and an exit leading out onto the open patio.

Her pants added to the dull pattering of rain. The light shower was a droning wash and was common here in England. Inside still, she could hear it louder than she ought to. As she came to the door, she stopped abruptly.

She'd revealed the errant discovery. The door here in the rear of the house, lay wide open. It hadn't been forgotten and left a crack. No, the door sat against the inside wall, still and unmoved by gentle winds outside.

Her heartbeat had increased as the strained notion resurfaced. It was more than a feeling; it was a strange sense that had even led her here. As if a beckoning memory, forced her to wake and find this very door.

A space between lips she stared down on the ground. The threshold was empty but not unmarked.

The house had more doors than she could count yet this one felt larger than any had ever. On the ground was not a gift, not a thing, however a message was there.

This door led out onto one of the terraces. One she liked playing on during the day. Outside the temperature wasn't cold but a soft drizzle quenched the sizable potted plants. Hundreds of them encircled one of two yards she spent hours in.

There was a footprint on the tile. Wet and waded in the light it was smaller than hers.

Looking through the opening, her gaze went high above. A moon unlike most, its face was dark yet still lit with a strained reddish shadow. Covered, it drifted behind clouds as they passed.

Standing for a count, she listened to the rhythmic tapping of the rain. It was soft as it hit the house's roof as well as other objects around her. A gentle misting, it was no different than any other that washed clean the world.

However, tonight a scent wafted alongside distant blossoming flowers. In it, it carried a memory as Simone grinned.

Taking another absent step, she moved into the open air. Stopped, she wanted to feel the drizzle. Head turned slightly up; her mouth dropped open. She was hoping to catch even the smallest of drops just for herself.

Eyes tired and almost closing, she felt a strange breath.

The mist, like the sensation, covered Simone as her head dropped. The feeling of eyes watching her was real. This was no dream. Looking to her right, it was a young girl that was watching her.

Standing in the rain, she presented a tilt of her own head back to her. Over thin lips she offered Simone a subtle grin. The colorless eyes narrowed as they met. "We can play hide and seek. Friend."

Darren DiGiovanni

Darren DiGiovanni